A TIME TO LIE

Simon BERTHON

ONE PLACE. MANY STORIES

HQ
An imprint of HarperCollins*Publishers* Ltd
1 London Bridge Street
London SE1 9GF

This edition 2020

1

First published in Great Britain by
HQ, an imprint of HarperCollins*Publishers* Ltd 2020

Copyright © Simon Berthon 2020

Simon Berthon asserts the moral right to be
identified as the author of this work.
A catalogue record for this book is
available from the British Library.

ISBN:
HB: 978-0-00-821446-3
TPB: 978-0-00-821447-0

MIX
Paper from
responsible sources
FSC
www.fsc.org   **FSC™ C007454**

Simon Berthon is a BAFTA award-winning and highly acclaimed investigative film-maker and journalist who lives in London.

He has spent much of his life delving into the secrets of state, and is also the author of three non-fiction books.

Also by
Simon
BERTHON

A TIME TO LIE
A SECRET WORTH KILLING FOR

Writing as Will Caine

THE INQUIRY

In loving memory of Hermione Young

'The role of non-military means of achieving political and strategic goals has grown'

VALERY GERASIMOV, HEAD OF RUSSIAN ARMED FORCES

'A new divide is opening up between anarchists – drawn to radical ideas about smashing everything up and starting over – and centrists. Remarkably the anarchists are more common on the British right than left'

MIRKO DRACA AND CARLO SCHWARZ, UNIVERSITY OF WARWICK

1

In a parched expanse of bankside wasteland only the cries of river traffic broke the silence. The foreman pointed to cracks in a swollen line of tar.

'Here,' he said. 'Careful when you hit it. It's just a service road. It wasn't laid that deep.'

The digger blade pounded into bitumen, descending easily through the layers – tar, concrete, gravel. Two feet down a workman knelt in the ditch to peel away hard core inch by inch.

His trowel tapped something hard. Gently he ran the tip along its curved and unbroken surface. This must be it – the pipe. Using his gloved hands, he burrowed around and beneath. There was no sign of fracture. Moving along, he exposed what seemed to be a fold of plastic. It was the tip of a package. He removed his gloves and prised it out with his nails. It extended to thirty, maybe thirty-five centimetres. One edge of the plastic wrapping was pierced with small metal rings. There was something familiar, domestic, about them.

An instinct told him its contents were precious, deserving of their private moment. He unwound the layers of wrapping. Now he understood the rings. This was a crudely cut section from a shower curtain.

He noticed shapes through the thinning plastic. Pale, straight but at different angles, disjointed. A slender outline of bones. An animal, someone's lost pet. He unpeeled the last fold to reveal a tightly bound, transparent display, like a vacuum pack. The bones took on a shape. More like fingers, splayed out. He flinched, dropping the package. My God. He turned away, then forced himself to pick it up again.

The outline of a human hand. Swallowing bile, he began to peel away the seal. A bone wriggled loose. He stopped.

Fingers, wrist bone, an element of forearm. There was no doubt. A hand, severed above the wrist. Who? That one simple question leapt at him. Who was this? He examined it more closely. Thin bones, a woman's bones, perhaps a girl's. Why packaged like this? Why here?

He stared, frozen in time, his eye drawn to the letters embossed on a faded silver ring dangling around the bone of the hand's fourth finger.

2

Two days later

The tall, lean figure of Robin Sandford loped into Birmingham's International Convention Centre, every inch the Lion King. Luxuriant wavy brown hair settled just above the collar. A white shirt beneath an expensively tailored suit so dark grey it seemed almost black. A silk tie of diagonal blue lines. A cheering, clapping crowd of three thousand mainly white, middle-class party members turned as one, their eyes following their leader's passage to the podium. The only hint of discord was standing in an aisle halfway back – an unsmiling, predominantly male group, their collars tieless, their patting of hands no more than obligatory.

Alongside Sandford, her elegant legs matching stride, one hand holding his, the other a smart phone, came his wife, Carol, her carefully highlighted fair hair falling on her shoulders; in their wake two daughters.

He released her, jumped ahead onto the platform, beckoned

his family to join him and waved his hands over the baying mob. It hushed.

'Thank you,' he said quietly.

The whooping restarted. He waved his hands again. 'Thank you so much.' He flashed a giant grin and lowered his hands. He paused. Faces merged into a featureless heap, sounds into a distant echo. Maintaining his smile but feeling a touch of giddiness, he imagined the sight before him as a giant anthill. He felt his hand being gently squeezed. He turned; Carol was looking up at him, that familiar encouragement in her eyes. He nodded as if to say, 'I'm OK' and gestured her and the girls to take their seats on the podium behind. He tapped the microphone, looked down at the lectern and waited for silence to fall.

'Friends and colleagues, we have faced a world and national crisis. A challenge to our country greater than any since the two world wars of the twentieth century. Now we are moving on. We are getting things done. The right things for ourselves and our country. As we said we would when the people of this United Kingdom gave this party, you, all those who worked with us, a landslide victory in a historic general election.'

A further roar. He repressed it with a firm, instant show of the palms. He spoke softly, only the flat 'a's and phonetic 'oo's betraying hints of class and origin. A state school boy who had traded up, not a public school boy who had traded down.

'Despite all that has happened, we must not forget why we won that election. We offered a coming together in a nation which, despite its name, had become disunited. We offered a clear path after Brexit. A better life for all our people. And

4

an end to the destruction threatened by a Marxist subset of self-serving London intellectuals. Let us never forget that.'

This time he allowed the applause, turning round to acknowledge the ministers and party officials sitting on the podium behind him. 'But, as we pick up the reins of our long-term ambitions, there is one value we never dared to stress enough. We must be a government that is not just practically good, but morally good. At this conference I commit myself to that. And I start with one particular ambition.'

The ears of Henry Morland-Cross, Deputy Prime Minister and Chancellor of the Exchequer, pricked. Until this moment, he had been trying to interpret that intimate exchange of looks between Mr and Mrs Prime Minister. Sandford had long been a colleague, but never a friend, and he sometimes wondered if all that glittered was truly gold. Was it put on for the cameras – or genuine affection and reassurance? If the latter, lucky man. Might he himself now be Prime Minister if he'd had a woman like that in his corner? The two daughters – adopted as 'Becca' and 'Bella' by the press – were in their teens. She was young enough – just – to have another child. Always a coup for a male Prime Minister. Youthful adoration of the golden boy leader would reach fever pitch. He pushed the irritating thought aside. Was Sandford actually about to say something interesting?

'The defence of our country,' continued the Prime Minister, 'is, and has always been, this party's priority. We need armed forces. We need arms. We need an arms industry. But...' He looked from one side of his audience to the other. 'There is nothing in today's world more wicked than the arming of evil states to impose terror on their neighbours – and on their own people. We have all seen too many images of innocent children and families being murdered by their own regimes.'

The audience was silent, knowing they were witnesses to a moment of drama. 'My commitment is this. My government must legislate to ban all arms sales by British companies to nations which do not adhere to the values of democracy, the rule of law and the freedom of the individual.'

There was a hush, then murmurings, followed by scattered applause. The standing group of informally dressed men exchanged puzzled looks.

'This ban,' continued Sandford, 'will also apply to the supplying of so-called military advisers, special forces, training personnel, mechanics – in other words, all types of mercenary that support such regimes. To repeat, a good government also means a moral government.'

The speech's end brought applause less ecstatic than at its beginning. Sandford turned to shake the hands of his government colleagues.

'Interesting, Robbie,' said Morland-Cross with a derogatory Etonian drawl. 'When was that morsel added to the speech?'

'Which morsel?' smiled Sandford.

'Oh, come on.'

'Last night actually. I've been mulling it over for a while. I gamed it with the team. And some colleagues, of course.'

'But not me.'

'No, M-C,' (as Morland-Cross was familiarly known), 'I wasn't sure you'd approve.'

Morland-Cross puffed himself up. 'Well, I must say...' he began, before, most unusually, holding himself in check.

'The team reckons the voters will like it,' said Sandford. He patted him on the shoulder and moved on, glad-handing his way along the podium, with a word here and there, and down the steps to the conference floor.

Morland-Cross watched him go. 'Bugger the voters,' he murmured. 'Bugger his fucking team.' He turned on his heel, dismounted the opposite end of the podium and headed towards the group halfway up the hall. A narrow-faced man left it and walked down towards him. Only when they were close enough not to be overheard, did he speak.

'What was that all about?' murmured Jed Fowkes, the Chancellor's special political adviser, or Spad as they were known – and feared – in Whitehall. By contrast to Morland-Cross's impressive girth, Fowkes was thin and tall, the line of his brown hair low on his forehead. He gave the impression of an intellectual – a thinker more comfortable poring over obscure treatises than greasing palms in the political merry-go-round. Unlike Morland-Cross – and more like Sandford – his accent revealed little, barring the occasional hint of Brummie.

'Perhaps he believes it,' replied Morland-Cross.

'Finally daring to show his true colours,' said Fowkes.

'Light blue verging to pink,' muttered Morland-Cross. 'Like that dress his wife's wearing.'

Fowkes glanced back at the group he had come from. 'You can be sure of one thing. Our side will never allow him to sell the pass.'

'No, Jed, we certainly won't.'

'I'd better go, I need a word with him. He won't blank me in front of this lot.'

*

Sandford pressed through the hall. He itched to be away, but this was a time for courtesies. He had almost reached the main exit when a familiar figure moved in to block him.

'Hello, Jed,' Sandford said, battling to hang onto the smile.

'Congratulations, Prime Minister,' said Fowkes.

'Yes. But none of the formality. I'm still just me. To you anyway.'

'Good. That helps.'

'Helps?'

Fowkes moved nearer. 'Robbie, I need a quick word in private.'

'Here? Now?'

'Thirty seconds.'

I can't refuse him, thought Sandford, can't afford the fuss. He waved away his entourage. 'Just give us a moment.'

'I'll need half an hour. Not right now, I know. But soon. I mean, really soon.'

'What about? M-C? The future?'

'No, the opposite. The past. Something's come back. Something bad.'

'What do you mean, Jed?'

'I can't say now. It's when we had the flat.'

'That was over thirty years ago.'

'I know. It's about someone we once knew.'

'Mikey?'

'No, not Mikey. One of the girls.'

'What do you mean, something bad?'

'Not now.' Fowkes glanced at the following group. 'But I'll need to discuss it with you. For both our sakes.'

'Jed, you're talking in riddles. This is not the time or place.'

'After the weekend then.'

Sandford made a show of looking at his watch. 'OK, I'll find space.'

Fowkes leant in and whispered in his ear. 'There's a question we have to answer.'

Sandford frowned. 'A question?'

'Yes. We have to know.' Fowkes paused. He looked around. No one was in earshot. He turned back, his breath hot against Sandford's skin. 'It's this, Robbie. Did we kill her?'

3

A twitch of the mouth, no interest in a reply, Fowkes marched off. Instantly, Carol was at Sandford's side. He stood stock still, his face a mask.

'Are you OK?'

'Yes, fine.' He forced a smile. 'Let's get out of here.'

As the four of them were travelling as a family, along with protection officer and driver, a stretch bullet-proofed Mercedes awaited. Sandford had tried to insist on a Ford people carrier. That was a battle lost but another had been won. To the dismay of civil servants, the Met protection unit and the Security Service, he and Carol had broken precedent. They were a family, he was a family man. They would stay living at the family home in Notting Hill that had been their main base since he was elected to Parliament. If the irregularity of his hours required him sometimes to stay over at the office, the Downing Street flat was always there. He had no urge to live above the shop, as Margaret Thatcher had once put it. Nor did he wish to end up like her, snared in the Downing Street cocoon, divorced from genuine human contact.

He glanced at his wife, sitting beside him. She turned and rested a hand on his thigh. He held it.

'I was worried it was happening again,' she said.

He smiled. 'I know you were, love. So was I for a moment. Being on stage. I sometimes still feel one could come.'

'It won't.'

'No.' He gently released his hand, pulled his briefcase onto his lap and opened it. He scanned the top papers, turned away and stared out of the window. She knew he needed quiet; the girls behind, sensing it too, were plugged into earphones.

Did we kill her? Totally weird. It was the *we* that stood out, the implication that he and Jed Fowkes were complicit. What on earth did he mean? He and Jed were not murderers. Could there possibly be someone they had made so unhappy that she had damaged herself? Committed suicide even? He certainly knew of no such thing. Mikey might have been callous at times, but that had never been part of his own nature with women. What about Jed? He had the ability to be insensitive, to put it mildly. But he had never developed relationships with women that went deep enough to cause hurt. That was always part of his problem.

After Carol and the girls were dropped off at the house in Salisbury Square, Sandford went on to Downing Street. The thought of the dinner with luminaries of British film and television, to which he had been looking forward, now irked him. There could be no pulling out.

11

Later that evening, as the guests finished off their meal, Sandford found he made one new friend. A director, who had devoted his life to making films on the wickedness of successive Conservative governments, congratulated him on his arms ban proposal. 'Quite agree, Prime Minister, sod the murdering capitalists, we'll make you a socialist yet.' Next he found himself with the BAFTA-winning producer of a feature documentary on a serial killer who had confessed to a nationwide spate of prostitute murders thirty years back.

'It was terrible,' she told him. 'Shocking. It felt like another poor young woman's bones were being dug up every week.'

'Awful,' he replied, Jed Fowkes's question ringing in his ears. 'To think our country could breed someone like that.'

Despite the temptation to make his excuses and leave, he stuck it till 11 p.m. Twenty minutes later he was deposited, this time by Prime Ministerial Jaguar, escort motorbikes in front and behind, outside another period townhouse that was home.

He opened the front door and shut it noiselessly behind him. One advantage at least of his new life was that he didn't need a key to unlock it; the house was under twenty-four-hour guard by armed policemen.

Carol was reading in bed, the girls sleeping, the house and square silent. She waited till he joined her.

'What was that about with Jed?' she asked.

He shook his head. 'I honestly don't know, love. He said he wanted a chat. Refused to say what about.'

'I thought you couldn't stand the sight of him.'

'He cornered me. I could hardly take him outside and chuck him into the canal.'

'That *would* have made a splash.' He smiled. 'Seriously though, he looked pretty frantic.'

'He's always like that.'

'He didn't say anything else?'

'No. Why should there be anything else?'

She hesitated. 'Indeed.'

He knew she didn't want to let it go. She was his closest confidante; normally he enjoyed her curiosity. Frustrating it made him uncomfortable.

She yawned noisily. 'I could see you were busy in the car, so I didn't say it then. But I'll say it now.' She paused. 'I truly admired you today. What you said.'

He frowned. 'Really?'

'It was brave. The good government. The moral government. Arms, mercenaries. It's right.'

'A lot of them won't like it.'

'That's just the party. Ordinary people will.'

'I'm the party's leader. As well as Prime Minister.'

'Yes. And it's your moment. You've earned it. Ditch the fanatics.'

His eyes widened. 'That's a big word. They consider themselves radicals. At least the ones with the brains behind them like a certain Jed Fowkes do.'

'It's not as if you're still friends.'

'No.' He paused. 'I sometimes wonder if we ever really were.'

Did we kill her? Was this the first move in some kind of

game? How twisted it seemed even to contemplate that. He remembered the instruction to his private office when he first stepped into Number 10. *On no account allow an unaccompanied Jed Fowkes to cross this threshold for as long as I am Prime Minister.* He must withdraw it. He had to know what madness was consuming Jed.

Jed Fowkes, once, a long time ago, the young meteoric riser. Sandford, two years junior and thrilled at landing a job as an MP's researcher, had held Jed in awe. An ordinary, working-class upbringing like his own but – and here was the difference – culminating in an Oxford double first and not afraid to show it. Jed had taken him under his wing, inviting him to share the flat he was about to rent on the Lewisham/Greenwich borders. There was a third bedroom and Jed suggested he find someone to fill it. Sandford's university friend, Mikey Miller, though he was on a much higher salary in the City, agreed. 'You might not be making money but you're making useful connections.' Three boys from ordinary backgrounds on the make, each bringing something to the party.

Then came the aftermath of the accident. Jed Fowkes saw it all. Jed, his guardian, the keeper of his secrets. Jed, whom he had tried to keep sweet even as, with the passing years and decades, their trajectories parted. There was never a fallout; it was just that he knew Jed would always see himself as the cleverer, the more serious, the more authentic. He came to realize that Jed had always condescended to him and would continue to do so, whatever their status. Ultimately, when he became party leader and then Prime Minister, he possessed the power to cut him out. Was that his pride? Was this now Jed's revenge?

Did we kill her? There had been bad times but, surely, nothing like that. He shut his eyes and told himself to block it out.

4

'Anything else, Mark?' asked Sandford, peering down at the tweet his thumbs were composing. Brilliant news, US President to visit UK, promising new friendship. Give a great British welcome to our greatest ally!

Friday evening, the week almost over, the weekend to come. Since he had taken office as Prime Minister, any difference between the two had become more illusory than ever. He checked his watch: 8.35 p.m. Time to let his principal private secretary escape. He looked up at the serious, still youthful face of Mark Burden and, as so often, thought how lucky he had been to inherit him. Even a year in, he still marvelled at how a civil servant this close to the centre of power had been able to transfer so seamlessly from the Prime Minister of one party to the newcomer of another. Mark was proof not just of impartiality but also of enduring loyalty. Sandford tried to imagine himself like that – the picture went blank.

'There *is* just one more thing, Prime Minister,' replied

Burden in a manner which, Sandford had come to understand, meant the 'thing' would not be a thing he wanted to hear.

'It's all right, Mark,' he said gently, 'there's always one, isn't there?'

Burden returned a limpid smile. 'Jed Fowkes has been phoning…'

'Ah.' Already? Surely he could have given him more than a single day.

'Of course I've remembered your instruction.'

'Sorry. I should have told you. He has a personal problem he wants to discuss with me. Instruction temporarily rescinded.'

Burden's eyebrows rose infinitesimally. 'Of course.'

'I'll see him in the flat first thing Monday. Seven forty-five. Fifteen minutes max.'

'I'll ring him.' Burden paused. 'He said there had been a development.'

'Well, I'll do what I can,' Sandford said, rising from his chair. 'Thanks, Mark. For everything. There's never any downtime…'

'It's worth it. You've built a strong team.'

'Let's hope enough of them go on kicking the ball in the same direction.' He sighed. 'At least till after the State Opening and Royal Speech.'

'Only a month to go then.' Burden attempted an encouraging smile.

'Sure,' said Sandford flatly.

'Final thing, Prime Minister, you had it in mind to be home in good time for dinner. I'm afraid we've overrun.'

'Yes.' He sighed, allowing the fatigue to show. 'It's OK, I'll phone.'

As the study door closed behind Burden, the prospect of being one-to-one with Fowkes loomed. He loved his family, but he was not yet ready to go home, to adjust to being the good husband and father. He walked up the stairs to the Number 10 flat. Man up, he told himself, don't be a coward. He dialled the number.

'Oh, hi,' said Carol. 'Have you done?'

'Not quite.'

'That's a shame. Everything's ready. The girls are dying to see you. Not to mention me. Anything serious?'

'World War Three's not imminent if that's what you mean. But something's come up. I need to think it through.'

'How long?'

'An hour. Hour and a half maybe.'

'Oh.' He heard her disappointment. 'Never mind,' she said brightly. 'I can come over if you want. At least we could be driven back here together.'

'Don't worry, love, it's one of those things I'd best sort myself.'

'All right. We'll see you when we see you.' The phone clicked.

There's been a development… Just like Jed to leave a sting in the tail. Here he was – the most powerful man in the land, still in the afterglow of his greatest triumph, paralysed by a secret he must keep to himself.

Sandford went into the flat's modest kitchen that led off the sitting room. He had asked that it be kept stocked with basic provisions. He opened the fridge. In addition to the red-topped pint of skimmed milk there was fizzy water and orange juice. He removed them both, took a glass tumbler and mixed them half-in-half, fighting to maintain calm.

What could a 'development' possibly be? Perhaps this girl had turned up in Tahiti safe and sound. No, whatever else, he knew it was not going to bring relief.

He needed mindless distraction and switched on the kitchen TV screen – a bleak-sounding drama with a police-man interrogating a father about his schoolgirl daughter who had gone missing. For God's sake… He finally alighted on an indoor tennis tournament. How long was it since he'd played? To remain sane, he must build in proper leisure time, time too with family and friends. They must make more use of Chequers as an escape. He would tell Mark first thing Monday that future diary planning must be based around a minimum of two weekends every month at the Prime Minister's country retreat.

He turned off the television and switched on the radio. Henry Morland-Cross pontificating on *Any Questions*. He tried to think of ways the evening could get worse and hit the off button on that too. In the silence he felt his heart thumping – all too audible in bullet- as well as sound-proofed Downing Street. The fear of its racing beat came back to him; the searching for the pulse, the not understanding why.

There was nothing to be achieved by delaying further. He must go home to his family.

5

'Hello,' he cried, closing the front door. He went down into the extended kitchen/dining room that occupied the semi-basement and a large swathe of former garden. Carol stood at the hob, the outline of her back and hips facing him.

She turned and looked down at her watch. 'Not too bad.'

'Sorry.'

She walked towards him; he didn't know what to expect. She put her hands on his shoulders and planted a light kiss on his lips. 'We'll talk later. The girls want to congratulate you properly.'

'Congratulate?'

'Of course. Your speech. You'll be glad to hear they approved.'

They had met in 2002. MPs and parliamentary candidates from the Bristol area had been invited to a presentation at the London HQ of a worldwide firm of recruitment consultants. Robin Sandford, thirty-four years old and just selected as his party's parliamentary candidate for the constituency of Bristol

20

Central – traditionally Conservative but lost to Labour in Blair's first two victories – was on the list. He had seemed an unusual selection – a Durham man in a west of England seat – but it turned out that the difference, the small lilt in the voice, the life narrative beginning 'born in a council house' had favoured him. A different sort of Tory to win the seat back.

Sandford noted that one of the two female speakers from the global headhunters was called Carol van Kroon – also the familiar name of a once modest Dutch family grocer that had relocated to Britain in the late 1930s and since grown into a vast, multinational food and drinks manufacturer.

Carol van Kroon spoke fluently and confidently, without a trace of nerves. She was in her mid to late twenties, Sandford judged, medium height, with blonde hair, expensive-looking designer spectacles, a black business skirt falling just above her knees, below which Betty Grable legs extended into black and white patterned, low-heeled shoes.

As she finished speaking, Sandford suddenly realized he was enthusiastically leading the applause. The crowd began to clear and he made his way over to her. 'Good speech,' he said. Close up, her glasses now off, he could see the deep brown of her eyes, so unusual and striking against her blonde hair.

'Thank you.' She peered at his name tag. 'And you are...'

'Robin Sandford,' he said, offering a hand. 'Usually known as Robbie.' She looked him up and down: over six foot, dark wavy hair in slight retreat each side of the widow's peak, and, above all, a smile that illuminated the entire room.

'Carol van Kroon.' She shook his hand. 'Usually known as Carol. So you're the new man for Bristol Central.'

21

'Well remembered.' They held each other's look for that split second that can change lives. 'We'll win it back next time.'

'Good. As it happens,' she said, 'I'm in line to head up our new operation out of Bristol. Great city.'

'I'm looking forward to getting to know it.'

'So, when will the election be?'

'Well, I guess Blair could go the full term but I expect he'll cut and run again after four years, so 2005.'

'And will they win again?'

'Sadly, but not by so much.' He smiled. 'Our trouble is Hague was bald, IDS is bald, and if we get Michael next, he's pretty hairless too. We'll never get in till we find a leader with hair.'

She laughed. 'Should be a good while before you have a problem there.' She brushed a speck of fluff off his breast pocket. 'Nice to meet you, Robbie. I'd better circulate.'

And she was off. For a second, he stood leaden-footed, the stroke of her hand like a bolt of lightning. A parliamentary colleague sidled up to him. 'Go for it, Robbie. She's a real van Kroon, she doesn't need the money. But you will.'

'Never occurred to me,' he replied without a beat. 'She's a bit of a goddess, isn't she?'

For him, it was a *coup de foudre.* He'd run naked to the North Pole if she felt anything like the same.

Watching her now move between oven and hob, he felt a surge of that adoration but also a twinge of sadness at a nervousness that had developed between them. The absences from home in a Prime Minister's life, the competing demands for his attention, the constant grind of meetings, never quite allowed the time to re-enter the innocence of early marriage. A voice within urged him to put his arms around her, to rest his face on her shoulder and close his eyes.

'Can I do anything?' he asked.

'It's fine. Just spag bol.' She suddenly turned. 'I need a hug.'

'So do I,' he said. Why couldn't he instantly revert to the ease they had once had? He shouldn't just blame it on the pressures of his success. Prime Ministers were like everyone else. They had no special immunity. He thought of Churchill and the 'black dog' of depression; Eden's bag of nerves; Wilson's early onset dementia. In his own case, however irrational it might be, the fear that the attacks could one day come back.

He had thought its origin would be the hardest thing to explain at their first date. She suggested the Italian place near the flat her parents had bought for her in Holland Park.

'What would you like to drink?' he asked, staring down at the wine list.

'You choose,' she answered. 'Red or white both fine by me.' Her eyes sparkled. 'Chianti perhaps? I'm sure we can manage a bottle.'

'As long as you drink most of it,' he said.

'Oh?' He soon found that this simple 'Oh?' with a soft smile and rise of inflection was her favoured mode of interrogation.

He grinned. 'Don't worry, I'm not a secret member of the temperance movement. I just don't do it so much these days.'

'I imagine you have to be careful in the limelight.'

'I'm nowhere near that yet.'

'It won't be long.'

They looked down at their menus. She needed no more than seconds, then examined him with a directness he found electric. He knew she had spotted it. Probably when she had first set eyes on him.

'This?' He ran a finger along it, a just visible, uneven semi-circle around the top of his forehead.

'Yes. You can hardly see it.'

'It's still there.' He paused. 'Car smash.'

'I'm sorry. Bad one?'

'Yes.'

'Do you want to talk about it?'

His smile waned. 'Not usually.'

'There's no need.'

'No, you've noticed. And it matters. It was after finals. Mid-morning. Clear summer's day. My best friend, Leo, was driving. We were going to pick up his girlfriend in Hampshire. On the way to the Isle of Wight festival. There was a girl in the front, Heather, who I'd invited. We'd met once or twice. The way she said yes sort of made us both think we could be getting together that weekend.

'Leo was well-off, I'd never had the money for a car. It was an Audi coupé. No back doors. It went fast. Too fast. We were on a road going south from Guildford through those pretty villages. Leo put his foot down and overtook on a straight. Then he went for the next car too. We were coming up to a blind corner. I thought of yelling, "Get in." But I didn't. I've never forgiven myself. A car came round. Leo tried to duck back in, but he was going over seventy. That poor guy in the other car… They crashed head-on, driver's side to driver's side.'

He stopped, caught in the horror of the moment. She moved a hand over the table and took his. 'You don't have to go on.'

'I feel I want to tell you. There were consequences.'

'All right. Only if you want.'

'I think I lost consciousness for a moment but then I remember the smell of burning, the hissing, then ambulance men and firemen. One of them was looking down at Leo. I'll never forget his words. "There's nothing we can do for this poor sod." They must have lifted Heather out. I guess I was trapped. There were grinding sounds. They cut me out and pulled me through the front door. I could smell burning, imagined the fire to come. My left leg had turned the wrong way round and been crushed. I remember how wrong it looked. There was blood on my face. They finally got me out. Still the smell of burning, but no fire. I was stretchered into an ambulance. That was it for a while. Morphine, I guess. I woke up to find I was in bed in a ward, my left leg hanging and stretched out on some contraption. Sorry, I'm saying too much.'

'No,' she replied firmly, 'I want to know everything.'

'I'd smashed my thigh, pulverized it. I had to lie there for four months. Otherwise I'd be Long John Silver today. Maybe not quite, but they said the leg would have been nine inches shorter. Soon after I woke, they told me Leo had died. Apparently his seatbelt couldn't have been properly fastened. The impact threw him at huge speed against the steering wheel. It fractured his aorta. The other driver died too, poor man. Heather broke a leg and wrist, more standard breaks than me, some cuts and bruises. She was properly strapped in, thank God.'

He ran his finger along the scar. 'They put a hundred stitches in that. They weren't sure if I'd smashed into the sunroof handle or been catapulted forward into the top of the windscreen. It was quite a mess. Heather was let out after a few weeks. She came to see me in my bed. I couldn't really face her. Not just because I knew I must look awful. It was because I'd brought her into this.'

'You couldn't blame yourself for that,' said Carol.

'You blame yourself for everything. I could have stopped the crash. Saved my best friend's life.'

'No, you can't think that.'

'When I got out, I thought of looking Heather up but I couldn't. Just couldn't.' He paused. 'I never saw her again.'

'That's sad. Perhaps you'd have ended up with her.'

He smiled. 'No. We were too young.'

She released his hand and sat up straight. 'Well, that's something. Otherwise we might not be sitting here.'

'And we haven't even ordered.'

'We'll do that in a minute. I want to know the aftermath.'

The bottle of wine had arrived. He poured into her glass – she didn't stop him filling it right up – and then a smaller amount into his own.

She took a large sip. 'Go on.'

'Before the crash, I'd had an interview with an MP to work on his team. I'd done my bit at Manchester. President of the Students' Union.'

'Not the Conservative Association?'

He grinned. 'You'd never get both. Not there, not then. Maybe at Oxford Tories were allowed.'

'As I well remember,' she said. A short silence fell. He wondered if she minded that he was a provincial. 'And I'm very

26

glad you're not from that Augean stable.' He relaxed. She had read him instantly. 'But difficult perhaps to hide your colours?'

'No, I was – am – pragmatic. Never an ideologue. The Conservatives seemed the party of power. I didn't spot Blair coming,' he said ruefully. 'I might have gone the other way.'

'We'll do politics next time. Go on.'

'Amazingly, lying in hospital, my parents brought me a letter. This MP had offered me a job as researcher. He was great about it, held the job for me for the time I needed to recover.' He took a sip of water and looked down at the table. 'And then, three months later, soon after I started, they began.'

6

Carol knew instinctively that whatever came next was central to his life. 'What began?'

He looked back up. 'The panic attacks. What do you know about how they work?'

'Assume nothing.'

'OK. The first time I was at a concert. A few weeks after I'd left hospital. I was in the middle of a row near the front. The hall seemed to go foggy. My pulse felt unbelievably fast. I was sweating, wanting to get out. It was chamber music. Even the slightest cough was a disturbance. The next ten minutes were agony. I thought I was going to die.'

'Die?'

'Yes, really. I assumed it was a heart attack. When the applause stopped, I pushed my way out, past the friend I was with. God knows what he thought. I phoned the next day to apologize. Put it down to a funny turn.

'Outside in the fresh air I slumped on the ledge of a pillar. I was sure I'd pass out. To my surprise I stayed conscious.

28

I couldn't face the second half. I couldn't walk to the tube. Or even get on a bus. My heart was still thumping. In the end I got a taxi back to the flat I was sharing with two guys. Jed Fowkes and Mikey Miller. They were both at home when I got back. Jed gave me a funny look. "I thought you were at a concert." "Yes," I said, "the lead violin was shit. I walked out."

'The attacks went on. Tube, theatre, in a car, flying. It didn't help if I'd drunk too much the night before.'

'Didn't you tell anyone?'

'I was sort of embarrassed. I didn't die when they happened, however much I thought I would. I didn't want to make a fuss. Then one Friday, I developed a headache. It got worse and worse over the next two days until by the end of Sunday I'd convinced myself it was a brain tumour. We had a friend, Suzy Lancaster...'

'The BBC reporter?'

'Yes, we met her when she was a trainee on attachment to Parliament and we became good mates. I told her what was happening. She was amazing. Carted me into a taxi, straight to casualty. I was examined in every possible way. Nothing physically wrong. The headache went. Fortunately there was a young doctor who got it and made an appointment for me to see a psychiatrist the next day.'

A waiter arrived. Sandford paused. 'I'm banging on, let's get some food.' They ordered. 'Haven't you had enough?' he asked, frowning. 'I'd much rather know about you.'

'Actually, no,' she said. 'I know this is the first time we've properly talked. I certainly didn't expect to be discussing this. I'm sure you didn't either. But if we want to know each

29

other – really know each other – then I think you should get to the end.'

'OK.' He touched his forehead. 'It's the scar, isn't it? You start with that, then one thing leads to another.'

'In that case, it has its uses – and you can only see it when you look really closely. As I'm afraid I'm inclined to do at most things.'

'You say that like it's a fault.'

She grinned. 'Is it?'

'Maybe I'll tell you in a few years.'

'Are you flirting or is that the quickest proposal in the history of marriage?' She saw the flash of alarm in his eyes. 'It's all right, Robbie, I'm joking.'

'Do you think I am?' he replied.

She did not answer and looked over his shoulder. 'Ah, olives.' A dish was placed between them. She poked an olive with a stick and plopped it into her mouth. 'So what happened?'

'The psychiatrist explained it to me. Anxiety disorder, plus depression—'

'Had you felt depressed?'

'Not that I was particularly aware of. He said they usually went together. In my case the crash might have been enough to trigger it. Combined with the stress of a new job and new home. Actually he called it hypochondriasis. I thought, hell, so I'm a bloody hypochondriac, am I? He said not at all. Everything you feel is happening to you physically. But it's a build-up of adrenalin caused by the mind working on itself and creating a vicious circle. He was an experienced guy – maybe a bit old-fashioned in retrospect – and put me on Valium and Librium. Seriously strong tranquillizers and anti-depressants.'

'That sounds drastic.'

'Yes, but it was still the go-to treatment in the first instance. SSRIs – you know, Prozac-type things – hadn't been around that long and were still viewed with some suspicion. And CBT—'

'Cognitive behaviour therapy—'

'Yes. It wasn't frontline treatment then.'

'Did the drugs cure it?'

'It's never fully "cured". They did control the attacks, but…' He hesitated, looked down and felt his glass of wine.

'But?'

'There were things you had to avoid eating with those drugs. I remember broad beans was one, heaven knows why. And they said you should be careful with alcohol. That was bloody difficult. There was a terrible drinking culture in the House of Commons. Still is, as I understand it. It was very male. Then at weekends at the flat it was always party-time. Mikey was a wild one. Great fun, but endless booze and, in his case, coke. I tried to be restrained, never did drugs, but on a few occasions the combination of too much alcohol with Librium and Valium was bad. Really bad. I mean, a few times I woke up on a Saturday or Sunday afternoon and couldn't remember anything from midway through the previous evening. Like, full-scale alcoholic black-outs. Except that I wasn't an alcoholic. After one of those, Suzy – the saviour again – took me to one side. She told me I needed to take care.

31

I wasn't sure why she chose that moment – I just hoped I'd never done anything really stupid or embarrassing.'

'Had you?' she asked sharply.

'No. Not as far as I know. No one ever said anything. But the thought of it made me wise up. Anyway, after a couple of years I came off the drugs. Did some CBT. To be honest, it's only the breathing exercises that really helped. I tried Prozac a couple of times for a few months. Helped a bit too – and no bad side effects.'

'And now?'

'Last three or four years have been fine. The odd attack, but milder. There are a couple of people close to me who fully understand it. Knowing they're there and I can lift the phone helps.'

'Well, I'm one now too.'

'Thank you.'

She raised her glass again. 'If you don't mind the irony, let's drink to that.'

They clinked glasses. 'You know something?' he said.

'Oh?'

'A scientific study has shown that a man only needs eight point two seconds to look at a woman to know he's fallen in love with her.'

'Really?' she laughed. She took a large glug of wine, looked straight into his eyes and broke into the biggest grin he'd ever seen. 'What on earth takes a man so long?'

7

'Good to see you, Jed.'

Sandford slapped an arm around his visitor's shoulder. Fowkes drew back with a frown. 'I sensed you'd been a bit withdrawn these past months.'

'No, not at all.' Sandford waved his arms around. 'It's just… everything's so… so busy.'

'Sure.' Fowkes's expression was a blank. 'How's the rich wife?'

Sandford forced a smile. 'Still rich. Look, sorry if I've been elusive. It's not meant.'

'It's fine. We all move on.'

'Let's sit in here.' Sandford gestured him into the 10 Downing Street flat's kitchen, indicated a wooden chair at the breakfast table, put on the kettle and sat down opposite him.

'But you, Jed… your wheel's come full circle,' said Sandford, rubbing his hands. 'Right-hand man to the Chancellor and Deputy Leader.'

'I wouldn't say that. I'm just a Spad.'

'But a powerful one. My civil servants tell me Spads have all the fun,' said Sandford lightly. 'Power without responsibility.'

Fowkes allowed a brief smile. 'I wouldn't listen too much to your civil servants, Robbie. They're a big part of the problem.'

'Maybe. But I've given M-C the Treasury. And that means you too.'

'You could hardly not. Better for you to have him inside pissing out, not outside pissing in.'

Sandford, his heart sinking, forced another smile. 'I reckon M-C doesn't mind where his piss goes.'

Fowkes had been shown through the door of the flat on the dot of 7.45 a.m. Sandford realized he must have arrived early to ensure that not a minute of the fifteen he had been given would be wasted. There was nothing new about the judgementalism. As young men, it had often seemed sharp, even funny. Less so now.

'Jed,' continued Sandford, 'you mentioned "something bad" in that quick chat we had in Birmingham. And you ended with a question which I assume you didn't mean literally. It was preposterous.'

'I wish it were so,' said Fowkes.

Sandford told himself not to react. 'Since then, you've told my PPS there's been a development.'

'I'll come to that.'

'As you wish.'

'First I want to ask you about a particular Friday night and the weekend that followed.'

'When?'

'In the flat of course.'

'That's thirty years ago. There were a lot of Friday nights and weekends that followed.'

'Quite.'

'Things get a bit blurry that far back.'

'This one was around November 1991,' said Fowkes. 'A Friday evening. You and I met Mikey in the pub round the corner from his bank.'

'We often met Mikey there.'

'Yes,' agreed Fowkes, 'bear with me.' Mikey, he related, had brought along a couple of girls from the bank – one was new, a sweet little Hungarian redhead called Andrea who was doing some waitressing and cleaning, the second a receptionist from Ireland called Roisin, pretty curls of dark hair and plenty of jokes.

'I remember Roisin,' said Sandford. 'I took her out for dinner a couple of times.' He smiled. 'She was a laugh.'

'I suspect that was after the evening I'm talking about. Maybe something was nagging you and you wanted to ask her about it.'

'I doubt it. I just liked her.'

'Perhaps.' Fowkes resumed his account. They drank and chatted, Roisin mainly, the petite Hungarian saying little – she had arrived in Britain only a couple of weeks before. A few others came and went; Mikey was sidetracked by a new girlfriend.

'It's weird,' said Jed, 'I can remember certain details like that, even picture Mikey's girl's face – and the two of them linking arms as they headed for the street. She was wearing a tight black leather skirt.' He paused, peering into Sandford's eyes. 'Bring anything back?'

'Can't say that does. Mikey always had a good-looking girl in tow. But yes, because of Roisin, I remember an evening out with her and her new friend. I don't remember the friend. Small maybe, young-looking?' Sandford looked at his watch. 'Any help?'

'Sorry, you're a busy man.' It had been nearing midnight, Fowkes continued, the pubs emptying, the city closing down for the weekend. 'Roisin said she was going to peel off.'

'I think I do remember that. I was disappointed.'

'OK,' said Fowkes. 'It's from now I'm really hoping you can keep bringing it back. Because, Robbie, it soon turned out your disappointment was short-lived. Unfortunately things turned out in a way that's come back to haunt me. And it has bad consequences for you. I mean, really bad.'

8

'Now I want to know all about you. Everything.'

'Everything?' she smiled. 'Are you sure?'

'Yes, please,' he said. The chianti bottle was empty and espressos on the way.

Carol took a deep breath. 'Well, I was born one Sunday at a quarter to midnight. Because I had my right hand stuck by my head, my poor mother's vagina had to be surgically widened to let me through. So I emerged into this world as a rather bloody mess.'

Sandford chuckled. 'All right, maybe not.'

'You see,' she said, 'I can be inclined to a certain precision at times.'

'I'll bear that in mind. I might learn from it.'

She took his hand and stroked the back of it. 'I was born lucky. My father is second-generation Dutch immigrant, married a soldier's daughter, he's now more English than the English. We had a house in Chelsea during the week, country house in Gloucestershire at weekends. Horses, swimming, tennis. I went to private day school in London, then boarding school when I was thirteen.'

'Your choice or your parents'?'

'Mine. Two of my best friends were going to the same place. I was OK, never unhappy or lonely. But it wasn't a clever girls' school and I was more academic than most of them. That could be frustrating.' She spoke with the same fluency and intelligence he had instantly admired at her presentation. 'But, my lucky star again, there was one wonderful teacher. He taught French and German. I was good at languages and, to everyone's surprise, I got into Oxford. The only one in my year – or the two years before and after, for that matter.'

'I knew it.' He turned his hand and held hers. 'Not just clever. But smart enough not to make a thing of it.'

'That's nice of you, Robbie. And then the summer after I did my "A"s we went as usual to Corfu, we had a villa there...' She tailed off, her face dropping, and retrieved a tissue from her bag.

'What is it?' he asked softly. 'You don't need to...'

She quickly dabbed an eye. 'No, it's fine. I had three brothers, one older, two younger. The older was Johann. They called him that as a sort of throwback to Holland, I think. Anyway, he was jet skiing. Going too fast, trying to be too clever. He turned it over and the front end somehow caught him just below the temples. It was bad luck. They quickly fished him out of the water, unconscious but still breathing. The Corfu town hospital at least had a CT scanner. They sent the result to Athens. It was what they call "unsurvivable". He had two days on a ventilator. We said goodbye, switched him off and that was it.'

38

'I'm so sorry.'

Under the cover of blowing her nose, she dabbed her eye again. 'The luck of life. Nine years ago now but I think of him every day. He was the golden boy. Rising through the company. Everyone knew he'd soon be running it.'

'Did that change things? Make you feel you should step up into his shoes?'

She smiled. 'I thought about it. I'm sure Dad did too. No. But it made me more determined. To get a first, to make my own way, my own career.' She paused. 'I suspect there was a traditional bit of me that thought the firm was for the male van Kroons. I became what we now call a headhunter.'

'Clearly with great success.'

'Yes,' she said with an openness he liked. 'It's gone well. The languages helped, I started off doing Europe. And now I'm starting a whole new operation in the West Country.'

'I'd always want to support you in your work,' he said.

Her brown eyes opened wide. 'Who knows what we'll all want to do?'

*

That first evening at the Italian restaurant rushed over them like a tidal wave. He walked her home and, somehow, knew that he should do no more than kiss her on the cheek and hold the door while she went inside.

The second date followed two days later, same place, same table. The forty-eight-hour wait was agonizing.

'I felt we'd hardly started,' Carol said.

39

'I know.' He slowly stretched a hand across the table. She took it and held it for a few seconds. Everything was going to be all right.

'Politics,' she said, as if turning the page to a new chapter. 'You said you could have gone either way. Please discuss.'

He grinned at the command. 'OK. I was never really an ideologue. But it always fascinated me and I was ambitious. Though I didn't have a photo taken on the steps of Number 10 when I was a boy—'

'Like Harold Wilson...'

'Yes, well remembered.'

'You don't need to sound so surprised, Robbie.'

'Sorry.' They laughed. 'Anyway I got involved in school debates, that sort of thing.'

'What about your parents?'

'I have to be careful with the humble boy made good narrative. Yes, we lived in a council house, a nice Victorian terrace in Durham as it happens. But my dad worked in the post office. We watched the Miners' Gala but I can't claim him as a miner. Then, under Thatcher's right to buy, he bought the house. Did well out of it. The Labour Party of the 1980s wasn't for me – Militant Tendency and all that. So I joined the Tories, the winners.'

'Now Blair's set in for ever as far as I can see.'

'May seem like that. But Brown's turned on the spending taps – second term, all shackles off – and it'll end in tears. Labour will win next time but heading towards 2010 there'll be a crash. No doubt about it. Then we'll win and have to sort out the mess. Like we always do.'

'Right,' she said, 'I'll hold you to that.'

He slapped the table with his palm. 'Good. Nothing's more certain.'

'And what about when you first were in Parliament? As a researcher, I mean.'

'It was a funny time. Thatcher had just been offed. I liked Major. Looking back, the seed of Jed and me eventually drifting apart was already sown.'

'Jed Fowkes...'

'Yes.'

'Your flatmate. You mentioned him.'

'Actually Jed was amazing in his way.' He collected his thoughts. 'His dad was on the shop floor at Longbridge. He was there when the first Minis came off the production line. He rose to be shop steward, and then a convenor. Fiery by all accounts. Jed, initially, inherited the politics. Even while at school, he joined the IS, International Socialists. Then in 1987 – the summer before his final year at Oxford – he went on a student visit to Leipzig. East Germany was still Communist. When he came back, he wrote an amazing piece in *Cherwell*. About how terrible life was there. The disillusion he felt. He also confessed – quite bravely, I thought – to how he'd been introduced to a man who turned out to be a senior Stasi officer and tried to recruit him. The article made him a student name. He ditched the left and joined the Tories.'

'And you met him...'

'Three and a half years later. When I arrived at Westminster in 1991. He was incredibly knowledgeable, full of ideas. I remember him saying something that turned out to be brilliant. "In future, there won't be general elections, there'll be a conglomeration of specific elections." Of course, we understood marginal seats were crucial. But – and the internet was just beginning – Jed was already outlining a future where data was king. We'd be able to know the preferences of every single voter. Whatever happened on the surface, electioneering would come down to who most effectively targeted each of those individuals with the right message.'

'That was smart,' she said.

'The problem was Jed was a preacher, an evangelical. Transmit, not receive.' He hesitated. 'I sometimes felt he should have been an academic. Then he could have kept banging on without people arguing with him.'

She smiled. 'That bad?'

'No, for a couple of years I enjoyed it. Well, put up with it. Because I was learning. But as I said, I was pro Major. Pragmatic, amiable, moderate. Jed joined the other side. The ideological right, the anti-Europeans, the lot Major called "the bastards". I suppose I'd had enough. He was more upset than I thought he'd be when I left the flat. Maybe he was always a bit on the spectrum, as we say these days. We bump into each other every now and then but he's part of my history now, not my present.' He stopped; she allowed him a moment.

'You know,' he eventually said, 'I think, politically, there was one big difference. When it came to the rich and poor, Jed felt the rich came first. I can see the argument – the logic – wealth trickling down. But it's inhuman. For me the poor always came first. Always will. Logic's not always for the best.'

He had finished. She looked at him, eyes shining. At that

moment, gazing back at her, he felt he was seeing the world afresh. He walked her home. This time, as she opened the front door, she took him by the hand and led him upstairs.

They married the Saturday before Christmas, just eight months after those first dates. The wedding, attended by three hundred guests, was a glittering occasion held at the village church in Gloucestershire followed by a reception in a huge, heated marquee on the front lawn of the van Kroon family home. They might not have forgotten Holland but they had left behind the austerity of Dutch Protestantism. The first Sandford daughter arrived so soon that some were tempted to count the months.

Jed Fowkes had been on the guest list. Sandford felt he had to be. His own selection as parliamentary candidate for a safe constituency had created a further awkwardness. Jed was a serial failure at selection meetings, unmarried, unattached, and now a rather anonymous figure in the party's policy unit. But Sandford remained grateful to him as a significant part of his early career. He made a point of seeking him out among the wedding throng.

'Hey, Jed, fantastic to see you,' he said, clubbing him on the shoulder. 'So good you could come.'

Fowkes did not return the gesture. He made a show of looking around the vast marquee. 'You struck gold, Robbie. Safe seat, rich wife.'

Sandford frowned. 'It's all luck. You know that.'

'Yeah, sure.'

'Anyway you're doing well. Crafting policy, preparing for our return.'

'It's all for show. You're fine, you'll get in. But we've no chance of winning while Blair's there.'

'If you think that, Jed, maybe you should get out, try something else.'

Fowkes took a step towards Sandford, matching him eye to eye. 'I'm a stayer, Robbie. It'll take time – ten, fifteen, even twenty years maybe – but there'll come a moment when we'll see what a proper government can do. Maggie was beginning to see it. Get out of Europe, it's corrupt to the core. Roll up the state. Build ourselves a country again. Mark my words, it'll come. And I've every intention of being there to see it happen.'

9

The kettle whistled. At least, thought Sandford, it allowed the menace of Fowkes's words to hang momentarily in the air. It was beginning to feel like Groundhog Day from that unpleasant – and unforgettable – exchange at the wedding eighteen years before. A scenario unfolding, a threat in its tail. Then it was just a wish, now it was clearly leading to something more.

'Tea or coffee?'

Fowkes shook his head dismissively. 'No. Let's get on.'

'Fine.'

'Right. Roisin gave a quick wave to the remaining three of us and went off. She asked the little Hungarian girl if she was going to be OK. Andrea said she was fine. Then she smiled at you and said, "Are you fine?" in a way that made me suspect exactly where the night might be heading. I wondered whether I should push off but, to be honest, I had nowhere to go that night. I hailed a black cab and piled into it with the two of you.' He paused again. 'Still with me, Robbie?'

Sandford frowned. 'I'll take your word for it.'

'I guess the girls were always eyeing you up. You were the one they went for.'

Sandford shrugged. 'I don't know about that. Where's this heading?'

'I'm sorry. This is difficult. But details and timings matter. There were the three of us in the cab. It seemed natural that you and she sat on the bench seat and me on a drop-down seat. We didn't say much. She stared out of the window. We drove across one of the bridges – London Bridge, I guess – and she said, "Wow, it is very beautiful." I felt she'd been rehearsing the sentence and finally had the opportunity to speak it. You had your arm round her. I can remember it like yesterday. You?'

'Jed, we met loads of girls.'

'Keep trying. The cab dropped us, we went up the stairs to the flat. I went to the kitchen, grabbed a couple of beers, she'd been drinking vodka and Coke. I probably thought she'd had enough and brought her something soft. You went into the kitchen. She kept her eyes on where you'd gone. You reappeared with a big glass of whisky.'

'You sure?' said Sandford. 'Unusual for me.'

'And not always a good idea.' Fowkes paused, extracting a tissue to clear his nose, as if to prepare himself for a development in the story that he needed courage to tell. 'I was beginning to feel like a wallflower so I made some excuse. But you stopped me, said, "Let's see if there's a movie on." I felt grateful to you, I didn't really want to go to bed but I didn't want to mess you around either. We always knew not to get in each other's way. Maybe that time, you felt it useful having

46

me there while you and she were working each other out. I got up, switched on the TV, flicked through the channels. I stopped at one playing a movie. It had a famous sex scene. That you might remember.'

'*Don't Look Now*?'

'Yes. Donald Sutherland and Julie Christie looking like they're really at it.'

'Everyone knows that scene.'

'But that night. Can you remember watching it that night?'

'Jed, how the hell can I begin to remember on which exact date a particular film was playing on late-night TV thirty years ago?'

Fowkes's eyes narrowed. 'I do, Robbie. That's the point. I do.'

'What are you implying?'

'I'm not implying anything. You were both watching the screen, laughing, and putting your arms round each other. I made my excuses and said goodnight. You seemed OK, though the whisky disappeared pretty fast.'

'I've no idea how you remember a detail like that.'

Fowkes raised a hand. 'Well, I do. You didn't usually drink too much but it was a Friday night, maybe you were tired, maybe it was the girl, I don't know. But you were certainly going for it.'

'I don't recall any of this.'

'Maybe that's why.'

Sandford looked at his watch again. 'Are we nearly done?'

'Yes,' replied Fowkes. 'We are – as you put it – nearly done. A while later, I don't know exactly how long, I needed to pee.

I crept out of my room. The sofa was bare, meaning you and she must be in your bedroom. On the way back, I heard what sounded like whimpering coming from behind your door. Then it suddenly stopped. I went back to my room. A minute or so later, you knocked at my door. Your eyes were wild, your face red. I'll never forget how you looked. "Something's happened," you said. I dragged myself out of bed and put on my boxers. You asked me to come and look, but you could hardly get the words out. We went into your bedroom and she was lying flat on her back, jeans and pants halfway down her thighs. Her head was on the sheet, one pillow beside her, a second pillow on the floor. "Something's happened to her," you said.

'I'm no medic but I picked up her arm and felt for a pulse. I wasn't sure. There didn't seem anything much there but maybe I was doing it wrong. Her chest and breasts seemed too still. I put on the top light. You were standing there motionless, like a marble statue. "What the fuck have you done?" I said. You said you thought she was going to scream, but when I asked you why, you kept saying you didn't know. "Was she asking you to stop?" I asked. "I don't know." It was the third time you'd said it. I wanted to call 999, but you wouldn't let me. You kept saying it was an accident but that you didn't know what happened.'

Fowkes stopped to draw breath. Sandford listened, expressionless, waves of nausea rising. 'I don't remember any of this. How can you know it happened?'

'I'll tell you how. Because she's reappeared.'

'What!' said Sandford.

48

'The girl. She's reappeared,' repeated Fowkes.

'The girl?'

'Her body.' He hesitated. 'I mean, a part of it.'

'What are you talking about? Jed, this is getting crazy.'

Fowkes took a folded piece of paper from his inside pocket and unrolled it. It was a page from the *Daily Mail.* 'Look at the date. The day before your conference speech. It was pushed through my letter box in an envelope. I've no idea who by.' He handed it to Sandford. 'Read the story at the bottom. Actually, first look at what's written below it.'

Handwritten in the bottom margin in red capitals were six words. 'REMEMBER THE GIRL FROM HUNGARY, JED?'

'That's your new development. I could hardly show it to you in the conference hall, could I?' Imitating Sandford's previous gesture, Fowkes made a show of looking at his watch. 'The fifteen minutes you gave me is up. You need to remember this more than I do, Robbie. Let's meet again when you've had time to think about it.'

Before Sandford could speak, Fowkes had turned and was heading towards the door, shutting it behind him with a click that felt like the distant crack of a rifle.

10

Sandford crouched over the newspaper cutting lying flat across the kitchen table. 'SEVERED HAND MYSTERY'.

His hands were damp with sweat, his heart racing, worse than anything he had felt for years. He pushed away the cutting, sat down, hands on the table, and closed his eyes. Following his CBT training, he took deep breaths, concentrating solely on counting the seconds as he exhaled each one.

After a couple of minutes, he retrieved the article. It described Lewisham CID's mystification at the apparent burial, some twenty-five to thirty-five years ago, of a young woman's chopped-off right hand with a ring on the fourth finger. It had been wrapped in a piece of shower curtain and dumped on wasteland near the river, part of a huge proposed development west of Greenwich. Workmen had stumbled across it while checking a mains water pipe beneath a service road. The official police statement concluded: 'If you have information about a young woman who went missing in

South-East London between the mid-1980s and mid-1990s, please contact Lewisham police.' The newspaper article was more excited. 'It's a mystery straight out of a crime thriller. The remains, it seems, of a young woman brutally hacked to death and dismembered. The truth may only be revealed if further body parts are found.'

Sandford tried to remember the exact words Jed had used to describe the events of that evening. He wondered how much he had rehearsed them. He had taken his allotted time of fifteen minutes, almost to the second. A delivery with perfect timing, ending in the final sting as he handed over the article. An ending that required at least one further conversation, perhaps more.

Why now? What evidence did he really have that the hand had anything to do with some incident at the flat? He stared at the words in red, 'REMEMBER THE GIRL FROM HUNGARY, JED?' Could they have been written by Jed himself? Was the whole thing, sparked off by this chance discovery, his invention? If so, why alight on something so extreme? A girl apparently unconscious in their flat, her pants halfway down her legs. Who then disappeared.

Sandford saw the real threat. It was not possible to disprove it. It was Jed's word against the void in his own memory. Supported by a newspaper page with a message and the evidence of a severed hand. That ever-present fear that something shameful – or, perhaps, much worse – might have happened in that troubled period of his life was raging. But never, surely to God, anything like this.

He would never forget that first conversation with Carol at

the restaurant. He had told her about the panic attacks because they could always return. But he had not fully spelt out the wildness of those times.

Most weekends had been one long party, usually started by Mikey and his City friends. Sometimes newly met couples peeled off to his or Mikey's bedrooms, locking the door behind them. Other times, the big joke was to ask if he could remember who had tucked him up in bed. They would give him looks and murmured questions. 'Did you have a good time with her, Robbie?' A fragment of memory still made him shiver. A girl, out of it, visited by at least three or four males in succession. Had he tried to stop them? He had a vision of her lying there, legs sprawled. If he had gone in, surely it was only to comfort her. That was the trouble. As with Jed, 'sure' was the impossible word until truth could be proved.

Jed, the one person who never fully joined the party, never had a girl in his bed, never seemed out of control. Always watching.

Suzy Lancaster, having first made him seek treatment for the panic attacks, was the one who took him aside again.

'My dearest Robbie,' he would never forget her saying, those deep blue eyes bearing in on him, 'you need to get away for a while.'

'I can't. I've got a job,' he'd replied. 'A really good one.'

'You'll lose it if you don't take a break and sort yourself out. It's not your fault. You've been through a trauma.'

'If I duck out now, I'll never catch up.'

She narrowed those big eyes. 'That's rubbish. Escape the Westminster bubble. See the real world. Trust me, it might actually help you. Most politicians have lived far too narrow lives and eventually it finds them out.'

He had the sense to know she was right and applied to VSO. He discovered how useless his skills were in the work – the real work – they did for people who truly needed help. He pleaded with them to take him on. He protested that he was fit, strong, healthy, could dig ditches, plant crops, whatever they wanted. Eventually they relented and he went to Malawi. Nine months later, he returned from this gentle, poor land to London, vowing that never again would alcohol and drugs interfere with his life and ambitions.

The first time he and Suzy met up after those months away, he decided he was in love with her. She could not be persuaded.

'I love you too, Robbie—'

'No, I'm in love with you.'

'It wouldn't work. It's not us. We're best friends, soul mates. Let's not do anything to ruin it.'

When he bumped into Carol a decade later, the mutual *coup de foudre* made him understand how right Suzy had been. He pictured her now, the hair blonder and more shining than ever, the eyes more sparkling. She had reached the summit, a lead presenter on the *Today* programme and big, political interviews on television. He looked at his watch – 8.20 a.m. – and turned on the radio. Not one of her mornings. Their contact was more fleeting now, both leading crammed lives. It momentarily saddened him. Two columnists were assessing prospects for the State Opening of Parliament and the Royal Speech.

He must not allow Jed to distract him from that speech. It was the defining moment, the route map of the next four years, his moment to see off the worst of the radicals in his party. Like Jed Fowkes and the Chancellor, who seemed to have become putty in his hands.

He needed to wrest control of Jed's story, to find out what lay behind it. He must find a strategy fast. He rang down and asked for the private office meeting to be pushed back till 8.45. That gave him twenty minutes. There were two traps to avoid. He could not allow Jed's story to become his own paranoia. And the story could not be allowed to fester unchallenged. Whatever risks the truth held, he had to know what really happened that night.

He could be the tactician not the investigator. He required an ally. An operative. A story digger. A confidant. There was certainly no political colleague he could confide in; they did not recognize words like 'trust', 'loyalty', 'confidentiality'.

Friends? Posing the question deflated him. There had seemed no time for friends, even his closest and oldest. Maybe it was his error – he had failed to insist on making that time. How many conversations must he have had with Carol when she pleaded with him to take it easy, to catch up with old friends? Almost imperceptibly a distance had grown. Perhaps he had too blithely assumed it would be easy enough to retrieve those friendships.

Carol herself? Out of the question. She must never know, never catch a single hint of it. Ever. The temptation to confide or confess to the person you wanted to share everything with could easily become overwhelming.

54

He understood one overarching rule. Only one other person could be allowed to know everything Jed had told him. It was the law of secrets – once they went beyond a single individual, the secret went too. If that individual needed others to help, they could not be given the full picture.

'Trust'. 'Loyalty'. 'Confidentiality'. The words jumped at him again. Who might any previous Prime Minister immediately think of? His most senior civil servant – the Cabinet Secretary? The ultimate crutch to lean on, an unbreakable mix of discretion and trouble-shooting, the Prime Minister's link to the intelligence services. He pictured the rotund shape and beaming face of the present incumbent, Sir Kevin Long, whom he would be seeing in a few minutes. He could not begin to imagine discussing this with him. Forget it.

Before he saw Sir Kevin, he would exchange words with one calming figure of indisputable loyalty. The principal private secretary to the Prime Minister was the person he spent more Downing Street time with than any other. Mark Burden was not just trustworthy, he was also likeable, fun even. Occasionally they had joked about his name – the 'burden' of office, the 'mark' of Cain – and mused about who they would both like to be rid of. But if he approached Mark with his dilemma, he would be placing him in an impossible position. He might feel obligated to pass on this secret, if only to his ultimate boss, the Cabinet Secretary. There was a further practical obstacle. If Mark was bound by confidence, what was there he could actually do from the confines of the private office? No. Wherever this might lead, none of it could – yet – be allowed within Downing Street or Whitehall beyond.

There must be someone. Someone at one remove. He retrieved the morning papers from the flat's front door. He turned to Adam Billing's column in *The Post* – an analysis of the motivation behind his initiative on arms sales and mercenaries. 'IS THIS THE REAL ROBBIE SANDFORD?' read the headline. Billing was fine, he reflected – and that particular question a reasonable one for a commentator to raise. But he did not begin to compare with his predecessor – a man for whom the word 'confidential' meant precisely that. How sad that someone he had so liked and admired was now out of the picture.

The thought lingered. 'Trust'. Yes. 'Confidentiality'. Yes. 'Loyalty'. Irrelevant, not the way he would think, outweighed by the other two.

Was it possible? Were there any other ideas even remotely worth considering at this point?

He opened the fridge, grabbed two oranges, went to the bathroom to check his hair and teeth, then down to the private office.

Mark Burden was waiting. 'Good morning, Prime Minister.'

'Morning, Mark.' He rubbed his hands. 'Right, I have a task for you. As and when you can fit it in. If you need any assistance, no one must know the request has come from me.'

'What should I say?'

'Oh, you'll find a way round it.' He paused, lowering his voice. 'Do you happen to know where Quine is these days?'

The PPS appeared puzzled, then smiled. 'Hiding from his creditors, I dare say.'

'Yes, that was an injustice. I want you to find him. I want

to meet him. Privately. You can know. No one else. Give him a codename if you want. Me too.'

'I'm not really suited to subterfuge—'

'Make yourself suited, Mark.'

'Yes, Prime Minister. But you do realize he is seen by most people as damaged goods.'

'You know something? I really couldn't give a damn.'

11

Quine gazed at the spectacle that had captivated him the moment he first caught sight of it.

He had gone west in Beatrice, his vintage VW camper van, one of the few treasured possessions he had managed to hang onto after the disaster, aiming for the seaside village he remembered loving as a boy. The broad beach was the same but now its smattering of shops and shacks were boarded up or closed. The bungalows rising above were gloomy and empty-looking as winter clouds rolled in across the sky. But then, looking out at low tide over the great stretch of sand, greying in the autumnal light, his eye was drawn to the cliff edge on its northern side, extending and rising to a headland in the far distance.

A mile along the cliff face was a cluster of dwellings, standing sentinel over the waves beating onto rocks below. He hurried back to Beatrice, turned round and retraced his route, chugging up the steep hill and onto a track. The camper van struggled through its dips, kerbs and potholes, until it joined a tarmacked lane. Half a mile later he descended through a group of houses that stretched all the way to the edge of the cliff. He walked over a band of mossy grass to a marble bench, inscribed with two names. 'At peace with the waves they loved'. The inscription showed they had drowned ten years before.

The air was cold, the chill coming from an east wind. The sandy beach Quine had seen from sea level had given way to rolling foam. On its other side, was a further long spur of cliff, tipped by a lighthouse. He moved his eyes to the water below him. Two black-suited figures lying on surfboards were paddling out, breasting the swell. Finally they stopped, turned, lay motionless, waiting for the perfect wave.

He sat on the bench, a tear in his eye, and watched. The troubles of his life, here and now in this moment, were as nothing. This was the place he would resolve them.

Dragging himself away, he drove slowly back up the lane, in search of a sign displaying 'Vacancy' among windows of pebble-dashed cottages. He neither wanted nor could afford luxury or even comfort. He needed only space.

It was late afternoon but the place was asleep. Perhaps no one came here outside the summer months. Then he saw not just a sign, but a porch light illuminated. A nameplate on the entrance gate said, '7, The Waves'. He drew up outside and knocked on the door. A tall, grey-haired woman, cigarette in hand – in her seventies, he guessed – answered.

'Yes?'

'I wondered if you have a room?' He paused. 'For the next year or so.'

'Good heavens,' she rasped, looking down on him. 'Why

didn't you phone, dear? There's a thing called the internet too.'

'There was no point,' he said. 'I could only know the place I wanted when I saw it. I've found it here. On this cliff.'

'What a strange-sounding man you are. All right, come in.' She inspected him. 'I'm Barbara Trelight.' She pronounced it as 'relict'. 'Spelt like delight.'

He offered a hand. 'Then I'm delighted to meet you, Mrs Trelight.'

She wheezed with a certain pleasure. 'As it happens, Mrs is correct. But he's dead.'

'I'm sorry.'

'No need. I'm better off without him.' She flicked ash on the gravel drive. 'A cup of tea, Mr...'

'Thank you. Quine. Joseph Quine. People tend to call me Joe—'

'Best stick to the formalities for the moment. I'll need to know a great deal more about you, Mr Quine. For example, will you pay weekly on time? Do you have antisocial habits? Or a criminal record?' She paused, leaning to stub the cigarette on the sole of her shoe, then rose to pat her hair down. 'I have to be careful, you know, a woman living on her own.'

Quine repressed a smile. 'Of course. I've an up-to-date passport, a clean driving licence and a recent bank statement.'

'I take little notice of such things, Mr Quine. I look at the person instead.'

This time Quine did smile. 'I intend to lose weight over these months.' He knew he did not cut an enticing figure. His round face and chubby cheeks, the blue eyes which once glinted, the mind which once devoured everything – from the tiniest item of gossip to the highest matter of state – were all dulled. Even his good head of hair felt lank. Judging that respectability might count in his favour as he sought his new accommodation, he was wearing the grey suit, white shirt, salmon tie and black shoes that had once been the uniform of his profession. The first was more crumpled than it should have been and the last less shiny.

The silent inspection lasted several seconds, then she lit another cigarette and waved it around. 'Will you mind the house smelling of this?'

'No. I might feel envy though,' he replied with relief. It seemed he had passed. 'Much of my life has been spent in smoke-filled rooms and bars.'

'Bars?'

'Yes. I used to conduct business in them.'

'And what is your business?'

Quine hesitated. 'I write.'

'A writer! Have I read your books? I enjoy a good detective story.'

His smile faltered. 'I'm afraid not, Mrs Trelight. I am... was... a journalist,' he said.

'Oh...' Her tone contained a hint of revulsion.

'What did I tell you?'

'Oh no, I don't mean to—'

'It's all right,' he said, 'most people dislike us. But that's not why I'm here. I have a project. A history to write. I expect it to take me the best part of a year. I need space and seclusion.'

'How much space?'

'A room large enough for a bed, my desk and four filing cabinets. I have brought those last two with me.'

'I might have to clear one or two things out…'

'And most importantly,' he continued, 'a bare wall on which I can attach a large cork board.'

'What do you want a cork board for?'

'Not for throwing darts.' His reply brought a twinkle to her pale green eyes.

'In that case, I'll show you what I have.'

She led him to the back of the bungalow; stairs rose to a spacious loft conversion with two windows overlooking a short garden and fields beyond.

'I have my own bathroom,' she said, 'you have access to the ground-floor toilet and shower. As you see,' she continued, looking out of the loft windows, 'no view of the sea or headland. Makes it cheaper.'

'As long as we can get my desk and board up the stairs, it will suit me perfectly,' said Quine. 'You said you have wi-fi?'

'Of course. But the phone signal varies.'

'I'm not expecting calls.'

'I can offer you a special rate if you take the full eight months from today till mid-summer when the season starts. Six hundred pounds a month. Breakfast included. No guarantees after that.'

'Thank you, that sounds most reasonable.'

She gave him a final inspection. 'Yes, it is. I don't mind having a young man in the house. But no loud music please.'

'I'm not that young.' He offered his hand. 'Do we have a deal?'

She took it. 'Yes, Mr Quine, we do.'

He vowed to transform himself and, over the coming months, kept to it. The stationary years of tobacco, whisky and wine, lunches and dinners, were replaced by the daily march to the point of the cliff and, on Saturday evenings, a single half-pint of Cornish bitter in the nearby Cross Keys pub. He bought a pedometer; the distance to the headland and back was 8.7 miles, the total ascent, with the ups and downs, just over 2,000 feet. After three months, the walk turned into a jog and he could do it in under an hour and a half. He found a gym at the nearest town, pumped iron and shadow-boxed. He ate Mrs Trelight's breakfast and one other meal only. And he spent the other waking hours of every day embarking on the book-length 'history' which was to be his revenge.

The exotically named Quentin Deschevaux had arrived in the House of Commons in 2015 as the newly elected MP for East Somerset. He was in his late fifties, a late-comer to Parliament, and conspicuously rich – at times he gave the impression of representing not just his constituency but owning most of it too. He was bombastic and national-ist. When challenged about his own name and origins, he claimed his family came over with the Normans and never regretted leaving the sewer that was Europe for the green land of England. His growing host of admirers loved him and he became a leading performer in the Leave campaign during the 2016 Brexit referendum.

Joe Quine, political editor of *The Post* at Westminster, had instinctively seen Deschevaux as a fraud and then, as his renown grew in the post-Brexit vote cacophany, as a danger. He wrote two brief pieces in his Saturday political diary column in *The Post*. The first analysed the reasons for Deschevaux's popularity with the grassroots of his party. The second commented on the mystery of his origins and wealth. Quine noted that Deschevaux's declarations of earnings and shareholdings in the House of Commons register were confined largely to his UK residential properties, and homes in France, South Africa and the Caribbean. Quine wrote to him asking for a fuller explanation of his wealth. Deschevaux's office replied that all his other investments had been placed in trusts managed at arm's length by independent trustees and that the MP was 'a free man, beholden to no persons and no interests'.

Two weeks after the second article, an envelope arrived at *The Post*, marked 'Private and Confidential' and 'for the attention of Joseph Quine'. There was no letter inside, just a single document. It was a copy of the latest annual accounts submitted to Companies House of a private company called IPRM. The headline figures were unremarkable – an operating profit of some fifteen million pounds on a turnover of just under seventy million. Quine ran an online check of IPRM on the Companies House website. It had been incorporated in 1992 as 'International Personnel and Resource Management'. Its initial share subscribers and directors were named as Lyle Grainger and Dieter Schmidt. Its business activities were described as the 'recruitment of personnel to assist British and other companies explore business opportunities in new markets opening up as a result of geo-political change'. There were several entries in the 1990s for 'New director appointed' and 'Director resigned' that were unavailable for online inspection. In 1997 the company name was formally abbreviated to IPRM which it had remained since. Among directors appointed in more recent years, available for inspection online, were two names indicating IPRM's global expansion – Daniel Vitaly and Michael Ho.

Quine visited Companies House in person to search the undigitized files. In 1998 Grainger and Schmidt resigned as directors. The 'New Director' appointed in 1993 was named Quentin Deschevaux. The director who resigned in late 1997, around the time the company name was abbreviated, was also Quentin Deschevaux. It was a tantalizing find.

He needed somehow to communicate his appetite for further information to the anonymous sender. This first offering was just enough for a further, more precise paragraph in his Saturday diary.

*

The mystery of Quentin Deschevaux's origins remains as elusive as ever. Perhaps one clue might be found in his association from 1993–97 with 'International Personnel and Resource

Management', now known as IPRM. What new markets in what exotic territories was Deschevaux opening up?

*

His informant took note.

Three further envelopes arrived. They contained copies of internal company accounts and documents showing transactions between IPRM and companies in different countries. There were also copies of receipts. One chain showed a significant travel pattern of IPRM staff between Britain and the new former Soviet states of Azerbaijan and Kazakhstan in the early 1990s. Another indicated frequent contact with Sofia, the capital of Bulgaria, and Tirana, the capital of Albania. A third chain showed a presence in west Africa from the mid-1990s to early 2000s, mainly in Sierra Leone and Liberia. Quine checked the state of those two countries over those years; both were being torn apart by civil wars. It allowed another Saturday diary story, which outlined IPRM's *'mystery contacts and activities in west Africa and behind the former Iron Curtain...'*

A few weeks later, Quine received a game-changing letter. It gave a date, a time of deliberate precision – 4.53 p.m. – and a place, the first-floor bar of a pub in Kilburn. On the day, Quine checked his watch against Big Ben, travelled to the location in good time and mounted the pub stairs to its first floor. In front of him was a row of booths. He waited. A single, male face peered out from one of them. He went and sat down opposite it.

'I'm Joseph Quine.'

'Yes. You are.'

'And may I ask who—'

'No. Not yet.'

12

He was, Quine judged, in his early sixties, gaunt, sallow cheeks, dark grey hair neatly parted and brushed back, bulbous nose. He wore a dark suit, white shirt and plain tie. A walking stick was propped up against the table. He had a glass in front of him that appeared to contain a remnant of juice.

'May I get you another?' Quine asked.

'Not yet.' He peered out of the booth again. 'You came alone.'

'Yes.'

Quine smiled. The man noticed. 'Something amusing you?'

'Not at all.'

'Good.' He pushed his glass towards Quine. 'Just a pineapple juice.'

Quine headed towards the bar. Two old men in black jackets and cloth caps sat in the open area, toying with pints of Guinness. Quine ordered a pineapple juice and half a bitter, and returned to the booth.

'Lively place,' he said.

No reaction. Finally the man replied, 'It'll do.' He sipped slowly, looked down at his juice with a hint of contempt, then up at Quine. 'Stanley,' he said, offering a weathered hand with nicotine-stained fingers.

Quine took it. 'Good to meet you, Stanley.'

'You got my letters.'

'Yes.'

'I'd guessed you suspected that man. That's why I wrote. And why you're here. Correct?'

'Correct.'

'Have you worked out what he was doing?'

'I can make guesses.'

'Just guesses?'

'Guesses don't make a story.'

'You have a name. You have a company. You have a description of its business.'

'It's too vague.'

Stanley eased closer to Quine. 'This goes no further than us. And stays that way.'

'Of course.'

'OK.' Except for the occasional clink of glass, the bar remained as silent as death. Stanley visibly relaxed, as if he'd made a decision. 'I was hired by International Personnel and Resource Management in 1994, two years after it was formed. I retired three years ago. A long time later than I should have done.'

Quine, instantly excited, raised only an eyebrow.

'When I joined up,' Stanley continued, 'they were a small, specialist company. They provided security personnel for oligarchs and the like. Or governments that needed them. Initially they concentrated on former Soviet republics.'

'Like Azerbaijan and Kazakhstan.'

'Yes. Security personnel began to mean mercenaries too. They seemed to have contacts everywhere. There were three directors and shareholders. You know their names. Grainger an American, Schmidt a German, and Deschevaux. He said he'd once been in the army. I could believe it. I'd been a soldier myself, knew his type.'

'Was he special forces?' asked Quine.

'May have been. I never knew.'

'Were you?'

'None of your business. He and I spent time together but never "conversed". It was a hierarchy, he was the boss. There's a four-letter word to describe him that begins with "c" and ends with "t".'

'You didn't like him.'

'I didn't need to like him.' Glancing at a man who had just entered the pub and made his way to a booth nearby, Stanley lowered his voice. 'Move to the park?'

He slowly stood, grabbed his stick, and walked with a pronounced limp towards the stairs. Quine followed. Stanley descended them with surprising agility, exited the pub and set off without resuming the conversation. After a hundred yards he stopped abruptly, looked behind, then moved on. They cleared the Victorian streets of Queen's Park and entered the park itself, settling on a bench. A coughing spasm interrupted him. Quine guessed it had been brought on by the burst of activity.

He gestured Quine to sit beside him and watched the passing mothers and toddlers. The cough subsided. 'They started doing business in other parts of Europe,' continued Stanley as if there had been no interruption, 'and then Africa. That's where I saw him close up. Getting it now?'

'Sierra Leone and Liberia. Civil wars in both.'

'Good for business. We were in Freetown in '97.'

'Who?'

'Him. And me and another bloke as his number twos.'

'Who was the other bloke?'

'I won't involve him.'

Quine let it go. He would return to it later.

'We were offered some locals by the client to help do the job.'

'Job?'

'You can read the history. Rebels were marching on the capital. The government needed help. Wanted us to take out the rebel leadership. They gave us ten of their "finest" – as they called them – to form a squad. It was an effing disaster. During one try we took a few prisoners and packed them in a basement. What do we do with them? He's in charge.'

'He?'

'Who do you think?'

'What *did* he do?'

'Spoke to the leader of the "finest".'

'In what language?'

'English.'

'And you heard?'

'Yep.'

'What did he say?'

'He said, "We need to get rid of them. Take two of your boys." Exact words. The leader picked out two and spoke to them in Krio.'

'It's a sort of pidgin English, isn't it?'

'There's lots of different stuff in it. But yes, some English.'

'Did you hear anything? Could you make out what the "leader" said?'

'"Keeal" came through a couple of times. "Kill" I remember thinking. But I don't know that for sure.'

'Fine. We shouldn't need that.'

'No,' said Stanley. He fished something out of his coat pocket. It was a single page of the *Guardian*'s foreign section from a few months earlier. Stanley pointed to a headline. 'MASS GRAVE FOUND IN FREETOWN BASEMENT'. It described how more than twenty years after the civil war ended, twelve male skeletons had been found lying together, all with evidence of bullet holes in the skull. 'Not now they've found the bodies,' continued Stanley.

Quine read the article twice, with a mounting surge of anger and exhilaration. He tried not to show it. 'Your recollection is the only proof of Deschevaux's involvement.'

'Wrong. The leader, his two boys and Deschevaux himself went into the basement together. We heard shots. Over thirty, three for each to make sure. Then they came out. That bastard looked almost happy. Like he'd been having a good time.'

'That could have been your imagination.'

'Yes, could have. It wasn't.'

'And then?'

'The rebels were overrunning the place. We got out of Freetown just in time. So did the President.'

'Did you discuss the incident?'

'Never with him. Not really with the other bloke either. What was there to say?'

'Why are you telling me now?'

'I told you. He's a cunt. Now he's lording it over the nation.'

'Unless anyone on the ground remembers – and that may involve a difficult investigation – you and the other bloke are the only witnesses. You could be incriminating yourself. Knowing a murder was about to take place and failing to intervene.'

'I'll take that risk.'

'If it comes to it, will you testify to all this in court?' Stanley did not answer. Quine realized his mistake. 'I'm sorry, I'm jumping ahead.' A further silence fell. He looked down at Stanley's right leg. 'What happened?'

'What happened is I shattered my leg making that bastard rich.' He coughed again. 'We were in Liberia after that. Effing landmine.'

'That must have been tough.'

'It happens. I heard he wanted rid of me, but the others persuaded him to find me a job. They retrained me, put me into accounts. I got into a habit of copying certain documents. Building my private file.'

'Why? You'd have been sacked on the spot.'

'Curiosity. I wanted to know everything I could about them.

73

Then it was for leverage. Something to use against him. I don't see myself as a nice person either.'

'Are there any other illegalities you can prove are connected to IPRM?'

'You don't tend to spread the word when you're doing jobs.'

'Jobs?'

'Hits. Assassinations. After the Wall fell, Russia and half of Europe was gangster land. Remember?'

'I remember.' Quine paused. 'Did you ever do a job, Stanley?'

He ignored the question.

'What about more recently at IPRM?' asked Quine.

'Try Mexico. A lot of drug cash and a lot of bodies.'

'Where else?'

'Every effing where else. Where there's trouble in the world, IPRM's there. And where isn't there trouble? The British company's just for show. The big money's parcelled all over the globe. Shell companies, off-shore trusts, untrackable. Billions' worth. Deschevaux's still a main stakeholder. Though you won't find it on any piece of paper connecting to him or IPRM.' Another cough interrupted him. 'Nothing's provable. Except that we now have a mass grave in Sierra Leone.'

'What do you really want out of this, Stanley?'

'I want him.'

'Just him?' Stanley did not answer. 'I need to ask,' continued Quine, 'do you want money too?'

He shifted uneasily. 'I won't refuse.'

'It would have to be much further down the line. When I know what it all adds up to. Even then, I can't be sure.'

'I'll have to trust you then.' He rose without warning. 'I'll be in touch,' and, stick in his right hand, he moved unevenly towards the gate. Quine remained on the bench.

A week later, there was a further letter with a time and place. It was a Victorian terrace in Tooting, South London, some single houses, others built as two flats with separate front doors. Quine rang the bell of the given number. Through frosted glass he saw a figure slowly descending the stairs. The door opened to reveal Stanley, wearing a white shirt, braces holding up striped black trousers, traces of whisky and tobacco on his breath. So much for the pineapple juice.

He led him upstairs to a tidy sitting room decorated in shades of fading browns. In one corner several boxes of files were neatly arranged.

'You brought a car?' said Stanley.

'Yes,' replied Quine.

He nodded at the boxes. 'This will take us a few sessions. They'll give you a general picture of IPRM's reach. A few clients are identifiable. Most are shells or cover names. I've included some crime scene photographs of men found shot or poisoned. There's no proof – never will be. You can't use them. There are receipts that put him, me and the other bloke in Sierra Leone at the right time. You can keep it all. It's no use to me now.'

Quine paid three further visits to confirm points of detail with Stanley and, more importantly, to make a final judgement on his trustworthiness. In the third visit, he raised the most difficult questions of all.

'Stanley, we have the information. It's now about you.

I have three things I need to ask you. You can be an anonymous source for the newspaper story. But our lawyers will need you to sign a sworn affidavit with your account of what happened in Freetown. Are you OK to do that?'

'Yes, Joe, I am.' By now they were on friendly terms.

'Second. If Deschevaux sues for libel and it comes to trial, we'll need you to be our witness in court.'

'I know, you mentioned it. I've thought about it. The answer is yes.'

'Third, will you handwrite me a personal letter promising me that you'll turn up in court?'

Stanley smiled. 'You don't trust me?'

'I do. But this isn't just about me.'

'OK, I'll write you the letter.'

He fetched some paper and slowly wrote his address and the date at the top. 'I'm not much of a writer, you give me the words.' An hour later, it was done, rounded off by Stanley's cramped but legible signature.

'Actually, Stanley,' said Quine, 'there's just one more question.'

'Ask it then.'

'It's just this. Are you a well man?'

Stanley spluttered. 'I may look and sound a wreck, but don't you worry. I won't be pegging out anytime soon.'

Four weeks later *The Post* published a front-page splash telling how Quentin Deschevaux MP had ordered the summary execution of twelve prisoners in a basement in Freetown. It was accompanied by a two-part profile in the paper's feature section on the origins, activities and global expansion of IPRM.

Quine had tried to explore Deschevaux's past before he joined IPRM but every avenue ended in a cul-de-sac. *The Post*'s lawyers allowed him a small amount of speculation – including that he might at one time have had a military connection – but Deschevaux's early years remained unexplained.

Deschevaux responded that the massacre story was a lie and sued both *The Post* and Quine personally. *The Post*'s in-house lawyer who, on the back of the documentation and affidavit from Stanley, had cleared Quine's articles for publication took advice from a top libel QC. The QC had no doubts – they should fight and they would win.

Thirteen months later, the case came to court. Throughout the long months leading up to the trial, Quine kept in regular, fortnightly touch with Stanley. When he took the stand as *The Post*'s star witness, it had been ten days since their last meeting.

Stanley, dressed in a familiar dark suit, no doubt with the usual braces concealed inside the jacket, hobbled the two steps up to the box and turned to face the court. He caught Quine's eye.

There was an impenetrability in his expression that gave Quine a sudden, ghastly premonition.

Something was wrong. Badly wrong.

13

'I've examined the article,' said Sandford, handing it over to Fowkes.

It was late afternoon, two days after their previous meeting. They sat in the Number 10 flat's sitting room, Fowkes on an armchair, Sandford on the sofa. He did not offer to put the kettle on. He had not set a specific time limit.

'And?' said Fowkes.

'You don't need to worry about it.'

'What do you mean – not worry? A girl's dead. A girl we knew.'

'There is no evidence this severed hand comes from a girl we ever knew. Do you seriously think we had something to do with it?'

'I told you. I remember what happened that evening. You appear not to.'

'I remember bits of it. But you went on to describe stuff that's just not credible.'

'Robbie,' said Fowkes quietly. 'Do you think I've made this up?'

'Not deliberately. Imagination can do strange things. Perhaps there was something you once witnessed, which grew in your mind and then this hand was found...'

'How can you honestly believe I'd invent something like this?' Fowkes coughed. 'Can I have a glass of water? I've got a sore throat.'

Sandford rose and went into the kitchen. His eye was caught by the kitchen knives in their wooden block. A severed hand. Jesus. He ran the cold tap and filled a glass. Was Jed concealing a buried rage? Perhaps over the years he had learned to. He wished he knew what sort of person he had become. Or, perhaps, always had been.

He returned with a filled glass. 'I may have Strepsils.'

'It's OK, thanks.' Fowkes took a gulp of water, set the glass down and wiped his mouth with the back of his hand. 'Right, I'll try something else to jog your memory. You must remember Suzy suggesting you take a break, go away for a while?'

'Of course.' Sandford frowned.

'Do you recall when that was?'

'Roughly. 1991, November-ish. The year before the '92 surprise victory.'

'That's right. But there's another way of dating it. It was the Tuesday evening after the weekend I'm talking about. I phoned Suzy on the Sunday. Didn't say what had happened, just that she needed to talk to you again. I knew you trusted her as she was the one who helped you find a way through the panic attacks—'

'How did you know that?'

'Come on, Robbie. After you sought help, you told Mikey and me about them. You said it helped that people close to you knew. So we discussed it with her. Briefly and just once.'

'You were all talking, were you?'

'We weren't "talking". Certainly not her. We just wanted to be there for you.'

Sandford sighed. 'Jed, just get to the point.'

'Good idea. Let's go back to that evening. We've agreed we spent it with a girl called Andrea.'

'And Roisin.'

'Yes. Until she left. And then Andrea came back to the flat with us in a taxi.'

'Yes.'

'OK. Do you remember her leaving?'

'No.'

'Was she in the flat next morning? On the sofa perhaps? Or in your bed?'

'Not that I remember. She must have left.'

'When you were back functioning the next day, I told you I'd managed to sort the girl out. Get her out of the flat. And I said something like, "You just be fucking careful in future, I'm not going to do this for you again."'

'No, Jed. And you've offered no material evidence that this hand has any connection with a Hungarian girl called Andrea.'

Fowkes sighed and looked at his watch. 'How long have we got?'

'As long as you want. If I'd known last time why you were coming, I'd have given you longer then. Unless you planned it this way.'

'I dislike the implications of that remark.' He seemed about to say more but stopped himself. Silence fell. He took another sip of water. Sandford waited. 'I'd rather you didn't try to provoke me,' Fowkes continued quietly.

'Are you still easily provoked?'

Fowkes closed his eyes and took a deep breath. 'I can see I need to explain what happened next. Before you ask me why I've waited thirty years, the answer is that I've always wanted to protect you. You didn't remember, you didn't need to. The important thing was that you sorted yourself out. Which you began to do. So why should I worry you with it?'

'Go on.'

'We had a girl in our flat in a seriously bad way. You were afraid to call an ambulance. Meaning you must have done something to her. She might even be dead. Whatever your state of mind, you knew you'd be questioned about what happened. You were talented, possibly a future star. I didn't want to see you in trouble. And yes, I knew I'd have questions to answer too. On the spur of the moment I did something I came to regret. I looked down at the girl. I thought to myself she's only just arrived in the country. She's doing a temp job. No one here really knows her. Her family don't expect to hear much from her. This is long before FaceTime and all that. She's just another post-1989 migrant worker from eastern Europe, bunking off from one job to another.

'She was small. Easy to carry. At that time I had a friend

from a different world to ours who would know what to do. I phoned him, he was at home. I said I had a problem, could he come round? He lived only twenty minutes' drive away. He came straightaway. With another guy. I didn't know him. I said maybe they could leave her outside a hospital. "Sure," he said. "I'll do what's best." The next time I saw him I asked how it turned out. "Fine," he said, "we disposed of her." I didn't ask him how. It seemed the best way.'

Sandford tried to keep his face neutral. 'Let's say this did happen. Maybe he was using tough guy language. He probably just dropped her at a hospital and she ended up fine. Assuming so, why didn't she report us? Why didn't something come out?'

'No reason for it to. She was so far gone she probably wouldn't have remembered much, if anything. If she did, she'd keep it quiet. She'd be too embarrassed to tell anyone. And she'd be too scared to go to the police. It was a different world for women then.'

'Right. That's what happened. And she probably spent a few more months here and then went home.'

'But there's an alternative, isn't there?' said Fowkes.

'Alternative?'

'She disappeared. She was a nobody. In this country anyway. And now she's reappeared. Her severed hand anyway.'

'There's no evidence,' said Sandford.

Fowkes felt for something in his inside pocket. 'Another cutting came through my door.' He produced a folded newspaper page and handed it to Sandford. 'Read that.'

This time Fowkes waited. Sandford put his reading glasses on. The headline was 'CLUE TO MYSTERY HAND'.

*

Lewisham CID say the ring found on a severed hand in Old Deptford Dockyard last week may help to narrow the search for the victim. The ring turns out to be of Hungarian origin. It was made from a Hungarian one-korona silver coin, its inside band marked with the name Ferenc József – the Austro-Hungarian emperor who died in 1916. Its age suggests it may be an heirloom handed down the generations of one family. Police have asked anyone with information about the unexplained disappearance of a young Hungarian woman in London between twenty-five and thirty-five years ago to contact them.

*

Beneath the article in red capitals was a handwritten message. 'SHE'S GETTING CLOSER, JED.'

Sandford put the cutting down on the sofa cushion beside him. 'That may point to the girl being Hungarian – but not to it being this girl.'

'And what about the messages?'

'Probably just some nutter you've fallen out with trying to wind you up.'

Fowkes stood up, leant over and retrieved the cutting.

'Jesus, Robbie, think about it. If it's just some nutter, how would he know about the girl?'

Sandford hesitated. He decided he had to say it. 'Unless, Jed, you're writing those messages to yourself.'

Fowkes buried his face in his hands, rubbed his eyes, then looked up. 'I honestly can't believe you said that, Robbie.'

Silence fell. But you haven't denied it either, have you, thought Sandford. 'OK, sorry. But if any of this is true, Jed… when you found her in that state, you should have called the emergency services there and then. Whatever I might have said.'

'You're still not listening. It's the question I asked you before. Did we kill her? Did *you* kill her, Robbie? Because that means I'm complicit in murder. It's always the cover-up, isn't it? That's what always gets you. So right now, I need you to tell me what to do.'

Sandford allowed himself a moment. He calculated that, whatever game Jed Fowkes was playing, his advice would be the last thing he would follow.

'Jed, let me be clear. If you believe this severed hand belongs to a young woman who was the victim of an accident – or something worse – in our flat some thirty years ago, you have to go straight to the police. Report your concerns, describe the whole of that evening as you've described it to me. Give the identity of the person who came to help remove Andrea from the flat. My own position is I don't find your story credible and have no recollection of any such incident.'

Fowkes stood up. 'Are you recording this?'

'Don't be daft.'

'Just wondering.' He sighed and slowly shook his head just once. 'Thank you for your advice, Prime Minister.' Without a further word, he turned and left the room. Sandford heard the front door of the flat shut quietly behind him.

14

The Prime Minister had five minutes till his next appointment. Whatever was true or false in Fowkes's account, this was not going away. Fowkes presented potentially terminal danger. The best defence – maybe the only defence – remained to discover the truth. Unless the truth…

That way madness lay. He needed to hold onto fact. He had not smacked his children – maybe just a couple of times when they wouldn't shut up in the back of the car. He had never hit his wife. Nor anyone else as far as he could remember. He had never killed anyone, never thought of killing anyone, never had any personal involvement in someone's death. Except the car crash.

Why was Jed doing this? The frightening thing was that Jed was so plausible, so apparently rational, that you could easily believe him.

The flat's phone rang. 'Yes, Mark, I'm on my way.'

A minute after 6 p.m., he was entering the office. The

Cabinet Secretary, PPS, and the Number 10 special economic adviser were waiting. 'We're in the study, aren't we, Mark?'

'Yes, Prime Minister.' They filed in after him.

'Thanks for coming,' said Sandford. 'I want this to be a private meeting, kept confidential and unminuted. Anyone unhappy about that has my permission to leave.'

The other three, surprised by the peremptory tone, exchanged puzzled looks and stayed silent.

'Good.' The Prime Minister gave a short smile. 'As my PPS is prone to remind me,' he nodded at Burden, 'we have less than four weeks till the State Opening and the Royal Speech. For several reasons, I want a new procedure this year for that speech. As always, we will take submissions from all departments. But the final drafting will take place here, within this office.' He paused. 'And, until the moment of printing, it will be confined to us four. There'll be no sharing with any other. Including the Treasury.'

'That will ruffle feathers,' said Sir Kevin Long.

'Tough,' said Sandford.

'I'll have no problem on the economic side without them,' said the special economic adviser.

'Thanks, Tim. Mark?'

'It's a short speech. There are no practical issues if we have departmental briefs.'

'Yes, short. But setting our agenda for the next four years. I'll be heavily involved in aspects of the drafting myself.' He looked around the room. 'I would also ask the three of you not to discuss my possible reasons with each other. Do I have the agreement and full support of all of you?'

Three voices in turn said, 'Yes, Prime Minister.'

Mark Burden checked his watch. 'Six fifteen, the guests will have arrived.'

Sandford stood. 'Let's go.'

It was a Downing Street drinks reception for champions of sport. Normally he would enjoy it – a chance to meet people he genuinely admired – but, as he entered the room, he felt a need to be with his family. He shut it out. He was the Prime Minister.

He joined a former manager of Newcastle United who had spent a brief period as England boss.

'Hello, Ron,' he said, stretching out a hand. 'You know I went to St James's Park when Keegan was playing.'

'Oh really! When Kev became manager, he got more out of that club than I ever did.'

'Why *did* Newcastle United,' Sandford's flat 'a' in 'castle' was more pronounced than usual, 'always seem such a basket case? All those fans. All that enthusiasm.'

'Well, Prime Minister,' said the manager, 'you should know this better than anyone. It always starts at the top, doesn't it?'

Sandford laughed. 'Good to catch up with you.' He moved on to a former Wimbledon Women's Wheelchair doubles winner. He knelt down and shook her hand. 'I love your sport,' he said.

'People find it too slow.'

'Well I don't agree with "people",' replied Sandford. 'You're subtle, every different type of spin, playing all the angles, more like a chess game, it's great stuff.'

'Oh!' she beamed. 'I'll pass that on. Do you play?'

'Used to. With the kids.' He waved his hands around. 'Never seems time for it now.'

'You're a busy man. I mustn't monopolize you.'

'It's been a privilege.'

For those ninety minutes, the vision of Jed Fowkes disappeared. Back in the car taking him home, it returned. The driver and bodyguard noted his unusual distance – he hardly managed to say hello.

At Salisbury Square, they had not yet started supper.

'You're early!' exclaimed Carol.

'I thought you'd be pleased,' he said with tragic theatricality.

His daughters frowned at him. 'Course we're pleased to see you, Dad, you muppet,' said Becca, the oldest. He looked at her, seventeen now but the shorter and broader of the two, wavy brown hair, athletic, on the loud side. Bella, four years younger, was thin and graceful, straight fair hair, more subdued, more serious, more intuitive. If either were to inherit his anxiety gene, it would be her. Because they were so different, it was easy to love them equally. He could not stop himself trying to picture the Hungarian girl. She would probably have been only a year or two older than Becca.

'What's wrong, Dad?' asked Bella quietly.

He forced a smile. Carol moved beside him and pecked him on the cheek. 'Who'd be a Prime Minister, eh?'

'Perhaps I'll just do one term. Get out before the next election. That would surprise them.'

Carol gave him an odd look. 'There are still times when I'm not a hundred per cent sure whether you're joking.'

'Me neither.' He grinned and rubbed his hands together. 'Right, I'm hungry.'

'Lucky you, your timing's perfect,' said Carol.

Home. He knew how fortunate he was. Carol's wealth had enabled them to buy a house in his Bristol constituency's most expensive address, Royal York Crescent in Clifton, and then his scruffy two-bedroomed flat in Lewisham to be replaced by this house. Not once in their occasional marital rows had Carol resorted to reminding him that her money had made it all possible.

Supper was a tray bake of chicken with a mound of roasted vegetables. 'Wow,' he said. 'An escape from the sandwich.'

'How was the drinks?' asked Carol.

'Really enjoyable,' he replied. As they ate, he told them about the wheelchair tennis champion. 'Seems an age since we played. How about next time we're all together at Chequers?' He looked up at Becca. 'Did you decide about Oxbridge?'

'Yeah,' she replied. 'I don't think I should go for it.'

'Oh.' He frowned. 'I thought you liked Oxford.'

'Sure, the city's OK. But the university's kind of elitist, not to mention all that work.'

'But you're clever.'

'I don't know about that. Anyway I wouldn't want to get in just because I'm the Prime Minister's daughter.'

He smiled at her. 'It'd be just the opposite. Nothing they'd like better than to turn the PM's daughter down. Maybe that plus us sending you to private school makes it impossible anyway.' He paused. 'Perhaps it's just too hard.'

'Too hard! No, it's not too *hard*, Dad. It's too sniffy. Anyway you didn't go to Oxbridge.'

'I wasn't clever like you.' He looked at Carol. 'There's the Oxford girl – where the brains come from.'

'Well, in the end, it's up to Becca herself,' said Carol.

'Of course it is,' said Sandford. 'Anyway, if it's too hard, fine, I get it.'

*

'That was rather naughty of you with Becca,' said Carol, putting aside her book as they lay in bed.

'Oh?'

'She sidled up to me after you'd gone to the study. "How could he think it's too hard for me?" she said. She was deliciously cross with you. I told her that's how it could look to some people. She harrumphed and walked out.'

'Do you think she'll go for it?'

She grinned. 'Almost certainly. Well done, my darling.' She resumed her book.

'Good.' He smiled briefly. Flopping flat on his back, staring at the ceiling, his face sagged.

She put her book back down, removed her spectacles and leant on an elbow. 'What's wrong?'

He glanced at her, then back to the ceiling. 'It's fine. I'm fine.'

'You're not.' He did not respond. 'Is it Jed?'

He sat up. 'Not directly. I did meet him briefly. He said he'd heard something bad about a very senior colleague.'

91

'Who?'

'On this one, I'd rather not.'

'You've never held out on me before.' She placed a hand on his chest. 'Not that I know of anyway.'

'No, I haven't.'

'If not the person, at least the deed.'

'I can't. It'd make me feel dirty.'

'It's worrying you. So there's a chance it might be true.'

'I guess so.' His heart was thumping.

'Right then, it's come from Jed,' she persisted. 'A very senior colleague. Is it Morland-Cross?'

'Carol, I can't—'

'It is, isn't it? Henry bloody M-C. That might not be so bad for you.'

'It's always bad. For the government. And the party. And him. He's stayed in his box, I owe him.'

'Who says he'll never jump out of it?' She sat up beside him. 'Robbie, if M-C is up to no good, you should be using it. You only just beat him in the leadership contest. He's still got his power base. He's the only one who can undermine you.'

Sandford said nothing. A conversation he would have preferred to duck had, through Carol's tenacity, taken an unusual turn. But not in the way she intended. The germ of an idea was forming. He could not just sit back and defend, he needed to attack. Against Jed, not Morland-Cross. But perhaps M-C could be deployed as his unwitting weapon.

'I've got you thinking, haven't I?' Carol said with a note of triumph. 'It *is* him, isn't it?'

'Maybe.'

'Ha! What's the old goat been up to?'

'I don't fully know. Nor does anyone else yet.'

She grinned. 'You're teasing. Lie back.' She moved her hand down from his chest to his stomach, not stopping there.

'Carol, I can't.'

'What do you mean, you can't!' Her hand cupped him.

He pointed a finger to his head. 'I'm done for. Too much going on up there.'

'Then let down there take over.' He put his hand over hers. 'Robbie, if you can't manage this once in a while, I might start thinking you're shagging the Downing Street cook.'

He laughed. God, he was stupid sometimes. There was only one response. He felt her. 'Go for it,' she said. 'The way you really like.' She turned onto her front and raised her thighs. As he entered, he put his arms around her, grabbing both breasts and squeezing hard. Harder than he meant. She gasped. 'Careful.' He loosened his grip and explored her all over, allowing himself to go with an intensity he had not felt for a long time.   From nowhere, the image of the girl lying, legs sprawled, exhausted, sweating, flashed before him. He shut his eyes and pushed harder. He came quickly. When he had finished, she rolled onto her back and he lay beside her, his face buried in her neck and hair, her hand stroking the top of his head. He tried to hold back tears. They lay together in a silence both seemed to want.

He eased away and went to the bathroom. He washed the sweat from his face and salt from his eyes. As he returned, she took his place. After a few minutes, she was back in a towel gown and lay down beside him.

'God, darling, that was something.'

'Yes, love. Thank you. I was being selfish.'

'No,' she protested. 'I wanted you to be. You haven't been like that for ages. It was nice. Not every time, but this time.'

Seconds passed. He decided to try something. 'Can we talk more?'

'I'm not sure I'll make any sense after that,' she said, yawning.

'Jed...' he said.

'We should forget about Jed.'

'Just one thing. I'm worried he's not telling the truth.'

'You know him better than me.'

'But you have good instincts.'

'I wouldn't want to guess.' She stirred herself and sat up. 'Shall I tell you a story about Jed?'

'Go on.'

'At conference two years ago, I found myself briefly alone with him. It was after we'd had a tiff, maybe I was showing it. "Hope things are all right with you and Robbie," he said. "Fine," I said lightly. "Just the ups and downs of life. Not been easy for him." I tried to close it down and move away. He touched me on my arm. "Look," he said, "Robbie's still my oldest friend, just want to make sure things are all right." Then he hesitated, locking eyes with me. "If you ever need a shoulder to cry on or someone to help with him, you know where to come." I said I really appreciated it. Never quite knew what to make of it.'

'Weird. You never told me that.'

'No, at the time I didn't see the point.'

'Was he trying to come on to you?'

'I'm honestly not sure.' She paused. 'God, can you imagine it? I'm not even sure he likes women. No, I don't think it was that. I thought that, in some odd way, he missed you. Maybe wanted to find a way back to you.'

'That *is* weird.'

'Yes. You mentioned instinct. That's all this is. I suspect Jed would find it hard to lie. He may be very clever. But you could never accuse him of having an overactive imagination. All that frustration. All arising from others not seeing his logic, not agreeing with him. I always felt I could see right through him except for that one conversation. And that wasn't to do with lying. It was more he couldn't for once bring himself to say what he really meant. Perhaps because it was about emotion, not reason.'

'Hmm…' he murmured. He wished she had answered the question differently. He wished now that he had never asked it. He had nearly allowed his guard to drop.

He needed that ally. Why was Mark taking so long to come back to him about Quine?

'Yes,' she said, 'I truly think that's what it was with Jed. Not trying it on with me, but trying to find a route to you.'

15

'The defence calls Stanley Hull to the stand.'

Words that Quine would never forget, spoken on that defining day in the Royal Courts of Justice by his and *The Post*'s QC. Words followed by that blank look from Stanley and his own sudden presentiment.

'Could you please give your full name?' continued the QC.

'Stanley Norman Hull.'

'Could you describe your employment at the company called IPRM?'

'Yes, I was a field adviser at International Personnel and Resource Management, later IPRM, from 1994 to 1998. After losing half my leg in a landmine explosion in Liberia, I became an accounts clerk. I continued at IPRM in that role until 2017.'

'After your retirement, you began a correspondence with Joseph Quine, political editor of *The Post* newspaper.'

'Correct.'

'Why?'

'He seemed interested in Quentin Deschevaux. I had

information of value to him. Initially I sent him the odd thing anonymously.'

'Why so?'

'To test his interest.'

'Did it?'

'Yes. He wrote a couple of stories based on what I sent him.'

'And then?'

'I decided to meet him.'

'What was your primary motive?'

'As I said, I believed I had information of value.'

'You mean journalistic value. Public interest value.'

'Well, not just that.'

'Excuse me, Mr Hull, could you explain?'

'Well, I reckoned there was financial value too. Not just for me but for Mr Quine, too, and his newspaper. To sell copies.'

The QC cast Quine a worried glance. Quine shook his head. It was the first drip of poison.

'Are you claiming that the issue of money was included in your conversations?'

'Yes, he asked me himself. Did I want money? I said I wouldn't refuse. He said it could only happen further down the line when he'd studied all the material.'

'Did you ever receive money from Mr Quine or *The Post*?'

'No,' replied Stanley. 'I'm still waiting.'

There were sniggers in court. Quine's head drooped, his heart sinking. Stanley had never mentioned money again after that first meeting. It had all been about exposing Deschevaux's crime. He was sure Stanley had not been faking that. His loathing had been real. He thought back to their last meeting two weeks before. Everything had seemed on track. As a final reassurance, with two days to go, he'd called round to the flat. There was no answer, so he'd texted. A reply had come back instantly. See you in court, am prepared. He'd had no tremor of concern. Perhaps he should have stuck around and waited for Stanley's return, but there had seemed no need.

'Very amusing, Mr Hull,' said the QC, trying to ride over the sniggering. 'In fact, you were always clear with Mr Quine that your motive was entirely to help expose a multiple murder which took place under Mr Deschevaux's command in Sierra Leone in 1997. Were you not?'

'I'm not sure I'd put it quite like that.'

The QC ploughed on, as if he had not heard him. 'In fact so clear – and you are to be applauded for this selfless act in the public interest – that you not only provided Mr Quine with a detailed affidavit and precise geography and timing of this crime, you also supplied a large quantity of documents to Mr Quine to explain the global scope of IPRM's activities and the nature of the work the company did in Liberia and other countries.'

'Yes. Well,' he paused, 'at the time, that was how I interpreted it.'

Quine instantly saw it. The train was approaching, he was chained to the line, in seconds he'd be crushed under its wheels. From now on, it seemed to happen in slow motion.

'At the time, Mr Hull?' asked the QC, the scales falling from his eyes too.

Stanley fidgeted, a hush fell, each person in the courtroom aware only of their own breaths. 'Yes. In recent days I have had cause to reconsider my understanding of certain matters.' It was as if Stanley had been scripted and was trying to remember his words. 'I must apologize both to Mr Quine and to Mr Deschevaux – I have realized I misunderstood a key moment. I have now been told that Mr Deschevaux's instruction to the leader of the squad of government soldiers attached to us was different to what I thought I'd heard. It appears that Mr Deschevaux's instruction was that these prisoners needed to be handed over to Freetown police and that they should remain under guard until the police arrived.'

'But, Mr Hull, as you swore in your affidavit, by this time there was no government in any serious sense, nor police.'

'Yes, sir. And it remains the case that the massacre took place. However, this was by the order and under the leadership of the government army officer attached to us. Perhaps he understood the collapse was imminent. In any event he made his own decision. He did not follow Mr Deschevaux's order. The instruction he passed on to his squad in Krio was the opposite – it was to execute the prisoners. The executions must have taken place after Mr Deschevaux, I and another colleague had left the scene.'

'Your original account to Mr Quine was totally different. Why have you changed it, Mr Hull?'

'As I've said, my original account was wrong and I apologize.'

'Come on, Mr Hull, why have you gone back on the true account you gave Mr Quine?'

'It was not the true account, sir. I am sorry for my error.'

There was a brief, shocked silence, broken by mutterings

from the court. 'I see. Thank you, Mr Hull.' The QC addressed the judge. 'My Lord, may I request an adjournment to seek instructions from my clients?'

'You most certainly may,' replied the judge caustically.

The withdrawal to a meeting room of the QC, his junior, *The Post*'s editor, its financial director and himself was the most dispiriting walk of Quine's life.

'Nobbled,' he said as they slumped into chairs around the table.

'Unless he was playing you all along, Joe,' said the financial director harshly.

'That's impossible,' said Quine. 'He's not showing it, but he's terrified. It's all rehearsed.'

'Unless he's been bought,' said the junior.

'Makes no difference now, does it?' said Quine. 'Either way, it won't be visible. IPRM act without trace. It's their business, isn't it?'

'Don't beat yourself up, Joe,' said the editor. 'We should have had a twenty-four-hour guard on him.' He glanced at the financial director. 'I suggested it. I was told it was not a good use of resources. Bit of a misjudgement there, I'd say.'

'Post-mortem for another day,' said the QC. 'We have to offer to apologize and settle immediately. I'll open negotiations.'

'No,' said Quine. It was a cry from the heart. 'I can't give in. Not to that man. He's evil.'

'You have to.' They said it as one.

'I don't have to.' He looked at the editor. '*The Post* can settle. I'll fight on even if it breaks me.' He turned to the junior barrister with whom he'd spent so many hours preparing the case. 'Fiona?'

The junior looked from Quine to her QC. He shrugged his shoulders. 'Tell Joe what you think.'

'I'm sorry, Joe,' she said, a soft, evenly modulated voice which could hit the volume button if needed.

'Is it all over?'

'In one sense, yes.'

'What sense?'

'In front of this judge, I can't see you winning.'

'And another sense?'

'Joe, we both know Stanley's been "nobbled" as you put it. One way or another, maybe a bit of both. You and I spent enough time with him to know his story's genuine. We also know that IPRM is a deeply unpleasant organization. Because in civil proceedings "hearsay" evidence is admissible,' she glanced at the QC who nodded in agreement, 'you can continue your defence against the libel action. We can produce Stanley's affidavit, you can describe your conversations with him, we can try to demonstrate what sort of organization IPRM is.'

'Then,' said the QC, 'they'll bring Stanley back, perhaps even Deschevaux himself. And they'll rebut it all. The judge you're in front of is a crusty old bastard. You saw just now he's not interested in hearing another word.'

'I agree,' said Fiona. 'I don't want to stop you, Joe. However, Deschevaux's true role in the massacre might come to light eventually. Africa has changed. This atrocity will be investigated on the ground – something I only wish we had been given the resources to do ourselves.'

'You were right,' said Quine, 'I should have paid for it myself.'

'No. Your paper should have done.' She glanced at *The Post*'s editor and financial director. 'As I said months ago. But that is past. Now, if you go on, you have a ninety-nine per cent chance of losing and it will probably bankrupt you. If the trial is later shown to be a miscarriage of justice and a witness has been suborned, you may be compensated. But the odds aren't good.'

Quine looked round the four blank faces in the room. The two men from *The Post* were looking at the floor. 'I'm in,' he said at last. 'I want to fight. If I go bust, so what. I'm broken anyway.' He looked at the junior.

'OK,' said Fiona. 'I'll do it. Pro bono. Because it's right. Because it's you. And because he's evil. It's easier for me. I won't lose money, just the case.'

*

She – all of them – were right. Deschevaux agreed a modest settlement of fifty thousand pounds with *The Post*; it printed a grovelling apology. Quine was not only required to resign from the paper, he was also hit with 'exemplary' damages by the judge for 'wasting the court's time in a futile pursuit of self-justification', amounting to over two hundred thousand pounds and costs of three times that. In the final settlement, Quine agreed to sell his London flat to foot most of the bill but was allowed to keep a small amount of cash and a few possessions, including his camper van. *The Post* did at least not contest his company pension although the early severance devalued it.

He was indeed a broken man. But there was a postscript.

It began with a final communication to him via *The Post* which could only have come from Stanley. It was a plain card with a typed name and address label stuck on it. The name was Jack Edgerley, the place Faversham in Kent. There was only one person it could be. The 'other bloke'. In this desolate period when he was wondering what to do with his shattered life, Quine caught the train to Kent, walked to the old part of Faversham, a terrace of Victorian houses leading down to the river, and rang the bell of one of them.

A burly man opened it. He seemed mid to late sixties, bald with a circle of close-cropped hair, dressed in a T-shirt revealing muscular arms. He glanced at Quine then up and down the street.

'Yes?'

'I'm sorry to trouble you. Are you Jack Edgerley?'

'What if I am?'

'My name is Joseph Quine. I was sent your name and address. Anonymously.' He lowered his voice. 'But I know it came from Stanley Hull.'

'Fucking hell,' the man murmured. 'Get inside.'

Quine followed him into a small front sitting room, its only noticeable feature two prints of sailing boats either side of a fireplace.

'Who is it?' came a female voice from upstairs.

'It's all right, I'll deal with it.' The man's accent had a mild man of Kent twang. He did not offer Quine a seat. 'I can't talk to you.'

'I understand,' said Quine.

'No, I mean it, I can't talk to you.'

'OK. I want you to allow me to ask a few questions. Then I'll be off. I only ask you to nod or shake your head in reply. I'm not recording anything, we're past all that. But at least this way you can say you never spoke to me.'

The man, clearly Jack Edgerley, took a deep breath. 'For the third time, I can't talk to you.'

'I'm not asking you to. Just listen. Question one. Were my articles both true and accurate?'

Edgerley buried his face in his hands. Time passed. He abruptly turned and left the room. Quine waited. Sounds of toilet flushing and water running. He returned. 'Jesus Christ.' He looked out of the window. 'Stanley fucking Hull, where are you now?' he murmured. 'Leaving me on my own, you old bastard.'

He turned back to Quine. He nodded.

'Question two. Another way of putting it. Did Deschevaux personally order the executions?'

He nodded again.

'Question three. Did Deschevaux personally take part in the executions?'

His head wobbled.

'As far as you were able to see and hear, did Deschevaux personally take part in the executions?'

He nodded.

'Question four. After the massacre, did Deschevaux

continue to be a central presence at IPRM, even if no longer a named director or shareholder?'

Another nod.

'Question five. Does Deschevaux continue to have substantial interests in IPRM globally via shell companies or other unidentifiable vehicles?'

This time, Edgerley grimaced, apparently unsure which way to go.

'Are you pretty sure he does but don't have the inside knowledge to say for certain?'

He nodded.

'Thank you,' said Quine. 'That conversation never took place. I'd like to continue. Would you be willing to do that?'

He shook his head.

'OK, I'll leave.'

Edgerley led him to the front door, opened it and checked the street. Quine exited and walked fast to be clear of the terrace. He felt transformed, energy rushing into every part of his body. Two weeks later he made the journey to Cornwall and installed himself at 7, The Waves.

To record the truth about Quentin Deschevaux felt like the overriding mission of his life. To keep himself on track he placed a large photograph of his target at the centre of his cork board, attaching it not with darts but with five drawing pins – one for each eyeball, the third for the centre of the forehead, the fourth through the tip of his nose and the fifth driven into the pronounced dimple on the chin. He then drew two dark red lines – one vertical, the second horizontal – to join the pins.

A crucifixion. Nothing less than Deschevaux deserved.

Every day Quine glared at the now quartered face – its glinting eyes, glossy brown hair, military moustache.

Then, as the months passed and words were laid down, his mood changed. The simplicity of his new life, the sweep of the coast and power of the sea, calmed him. The book began to turn into his own journey. Mrs Trelight must have intuited a change in him and started occasionally looking into his room for a quick chat. He found himself welcoming it. He knew she would have checked him out on the net and read every piece she could find on the libel trial.

'Is it satisfying, Mr Q?' she asked one morning. Almost without noticing, they had found themselves addressing each other this way. 'I mean, is the treatment working?'

It was an extraordinarily perceptive question. 'Yes, I think it is, Mrs T,' he replied.

'Good. And you look so well too.' She hesitated, wondering whether to go further. 'It must have been such an interesting life. Knowing all those politicians.'

'I was lucky. But I'm not sure I ever really got to know them. It was a professional relationship.'

'Oh, I'm sure it was more than that.'

Quine smiled. 'You'd have to ask them.'

'Perhaps one day, you'll introduce me.'

'I'll see what I can do.'

'Now, don't you overdo it. He's a bad, bad man. But you don't need to carry the sins of the world.'

She was right. It was just a story among millions of stories. One about a particularly dangerous creature in the strange ocean of politics Quine had swum in. About how he had allowed himself to become obsessed – at a huge cost, not just materially, but mentally too. And how this year by the sea became a time of atonement. The book became a human story of events leading to a defeat which had nothing to do with truth.

His work was done. The time might one day come when it would see the light of day. Winter was long gone, spring had evolved into summer, Mrs Trelight allowed him to stay on in the high season and complete the yearly cycle. Fair-weather residents and holiday-makers arrived, the green of cliff tops burned to brown, the sand bleached and sea warmed, pleasure boats cluttered the estuary. Now, with autumn's arrival, it was empty again, just as Quine had first found it. He allowed himself a few days to enjoy the peace but knew it was time to move on.

'Where next?' he repeated to himself.

The immediate answer was the Cross Keys. He walked up the lane and climbed into Beatrice, turning the key several times in the ignition. After showing a certain regret at her slumber being disturbed, the camper van stirred herself into action and trundled inland.

When he had been briefly lured into conversation by the Cross Keys landlord on his first Saturday evening visit, he had answered the inevitable inquiry by saying, 'I'm working on a book.' On each succeeding Saturday he had been greeted with the predictable cry of 'Here's Tolstoy'. Arriving now on a weekday evening, the landlord frowned. 'What are you doing here, Tolstoy?' he said.

To which he replied, 'I finished my work last week. I've come to say goodbye.'

'Oh. Where are you going?'

'If only I knew.' And then his phone rang.

He picked it out of his jacket pocket and examined it as if it were an alien object. It was not the first call from this number; it had been trying him once an hour throughout the day. He assumed it was a cold call and hesitated to answer. The landlord glared at him. 'Aren't you going to answer it?'

He did. 'Hello?'

'Is that Joseph Quine?'

'Who's calling?'

'Can I take it this *is* Mr Quine?'

'You can take it any way you want. I asked who's calling.'

'Mr Quine, I realize this may be unexpected. My name is Mark Burden. I am principal private secretary to the Prime Minister and I am ringing you from Whitehall on his behalf.'

'You're not phoning from a Downing Street number.'

'I am using what I believe is called a burner phone.'

'How do I know this isn't a hoax? What did you say your name was?'

'Mark Burden. B U R D E N.'

'You're going to have to do better than spell your name.'

'I understand that.' The voice seemed to be readying itself for a prepared statement. 'The Prime Minister has asked me to remind you of a one-to-one lunch he had with you in the snug of the Royal Oak, Clifton, on Friday February the nineteenth, 2016. This was a lunch neither of you revealed to anyone. At it, he told you the then Prime Minister would announce the next day, Saturday the twentieth of February, a referendum on whether to stay in or leave the European Union. The story you wrote following that lunch enabled you to steal a march on your newspaper rivals.'

'All right, carry on.'

'The Prime Minister urgently wishes to meet you to discuss a confidential matter. He hasn't told me what this is. He'd like to meet you tomorrow, Friday, for lunch at that same venue in Bristol.'

'Tomorrow!'

'Yes, my apologies for the short notice.'

'Look, I'm out of it all now, he knows that. And it's two years since we last met.'

'The Prime Minister asked me, if necessary, to plead with you to come without delay. He said you would have his undying gratitude.'

'Then I must say yes, mustn't I,' said Quine. Without waiting for a 'thank you' or 'goodbye', he cut the call, looked up at the landlord and said, 'I think I'll have the other half.'

'Old flame, was it?' asked the landlord.

His phone pinged. It was from the same number. **For the purposes of this exercise, you are Jonathan Moore, he is Paul Reynolds.**

Quine hit reply. OK, suggest you now get new phone.

Second half-pint quickly downed, Quine rose to leave the Cross Keys.

'Will we be seeing you again, Tolstoy?'

Quine stopped in his stride. He thought for a few seconds. 'I promise I'll come back here to die.'

Mrs Trelight was in the kitchen when he arrived at the

bungalow. 'I have to make a day trip tomorrow,' he said. 'I'll be back to clear my stuff after that.'

'I'll miss you, Mr Q.'

'And me you, Mrs T. '

'Times pass.' She was inspecting him just as on that first encounter a year before. 'Who are you off to see?'

'Oh, the Prime Minister.'

She smiled, tapping ash into the kitchen sink. 'Give him my regards.'

16

Entering the crowded lounge bar of the Royal Oak, Quine was intercepted by a man in his early forties with the unmistakeable manner of a private office civil servant.

'Jonathan Moore?' he asked, stretching out a hand.

'Yes,' said Quine, accepting it.

'Your host is here. Perhaps you can remember the room?'

Quine climbed a set of stairs leading to a landing. On a chaise-longue a dark-suited figure, reading a newspaper, glanced at him. Close security but as discreet as possible. The figure nodded him towards the end of the corridor.

A door was half open, Quine entered. Sandford was sitting alone at a rectangular mahogany table for eight. Two places were laid for lunch. He rose.

'Hello, Joe, good to see you.'

'You too, Prime—'

'I'm still Robbie to you. Been a while. Too much water under the bridge. For both of us.' Rather than offer a hand, he gave him a friendly pat on the shoulder and sat back down. 'Pint? Glass of wine?'

'I've been cutting down.'

'You have, haven't you? You must have shed stones.'

'Yes, two.'

'Good man.' Sandford grinned. Quine remembered his enviable knack of making every individual he talked to feel like they were the centre of the universe. 'Have a half. They do St Austell's on tap.'

'Thanks. What about you?'

'Trying not to. Even if my party would turn sane men to drink.' He picked up the menu. 'Let's order. I'm having kidneys. High-cholesterol treat when the cat's away.'

'How is Carol?' asked Quine, peering over his own menu.

'A marvel as always.'

Quine repressed his impatience to know the reason for their meeting. During the journey, images of Sandford's upward progress had flashed before him like scratchy old home movies – initially as the parliamentary candidate he had first come to know when he was political editor for the group of local and regional newspapers owned by MetroWestern plc. They had got on immediately. Politically, the MetroWestern group, focusing on local issues, had no ideological axe to grind. Quine had seen Sandford as a decent man with a more visible heart than the usual Tory candidate; he had written fairly about him. Trust had grown. Off the record meant just that. A secret was a secret, background meant background.

Shortly after Sandford's election to Parliament in 2005, Quine was offered the job of chief political correspondent, based in Westminster, for the *Daily Post*, a national paper. Then came a seminal moment in their relationship. *The Post*'s editor was approached by a freelance investigative journalist with a shocking story. He said that two young men who had recently left a residential care home in Bristol had been the victims of long-term abuse by Alan Griffiths, the Defence Secretary in the then Labour government. Quine, with both his Bristol and parliamentary connections, was asked to check it out. Griffiths was married with two children and there had never been a hint of scandal. If the story stacked up, it would destroy his career and perhaps his life too.

The journalist arranged for Quine to meet the young men. What they told him was appalling. Griffiths, as the local MP, was a trustee of the home and a frequent visitor. The accusers, now nineteen, said he was initially charming and helpful, offering support and mentoring to them. He first invited them when they were fifteen to the rented flat he kept in the constituency. A friendship grew. After several visits Griffiths wanted to make their friendship physical too. They said they tried to fend this off but he threatened to withdraw all favours. They both clearly remembered him saying, 'You know, lads, I can break you as well as make you.' From their family and social care backgrounds, the boys were accustomed to both hetero and homosexual sex. Griffiths said that as the three of them had all become friends, they should enjoy each other together. The young men, who were sixteen when they said the abuse started, described graphically what Griffiths had made them do.

After they left the care home at eighteen, they said Griffiths ceased all contact. He no longer responded to their messages. They rang the bell of his flat a few times but it appeared empty. One of the boys had read an article about the care home's authoritarian regime and sought out the journalist, who saw the claims as a major story that he could sell to a national newspaper.

Quine believed the story. It was unusual to have two witnesses corroborating each other in this way. Their knowledge of the rented flat and what had taken place inside it was detailed. One of them had begun to keep a contemporaneous diary of their encounters with Griffiths. The dates were all plausible, there was no evidence of retrospective entries after the event. Quine recommended publishing and *The Post*'s editor and lawyer were on-side.

At the last moment, even as he was rewriting the freelancer's initial draft, Quine decided, as a final check, to run it by Robin Sandford. Though Sandford and Griffiths were on opposite political sides, he knew they were friendly, or at least on speaking terms. Sandford agreed to find a way of raising the allegation with Griffiths without jeopardizing the story if it were true. Two days later, Sandford invited Quine to his Notting Hill home. When Quine arrived, he was suitably impressed by Sandford's financial windfall, courtesy of the van Kroon marriage.

'This is tricky, Joe,' said Sandford, stirring his cup of tea and munching a biscuit. 'You believe the two boys, don't you?'

'Yes,' replied Quine. 'Yes, I do.'

'If you're a hundred per cent sure, why approach me?'

'Because nothing is ever a hundred per cent.'

'The story will destroy Alan. On the other hand, though Alan and I are sort of friends, there's always political advantage with scandal in the opposition. I'm trying not to allow any of that to influence me. You just want my honest view.'

Quine felt a slight sinking. 'Yes. Be frank.'

'I didn't give Alan names or mention you – but I was very clear about the nature of the allegation.' He rubbed his forehead and sighed. 'Joe, you won't love me for this. I don't think it's true. This isn't Alan. Just isn't. He guessed the source. He put two and two together and named these two young men. He said they'd turned out to be a disappointment to him. So he'd broken off contact.'

'Why did he move flat?'

'I asked him that. He laughed and said it was a shit-hole. He'd been meaning to get something better for ages.'

Quine stayed silent.

'Look,' said Sandford, 'you could run it. It would be their word against his. I can't be a hundred per cent sure either. But if you run it, another truth could emerge. And that could rebound on you.'

Quine changed his mind and *The Post* passed on the story. Two months later it appeared in a rival newspaper. One year later, the two young men appeared in court, charged with attempting to pervert the course of justice. One of the many diary entries gave a date on which Griffiths could not possibly have been in Bristol. From this single error, their story had unravelled. It turned out they had stolen a small amount of cash and a watch from Griffiths's flat. Rather than report them, with the ensuing stigma of a criminal conviction damaging their future prospects, Griffiths told them he would never see them again.

Quine gave Sandford his heartfelt thanks and said he owed him. Sandford told him he didn't think like that. When David Cameron made Sandford Social Security Minister after the 2015 election, Quine was promoted to be *The Post*'s political editor. Their intertwined ascents would have continued, if it had not been for Deschevaux.

'You all right, Joe?' said Sandford.

Quine looked up from the menu. 'Sorry, just thinking about old times.'

'Not too bad, I hope.'

'Not at all.'

Perhaps they had been good for Sandford too. The youthful vigour and charm still evident on TV was, on close inspection, marked by strain. A touch more flesh around the chin and jowls, lines across the forehead, hair retreating a little further. It was hardly surprising – fatigue, anxiety, pressures known and unknown. Quine thought of other Prime Ministers. Blair had lost some of his gloss but only towards the end of his ten years; Brown was always a bag of nerves; Cameron seemed to rise above it all – whatever sense of failure he must feel, the skin was as baby-like as ever. The change in Sandford seemed more rapid, more marked. Was there something more than the daily grind of his office? Was that why he was here?

'Yes,' said Quine, 'kidneys. I'll spoil myself too.'

Sandford grinned. 'So... tough times.'

'Don't worry about me. A year ago, when I'd lost everything,

116

I went away and wrote the full story. To get it out of the system, I guess. I don't imagine anyone will publish it.'

'I don't know how that man was ever allowed into our party. Let alone selected as a candidate.'

Quine smiled. 'Isn't that local democracy?'

'I guess so.' He grinned back. 'What *is* it about Somerset?'

'I take it Deschevaux will never be part of your government.'

'Over my dead body.'

The door opened, two plates of veal kidneys, sides of vegetables and a half of bitter were set in front of them. 'Let's enjoy this,' said Sandford.

They skipped dessert and ordered coffee. After it arrived and they were alone with the door firmly shut, Sandford began. 'Joe, I have a problem. A weird one.' He paused, steeling himself. 'Over the years you and I grew to understand each other. If I tell you this, it will be by far the greatest confidence I've ever shared with you. Is that all right?'

'Of course,' replied Quine without hesitation. 'But why me?'

'Because I need an ally and you have the necessary skills. Because – I know this sounds odd – I'm alone. And powerless. Ultimately it's because there's no one in the world, including my wife and daughters, that I trust more than you.'

'I feel humbled.'

'It's true. I'm putting myself in your hands. In your power, if you like.'

'Power is not a word I would ever use in our relationship.'

'No. Nor me.' Sandford took a sip of coffee, put the cup

down, closed his eyes for a second and took a deep breath. 'OK. A few days ago, I was visited by Jed Fowkes.'

'Fowkes? I thought you'd pretty much cut ties with him.'

'I thought I had too.'

Sandford told, unedited and with a brutal clarity, the story of his encounters with Fowkes, both after his conference speech and in the Number 10 flat. He described the difficult period in his life which had caused occasional black-outs. He repeated Fowkes's description of the removal of the Hungarian girl from their flat. He related the newspaper stories of the young woman's hand. He finished by saying, 'I need to know the truth about what happened, Joe. It's the only way to get rid of this. And I want you to find it for me.'

Quine tried to hide his rising astonishment. As Sandford fell silent, he told himself not to show alarm. 'OK, Robbie, first things first. All this, right now, is just a story. It's very probably one fabricated by Jed Fowkes for reasons we don't know. There may be no "truth". The girl was probably fine, caught a late-night bus or cab home. And, however weirdly it's come about, the severed hand has given Fowkes an opportunity.'

Sandford sighed. 'Yes. It's impossible that a girl died in my bed. But let's take this in stages. Why would he come up with this story? I see two reasons. He's genuinely scared about something bad he believes might have happened. Or he's using it to scare me. And soon enough I'll know why. But just say he ever decided to go public. Or tell the police. It might destroy him, but sure as hell it would destroy me.'

'No one would believe him.'

'Think what the police have believed at times. You

remember the fantasist who told them about a paedophile murder ring of politicians and generals operating in Central London. Or the millions of pounds they spent investigating one former Prime Minister, Edward Heath, without a thread of proper evidence. Whatever they now say, the culture is still to trust the accuser.'

'Perhaps Fowkes himself is being blackmailed. Maybe someone's using him to exert leverage over you. So he's come up with this story.'

'Doesn't help. Because it doesn't kill the story.'

Quine looked hard into Sandford's eyes. 'Robbie, shouldn't you involve MI5? This is the security of the state, surely they can find a discreet way of dealing with Jed Fowkes?'

'If only. Once maybe, not today. Can you imagine me telling all this to Sir Kevin Long or to Dame Isobel Le Marchant? I'd never be able to look them in the face again. Whatever the truth, it'd always be no smoke without fire.' Quine could find no answer. Sandford paused, his worry lines more pronounced. 'I don't know,' he continued. 'Maybe Jed's got to some warped point in his life. He's so jealous, it's worth his own destruction to bring about mine. Maybe I shouldn't have shut myself off from him.' He stirred the dregs in his coffee cup with a teaspoon.

'You can't think like that,' said Quine. 'You've said it yourself. This didn't happen. Call his bluff. Dare him to do his worst.'

'I wish I was brave enough.' He covered his face with his hands. 'But I can't guarantee the outcome. I can't be one hundred per cent sure there isn't some tiny grain of truth in what he's saying. That's the nightmare. My rational mind tells me it can't be. But because of the memory loss, there's nothing I can say to prove it.' He removed his hands and looked up. 'To return to first base, the only way out is to find the truth. What's true, what's invented, what's Jed's motive. And I'm asking you to do that for me, Joe.'

Quine stared at him for a second. 'You don't ask for much, do you?'

Sandford slumped back in his chair; he'd shot his bolt. Quine felt the weight he must be carrying. And the loneliness. He also knew he could not refuse him, however inadequate he was for the task. It was not just that he owed him – even if Sandford didn't see favours as trades – but that he was fond of him. He was a decent man. A good Prime Minister.

'Of course, I'll help,' he found himself saying. 'Succeeding is another thing.'

'Thank you,' said Sandford. He sat up with relief and pressed his shoulders back. 'Thank you so much.'

17

Sandford peered out into the corridor and signalled thirty minutes to the bodyguard. Returning to his chair, he unwrapped the small red square beside his saucer, removed the piece of chocolate within, and silently revolved it in his mouth.

'What do you need?'

'Luck,' said Quine.

Sandford laughed. 'Controllables first. Money.'

'I don't want money,' said Quine.

'We're entering a professional relationship.' He grinned. 'I hereby commission you to write a quick-turnaround biography of the Prime Minister. The Prime Minister will give you every assistance. He will tell his friends to speak honestly with you. Particularly those who knew him during that sometimes difficult period when he shared a flat with Jed Fowkes. You'll be paid a monthly retainer and all reasonable expenses—'

'Reasonable?' Quine was enjoying the performance.

'Only the best wine. Business class should you need to

travel within Europe. Front of plane for intercontinental. The Prime Minister has a rich wife.'

'Does she know?

'Not yet.'

'Sounds a good deal. I could do with the work. Do I get to take it to a publisher when it's finished?'

'Depends on what your research unearths.'

Silence fell, the game over. 'This needs more than a biographer,' said Quine. 'It needs a strategy and resources. We have to investigate Fowkes, track him in the present, delve into his past.'

Sandford frowned in concentration. 'I agree. All my instincts tell me there's more to come. He's setting up a drip-feed. He's precise. He plans. He plays a long game. I need to go on the attack. Unsettle him. Flush him out.'

'How?'

'I've had one thought. Came from something Carol said.'

'Can you share?'

'Jed's power rests on Morland-Cross. Unless he's got a hold over him too, of course. I wouldn't put that past him. Assuming not, I want to drive a wedge between them.'

'How?'

'Not sure. Leave it with me.'

'Fine. As and when.' Quine hid his disappointment. He suspected Sandford's plan was more advanced than he was letting on.

'Joe, you mentioned tracking Fowkes in the present. Meaning?'

'Meaning this requires professional surveillance.'

'As I've said, I can't bring in MI5. Not yet anyway. You're a journalist. You've tracked people.'

'I'm not a spy.'

'No, but—'

'I'm a one-man band, a discredited hack. It won't fly. You need a professional.'

'Any ideas?'

Quine looked down at his lukewarm coffee. 'Let me think,' he said.

'OK. I'll leave that with you.'

'I guess the final thing,' said Quine, 'is how we communicate.'

'There's no problem people knowing you're doing a biography of me. You could tell your agent—'

'If he's still speaking to me...'

'He will when he hears the Prime Minister is giving you full access. Say the deal is you write it first. You allow me to comment, though editorial control is yours. He flogs it for a vast sum to his favourite publisher.'

'He'll be even more pissed off if I then don't deliver.'

Sandford got up again, went to the window and stared down at the street. He swung round. 'Then let's do it for real. Think of it, Joe, you'd be right back in the mainstream.'

'Do I want to be?'

'Course you do. I'm serious.'

'One step at a time,' said Quine. 'We were discussing communication.'

'Yes. The biography gives a cover. But my email, office

123

phone and mobile are no good. The only safe conversation is face to face.'

'We need a private email. Just short, sensibly coded messages.'

'How?'

'Let me think.' Quine hesitated. 'However I set it up, we can keep the names we're using today. And put numbers or extra letters between the first and last names as they're quite common. I'll do 1234. So I'm jonathan1234moore. All lower case. You do abcd.'

'OK,' said Sandford, 'do we have a deal?'

'I need to nip out and get something. Have you got time?'

Sandford looked puzzled. 'I guess ...' he began, but Quine was already out of his seat.

Five minutes later, he returned and showed Sandford two small mobile phones. 'There was a phone shop in the high street. One for you, one for me. I've loaded a few quid credit on them.' He handed one to Sandford. 'There's one contact I've added to yours – the number of the phone I'm keeping. I've added your number in mine. It's one-off use only, then you chuck it.'

'I know what a burner phone is.'

'So you know the rule. One call or text only. More than that and a traceable pattern begins to emerge.'

Sandford stared down at the black object he was holding. 'You know what they say. A secret remains a secret between two, but when it's passed to a third, it's no longer a secret.'

'I understand.' Quine extended his hand. Sandford shook it. There were no smiles now. 'There's one thing,' he continued.

'What happens in the hugely unlikely event... I mean it must be impossible...'

'... that Jed Fowkes's story is true,' said Sandford. 'That a girl died in my bed. That I caused her death in a black-out.'

Quine stayed silent. 'If that proves to be the case,' continued the Prime Minister, 'then you'll be sitting on the greatest political scoop of all time. With a best-selling book to follow on the destruction of a Prime Minister.'

*

'You're awake again.' Carol stirred. 'What's the time?'

'Dunno.' He was sitting up, brain whirring.

'Come on, it's the middle of the night. You need to sleep.'

'Thatcher didn't.'

She turned to lean on her elbow and face him. 'Not a good role model.'

Silence fell momentarily. 'Actually...' he began.

She now sat up, matching him. 'Actually what?'

'I had lunch with Joe Quine today.'

'Why on earth would you do that? He's damaged goods.'

Exactly the same words Mark Burden had used. 'I thought you'd react that way. It's why I didn't tell you.'

'Thanks for that.'

'My pleasure.' He said it lightly; she did not respond. 'May I ask you one favour, love?'

'Now?'

'Yes. While we're alone.'

125

'All right.'

'Can you set up a private email account for me on your computer, under the name of Paul Reynolds, to communicate with Joe? We've agreed a name for him too.'

'What!'

'Nothing illegal. He's going to do some research for me. I need to go off-piste for it.'

'Is it connected with the story you've been told?'

'Yes, sort of. Best for now to keep it in the family – if you get my drift.'

'Hillary Clinton lost the presidency because she ran a private email.'

'This isn't the same. It's temporary. Just for one thing.'

'Why not do it through Mark Burden?'

'I don't want this anywhere near Whitehall. The time may come.'

'You're being evasive, Robbie.'

'Sorry. I don't like it either.'

'OK. I'll set it up. What do you want your password to be?'

'Carol.'

'I suppose I should be flattered.'

He smiled weakly. 'Because they're common names we agreed some digits and letters to add.' He wrote them on a piece of notepaper on his bedside table and handed it to her. 'Just one more thing.'

'What?'

'Joe's broke.'

'Not news.'

'So the deal is I'm hiring him to write an authorized biography.'

'Bit premature, isn't it?'

'A week is a long time in politics.'

'Now you're being irritating—'

'Could you organize payments to him? Advance five thousand to get him going.'

'Five K!'

'We … we're hardly short.'

'Why won't you tell me?'

'I will. Soon as. It's an unusual situation. But done like this, nothing improper. I promise.'

'Then at least before we make any further payments.'

'OK.' He turned on his pleading smile. 'You're a wonder, Carol. I mean it. I don't know what I'd do without you.'

'The trouble with you, my darling, is that you're now too powerful to refuse.'

She rolled away, her back to him. He slid down and snuggled up, putting an arm around her. She patted his hand then gently moved the arm away. He knew he'd upset her, but he could see no other way.

He lay still for a few minutes until, as usual, a soft snoring broke the silence. As quietly as he could, he rolled back his side of the duvet, slid his legs out and tiptoed towards the door. He headed down half a flight of stairs into Carol's study overlooking the garden – in easier times, the refuge where they'd snuggled up and watched TV.

His world felt pitched into uncertainty. What if somewhere out there lay concrete evidence or a credible witness?

What he could never tell Joe was a calculation that he disliked himself for making. If Quine found Fowkes guilty of a malicious conspiracy, Sandford was a free man. He might even gain sympathy.

If Quine found evidence against him – and tried to interest the media in his story – might not people mutter, poor old Joe Quine, he's discredited, isn't he? The loser of the biggest libel case in recent British history. The guy who was hoodwinked by one liar has fallen for another.

Win-win. The name of the game.

18

That, reflected Quine, was the most bizarre conversation of my life. He felt a surge of sympathy for Sandford. To be unable to dismiss the possibility of something so horrible must be terrifying. He was also beginning to feel contempt for Sandford's tormentors, whether Fowkes was acting alone or being used by others.

Out in the street, he made two immediate calls. The first to the one person in the world he both trusted unreservedly and who might have a private link to the sort of help he needed. She suggested he come to lunch the next day. The second to Mrs Trelight to say he'd be away for a short while.

'I'm missing you already, Mr Q,' she said. 'Did you have a nice time with the Prime Minister?'

'He wants to make me Foreign Secretary.'

'Don't take us into any wars, please. Oh, someone called round to see you this afternoon.'

'Really?'

'Yes, he said he worked for your publisher – or did he say agent?'

'What did he want to know?'

'He wanted to speak to you – said he had tried calling you.'

Quine was sure there were no missed calls except for Sandford's PPS. 'Did you tell him anything?'

'Good heavens, no! I said you were a law unto yourself. Never knew where you might be from one day to the next.'

'Thank you.'

It was the second time in an hour his agent had come up. He recalled his last contact with Riley Trueman a few days after the court case was over, when he had been preparing to go to ground.

'Well, Joe, what are we to do with you?' Riley had asked. 'I'm still your agent and you're still a great scribe. I can get you some ghosting. You'll need to earn.'

'Not interested, Riley.'

'Or write one of your biographies. You could churn out a quickie on Theresa.'

'Yes, quick and empty. Nothing there that interests me.'

'You always manage to find something new with your subjects.'

'Riley, I appreciate it. But I'm going to bed down for a while. Still got the camper van. And a few quid somewhere.'

'It's your life. Just promise me you'll never write another word about Quentin Deschevaux.'

That was it. Quine couldn't imagine what Riley would want from him now. Anyway he never left London. Perhaps he'd sent a minion. Or a tabloid sneak had sussed him out. Though he couldn't imagine why.

Being confronted by London after so long away disconcerted him. He arrived at Paddington mid-morning, took the tube to Earl's Court and a detour around the billionaires' curves of The Boltons. The gate into the garden by St Mary's Church was open; he entered and, finding himself alone, sat down on a bench, gazing at the dappled light filtering through the shrubbery. Did any resident of the encircling palatial villas ever enter this church or even this garden? How many of those houses were actually lived in? The oddity of the new global class of super-rich struck him. They dug down and down to give themselves space for cinemas, swimming pools, art collections – not to mention elevators designed to lower the Bentley to its temperature-controlled car suite. All to prevent the world around impinging no further than the walls they hid behind.

So much of this city had become impenetrable, lives lived, deals made, power exchanged, money appearing and vanishing behind a barrier of shadows. Could his book, his tiny gesture against this mockery of humanity, ever see the light of day? Back here, he was seized by a sense of his own irrelevance – the sheer impossibility of the task ahead of him.

He rose with a jerk. You can't give up before you even start. View it as a privilege – a commission from the Prime Minister himself. Yet all he could now see was a diffused image of a girl lying dead and half-undressed on a dishevelled bed. He rubbed his eyes and headed back to the crossroads. Stopping only at

Earl's Court Road to buy a bunch of flowers, he arrived at West Kensington's blocks of Victorian mansion flats.

'Come in,' yelled a voice.

The door buzzed and he floated up four flights of stairs. A year ago, he had been breathless at the first half landing. Now, he did not break sweat. The latch clicked and the door opened to reveal a familiar figure.

'Dad!' she cried with delight, flinging her arms around him.

'Sophie.'

Sophie Becker released her grip and inspected him. 'Wow, you look terrific.'

'I've been trying. Pretty good yourself.' His daughter was four inches shorter than him, curly blonde hair. 'What are those?' he said, staring at strawberry streaks running from the crown of her head.

'Like it?'

'It's different,' he said.

She smiled. 'I thought I needed definition.'

'You've never been short of that.'

She looked at him again. 'It's really good to see you. Sorry it couldn't be earlier. She was on duty yesterday evening and had a meeting this morning. She should be back soon.'

She led him into a short corridor, with doors on either side, and onwards to a sitting room with a triple window overlooking the garden square.

'It's nice, this square,' he said. 'Leaves turning, season changing.'

'Yes, we're lucky.'

'And how's married life?'

'Great. Actually we've been thinking about something.'

'Oh?'

'Maybe having a child.'

'Wow!' He gave himself a moment to take it in. 'Great!'

'You approve?'

'Of course. I'd love to be a granddad.'

Her eyes lit up. 'Brilliant. Because her work's so intense right now, I'll carry it. Then, if we have a second, maybe she can.'

'Do you have a donor?'

'Do you honestly want to know?'

'Not really. Just make sure it's someone as good-looking and clever as you.' He paused. 'And her, of course.'

'We've already selected him. Not that he knows it yet.'

'Lucky boy.'

She affectionately tapped his forearm. 'That's not the way to view it, Dad.' They fell into comfortable silence. 'Would it have made a difference if you and Mum had actually got married?' she suddenly asked.

He turned. 'Where on earth did that come from?'

'Just wondering. Thinking of us. Do you ever wish you had?'

'It wouldn't have stopped her leaving me and going home.'

'Maybe you should have tried following her.'

'You can't report Westminster from the Black Forest,' he said wistfully.

'No. That was always your first love, wasn't it?'

'Yes, I suppose it became obsessive. I couldn't let it go. How's your job?'

'Still looking for the next *Girl on the Train*.'

'I never read it.'

'It's OK, Dad, you're not the target market. What about your book?'

'Well, at least it's done.'

'Can I read?'

'Sure. But you're not the target publisher.'

They heard the front door open. Quine watched an elegant figure, taller and narrower than his daughter, enter the sitting room, shedding a long black coat as she moved. She flung it over a chair, embraced his daughter with a kiss on the lips and then turned to him.

'Hello, Isla.'

'Hello, Joe,' she said with a mild Scottish accent. 'Seems a long time. You can have a hug too.'

They stood back.

'You're a new man!'

'And you haven't changed a bit,' he said.

'I stopped by to get some lunch. Whatever else we're going to talk about, Joe, it's been over a year, I've just come off duty and there's a cold bottle of white wine in the fridge.'

*

'Right,' said Isla an hour later. Sophie had gone out for a breath of crisp autumnal air. 'Fire away.'

'Isla, I find myself in a most unusual predicament. Though we never talk about it, I'm aware of where you work. That *is* allowed, isn't it?'

'Sure. It works like this. When we married, I made Sophie my next of kin. I can in general terms talk to her about my workplace. After her mother went back to Germany, Sophie made you her next of kin. And she's been your next of kin for longer than that. So yes, she can tell you where her spouse works.'

'Good. I don't know if you can actually help, but I've got a problem. I've come across the odd person from your world over the years. But I *know* no one else but you. Certainly no one I can trust. Are you able to listen to me confidentially?'

'If it's an immediate life or death threat, like a terror attack, it can't be confidential.'

'It's not. There's no threat to life.'

'Then I can agree to that and we can discuss afterwards what to do.'

Quine breathed more easily. The first point of tension was resolved. It was now about exactly what, and how, he told her. 'This is very sensitive.'

'Yes, Sophie said you sounded a bit on edge. I'm sorry. I was working yesterday evening and this morning.'

'There's also a double catch. One. My informant, for want of a better word, has sworn me to confidentiality. But I don't have the resources to do what he needs. Two. MI5 does have the resources to do what he needs. But my informant's in a position where he feels that he can't involve either police or intelligence services.'

'I see.' There was a long silence. 'Can you tell me who your informant is?' Isla finally asked.

'No.'

'OK.'

'They say a secret remains a secret between two,' Quine said, remembering Sandford's words, 'but when it's passed to a third, it's no longer a secret.'

'If one of us happens to be that third person, in certain situations we're permitted to use our judgement.'

Quine hesitated. 'Right…' he murmured, then stopped. She waited. 'The Prime Minister of this country,' he saw Isla blink, 'is under a serious threat from a man called Jed Fowkes, the senior special adviser to the Chancellor of the Exchequer.'

She sat still as a rock. 'I know the name.' Quine was unsure whether he could continue. 'At this point, Joe, you're only telling me—'

'OK. Some thirty years ago,' resumed Quine, speaking flatly, without expression, 'Robin Sandford and Jed Fowkes shared a flat in South London…' He relayed the story as he had heard it from Sandford, holding nothing back, ending with the Prime Minister and Fowkes's most recent meeting. 'Through a particular connection I have been tasked to find the truth of what happened on this night thirty years ago as it seems the only way to resolve the problem. I can try to dig into the background, interview people who were around Sandford and Fowkes at the time. I may get somewhere. But we need to put Fowkes under surveillance. That, obviously, I can't do. I don't know exactly what it is but I'm sure there's real danger here. Tracking Fowkes can't wait.'

'I see,' said Isla coolly. 'Just a question or two.'

'I can't tell you more.'

'Call it clarification. One might expect a Prime Minister to

136

be sure that such an event did not happen and immediately bring in the police or security service to report what appears to be the onset of a blackmail attempt.'

'Yes, the problem is the gap in Sandford's memory caused by the black-outs. So he feels the only sure way to put the allegation to rest is to discover the truth. And that's needed because he fears that, for whatever reason, Fowkes might wish to damage him – perhaps destroy him – by going public.'

'Why is Fowkes so certain this severed hand has any connection to the Hungarian girl?'

Quine opened his case and pulled out the two *Mail* articles. He allowed her time to read. 'Fowkes seems to be implying that somebody out there knows he was complicit in getting rid of the body.'

'He could have written those words himself,' she said sharply.

'It's possible.'

'And if it's not him, it's likely to be the party or parties that took the girl away and disposed of her.'

'I assume so,' said Quine reluctantly. Isla's tone made it seem that one or two pieces of the jigsaw might be falling uncomfortably into place. 'But even if there was some kind of incident, there remains nothing to connect Sandford to it except for Fowkes's own account.'

'Quite,' said Isla. 'Just one further clarification. Does anyone else know about Fowkes's conversations with Sandford?'

Quine understood what the implication of his answer would be. He allowed himself time to think. 'Not as far as I know. Unless, I guess, there *is* someone threatening him.'

137

'OK. Joe, you were right to come to me. I agree about the immediacy. Why don't you take it easy, make up lost time with Sophie. I'll head straight back into the office.'

'You said we could discuss how you act on this information.'

'Sure.' She smiled gently. 'What do you want? That we just have this chat and I then sit on it?'

He closed his eyes and shook his head. 'No. There's no choice, is there?'

'Trust me. I'll go about it carefully. I promise.'

*

If it was said that a problem shared is a problem halved, Quine was feeling the opposite. Sharing this problem now seemed to have multiplied it a hundredfold. The train had left the station but neither he nor Sandford was in the driver's seat. Surely he had made it clear enough to the Prime Minister that there had to be some form of extra help. He felt a desperate need to do something useful himself. Checking out the severed hand story at least fell within his expertise.

The *Mail* story's by-line was the paper's crime correspondent. Quine had no wish to alert him – or the police – by asking for further background. Instead he searched local news sources in the Greenwich/Lewisham area. Nothing came up. It didn't surprise him – most local newspapers in Britain had been killed off. Instead he came across an intriguing header. 'RETIRED EDITOR AND DETECTIVE JOIN FORCES'. He hit the link to find an appeal to raise support for a new local news sheet and website to be called 'Creek News'. It proposed a community enterprise to fill the void left by the closure of the Deptford and Greenwich Press. There were email addresses for the former editor of the defunct paper, Geoffrey Boyes, and a retired Detective Inspector called Jim Letts. Quine knew Boyes would know his name from *The Post* and emailed him to say that something to their possible mutual advantage had arisen and perhaps they could meet in the next day or two. Within minutes, Boyes replied, giving an address in Greenwich and a time.

Sophie returned not long after Isla had left for her office.

'Did it go OK with Isla?' she asked.

'Yes. She was great.'

'Where is she?'

'Gone back to work.'

Sophie frowned. 'Because of what you told her?'

'Sorry, I've messed up your weekend.'

'It's fine, they've been messed up before. We've got a couple of friends coming for supper. You'll have to entertain them if she's not back.'

His eyebrows rose. 'Is that an invitation?'

'Looks like it. You can stay the night too.'

'There's a Premier Inn not far away. I was going to check in.'

'Don't do that. There's a sofa-bed. You can cook us breakfast in the morning.'

*

The next day, Quine explored the modest terrace of houses off Lewisham Way where Sandford, Jed Fowkes and Mikey Miller had lived. The change over a single generation was evident. Most were now smartened with freshly painted front doors – single dwellings occupied by well-off families comparatively outpriced by Peckham and Brixton. Even at dusk the street Sandford and Fowkes had lived in was deserted and silent, well away from bars and clubs. If you needed to get rid of a body in the small hours, you'd be extremely unlucky to run into anyone here. For the first time he sensed that it might not be easy to knock a hole in Jed Fowkes's story.

19

Monday morning, 7.45. 'I owe you an apology,' said the Prime Minister.

The Chancellor of the Exchequer's eyes shot up, the modishly cut head of blond hair, skilfully executed by his girlfriend's hair stylist, almost seeming to bounce. 'An apology?'

'Yes, I should have warned you about the arms ban.'

Henry Morland-Cross had been surprised enough in the first place by Sandford's call on the Sunday evening. 'Could you nip over to the flat first thing? Won't take long.' He was no less surprised to find himself alone with the Prime Minister who personally made coffee, assembled a tray with mugs and a pack of chocolate digestive biscuits, and then gestured him to sit down at the nondescript kitchen table of the 10 Downing Street flat.

The Chancellor puffed himself up. 'Well, yes, you should have told me. But I accept the apology. Are you actually serious about it?'

'Yes, I want it as a commitment in the Royal Speech if Cabinet supports me. Which it will.'

'Hmm,' mused Morland-Cross, 'the majority will. They're your people.' There was an awkward silence. They both took a sip from their mugs.

Sandford broke it. 'Look, M-C, these past couple of years haven't been easy.'

'Well, I don't know—'

'You won the Brexit argument, you expected to get the leadership too. You had every reason. You had the grassroots at your fingertips.'

'Ah, the fickle mob.'

'Seems they didn't mind drink, dope or divorce – just not so keen on cocaine.'

'Christ, it was a fair few years ago.'

'As you said. That's old ground. I've been thinking.' Sandford paused. Morland-Cross sensed the reason for the summons coming. 'I've told no one else this. I'm not going to fight another general election.'

'What!' Morland-Cross almost choked on his biscuit.

Sandford gave a watery smile. 'Odd, isn't it?'

'I should say so. You must have discussed it with Carol?'

'No.' He paused. 'You know why. Because my final decision depends on you.'

'Me!'

'I'll explain. I know I'm not fundamentally in tune with the direction the party's headed in. Sooner or later that'll rear up in a way that'll be damaging. To the party – and to me personally. I want to be gone before it does.'

'We managed to agree a manifesto,' said Morland-Cross.

Sandford saw the irony of his greatest rival apparently

trying to buttress him. He wondered what he was thinking. Much depended on it. 'We fudged everything. You and I know that. We both know what the majority of the party *really* want. Slash income and corporation tax, abolish inheritance tax, private health insurance, Singapore-on-Thames, business does what it wants, sod workers' rights, sod the poor and useless. And it sees the shock of the past year as offering the perfect time and opportunity. Debt's soared, the economy's tanked, radical therapy is needed. And that's what you want too.'

Morland-Cross grunted. 'Wrong on one thing. Sod the lazy and useless, not the poor.'

'I thought they were supposed to be one and the same.'

'We don't put it like that.'

'Whatever the details,' said Sandford, 'these pressures will build. So,' he paused, watching the mounting hunger in Morland-Cross's eyes, 'I have a proposal. I've been in office for almost a year. For the next three years, broadly speaking we follow my course. You understand what I mean by that.'

'Yes. Go gently.'

'If we do that, with you as my Chancellor and Deputy PM, I will then resign and support you unequivocally in the leadership election that follows. With my backing, you'll win. Past indiscretions will be forgotten. In their hearts they've always wanted you. I'll have had nearly a full term as Prime Minister trying to do things my way and going out on my terms. And you'll have a full year to run, if you want it, before the next election.'

'Hmm...' Morland-Cross was visibly calculating. 'How do I know you'll stick to it? Remember Blair and Brown.'

'Blair became a zealot. I never could be. More practically, I'll put it in writing here and now.' He looked up with a grin. 'We'll call it the "10 Downing Street Kitchen Declaration".'

Morland-Cross's cheeks twitched. 'Does the arms thing have to go in the Royal Speech? It sends such a bad message.'

'Yes,' said Sandford. 'And it won't harm us at the polls. But, now we've had this chat – and if we agree – I promise I won't spring any more surprises on you.'

'Hmm,' Morland-Cross repeated. 'It will bring difficulties with some of my people.'

'I know,' said Sandford. He made a show of hesitating. 'Can I help you with any of them?'

Morland-Cross shrugged. 'Jed Fowkes will be disappointed. More than that. Devastated. I owe him. He's odd at times but he has real flashes of insight. He more than anyone sees now as the big chance.'

'If there are any issues with Jed Fowkes, I will one hundred per cent support you. As you know, he and I go back.'

'Yes. But he won't like it.'

Sandford conveyed sympathy. 'Are you worried about how he'll react?'

'Not at all,' Morland-Cross protested.

'Then you and I have nothing to fear.' Simultaneously they checked the kitchen clock. Seconds ticked past.

'Right,' said Morland-Cross. 'I agree.'

'Excellent.' Sandford beamed. 'I've written out our agreement. Two copies. We can date and sign it right now. You take one with you. That is your guarantee. If you want, we can write something more elegant later.'

Sandford took two envelopes out of a kitchen dresser drawer. He handed both to Morland-Cross, who read them with careful deliberation. As the clock ticked towards 8.10 a.m., he signed both sheets of paper, handed them to Sandford who added his own signature, returning one copy to Morland-Cross. The transaction had taken twenty-five minutes.

They stood and shook hands.

'Deal,' said Sandford, face set firm.

'Deal,' replied Morland-Cross.

As Morland-Cross left the Number 10 flat, Sandford suspected he had not even the slightest inkling that both the conversation and the 'deal' were entirely about Jed Fowkes and had absolutely nothing to do with him.

Two minutes later, the flat's phone rang.

'Good morning, Prime Minister.'

'Yes, Mark.'

'The Cabinet Secretary has asked to see you urgently,' said his principal private secretary.

'Now?'

'If possible, yes.'

'OK, send him up. I've got a few minutes, haven't I?'

'Yes. If it takes longer, I'll rearrange.'

The chubby face of the most senior civil servant in the land seemed pinker than usual. 'I'll be brief, Prime Minister,' said Sir Kevin Long, perched on the edge of an armchair in the sitting room.

'I'm told I have time,' said Sandford, seated more languidly.

'A serious matter has arisen.'

'Go straight in, Kevin.'

The Cabinet Secretary composed himself. 'MI5 has discovered that the senior political adviser in the Treasury—'

'Jed Fowkes...'

'Yes. I realize you, er, know him.'

'Not much contact in recent years, thank God.'

'Good. Apparently Fowkes has fallen under suspicion of removing highly confidential documents from within the Treasury overnight and returning them the following morning. The suspicion is that he is either photocopying them or scanning them into a personal computer at his flat. His motive is yet to be determined. I understand the discovery of this is extremely recent. MI5 told me over the weekend they wished in the first instance for Fowkes to be observed from within the Treasury. With immediate effect. To that end I have agreed that an MI5 officer will begin a temporary attachment, with the cover of being a DTI civil servant, to the Treasury this morning. This person will be seated in the HMRC section, which neighbours the open-plan space alongside the permanent secretary and main Treasury officials. It offers a line of sight to the door into the special advisers' office and to the Chancellor's next along the corridor.'

'Extraordinary,' said Sandford, appearing baffled. 'Why would Fowkes do something like that?'

'That is what we need to find out. At this point MI5 do not recommend seeking warrants for electronic surveillance. The human factor should soon tell us if this is necessary.'

'Right,' said Sandford. 'Thank you for telling me, Kevin.'

'It is of course highly confidential.'

'Yes,' said Sandford. Sometimes his Cabinet Secretary seemed to think he had just wandered in off the street.

Long stood up, then hesitated. 'Forgive me for asking, Prime Minister. I just wondered if there is any connection between this and your instructions concerning the Royal Speech.'

'As I said, Kevin, at this point my reasons are not up for discussion.'

Long walked busily out of the flat. Sandford felt a frisson of pleasure that the Cabinet Secretary might think the Prime Minister had stolen a march on him. The truth – that there was no planned connection, just a fortuitous piece of timing – was more prosaic.

A secret is no longer a secret when it passes to a third person, he reflected. Quine had spoken to someone. Who? And what exactly had he told them?

20

Henry Morland-Cross was regretting that it had become accepted practice for his special advisers to pretty much stroll in and out of his office at their pleasure. More accurately, the regret was confined to one of them.

The less experienced Thomasina Bellingham was always welcome. She was a serious, idealistic young woman who, unlike his senior Spad, Jed Fowkes, tended to agree immediately with his pronouncements. She was also in her early thirties, with wavy brown hair and lips that had a certain lusciousness. He couldn't easily dismiss the gnawing truth that Patricia, his present 'squeeze' as the tabloids put it, was several years older and not wearing as well as she might. Drink was not helping.

There had been moments over the past few months when both he and Thomasina must have known they were on the cliff edge. Now, with the rekindled prospect of being a future Prime Minister, he ought to be careful. The thought of locking his office door while alone with her was fraught with unknown consequences. Leaving the door unlocked was risky beyond madness. And yet...

At least encounters with Fowkes were never coloured with any such overtones. On this morning, as the meeting wound up, he lingered.

'A quick word, M-C?'

'Of course, Jed.'

They resumed their seats at the oval table Morland-Cross used for meetings.

'We're being cut out of the Royal Speech,' said Fowkes.

'What do you mean?'

'I've asked for drafts. I've had nothing. Normally the Treasury's in on it throughout. I reckon Number 10's keeping to it themselves. What's in that speech will dictate the whole tenor of this government. They're back-tracking, I'm sure of it. The radical agenda's turning into liberal mush.'

'How?'

'Take this arms, private armies rubbish.'

'What about it?'

Fowkes looked puzzled at the response. 'I mean, is that going to be in it? Is he actually serious?'

Morland-Cross remembered how he had asked the Prime Minister exactly the same question an hour and a half ago. A torrent had passed under the bridge since then. 'It appears to mean a lot to him, Jed. We may have to let that one go.'

'Surely not,' Fowkes protested. 'We... you've got to stop him. It's not just the companies – I've had British Aerospace and Rolls-Royce shouting in my ear. "Are you seriously saying no more sales to the Saudis?" Not just them, Babcock, Serco,

QinetiQ, IPRM, the whole lot of them. We're supposed to free these guys up, not get in their way.'

'I agree completely,' said Morland-Cross.

'And what about everything else?' continued Fowkes. 'Tax cuts, stiffing the unions, private health, everything we've talked about. Because of the shit we're in, now's the time to go for it.'

'I know,' continued the Chancellor in the same soft tones.

'Look, there's only three weeks till the State Opening and that speech.'

'It's tricky.' Morland-Cross paused. 'It's all a matter of timing, isn't it?'

'Now's the time.'

'But is it? Is it really? Perhaps we should go more gently after all that's happened?'

Fowkes stared at him open-mouthed. 'We've discussed all this endlessly. The key is to strike fast now.'

'He's the PM. It's his Cabinet.'

Fowkes fell silent. Cat on a hot tin roof, thought Morland-Cross. Fowkes had once or twice displayed the fury of rejection, an experience that he himself was not unacquainted with, though from spurned mistresses. He wondered if another explosion was building.

'You have to move when the stars are aligned,' Fowkes continued coldly.

'Hmm…' mused Morland-Cross. The moment seemed to have passed. 'It's only about timing. Let's get halfway through the rest of this term, don't rock too many boats, and then, yes, we'll go radical.'

Fowkes stood slowly, half-turned, stopped and swung back. 'Have you been to see him?' His voice seemed near to cracking.

Morland-Cross looked at him with a puzzled smile. 'We *are* allowed to speak.'

'You've done a deal...'

Morland-Cross stood too. 'He's entitled to make arrangements with his colleagues.'

'I see.' Fowkes turned and, without a further word, walked out. Glowering, he marched the few yards into his office, closing the door behind him.

From her desk some twenty yards away in HMRC's tax collection policy unit – where she had arrived an hour and a half earlier on her first day on 'attachment from the Department of Trade and Industry' – Isla McDonald observed Jed Fowkes's passage down the corridor. There goes an angry man, she thought.

A fly on the wall would have found the conversation that had just taken place most interesting. But, for the moment, rather than the full story Quine had told her, she had confined her report to her head of desk to a cover story of suspected misconduct by Fowkes. That was not strong enough to justify bugs and taps. The coming days would dictate whether she would need to tell him more.

21

At 10 a.m. sharp Quine knocked on the black-painted front door of a narrow terraced house a few hundred yards uphill from the tourist bustle of Greenwich. It was opened by a crouching figure – early seventies, Quine reckoned – wearing a brown jacket, woollen tie and corduroy trousers.

'Joseph Quine, I take it,' he said, stretching out a hand.

'Yes,' said Quine. Wearing a suit was the right decision.

'Come in, meet Jim.' He led him into a sitting room with just enough space for a sofa and two chairs. A gas heater sat between the decorative tiles of the fireplace; on the wooden mantelpiece above, which had sustained chips at both corners, lay a couple of small china vases.

A second man rose, taller, a few years younger, with a neatly clipped moustache, also wearing jacket and tie. His whole being displayed the legacy of a lifetime of cigarettes.

Quine suspected that both lived alone. Two figures from a past world wanting, in their own way, to reconnect to the present.

'I could hardly believe it when I got your email, Mr Quine,' said Boyes.

'Joe. Please,' said Quine.

'In that case it's Jim and Geoff.' Boyes looked across at Letts and they exchanged an easy grin. They go back a long time, thought Quine.

'Of course, I knew the name, but never the face. I always enjoyed reading you.'

'Thank you.'

'What's brought you to these parts?' interrupted Betts, spotting the danger of old journalists reminiscing.

It was the obvious question and Quine had given thought to the answer. As always, a strong element of truth was best. 'I was directed,' he replied, 'to a *Mail* story about a young woman's hand being unearthed in this area.' There were two sharp intakes of breath. 'I wanted to ask you whether you've heard about this. And whether or not the reporting of the find is accurate.'

Boyes and Letts looked at each other and grinned.

'Have we heard about it?' said Letts.

'Is it true?' echoed Boyes. 'Jim was first to the story! Then I sold it to the *Mail* ahead of the official police statement.'

'Gosh, well done!' said Quine, genuinely surprised. 'How did you get it?'

'As you protect sources, so do we,' said Letts with quiet pride.

'Jim is former Lewisham CID and a popular copper with many friends still in the force,' said Boyes.

'I understand,' said Quine. 'Congratulations. A real scoop.'

'What's your interest?' asked Letts.

'The report said the remains were dated from twenty-five to thirty-five years ago...' Quine began.

'Their best guess,' said Boyes. 'The piece of shower curtain helped but there was nothing more precise.'

'And a young woman. Which takes us back to the late 1980s and early 90s,' said Quine. 'Strange times, the years after the Berlin Wall fell, the oligarchs taking over Russia. Smuggled cigarettes paying no tax, mountains of cocaine, Mercedes 600s stolen to order.' He paused. 'I've been commissioned to write a book about that era. And no, the name Deschevaux won't be appearing in it.'

'I imagine not,' said Boyes.

'Even if it should be. But during my researches, I've accumulated a great deal of knowledge. Particularly about the worst trade of the lot.' He looked at his two listeners.

'Yes,' said Letts, a sadness in his eyes.

'The nastiest,' agreed Boyes.

'Exactly,' continued Quine. 'Human trafficking. Prostitutes. No, they weren't usually that. More likely, innocent girls kidnapped and imprisoned as sex slaves. Lives that were stubbed out as cheaply as a rolled-up cigarette.'

'You can speculate,' said Letts, 'but it doesn't give us anything concrete about our hand.'

'No,' said Quine. 'But the decade, the ring of Hungarian origin, the grisly death at the very least add up to an intriguing story about that era.'

'If the hand can ever be identified,' said Boyes.

'That may depend on the rest of the body turning up,' said Quine. 'But first, can I ask you a favour?'

'Of course,' said Boyes.

'I traipsed all over this area yesterday but it's covered with new blocks of flats and heaven knows what else. Where's the wasteland?'

Boyes chuckled. 'You missed the biggest development opportunity left on the Thames. I'll ring security there to see if we can have a dekko.'

As he shuffled to a landline, Quine judged that his pitch had worked. He tried to imagine the shock of these well-meaning men if he had given them the full story – that the British Prime Minister might somehow be connected to a severed hand.

Boyes came off the phone. 'It's locked up today. He'll be there tomorrow. Two p.m. OK?'

*

Not allowing his frustration at the delay to show, Quine went knocking on doors in the street where Sandford and Fowkes had lived, saying he was compiling a local history of the area. Only one person who answered had lived there in 1991. She remembered nothing of the young men who had lived in Sandford's flat.

He arrived back in West Kensington around 7 p.m. Sophie was home. He wished he could tell her what he had been up to. Isla arrived an hour later. After a brief greeting, his daughter left him and Isla alone – he wondered how much Isla had told her.

'Are we allowed to exchange information?' he asked.

155

'Yes,' Isla answered. 'To a certain extent. First, you're the only one who can feed back to your "informant". Second, the cover story I've given my head of section is that there's evidence of Fowkes removing confidential documents from the Treasury and copying them. It's the sort of thing that crops up now and again and we're always brought in if it's high level.'

'That's good, thanks.'

'The problem is, at this stage, that doesn't justify bugging or a team of watchers. I'm on my own, just eyes and ears. I'll need your help.'

'I've not got much yet,' said Quine. 'Nothing from neighbours in range of the flat at that time. I'm having a tour of the site where the hand was found tomorrow. You?'

She told him about the line of sight her desk gave her and Fowkes's angry expression as he left the Chancellor's office.

'Interesting,' he said.

'Why?'

'I was told all this in confidence. There was a thought of trying to rattle Fowkes. Destabilize him. Drive a wedge between him and Morland-Cross. I wasn't given details.'

'Whatever it is, it sounds like it's drawn blood.' Isla frowned. 'By the way, there's something I never realized. The Treasury's an open door. Not like Number 10. No searches, just wave a pass and through you go with any guest you want. Totally unchecked.'

*

Just before midnight, before turning in, Quine decided to try emailing Sandford.

*

JONATHAN MOORE
To: paulabcdreynolds@gmail.com
Re: update

Hi Paul

You might be interested to know that today our friend left his boss's office looking upset. Sounds as if there'd been an angry discussion.

Cheers
Jonathan

PAUL REYNOLDS
To: jonathan1234moore@gmail.com
Re: update

Hi Jonathan
Thanks.

Cheers
Paul

*

If nothing else, it showed the email link was working and Sandford was at home – though in front of a screen rather than in bed with his wife. Assuming they still shared one, Quine suddenly thought.

*

Sandford shut down Carol's computer. It appeared his first move was having repercussions already. Over the weekend Carol had not been herself. He knew she was still disturbed by his request for the private email. He must reassure her. He stood tall, took a deep breath and stretched back his shoulders. He checked his watch – only a couple of minutes past midnight. She would still be reading. It was time to disturb her more affectionately and, this time, more lovingly.

22

'I'd no idea,' said Quine.

The three of them stood surveying the vast expanse of what, once upon a time, had been the backbone of the British Navy – Deptford Dockyard.

'Most people don't,' said Boyes. 'Unless you're born and bred in these parts.'

'That's because speculators and planners have been sitting on it,' added Letts. 'Not to mention the Mayors of London.'

'The big slab of grey is where Murdoch stored newsprint for a while,' said Boyes. 'He bought the site back in 1980 and demolished the Great Store House. No one seemed to give a damn about heritage then.'

'Presumably they didn't still have ships here.'

'Heavens, no. Henry the Eighth started it in 1513. The land that gave birth to the Royal Navy. *Golden Hind*, *Mary Rose*, you name them. Slow decline ever since.' His voice faded away across the unkempt grass and weeds stirring sorrowfully in the off-river breeze, broken up by slabs of brick and concrete that had once been slipways and basins servicing a maritime empire. Quine stood silently – there was a time to speak and a time to listen.

'Onwards,' said Boyes, perking up. 'You didn't come here for a history lesson.'

'Follow me,' said Letts, striding towards the perimeter. 'The plan is to build three and half thousand homes here. There've been arguments about it for years but it looks like we're getting some action now.' He stopped by a newly laid, single-lane tarmac road. 'They were repairing this service road – apparently they were worried about some sinking beneath. They found it here, a couple of feet under.'

'Who found it?'

'A workman. As I heard it, he called the foreman over and he rang the police.'

'What then?'

'Forensics dug up the area all around. You can see where.' He pointed to a square of ground both sides of the new lane. 'Found nothing more. Just the hand.'

'Any useful clues from the ring?'

'No. It was old, goes back to the last Emperor. But not that rare.'

'Where are the remains now?'

'In an evidence bag at Lewisham.'

'And that's it?'

'Seems so.'

'It's a mystery till it's not,' said Boyes.

'One thing's not a mystery,' said Quine. 'A young woman's body was mutilated.' He dished out two cards from his wallet.

'I'm staying with friends. You have my email – that's on here with my mobile. If there are any developments—'

'Absolutely,' said Boyes. 'We'd be happy to collaborate, wouldn't we, Jim?' Quine assumed the retired policeman's immobile expression meant agreement. He must have been a poker-faced interrogator. 'Perhaps,' added Boyes, 'you might give Jim and me a mention in your book.'

*

Three hours later, just before 6 p.m., Isla McDonald watched Jed Fowkes walk out of his office. He was carrying an overcoat. From everything she had so far gathered, it was unusually early for him.

She gathered her own coat and handbag containing hat, scarf and different glasses. It was a good time to follow – nothing unusual about this moment to be packing up for the day.

Lingering inside, fiddling with her bag, she watched him leave the building and turn left. She walked out fast, donning the hat and changing spectacles, catching the back of him at the south-east corner of St James's Park. He crossed Birdcage Walk, turned left on the opposite pavement, then right into Storey's Gate. There was enough bustle of office workers heading for tubes to merge into them. He walked past the Westminster Arms, the smokers already outside, and Central Hall. Sounds from a practice session on the giant organ drifted faintly above. He turned right into Victoria Street and, slipping between stationary buses, crossed the road. She stayed on its north side. He walked with a committed stride. She guessed he was heading towards Victoria station. The crowds there would be helpful for cover, the many transport choices not so for pursuit. The trainers had always said solo pursuits on foot were the most difficult of all. Maybe she would never be able to do anything more than monitor him within the Treasury.

He halted and glanced around. The flash of his eyes was too quick to take anything in – certainly not her, thirty yards back on the other side of the road. He opened a door and entered.

Pizza Express. Somehow she had expected a darkened room in a dingy pub. She walked on past the restaurant on the other side of the road, flicking a quick look across, seeing only that he was sitting with a woman near the back. The place was almost empty. If she were to maintain her watch, she would have to circulate on the street. Maybe there was a wall to sit on offering a line of sight.

How long to eat a pizza? Her stint on a watcher team had showed her that boredom, leading to lack of concentration, was always the enemy. It was nearly two years since she had joined the anti-money-laundering desk; there the work was carried out behind digital firewalls, not on the street. Her boss had agreed she could be the field agent on this assignment because of its delicacy and the confidentiality of her source. She hoped she hadn't lost her edge. She checked her watch. Ninety minutes.

He and the woman were leaving. Talking to each other. She removed her smart phone with its adapted and enhanced camera. Holding it in her left hand down by her side, she walked towards them, still keeping to the opposite pavement. As they neared she tapped a button, initiating a flurry of photographs. She was close enough to have a good chance of a recognizable image. The woman had fair to blonde hair. After passing them, she walked a further twenty yards and turned to retrace her steps. She speeded up to draw nearer. They stopped and turned into a small alley. She held back. A couple of minutes later he reappeared without the woman and walked in the direction of the Treasury.

Twenty yards up the road, Fowkes abruptly halted. She froze, thinking he was about to turn. Instead, he took his phone from an inside jacket, hit a number and bent his head away from the traffic. She would have needed to be on top of him to hear anything, but she could at least deduce that his meeting with the woman had triggered the call. She watched him enter the Treasury. To follow suit herself would invite suspicion. She returned to the alley where Fowkes had parted from the woman and inspected the few office nameplates. The likeliest one to house someone known to Jed Fowkes read 'Freedom Research and Policy'. She photographed it.

*

Back at the Treasury Fowkes entered the empty Spads' office; Thomasina's desk light was still on, her handbag by the side of her chair. He returned to the corridor and knocked on the Chancellor's door. No response. He was probably at an evening function. Thomasina must have nipped to the toilet or coffee bar. He thought he heard a rustling; he stood stock-still, holding his breath. The open-area sections both of Treasury civil servants and HMRC staff were deserted. He crept to the end of the corridor, switched off all the lights and returned to the Chancellor's door. A shaft of light was just visible. He knelt down, his eye to the floor. A lamp was alight in a corner. It might mean nothing, just no one bothering to switch it off. He shuffled and put his ear to the ground. Could he hear breathing? A short gasp? There was someone, more than one person inside. He stood and tried the door. Locked.

'M-C?' he said softly. 'Are you there?'

No answer.

He asked again, much louder. Still no answer. He weighed up the possibilities; there was no need to rush. He retreated and concealed himself behind a desk in the open-plan area, some fifteen yards from the Chancellor's office door with a direct line of sight. The corridor remained dark, the lights still switched off.

He waited, buzzing with an unfamiliar excitement.

It did not take long. The door edged slowly open, a head peered round, glancing from side to side. A female figure slipped out in the shadows and padded into the Spads' office. A second figure, male, emerged and, with a quick glance, strode off down the corridor.

Fowkes gave it a couple of minutes, switched the corridor lights on and breezed into the Spads' office. She was applying make-up, her hair still ruffled. She looked up, terror in her eyes.

'Oh, hi, Thomasina,' he said with untypical good humour, 'working late?'

*

164

Sophie and Isla had jointly persuaded Quine to stay on in the flat, both enjoying his company and Isla realizing he could be of use. While Sophie withdrew to wash her hair, the other two exchanged updates.

Isla refused to jump to conclusions from her evening's observation.

'There's no evidence Fowkes was engaged in anything irregular. He's allowed to have female friends and to have pizzas with them.'

'Sure,' said Quine. 'Though apparently he was a bit of a failure in that department.'

'Maybe he's gay,' said Isla.

The ease with which she said it jolted Quine into remembering when his daughter first told him about Isla. Even though she was in her late twenties, Sophie had never said she was gay and he'd had no reason to suspect it. He had assumed she wanted to keep her boyfriends to herself and had never felt any entitlement to pry into her love life. When she did tell him, her eyes bright with happiness, not just about her sexuality but that she was in love, his heart had skipped a beat. There was an element of surprise but none at all of shock.

'Maybe,' he replied. 'More likely he's just married to the cause. Mind you, if he was gay, he'd have felt out of place in that flat thirty years ago.' She fell quiet. 'You're thinking something, Isla.'

'Yes. I got this feeling he knows how to look after himself on the street.'

Quine's eyes narrowed. 'Really.'

'Yes. Only a feeling. The way he stopped once or twice and

glanced round. Changes in pace. Probably nothing. Maybe he's a bit paranoid.'

'Or he knew he was doing something underhand.'

'I suspect we're clutching at straws. Time for a nightcap.' She rose and headed for the kitchen.

Quine opened his laptop.

*

JONATHAN MOORE
To: paulabcdreynolds@gmail.com
Re: update

Hi Paul

1. Artefact. No sign of other supporting material. A mystery but on its own an unimportant one that leads nowhere. Our friend exploiting emergence of artefact for own purposes seems best working hypothesis.

2. In the evening friend left unusually early for meeting with female maybe from organization called 'Freedom Policy and Research'. No evidence yet anything more than social.

Cheers
Jonathan

*

Quine had the sense he was observing a duel being fought at one remove between two opponents with matching skills. Sandford and Fowkes were chess players planning moves far ahead – but he suspected the endgame would play out with loaded weapons and one king lying on his back, bleeding to death.

His job had a certain simplicity – to dig out information. What was Sandford planning?

23

Good morning, this is Today on a gloomy autumnal morning…

*

The recorded bongs of Big Ben (the clock itself, still under repair, was silent) sounded 7 a.m. The newsreader read the headlines.

*

And finally, we've just heard that a *Panorama* special will replace the scheduled programme at nine o'clock on BBC1 tonight with what it describes as an extraordinary revelation. Here's our political editor, Suzy Lancaster.

*

Carol glanced at Sandford who, unusually, was still lying beside her in bed. He shrugged his shoulders. She turned up the volume. A familiar voice came on air.

*

Good morning, thank you. There's a limit to what I can tell you right now as the full story must wait for the transmission of tonight's programme. Two days ago I was rung by a highly trusted contact. He introduced me to someone he had come to know well over the past sixteen years. This person gave me an account of a particular evening which amounts to a sensational revelation – I don't use those words lightly – about a major national figure. Her story remains strictly embargoed until nine o'clock this evening on BBC1. It is of major national interest and I urge you to watch. Now, back to Nick in the studio.

Right, doesn't sound like we'll get more on that for the moment...

*

Carol turned it down. As the presenter's voice faded, she put an arm round her husband. 'It must be huge. Even the BBC couldn't hype like that otherwise.' She hesitated, showing unaccustomed nervousness. 'Is it connected with what's been worrying you?'

He shrugged his shoulders. 'I don't know.'

'But not about you, at least.' She grinned.

He grinned back. 'If it is, no one's bothered to tell me.'

If she had studied him more deeply, she would have seen that, beneath the apparent levity, he was shaking. He composed a curt message on his personal mobile, simply **WTF??!!**, and sent it to Suzy Lancaster.

What if it was Jed? And Suzy and her BBC bosses – the Director-General himself would have to be in on this – had found his story so plausible and convincing that they were prepared to run it. Should he text the D-G? He told himself there was still no hard evidence for anything.

The drive from Salisbury Square to Downing Street was nightmarish. A childhood memory of a butcher stripping a pig's carcass gave way to a handsaw grinding through a human arm. He had visions of a lean girl with long red hair he had once made love to lying beneath him. Then a judge pronouncing his sentence. He was sweating and his heart racing – signs of a panic attack. He closed his eyes and made himself take long, deep breaths. He began to calm, the pulse slowing, the heart beating more normally. He wiped the sweat off his forehead. The car entered the back security gate of Number 10. He checked his mobile. Nothing from Suzy Lancaster.

*

It was a close, muggy day in Central London, reflecting the oppressive atmosphere in the rooms and corridors of Westminster and Whitehall. Whispered conversations buzzed around like wasps in search of marmalade. Aides skulked in corners. Taps were turned on in toilets to cover the sounds of voices.

The BBC was playing a tight game. Its press office, which itself had been given not a hint of the story's contents, could only tell inquirers to wait for the broadcast. The *London Standard*'s front-page headline attempted speculation – as did television, radio and online news websites. All suffered from the same drawback. They could not start tossing names in the air of which 'major national figure' was involved for fear of inviting libel suits. One site daringly asked, 'Is it royalty or politics, sport or showbiz?' failing to observe that one glaring clue was Suzy Lancaster's long career as a political journalist.

Downing Street knew no more than anywhere else.

'Any straws in the wind?' Sandford asked Mark Burden, affecting a carefree tone.

'There aren't even rumours,' replied his principal private secretary. 'It's curious. Normally they'd be promoting it with clips from the interview, whoever it is. Don't even know if it's male or female.' He paused. 'Maybe the "interviewee" isn't sure of that either.'

The dryness of his PPS's barb was unexpected. Sandford wished he could be so sanguine. He had been texting Suzy Lancaster every hour on the hour. Still no reply. Surely if it was anything to do with him, they would have offered a right of reply. Unless it really was Jed and the story was so sensational that they feared he would attempt – and succeed in – a court injunction. Not once since he had entered Parliament – let alone become Prime Minister – had she not replied within minutes to a text from his private phone.

171

He cancelled his evening engagement to watch the pro-gramme live. There was no avoiding it. He could not decide whether to stay alone in Downing Street or return to Notting Hill and watch it with Carol.

Next door at 11 Downing Street, the tension was more overt. Henry Morland-Cross, unprompted, stalked into the Spads' office.

'Where's Thomasina?' he asked Jed Fowkes, glaring at her empty desk.

'Didn't you tell her to go to that economic forum in Birmingham?'

The Chancellor stopped in his tracks. 'So I did. Means we can chat here.'

'Chat?'

'Come on, Jed, what the fuck's going on? You always know everything.'

'Not this time.'

'All right then, guess.'

Fowkes stared up at the ceiling. 'Well, the great Ms Lancaster referred to her most trusted contact. We could start by asking who that might be.'

Morland-Cross frowned. 'Sandford?'

'You said it. The man himself.'

'Good God…'

Fowkes looked at his watch. 'Just a few hours till we find out.'

Morland-Cross sighed. 'What's that duplicitous bastard up to?' He walked over to Fowkes and looked him in the eye. 'You and I are OK, aren't we?'

'Course we're OK.'

'It was a bit of a barney we had.'

'I've already forgotten it.'

*

Quine, Sophie and Isla were all back in good time to watch the programme. The BBC as an organization hyped like crazy, but he knew Suzy Lancaster was one of the few still inside who refused to go along with it. She would not use the word 'sensational' if it were not true. He pleaded with the gods of journalism that she had not somehow got one step ahead of him on the Sandford story.

'Fowkes headed off around seven,' said Isla. 'No indication he wasn't going home to watch the show. You heard anything?'

'No,' said Quine. 'I'm out of it now.' Was that something to feel pleased about or not?

*

Sandford arrived home at Salisbury Square at 8.45 p.m. The thought of watching alone had become unbearable. He checked the email link to Quine. No further news. No text from Suzy.

At 8.55 p.m. Carol joined him in the study. She carried a tray with the TV supper she had promised him. He hoped the programme would not make him throw it up.

As second hands ticked round to 9 p.m., pairs of eyes, some alone, some alongside the eyes of partners or collaborators, others in restaurants, bank trading floors and heaving Northern pubs, focused on televisions and screens across the nation. A single BBC press officer, seconded for the day to this one project, prepared to email, page by page and in concert with its real-time unfolding on air, a full transcript to every national newspaper.

At 9.01 p.m., sixty seconds after the broadcasting watershed, *Panorama*'s opening titles rolled. Robbie and Carol Sandford sat side by side, plates of smoked salmon and salad on their laps.

'Quite like old times,' she said, sipping a large glass of Macon with one hand and squeezing Robbie's arm with the other.

The picture cut from the titles to Suzy Lancaster, sitting alone at a studio desk. The camera slowly closed in on her.

*

SL: Good evening, I'm Suzy Lancaster. Tonight's *Panorama* reveals a story which concerns an extremely senior and powerful figure. It is a story of significant public interest and has taken great courage to tell.

*

The screen now showed a wider shot of what looked like a hotel room. A figure with blonde hair was seated in a chair in the foreground. Suzy Lancaster, beyond, faced the figure.

As her introduction continued, the camera crept around to reveal more of the face opposite.

*

SL: Yesterday morning I was introduced by a trusted contact to a woman in her mid-thirties. She told me a story which included a serious allegation against a major national figure. Throughout yesterday, I verified the date, place and time of the encounter. I was able to confirm through witnesses present that her recollection of these core facts is correct. The incident itself took place without others present. I believed her account credible and yesterday evening recorded an interview with her. This, unedited, is what she told me.

*

By now the face was fully revealed.

'Rather attractive woman,' said Carol, taking a glug, enjoying herself.

Sandford was staring at the screen, his cheeks whitening. 'Yes, not bad,' he said, trying not to show the shock. He recognized the face. Where from? Carol was glued to the screen, too rapt to notice his reaction. Please, God, let this not be me.

24

SL: First, could you tell me a little about yourself?

CP: My name is Christine Patterson.

*

'Nicely spoken,' said Carol, continuing her commentary and pouring herself another glass. 'Doesn't seem a victim type.'

*

SL: And your background?

CP: Middle-class, I suppose. My father was an accountant, my mother trained as a physiotherapist.

SL: And now?

CP: I'm a research consultant and planner for Freedom Policy and Research.

SL: And they are?

CP: A think-tank, encouraging new and radical ideas to further democratic capitalism in today's world.

SL: Where did this interest in politics begin?

CP: It was always there. But it came together at Oxford.

SL: Oxford University?

CP: Yes, Somerville. My degree was chemistry.

SL: In the footsteps of Margaret Thatcher.

CP: If only.

SL: What years are we talking about?

CP: 2005 to 2008. When David Cameron became our leader. I joined up and in my second year became secretary of the Oxford University Conservative Association.

SL: Did you think of becoming president of the Association?

CP: Ha! Of course. But it was a very male world. Still is, I'm afraid. Plenty of women have been secretary. Doing the real work.

*

'Nice one!' exclaimed Carol. She flicked a look at her silent husband.

'Sorry.' He perked up. 'My mind was wandering. Jog me when they finally get on with it.' Carol had already turned back to the screen.

He wished he could place the woman. It was a long time ago. What had she just said? Cameron's first years as leader? '05 to '08. His first years as an MP. Two years in he had already made an impression. The *Telegraph* had even run an article. 'A LEADER ONE DAY?' A time when he was not just working

177

his constituency but trying to branch out to the nation beyond. Oxford. Of course he'd done visits there.

*

SL: So we're talking...

CP: Autumn 2007.

SL: How old were you?

CP: Just turned twenty. I didn't take a gap year. I wanted to get on with life.

SL: What were your plans that autumn for the Association?

CP: I wanted to persuade those I saw as potential long-term leaders to come and speak to us.

SL: Right. There was one person above all you believed, even back then, could be a future leader, perhaps even Prime Minister.

CP: Yes. I rang his Westminster office to invite him to address us, and he—

SL: It was a he?

CP: Yes... he asked me to send a photograph of the Association's officers. So 'my man will know who he's meeting'—

SL: Was that usual?

CP: I was new to this but I thought nothing of it.

SL: It didn't strike you as odd?

CP: No. Why should it? Anyway they got straight back that afternoon, said he'd be delighted. And we fixed a date.

*

'Robbie?' Carol glanced at her husband.

'Yes?' His eyes remained fixed on the interview, trying to listen even as he spoke.

'Why on earth would anyone ask for photographs?'

'God knows.'

'Did you ever?'

'Course not.' Why lie? He had several times, it was useful preparation. 'Can we watch?'

She sniffed and turned back to the screen.

*

SL: Let's move on to the evening itself.

CP: Actually I was panicking, he arrived literally with minutes to spare. He had an assistant with him—

SL: Can you tell us who?

CP: I've thought about that and would rather not name them. If that's all right?

SL: Yes, there's no need. We have their statement confirming the evening and people present.

*

'His assistant'. Sandford tried to remember who used to travel with him. Obviously at that time not Carol as she was at home with the girls. It was never one person in particular, just whoever was free and fancied the outing. He hoped he would not need to call on any of them.

179

SL: Please go on.

CP: It was brilliant. He was inspiring, responded to all the questions. I thought – I think everyone thought – this is possible, this man can really make a difference. Good speaker, attractive…

SL: In what way attractive?

CP: Good-looking, funny, still young enough but gave you a sense of experience.

SL: So when the ninety minutes were up…

CP: Actually we overran. Went on till around ten to ten, I think. I said I'd reserved a space in the bar if he was able to spare the time to carry on informally. He said, 'I'm all yours, I've booked into the Randolph for the night—'

SL: The hotel.

CP: Yes.

SL: Had you known that?

CP: No. But I said, 'Great, I know lots of them will want to continue the discussion.' And it *was* great. The bar closed at eleven thirty and people began to drift off. Within a few minutes it was just me, him, the vice-president and treasurer. He said, 'We don't have to stop the discussion there, do we? Come back to the Randolph, drinks on me.' I looked at the other two, we sort of shrugged shoulders and I think it was the treasurer who agreed. He was an old Etonian. It was such an opportunity. We were close up, face to face with someone who one day could be our party leader.

SL: What then?

CP: We got to the Randolph. He said he was worried about journalists and photographers and suggested we should go to his room. We could raid the minibar or order room service.

SL: Didn't that seem an odd request? Inappropriate even?

CP: Actually no, it seemed to make perfect sense, the way he put it. And there were the three of us.

SL: Were you finding him attractive?

CP: *(A long pause.)*

*

Sandford felt Carol stiffening beside him. She had put her glass down and fallen silent, concentrating more fiercely on the interview. Had she begun to grasp where this might possibly be heading? He itched to seek out his old diaries – they sat in the desk at the end of the room. At all costs he must forestall a panic attack. He began the slow rhythmic breathing, keeping it as quiet as he could.

Oxford. Yes, he had been a guest of both the Union and the Conservative Association more than once. He could not remember the dates. And the woman – she was definitely familiar.

*

CP: Yes. Yes, I was finding him attractive.

SL: And you'd had more to drink than you were used to.

181

CP: Perhaps. But I wasn't drunk. I'm not going to say that.

SL: So you went to his room.

CP: Yes. It was more like a suite. He clearly had money. It was all so unreal. He was already on the phone to room service ordering sandwiches, crisps and a couple of bottles of wine. He put the phone down and got us all drinks from the minibar.

SL: What did you discuss?

CP: Everything. He asked about our ambitions, said he'd always be delighted to help, he was funny about Blair and Brown – called them 'Noddy and Big Ears'.

*

'Didn't you used to say that, Robbie?'

Quick. Think. Reply. 'Probably,' he said smoothly, 'it was pretty common. It did suit them.'

'Hmm, I thought it was one of yours…'

'May well have been. It certainly spread.'

*

CP: There was serious stuff too – what he'd really do to 'set the country free', as he put it. Sorry, this is rather detailed…

SL: Not at all. It shows how good your recall is.

CP: We must have chatted for at least an hour, then the treasurer finished his drink and called it a night. The vice-president did too. And even though I was really enjoying it, I said, 'Guess I should go too.' He said, 'Me too, I'm pretty much done for.' But then he turned to me and asked if I could stay to discuss getting our committee down to Westminster. I thought, fine. There seemed nothing to it. The other two left. I don't know what they were thinking, whether they thought I was up for something or what.

SL: What *were* you thinking?

CP: I thought he wanted – as he'd said – to discuss our trip to the Commons and then he'd want to get some sleep.

SL: What did happen?

CP: He sort of collapsed on an armchair – I was sitting on the sofa. Then he got up, walked over to the minibar, returned with a bottle of white wine, pulled out the cork and flopped down beside me.

SL: Did he join you in a drink?

CP: Actually, now you mention it, I'm not sure how much he was drinking. Then, this was where it sort of turned. He walked over to his case and took out a washbag. He took a tube from it and a razor blade. He poured a line of white powder on the table, splitting it into small sections. I was a bit stunned and said nothing. He rolled up a note and offered it to me. I said no and he took two huge sniffs. 'Have a go,' he said. 'Nothing to be frightened of.'

*

At the mention of white powder, Carol cast him another quick glance.

She knew, as he'd told her, about Mikey using it in the flat. But he hadn't. Not cocaine.

Was this a set-up? Perhaps they'd somehow matched his dates. He'd certainly stayed at the Randolph a couple of times. But, watching the woman, a different memory was coming back. These were the months after Bella's birth, Carol wrapped up in her, not him. Sometimes getting away from home and his own tiring responsibilities for Becca had felt like freedom.

'I've been realizing something,' Carol said. 'This was the period just after Bella was born, wasn't it?' My God, she was thinking the same thing. What had begun as enjoyment of a juicy piece of scandal was turning into cold calculation. For both of them.

He tried to smile. 'Maybe. Don't know. She's certainly telling some story.'

'Yes, she is.'

*

SL: Christine, you're in a hotel room alone, one o'clock at night, with a man who must have been considerably older than you. He's offering you cocaine. Didn't you think of running?

CP: I don't know. I just don't know. I think I thought it would be rude.

SL: Rude?

CP: I know. It sounds ridiculous. I didn't want to spoil the evening. He told me what a great future I could have, how he'd like to help me. I said that was really kind but maybe

184

we should just sort out the Westminster arrangements. He said there was no need to rush. Then he took my hand, I tried to pull it away, he gripped tighter and said, 'Don't be a tease.'

SL: Were you teasing?

CP: Maybe there'd been smiles between us but we were enjoying the discussion together.

SL: But no more?

CP: No. As I said, he was attractive, but there was nothing more in it.

SL: Christine, I need you to explain exactly what happened.

CP: So he had my hand and moved it over the bulge of his crotch. I finally faced up to what was happening. 'I need to leave now,' I said. 'This isn't a good idea.'

SL: At that point, you were clearly saying no.

CP: Yes.

SL: Not teasing?

CP: No! I tried to wrench my hand away but he wouldn't have it. He was strong. And then I remember him saying that he needed this, he was bursting. He said I owed it to him.

*

Carol stood up. 'I don't want to hear all this.' She was watching him with an unreadable expression. She wiped an eye with a handkerchief.

'I agree,' he said. 'I'm not sure I believe her anyway.'

'She's completely convincing.'

She moved to the door and hovered.

SL: Couldn't you have shaken him off?

CP: I couldn't. I was frightened. Then he moved one hand and grabbed my head. Forced me down. I suppose I could have tried to kick and scream. But all the consequences of that flashed through my mind. The shame of it. Police getting involved. The scandal. I felt it would have been the end of me. I surrendered. Gave in.

SL: Gave in?

CP: He guided my hand over his bulge, then up to the zip. I undid his trousers, took his thing out of his pants and went down on him.

SL: Had you ever done this before?

CP: No. I'd read about it. I knew what to do. I just got it over as quickly as I could.

SL: And when it was over?

CP: He sort of flopped and let me go. I went to the bathroom, washed my mouth out and cleaned my hands. I came back through the bedroom, walked straight to the door and left.

SL: Did he say anything else?

CP: He was spread over the sofa, eyes half-closed. As I was opening the door, he looked up, told me to ring the office and we'd sort out that Westminster visit.

SL: That's all he said?

CP: Yes. Like it was nothing to him.

*

Yes, it was at the Randolph, the date he couldn't be sure of. But, as the woman told her story, more details of that evening were returning. A group of them had retired there for one more drink which he had bought them in the bar. They all drifted off except her. He had wanted to go up to bed but she had lingered. They'd been sitting on a sofa in a corner. She'd moved closer to him, looked around, then suddenly tried to thrust her hand inside his pants.

'Hey,' she'd said. 'What's this?'

He'd tried to edge away. 'It's all right,' she'd said, 'no one will ever know. Shall we go upstairs to your room?'

And he'd submitted. He'd enjoyed it – and felt a terrible guilt afterwards.

He looked at her now. He wondered if there was a single male guest of the Oxford University Conservative Association during her tenure as secretary she had not tried it on with.

If this was him, it was almost entirely a fabrication invented by Jed. Including the cocaine to ratchet it up. Surely he wasn't that vengeful.

He was desperate to run from the room. He had at least to move. He felt an attack might be coming. He gambled. He stood up, moved alongside Carol and put his arm round her. 'What's the problem, love?'

'I don't know,' she said, 'is there a problem?'

Whatever the outcome, at this moment holding her helped.

*

187

SL: Now, Christine, this is perhaps the most difficult part of it. You told me you first wanted to tell the story and then you thought you would know how you felt about naming this person.

CP: Yes.

SL: And?

CP: It's difficult...

SL: No one is forcing you. You can change your mind and we can stop filming now. We don't need to broadcast any of this. It's your decision.

CP: No, I'm going to do it. It's important. If someone like me won't speak out, who will?

SL: You're one hundred per cent sure?

CP: Yes.

SL: In that case, may I ask you who this person was?

CP: It was Henry Morland-Cross.

SL: The present Chancellor of the Exchequer and Deputy Prime Minister.

CP: Yes.

*

He felt her slumping beside him. 'God, Carol, you didn't...'

'Didn't what...'

'Nothing,' he said. 'Just something silly. Stupid even to think of it.' He hoped she was too off-balance to notice the colour returning to his cheeks.

*

SL: Do you have concrete evidence of this visit?

CP: As I told you before we started this I've kept all my diaries. I have that year's with me.

SL: Perhaps you could show it to the camera and read what it says.

CP: If you want me to. It says, '8 p.m. Henry Morland-Cross talk. Room A3. 9.30–11.00 p.m. space in bar reserved.'

SL: You wrote that in blue?

CP: Yes. Just anything to do with the Association. Colour coding.

SL: I must ask this. Why now? Why have you decided to speak out now?

CP: I should have spoken out years ago.

SL: Yes but—

CP: I understand. People will ask. I failed. When Henry Morland-Cross became Chancellor, I knew I should say something but failed again. Now, the government is preparing for the next four years. A new Parliament. About to set out its agenda. It's a really important time. People have the right to know exactly what sort of man is deciding our country's economic future.

SL: Finally, has anyone put pressure on you to come forward and speak out?

CP: No, not at all. I'd never allow that. I'm the only person responsible for my life and my decisions.

SL: Christine Patterson, thank you.

*

The credits rolled. Carol returned to the table, poured herself a third glass of wine and took a large gulp. 'Didn't you visit Oxford a couple of times?'

'Yes, more than a couple. It was the one invite worth accepting.'

'She *was* convincing, wasn't she?'

'Yes, by the end.' He sat down beside her. 'M-C's in a spot, that's for sure.'

'I've no sympathy,' she said fiercely. 'If he behaved like that, he can go to hell.'

'There could be another way of seeing it.'

'Meaning?'

'Maybe she's overegging it. She could have been primed.'

'What do you mean primed?'

'She might not be acting alone.'

'Either way, she can still be telling the truth. So,' she screwed up her eyes, 'I was right. M-C. You – Jed Fowkes rather – suspected something. Quine. The secrecy, the private email. That's why you've been so out of it.'

'Perhaps,' he replied cautiously. 'I mean, no one minds M-C being a shagger but force is different.'

'It's more than force, it's rape,' Carol said.

'If true. Her word against his. The coke could be more damaging. He gave solemn assurances he'd never used it after he became an MP.'

'At least it's all out in the open now and you can restore order.'

'If only,' he said mysteriously. 'It may just be the beginning.' With that, he went into the bathroom, the convenient bolt-hole.

Action, reaction. Jed had lit the fuse; he had counter-attacked through the unwitting proxy of Henry Morland-Cross. If this was Jed's next move, where was it leading?

His mobile bleeped – a text from Suzy Lancaster.

Hi Robbie, Sorry, I was in lockdown. Orders from on high. Hey, you didn't ever think… no, course you didn't, you silly boy. Love, Suzy xx

25

One person had been informed in advance of the identity of the 'major national figure', but by phone not text. The call took place at 3 p.m., six hours before transmission. The recipient was Henry Morland-Cross. The moment had been carefully chosen to allow him the opportunity to respond, but limited time to mount an offensive in advance against the programme.

'Hello,' Morland-Cross had answered weakly, seeing a familiar name on his phone screen.

'It's Roger Boyd, BBC Head of News, here. I take it this is Henry Morland-Cross.'

'Yes, Roger, you know it is.'

'Chancellor—'

'Cut the crap.'

'Look, this is difficult for me too. I have to keep an element of formality.'

'Go on then, who's been sneaking?'

'May I come to that? M-C, this is primarily a courtesy call to tell you that a letter for your personal attention has just been hand-delivered to Treasury reception and is awaiting your collection. Because this is not a government matter it's not going via the press office. It describes an allegation that will be made in tonight's *Panorama* by a woman called Christine Patterson—'

'Never heard of her.'

'May I just finish?'

'Sure. Whatever you say, she's lying, whoever she is.'

'Thank you. Ms Patterson has made an allegation of sexual assault by you against her, which occurred around one thirty a.m. on Tuesday the twenty-third of October, 2007, in your room at the Randolph Hotel, Oxford. In addition she says that you used cocaine in her presence.'

'That,' growled Morland-Cross, 'is a total, fucking lie. As for the former, she'd have been gagging for it. Like all the many others who've never made any complaints.'

'If you would like to make that rebuttal, Suzy Lancaster is available right now to film an interview.'

'You can tell that dirty, glory-seeking, low-life cunt that I hope she fries in hell.'

'Chancellor, do I take it then that you are declining that offer? Alternatively we'd be willing to allow you to watch the programme live in the studio and respond immediately following it.'

'How about you have the decency to show me the programme right now? I'll cancel engagements and be at New BH in half an hour.'

'M-C, you know we wouldn't do that.'

'Why not?'

'We have the interviewee's interests to respect too.'

'But not mine.'

'I assure you the allegation is sufficiently described in the letter.'

'You really are shits,' said Morland-Cross. 'Roger, would you mind just fucking off? I'll watch it, see what lies this woman's inventing and take it from there.'

'You don't wish to include a statement?'

'You know what, I wouldn't give you the pleasure. And when I expose this person's lies, it won't be in an interview with the BBC. I'll tell you something else. Whether I'm here or not to see to it, your licence fee's fucked. And that means your pensions will all be fucked too. Goodbye.'

Morland-Cross cut the phone. The same number rang again twice. He did not answer. October 2007. He tried to remember what that particular Oxford girl was like. He had visited that Association several times – on each occasion, as far as he could remember, there was at least one young lady up for it. Like every other university he had visited. Trouble was there were far too many for any one individual to stand out.

Surely Jed must have had a whisper. Had he come up to Oxford with him that evening? Someone was playing games, and he was the loser.

He looked at his watch: 3.20 p.m. Sod it. He fetched a bottle of whisky and poured himself a tumbler. God, a snort would help now. That really was a lie, he'd been clean since 2005. Meaning never in the presence of another. Well, maybe once or twice with willing partners. Which that girl would have been of course...

What to do? He had better read the letter. He asked a secretary to collect it from reception. Whatever it contained, he couldn't watch the programme with Patricia.

He read it. It was the woman's word against his. He wouldn't dispute the timings, dates and places – the BBC would have checked those out. There was no suggestion that she had ever reported the incident or any evidence of physical injury. The worst thing he could do was phone his lawyers and go for an emergency injunction. All he'd achieve was more media hype and sensation.

He needed a friend. Someone to confide in at least. He checked his watch. Five and a half hours to go until his public humiliation. He was normally the joker. Now, how the world would laugh. How his enemies – his friends too, probably – would wallow in it. He wondered if Thomasina was back from Birmingham. If so, she would probably look in to the Spads' office. He made an instinctive decision and rang the number.

'Hello.' Her voice.

'Hi. Good trip?'

'Yes, thanks, I just got back to see if anything needed doing.'

'Actually, have you got a minute?'

'Of course.'

She entered his office. Unusually for when he was expecting her, he was seated at his desk. He gestured to her to sit down opposite.

'Thomasina,' he began hesitantly, 'something unpleasant is going on. I want you to be the first to know. Probably the only person to know. Until the whole world does.' She said nothing. 'This BBC programme tonight is about me.'

'I'm so sorry,' she said. He filled her in on the details of the allegations. 'What she says about the use of force and cocaine are both utter lies,' he concluded. 'But it's her word against mine.'

'Can you try to stop it?'

'It would only make it worse.' He hesitated. 'I just want to say this. I'll understand if after the programme you won't want to be with me any more.'

'Thank you for telling me,' she said flatly. 'I'll watch it and take it from there.'

She stood, forced a quick smile, and turned. As she was closing the door, he thought he saw her raising a hand to an eye.

*

Isla McDonald, Sophie Becker and Joe Quine watched together. At the moment Christine Patterson's face was revealed, Isla said, 'Fucking hell' under her breath. Quine turned sharply to her. She put a finger to her lips, nodding almost imperceptibly in Sophie's direction.

At the end of the programme, Sophie disappeared to make coffee. Quine was impressed by his daughter's tact, though it must come with the relationship. Isla took her smart phone from her bag. She retrieved a slightly blurred photograph of a blonde-haired woman. A second photograph showed a man conversing with her. Jed Fowkes.

'It's the same woman.'

Quine peered at both photographs. 'You can't be sure from those.'

She swiped to a third photograph. 'That's the woman turning into the alleyway he dropped her off at.' She swiped again. 'That's the "Freedom Policy and Research" nameplate. Put them all together and there's no doubt.'

He frowned. 'You didn't tell me you'd actually photographed them.'

'Don't worry, I'll tell you what you need to know when you need to know it. What you then pass back to your "informant" is up to you.'

'Did you catch anything they said?'

'No. I'd have exposed myself if I'd tried to get closer. As I mentioned before, he tends to keep an eye on what's going on behind him.'

'Perhaps it's because he's stabbed so many in the back himself,' said Quine.

Isla returned a short smile. 'There's no evidence yet that he's actually done anything wrong. But yes, he and the woman we now know to be Christine Patterson had a ninety-minute meeting. We still don't know who was saying what.'

'Not too tricky to work that one out.'

'You're a journalist, Joe. I'm an intelligence officer. I don't jump to conclusions.'

Quine's final act of a momentous day was to email Paul
Reynolds with a report on what Isla had just told him.

JONATHAN MOORE
To: paulabcdreynolds@gmail.com
Re: update

Hi Paul

Just thought you might be interested to know there is
photographic confirmation that the young woman from
"Freedom Research and Policy" party and our friend
were the couple meeting at the pizza place earlier this
week.

Cheers
Jonathan

*

It was Sandford's final act of the day to read the email. He
couldn't help feeling a reluctant admiration for Fowkes's cunning. It had been his plan to unsettle him with a divide-and-
rule manoeuvre between him and Morland-Cross. It appeared
Jed had now raised the stakes dramatically.

Surely Morland-Cross had explained to him that all he
needed to do was sit and wait three years for all his policy
desires to be fulfilled. Why was he so impatient?

And what, if any, was the connection between this scheming against Morland-Cross and his story of the girl in the flat? It remained possible there was none. Sometimes the simple explanation was the best.

And yet, this did not feel simple at all.

26

Immediately after the broadcast, Thomasina Bellingham rang Henry Morland-Cross offering help with his rebuttal. Within half an hour she issued a personal statement by him to all UK and major international news outlets.

*

I have been unable to respond until now to the allegations made in this evening's Panorama *owing to the BBC's wholly unreasonable refusal to allow me to view these allegations in advance of transmission. The allegations are one hundred per cent untrue. I have never – not once – in my life used any form of force or violence against any woman. I have previously admitted to using cocaine in the past. However, as previously stated, I have not used it since entering the House of Commons. While I shall be taking legal advice about suing the BBC, I will certainly not be suing or in any way seeking recompense from this most unfortunate woman who, for whatever reason, has ended up telling these terrible lies.*

*

The night hours that followed saw a Twitter storm and over three million hits on the YouTube highlight clip showing Christine Patterson's account of the sex act and coke snorting.

'The coke was sheer invention,' said Morland-Cross. 'I've not lied. I'm clean since I entered the Commons.'

'And the other?' asked Sandford, showing no sign of his scepticism.

This conversation first thing the next morning was, unlike their previous one, taking place in the PM's study in 10 Downing Street. It had an edge of formality.

'It was one hundred per cent consensual. Every word in my press statement is true, I assure you of that. That girl was hot for it, Robbie. I've been thinking back. She's hardly changed. Hot, hot. They were all gagging for it.' Though he could never tell him why, Sandford knew he was telling the truth.

'"All". How many?'

'I don't know. That's the honest truth.'

'Single figures?' Morland-Cross shrugged. 'Double figures?' Sandford asked gently. Again, silence.

Morland-Cross looked up with a wan smile. 'The thing is – it was easy. And fun. They all wanted it, enjoyed it. They probably chalked it up on a ledger. Who could score the most and the best. Otherwise some of them would have spoken out.'

'Now one has,' said Sandford.

'And she's lying.'

'Her word against yours.'

'I realize that. Look, I'm no angel. I'm twice married and divorced. I'm a bachelor now. I committed no crime. None was ever under age. Never went younger than twenty as a matter of fact.'

'No crime committed didn't help Bill Clinton.'

'That was because he lied to Congress. Not the sex itself. I'm not lying to anyone.'

'Times are different.'

'Fine. Find something wrong I'm doing now. Don't crucify me for something all right that I did then.'

'Was it all right?' mused Sandford, thinking of himself too. Morland-Cross sighed, energy spent. 'It's Friday today,' Sandford continued, looking at his watch. 'Constituency day. I've got to go. You've done your statement. See how it plays over the weekend. Then meet me for breakfast, Monday. OK?'

'Thanks, Robbie, that's decent of you. I know we've never been friends—'

'"Friends"? In politics? Don't kid ourselves.' Both men stood. 'One thing,' continued Sandford. 'Jed Fowkes was seen having an animated conversation with Christine Patterson at Pizza Express on Victoria Street three evenings ago.'

'What!' Morland-Cross flushed with anger. 'How do you know that?'

'A friend spotted him. He phoned me after the programme.'

'I don't know where Fowkes would have got it from,' said Morland-Cross, 'but I wouldn't mind betting that bastard was paying her money. Plenty of it.'

*

Jed Fowkes delayed his arrival at the Treasury, listening to the early morning fallout on radio and television and scanning the papers. He varied his usual journey from his flat in Stockwell, staying on the tube till Green Park and enjoying a walk through the cool air and diagonal sun shafting through the plane trees of Green Park itself and St James's Park beyond. This approach gave him an early view of the reporters, photographers and television crews milling outside the Treasury's Horse Guards Parade entrance. He felt a moment of sympathy for Morland-Cross. It quickly passed. M-C's dirty compromise with Sandford – whatever it was – had disrupted carefully laid plans; something had had to be done. The years of collaboration, even friendship, could not stand in the way.

He brushed through the media throng. Some of them, mainly the financial and economics correspondents, tossed him questions. 'What next, Jed?' 'How's M-C this morning?' 'Will he resign?' A voice from an unknown sweaty-looking face topped by crinkly black hair yelled out from the back of the pack, 'Is the Chancellor a rapist?' 'Is he still snorting?' shouted another. The tabloids, never known to take a serious interest in the nation's finances, finally had a story from the Treasury.

Fowkes swiped his pass to enter the building and walked up to the first floor. Heads looked up from screens and quickly returned to them. There was that intangible air of trying to preserve normality in a micro-world that had been turned upside down. The Chancellor's door was open, his office empty. Thomasina looked up silently as Jed entered, closing the door behind him.

'Morning.'

'Have you seen him?' she asked.

'No. You?'

'I spoke to him after the programme.' She sniffed and blew her nose. 'Did you know anything about it?'

'You mean the allegation? Well, allegations plural now.'

'What else…'

'Henry has always been a serial shagger. Everyone knows that.'

'I didn't.'

'Well, you do now,' he said. She sniffed again. 'Sorry, I didn't mean it to come out like that.'

He sat down and fired up his computer, the silence hanging heavily. Finally she broke it. 'What happens to us? If he has to go, I mean.'

'When ministers resign, Spads get five minutes to clear out their office, hand in their passes and return jobless to whence they came. So we should make preparations.'

The door flew open without warning. Morland-Cross

stalked through it towards Fowkes's desk, pointing a finger at him.

'You. You did this!'

'What?' Fowkes replied quietly.

'You lined this girl up. I know you did.'

'Did I now?'

'Yes. You bloody well did.'

'Has it occurred to you that what actually might have happened was that it was the woman who asked to speak to me about what she was planning? And that I tried to talk her out of it.'

'No, that has not occurred to me. Because I'm damn sure it didn't happen like that.' He paused, narrowing his eyes. 'You're a sly bastard, Jed Fowkes. Too fucking clever for your own good.' With that, Morland-Cross turned, walked slowly away and closed the door silently, entering the corridor as a sea of faces turned away.

Fowkes turned to Thomasina. 'Will you stay with him?'

'What do you mean?'

'I'm neither blind nor an idiot, Thomasina. Look… he'll have to go. He knows that, I know that, the PM must know that. It won't be easy for him. One minute the world's knocking on your door. Everyone's your friend. Then suddenly, there's silence. You're a non-person. It's only power – and money – that bring friends. So when you're stripped of both and falling from the top of the mountain you need someone to catch you in their arms and comfort you. You'll be out of a job so you'll have time too. You could do that for him, couldn't you?'

'You're forgetting something, Jed,' said Thomasina with unusual steel.

'Oh?'

'I not only believe him, I happen to like him. And he happens to like me.'

27

Seven a.m. The headlines this Saturday morning. A second woman, a former student at Leeds University, has made a claim of sexual misconduct against the Chancellor, Henry Morland-Cross...

*

Quine, sitting in the kitchen, laptop open, paused to listen. As always, he was an early riser. The law of unintended consequences. Beneath the amiability, Sandford was often calculating and could sometimes be devious – otherwise he would never have risen to the top. But surely he had never intended the destabilizing of Jed Fowkes to lead to this.

His phone pinged with a text from Geoff Boyes.

Sorry so early. Get to Greenwich quick as you can. Tell me when you'll arrive – I'll be waiting in car. Geoff

Damn. He had booked a mid-morning train for a quick weekend trip to Cornwall to retrieve his belongings and boxes of research and drive Beatrice back to London with them. It was unfair to Mrs Trelight to use 7, The Waves as his private depository. Boyes's text allowed no choice; he must go straightaway. A quick search told him that the journey by tube and overland should take little more than an hour. He replied that he'd be there by 8.30 a.m.

Boyes was ready, jumping out to hold open the passenger door. 'Hop in, they're already digging,' he said, his eyes gleaming. Before Quine could reply, he was sprinting round the back of the car to the driver's side.

'Digging what?' asked Quine as Boyes dropped into his seat.

'I'll wind back. Yesterday afternoon, there was an anonymous delivery at my house. An A4-size envelope, thicker than a letter, thinner than a parcel. Hang on a minute, this roundabout's a nightmare.'

Boyes impatiently muscled his way through a scrum of Greenwich traffic. 'Right,' he continued, 'the trouble with Greenwich, even at this hour on a Saturday, is all the old geezers and girls who shouldn't be allowed on the road.' Quine tightened his seatbelt as the needle moved well over the speed limit and they crossed Deptford Creek. Boyes slammed on the brakes. They were following the same route as before.

'You were talking about a delivery,' Quine said.

'Yes, I opened it up. Inside was a sheet folded into eighths. I unravelled it. Guess what it was.'

'A map of Atlantis.'

'Not bad. It was a map. A large-scale one of the old dockyard. More like a drawing really. Something was stuck to it.

A narrow strip of plain paper, cut like the hand of a clock with an arrow at one end, and a message.'

'"Here be gold",' said Quine.

'Hah. Actually it just said, "TIP MARKS THE SPOT". Handwritten in red capitals. Someone out there must have become aware of my interest and saw me as a go-between.'

'They could have posted it direct to the police.'

'Perhaps they reckoned I'd make sure it got to the right person quickly. I rang the new head of CID. She doesn't hang about and asked me to come straight in. She ordered a search to start at daybreak. We should arrive just in time.'

'For what…'

'Has to be a pattern, doesn't there?'

Yes, Quine said to himself, there does. He began to assess the implications.

A single motorcycle policeman was stationed at the gated entrance. Boyes gave his name, referenced the head of CID, waited for a phone call to be made, and was waved through. The arrow on the map pointed to a corner of the outer pcrimeter wall by the former shipwright's quarters, the one remaining building from the old dockyard. An excavation area had been drawn, taking initially the first ten yards of the corner walls.

Boyes drove as near as he could along a dirt track and was greeted by a fast-approaching Jim Letts.

'Nothing yet. They've advanced a yard on each line.'

'Meaning they've covered a fifth of the area,' said Boyes, pleased with his speedy calculation.

'Edith's in charge,' said Letts, pointing to a strong-looking woman in overalls, who was alternating between two lines of four diggers.

A woman's shriek came from one of them. Edith was by her side in an instant and down on her knees, scraping away in the trench. She stood and marked the perimeter of a small area, around two by two yards.

'What's going on, Edith?' asked Letts.

'Not sure.'

'Can we get closer?' asked Quine.

'Leave them be for the moment,' replied Letts.

The three men waited and listened to the murmurs of quiet scraping and chipping as stones and earth were peeled away in narrow swathes. An hour passed. Thermoses of tea and coffee were produced. Then a second. At last Edith rose and walked over, addressing herself to Letts. 'I need to get a SOCO,' she said quietly.

'Can we?' asked Letts.

'I guess so, as you reported it. Just a quick peep.' They followed her to what they could now see had become a four-foot-deep hole in the ground. 'The initial finder hit what looked like a toe. Since then we've been able to expose the feet, and make our way up the body.'

Quine looked down. His eyes stopped at the waist and arm remains on each side.

Edith watched him. 'Yes. No right hand.'

Quine nodded. The skeleton was lying on what looked like a large section of a shower curtain. He frowned. 'What's... what's this?' His voice shook.

'Exactly,' said Edith. She paused. 'No head. No skull.'

'My God,' said Boyes, the triumphalism of the morning now subdued.

'I can give you some basics. A young woman. Small. Five two, maybe five three.'

'Any idea how long it's been here?' asked Quine.

'We'll need to work on that. Like the hand, I'd say within the last twenty to forty years. But, as with the hand, the section of shower curtain, assuming it's the same, will give us better idea. So twenty-five to thirty-five.'

'Is it possible that the skeleton is of that age, but has been buried here much more recently?'

'Why would anyone do that?' asked Edith. 'But since you ask… I've supervised this dig. I'd have noticed it a mile off.'

'And the original hand?'

'Maybe. I wasn't there. Mind you, the way those bones had been packed was a bit unusual. Didn't change what they were though.' She raised her eyes from the earth grave and skeleton that occupied it. 'Time's up.'

'What about the head?' asked Letts.

Edith shrugged. 'Let's assume – we still have to confirm it – the hand belongs. That came from half a mile over there,' she said, pointing across the empty ground. 'Let's further assume the skull is somewhere here. What would you have us do, Jim? Dig the whole place up? Probably quicker to wait till your friend with the map gives us another clue.'

*

211

'When it was just the hand with the ring, it may have been macabre,' said Boyes in his cluttered sitting room, 'but it somehow intrigued as well as repelled. Now...'

'Quite,' said Letts grimly, sipping his cup of tea. 'Somebody killed a young woman, dismembered her body, cut off her head and got rid of it.'

'Why?' asked Quine. 'Decapitation, for God's sake.'

In the hour that had passed since the discovery, he had felt the screw turning on the history the Prime Minister had asked him to explore. He urgently needed to tell Sandford, if only to prepare him for the headline splash that Geoff and Jim, despite their qualms, must be contemplating. How would – or could – Sandford react? Perhaps he would see this as evidence of something so impossible for him to be involved in that it could be encouraging. Against that, no word uttered by Jed Fowkes had yet been disproved. If anything, his allegation had gained weight.

'It removes dental evidence, doesn't it?' Letts sighed, as if nothing could be more obvious.

Boyes turned to Quine. 'What now, Joe?'

'You're first to a hell of a story. A participant in it, too, with the map. If you want that known.'

'Back to the *Mail*, I guess?'

'If it all helps to set up the newsletter, why not?'

Quine calculated. The police would soon issue a statement. It would hit the Sunday papers, come what may. There was no point in trying to prevent it. 'They should pay you properly this time,' he said. 'I know the *Mail on Sunday* editor.'

'How much, do you reckon?' asked Boyes.

'Five figures for sure,' replied Quine without a beat.

Eyebrows raised, Boyes and Letts looked at each other and exchanged a silent nod. 'Let's get writing,' said the old newspaperman, a veteran of print remounting his charger.

'I'll ring him now.' Quine made the call and fixed the price. The next move must follow fast. Sandford had to know before the Sundays began their print run.

28

Stretching out in the back of the Prime Minister's custom-built, armoured Jaguar, escorts in front and behind, Robin Sandford felt, for the first time since Jed Fowkes had stopped him at the party conference, that he might at last be ahead of the game.

Jed had acted impetuously towards Morland-Cross. His motives remained mysterious – for a moment Sandford wondered whether he had been diagnosed with advanced cancer or some other fatal prognosis and his story was a lever to exert power before he died. Perhaps he should ask him if he was all right.

Nothing made sense but, however scary these past days, he was still Prime Minister. There was an unexpected bonus. Even if Morland-Cross hung on as Chancellor, the grassroots would never make him leader now. He would not have the tricky job of reneging on their 'deal'.

The comforting stream of thoughts was interrupted by the beep of a text message. He hesitated; it was not the usual sounds of his mobile. Then he remembered – it was the 'burner'. He shuddered. The head of the protection officer sitting next to the driver in front whipped round. Sandford smiled sweetly back – the head reverted.

He took the phone from an inside jacket pocket.

Need to meet without any delay. It can't wait. Will travel anywhere. Am coming from London. Jonathan.

Quine had been clear the phone was for one-off emergency use only. What had come up? For sure, it wouldn't be good. If life had been easy, he could have just phoned back and asked. Sometimes he felt more like a prisoner than a Prime Minister.

It was an informal Chequers weekend – mainly friends of Carol, hospitality all paid for by her. She and the girls had driven down ahead and, if the usual pattern prevailed, her guests would be soon arriving for lunch. The idea of meeting Quine at the Prime Minister's official country house seemed inappropriate, not to mention the rushed preparations for Special Branch to clear him. There appeared to be no choice. He looked at his watch – just before noon – and texted back.

Has to be Chequers. We have guests arriving for informal weekend. Am on my way there now. Tell me when. Paul.

A few minutes passed, then another ping of a phone, this time his personal mobile. The screen showed a message from Joe Quine.

Just to remind, am looking forward to discussion re biography we arranged for early afternoon at Chequers. Arriving by taxi from

Wendover station. Should be around 2.30. No more than hour needed. If security needs to know, plan taxi to wait and take me on to Reading station. Best, Joe.

In addition to the confirmation, Sandford understood the implication. *Don't use the burner phone again.*

Half an hour later the Jaguar swished through the gates of Chequers. The mini-paradise of rural isolation in one of England's most enchanting landscapes held one illusion – constant armed watch was kept for snipers on hilltops and approaching drones. But from the house and garden and the estate beyond, you would never have known. The imposing mass of the grand Elizabethan house should have been a fortress against turbulence, the surrounding park-land and hills a folding embrace of comfort. A weekend here, unless it had to be spent pacifying a trouble-making Cabinet Minister or showing off the Nelson Room to visiting dignitaries, was meant to be a haven. Quine's text had put paid to all that.

The taxi arrived shortly after 2.30 p.m. and was asked to wait in a car park a short walk from the main entrance. In the few minutes' gap after Sandford's initial text reply, Quine had worked out that, by getting a train to Wendover, a taxi to Chequers and then on to Reading station – at the Prime Minister's expense – he should comfortably make it to Cornwall by late evening. The afternoon was grey, a chill wind coming from the north. He imagined well-fed guests settling by a glowing fire in front of the day's rugby inter-nationals.

Sandford met him in the lobby. 'Got a coat?'

'I left it in the taxi.'

'You'll manage. We're going for a walk.'

There was no small talk. Quine explained the discovery of the headless skeleton and the near certainty that it matched the hand with the ring.

'Hell,' said the Prime Minister under his breath. His first question was instant and simple. 'Does Jed know?'

'I've no idea.'

'How did they know where to dig?'

Quine had hoped he would not ask. He was tempted to say that, as with the initial discovery, a workman had come across some bones by chance.

Sandford sensed his reluctance. 'Just tell me.'

Quine explained the map that had been sent to Boyes, with its message in red ink. 'Presumably the same hand that sent the newspaper articles to Fowkes.' Quine described his collaboration with Boyes and Letts. 'I hadn't wanted to bother you with all that,' he concluded.

'I want to know everything,' said Sandford.

'They've sold the story to the *Mail on Sunday*. I expect it to be their splash tomorrow. I thought you had to know.'

Sandford stopped, looking up at the overhead gloom. 'What next?'

Quine could only shrug.

'Maybe,' Sandford continued, 'it's helpful. Even Jed won't blag he's been chopping off heads.'

Quine felt a curious satisfaction at Sandford having one

of the reactions he had forecast. 'Robbie, what, exactly, did he say about what happened to the girl after he'd called his "friend" to help? Can you remember?'

Sandford was silent for a few seconds. Quine shivered. 'Not every precise word but the content, yes. He said he had a "friend" from a different world to ours. And this friend, along with someone else he didn't then know, took the girl away. He suggested they drop her at a hospital. He said the friend later told him that they had "disposed of her". Those three words are precise. He said his friend never told him what they meant.'

'Some friend,' said Quine. 'Unless "friend" is actually a euphemism for Jed himself.'

'Jed dismember a body?'

'You're the one who knows him.'

Sandford shook his head. 'If this skeleton is really that girl, Jed must have had a bloody unusual friend.'

'In which case we need to dig deep into the Jed of thirty years ago,' said Quine.

'He never introduced any such friend to me.' Sandford, too, shivered. 'I ought to get back.'

'OK,' said Quine. 'It seems to me this is where we are. Right now Jed Fowkes is an undetonated bomb. We don't know for sure whether it's a dud or contains real explosive. We won't know till we have all the facts. So far there's a dismembered body, the place it was buried and a timescale. Beyond that we have a story told by Jed of how one particular evening played out. You agree how that evening started – you have no memory of how it ended. I'm going to be very honest, Robbie. Jed still holds the cards.'

'If he's daft enough to implicate himself in murder—'

'He'll have worked that out. His threat can always be that he'll plea-bargain with the police to give evidence against you in return for leniency towards himself—'

'He'd still have to be mad—'

'Yes, but that's not the point. The point is the threat. The hold he's trying to build. As I said, the unexploded bomb. Until we unearth the truth, we have to treat him as highly fragile. After the story comes out tomorrow, he'll want to see you, to frighten you more. Ride with it. Ride with whatever he wants. *Do* whatever he wants.'

'I can't do that,' Sandford protested.

'You have to,' said Quine. 'And I – and the MI5 officer attached—'

'Can you tell me?'

'Best not. I and she—'

'She?'

'Yes. We have to get to the bottom of all this, Fowkes's motives above all, before he can execute – or force you to execute – whatever plan he's got in mind.'

'How much time have we got?' asked Sandford.

'Don't know. I'm sure we're in a race of some kind or other. There has to be an endplay. But Jed himself may not yet know exactly what it is.'

'Next steps?'

'I need to get on with speaking to anyone who knew you then. Starting with Mikey Miller.'

'I'll ring him.'

'Good. And Robbie, ride with Jed. It's the only way.'

They were back at the front drive. 'Joe,' said Sandford softly, 'what do you think? I mean, really think?'

Quine, puzzled, replied, 'What do you mean?'

'I keep having nightmarish images.' His face sagged, his voice a murmur. 'I even have a half-memory of a girl lying semi-naked in my bedroom and blokes visiting her one by one. Could I have ever been part of that? Surely to God, that's not me. I can't stop asking myself. Did something bad actually happen?'

Quine hesitated. 'I think something bad did happen. And some kind of fallout is happening now. But you'd never be a bad man, Robbie. Not knowingly.'

Later, standing alone in front of a bathroom mirror, a distorted image of Jed Fowkes, face pinched and finger jabbing, flashed before Sandford. As the image faded, he reminded himself of Quine's mantra: *Ride with Jed*. Easy to give advice if you were not the one having to carry it out. *You'll have the greatest political scoop of all time*. It seemed clever at the time. Now it left him cold.

He walked into the kitchen, where Carol was inspecting the tea trolley. 'You were out for a while. Was it my friends?'

He tried to smile. 'No. I was having a catch-up with Joe Quine.'

She frowned. 'Couldn't it have waited?'

'No. Nothing's over till it's over.'

'Do you still mean M-C?'

'Joe reckons there may be more to come.'

She turned towards the fridge, then stopped. 'Just tell me,

my darling. You can't keep everything locked up inside. It's too much for one person to bear. That's why I'm here.'

He closed his eyes and sighed. 'There's nothing I want to do more, love. But this time I can't. I just can't.'

29

The taxi bringing Quine from Bodmin Parkway arrived at 7, The Waves, just before 10 p.m. No doubt alerted by its headlights, Mrs Trelight stood in the porch, ready to greet him as the prodigal son.

'You've been gone for an age, Mr Q.'

'Only just over a week, Mrs T.'

'Any news of your book?'

'Not yet, I'm afraid.'

'Well, I hope that person – whoever he was – will make sure it's a best-seller.'

'And I'll send you a signed copy. By the way what did my visitor look like?'

'Nice-looking, respectable, I'd say. Maybe in his forties? He wore a suit and spoke like a gentleman. It was just the hair. Rather "bouffant" for a man, I thought.' She sniffed. 'I even detected a touch of pomade.'

You truly do come out with some gems, thought Quine. 'Well, it will have to remain a mystery.' For sure, it was not

Riley Trueman. No description could have less suited the shambling, unkempt, overweight, wheezing figure he cut.

On the Sunday morning, Quine rose with the sun and, almost twelve months to the day since he arrived, embarked on his final trek to the point and back. He made a quick calculation for the period of what he now saw as his exile. Three thousand miles plus walked, some seven hundred thousand feet climbed, twenty-five Everests, give or take a foot or two. It was not just an exile, but a reinvention. The book was its physical manifestation. Starting out, he had seen himself as a latter-day Zola; the book his 'J'Accuse…!'. In the end, it was just another chapter in the long history of human injustice. His labour was not the crushing of rock but the tapping of keys. Now it was over. From here on his story would be in the hands of others. Whether or not it changed the world, he had set the record straight. That was what mattered.

He stepped onto the cairn that marked the summit of the headland, the ocean seven hundred feet below stretching immeasurably beyond the horizon. The sky was cloudless, transformed from the grey of the day before, the sun low behind him as he looked out. His favourite sight over the past year had been its evening setting. If there was no skein of cloud obscuring its final disappearance, he sometimes remembered the French film *The Green Ray* – two young lovers waiting for the flash at the moment of solar obliteration – and imagined Sophie and Isla standing beside him, arms around each other.

By the time he returned to the bench on the cliff, dawn had become day. He watched a black-suited figure turning its surfboard, a rising wave curling up behind, an avalanche of water about to thunder down.

At 9 a.m. he was ready to go, Mrs Trelight standing on the doorstep to wave him safely on his way. Their final exchange over his last breakfast had also not disappointed.

'So, that board of mine, Mrs T. I've removed what you might call the decorations but I said I'd take down the board too and repair the screw holes.'

'You don't need to do that, Mr Q!' He recalled the firmness with which she had insisted on it a year ago. 'It will be no trouble at all.'

'I promised I would.'

'What a gentleman you are. You just leave it with me. But…' he sensed her searching for the way to put something, 'what about all those "decorations" you mentioned, what will become of them? Will some of them go in your book perhaps?'

'They may indeed.'

She moved closer and lowered her voice to a confidential murmur. 'He's not just bad. He deserves to die.'

He paused. 'There *are* one or two things I'd prefer not to be carrying around.'

'Official secrets?'

'Sort of.'

'You give it to me. They'll be well-hidden.'

'Are you sure?'

'Yes,' she said fiercely.

He got out to open the back door, removed a few items and retrieved a brown box of files. From it he extracted six and handed them over. 'The crown jewels.'

'I'll guard them with my life.'

He returned to the driver's seat, fired the ignition and Beatrice spat into life. He knew some thought him silly for being sentimental about an old camper van, but Beatrice was, in many ways, his most loyal companion. In his darkest hour, when he thought he might have to sell her, he had checked the internet for the going rate. The results had been astonishing; the ugly old contraptions had achieved iconic status – prices from twenty thousand pounds up to fifty thousand. Beatrice, a 2006 VW Danbury Diamond, could fetch upward of twenty-seven thousand pounds!

He wound down his window.

'I'll be back, Mrs T.'

'And I'll be waiting for you. With the crown jewels.' She was wiping an eye. He held back a tear of his own. 'You take care.'

Beatrice eased up the lane and he cut through the fields to go by the village to get a *Mail on Sunday*. The newspaperman within him felt an itch to see whether headless torsos or more Morland-Cross revelations would be the headline.

He turned right off the track onto the 'main' road which narrowed to a single lane for the final descent. Shifting the gears and pushing up to forty miles an hour, the maximum speed he allowed Beatrice to go, he sat back, glancing at a passing field of cows and the grey sea beyond. The outcome of his strange collaboration with Sandford was unknowable. But an outcome there would be. He felt an excitement he thought he had lost for ever.

Ahead of the shallow incline leading to the village, he put the gear into neutral and raised his foot from the accelerator, swinging around the bend. Once over the brow Beatrice gathered speed on the final descent. As the road narrowed to a single lane, he applied the footbrake. Nothing. He slammed it down. Nothing. He was going faster. He changed down gears, the engine screaming. Frantically pushing the footbrake, he hoiked the handbrake up as far as he could. A smell of burning, the speedometer not slowing. If anything, gaining... fifteen, twenty, the needle moving upwards... at the bottom of the hill, the white concrete wall beside the fish and chip bar and the beach shops beyond. He turned the steering wheel towards the right verge. Beatrice began to overbalance. He straightened.

He opened his door. He saw his laptop on the passenger seat – he had to grab it. He jumped. As he rolled into the verge, his left leg felt a harsh crunch. Beatrice accelerated downhill. He prayed there was no one below.

30

Sunday was the one day that Sandford read the newspapers. On the other six, he scanned a digest from the Number 10 press office. Sometimes he caught a snatch of the *Today* programme if there was a lead interview with a big-name politician.

He particularly looked forward to a Sunday morning at Chequers; the papers neatly spread over one sideboard, a gloriously unhealthy English breakfast beckoning from hot plates on another. This one was ruined by the prospect of today's headlines. As Carol had come down with him, he glanced first at the *Sunday Times, Observer* and *Telegraph*. Then, idly holding up the *Mail on Sunday* – with its screaming headline 'HEADLESS TORSO MATCHES SEVERED HAND' and a small box at the foot of the front page announcing 'TWO MORE STUDENTS ACCUSE CHANCELLOR' – he turned to Carol. 'They've found something to outdo M-C!' he grinned, helping himself to a double ration of fried eggs, bacon and sausage.

'Something to be glad for, I suppose,' she replied. 'How high does the M-C score have to rise before this is all done?'

'Some might admire his prowess,' said Sandford, feigning good humour as he rifled the pages and, stomach churning, counted the number devoted to the torso.

'I'm not one of them,' said Carol at a sufficient volume to attract the attention of one guest already seated at the table, who wondered whether someone had got out of the wrong side of bed.

*

Dimmed light, a haze, nothing in focus. He tried to force his eyes open. Liquid trickled down them. He began to move his arm.

A voice. 'Stay still, my friend.' Who was calling him 'friend'? The fuzzy shape of a hand hovered over him. He felt touches on his forehead, around his eyes and nose. Then down to his mouth. Dabbing and wiping. 'Just a bit of blood. We're keeping you clean. We don't want you to move just yet.' He tried to concentrate on the figure above him – yellow jacket, big square face, eyes going in and out of focus.

Something touched his leg. Pain shot through him, he yelped.

'You've had a bash. It's good you can feel it.' Was the face trying to smile? 'Can you tell us your name?'

Of course I can tell you my fucking name. He began to form it with his mouth. 'J... J... J...'

'It's OK, don't push it.'

Why was nothing coming out? He forced himself, 'Joe.'

Had the word come out? He felt sick rising in his throat; he coughed, just a dribble.

The face came nearer. 'Did you say Joe?'

He faintly nodded his head. Too hard to speak.

'OK, Joe, you've had an accident but you're doing fine. Are you hearing me OK?'

'Yes,' he mumbled.

'I want you to relax. I'm going to give you a shot of something to ease the pain. Before I do that, do you have any friends or family nearby we can contact?'

Why? What were they…? He hadn't the energy to ask. 'Mrs T…'

'What was that you said, Joe? Mrs Something?'

He nodded. 'Mrs T. Tre…' He felt so tired, his head throbbing, his leg screaming.

The face looked upward and over him. He heard words. 'Sounds like Mrs T, maybe Mrs Tree. Ask in the shops. It's a small place.'

He caught the glint of a needle and started shaking his head. His neck hurt. 'It's OK.'

*

The call came around 5 p.m., while Robin and Carol Sandford were packing up for the drive back from Chequers to London.

'It's Mark,' said the familiar voice.

'I know it's you, Mark,' said Sandford, still wearing the smile he had somehow preserved through the day.

'Jed Fowkes has been on again,' continued Mark Burden. 'He insists on seeing you.'

'This time to discuss his boss, I presume. Seven more allegations, I make it. Though all but one saying it was consensual.'

'Yes.'

'I'll see Fowkes but I won't be hurried. Give it a couple of days. Then fit in the Chancellor afterwards. We'll see how he deals with it in the meantime.' He cut the call.

Carol appeared from the bathroom from where she had been eavesdropping.

'Whatever you can or can't tell me, surely M-C has to go.'

He looked at her, eyes narrowing. 'Sometimes in politics, as in life, it's best to allow solutions to find themselves.'

'And appear weak?'

'Look, love, we're not quite there yet.'

'Robbie, you're starting to talk in riddles. I've been trying to help you. Cash. The email. I know there may be confidences but it's never been like this before. It's not just about wanting to share, I think I've the right, too.'

He frowned. 'Do you think I'm covering something up?'

'No,' she replied softly. 'I just want you to be open with me. It's an old-fashioned word called "trust". I thought we were a partnership.' She moved to the window, surveying the Chilterns beyond. 'We've achieved all this together, haven't we?'

She had never before even hinted at the advantage her wealth had brought him. There was a change in tone. He told himself not to rise.

'Hello, Joe.' A bright light above, his head on something soft, a pillow. A needle stuck in an arm. A young woman's face looked over him, her hair gathered in a net and covered by a neat little bonnet. She wore a blue dress with a badge.

'What's the time?'

'Just after six.'

'Can't be. Where am I?'

'You're in Truro hospital. I'm Anna. You had an accident.'

'Yes, but that was this morning.'

'You remember it?' She sounded Welsh. What was she doing in Cornwall?

He felt his mind clicking into action, his memory catching up. 'Of course.'

'That's great you do.'

He frowned. 'What happened to my camper van?'

'There's someone waiting to see you.'

As she slipped through a gap, he took in more of his whereabouts. A bed surrounded by a pink plastic curtain, a strip light in the ceiling above. A TV screen, a bedside table. His head ached but he could see and hear normally. The burble of what must be a ward outside, the pings of monitors, the groans of patients. The nurse reappeared through the curtain, an instantly recognizable figure following her.

Quine's surprised grin was cut short by a jolt from his knee. 'Mrs T!'

She sat down. 'Oh dearie me.'

'It seems Beatrice let me down.'

'That old jalopy. Proper death trap.'

'I'm not dead.'

'You've had a lucky escape.'

'What's happened to Beatrice?'

'No need to worry about that.'

'It's all right, I know she's really just rivets and steel.'

'I'm afraid it caught fire.' He closed his eyes. 'Thank heavens you're alive. They said it can't have been going too fast when you jumped out.'

He looked at her, all trace of humour vanishing. 'Those brakes have never failed before.'

'Best not to think about that.' He could see she was not dismissing it.

'They won't come again.' He stopped himself. If she also was wondering who 'they' might be, she was considerate enough not to say so.

'And your book?'

'That's fine. Everything's backed up except what's in those files. All scanned.'

'Good.'

'Perhaps I should take them myself. I don't want to—'

'Don't you even think of it. Now, I need to hand you over. Family? Friend?'

'I have a daughter, lives in London. If my phone – or computer – survived, the number's saved there. She's in the contacts under "Sophie". Oh... Could you ask her to get a *Mail on Sunday* for me?'

*

She arrived at noon the next day.

'I didn't say you had to come.'

'Don't be silly, Dad.'

'I'm fine, just nothing fit to wear.' Quine, a large rectangular bandage on his forehead and dressed in striped pyjamas that made him look like a concentration camp inmate, rose from the wooden-armed chair by his bed to give Sophie a kiss.

'They've said you can leave?' she asked dubiously, inspecting the bandage.

'I was lucky. Mild concussion but CT scan shows nothing more. Just cuts and bruises. This one,' he waved a hand at his forehead, 'has a few stitches.'

He gathered his computer and phone, stood up and pointed to a plastic bag. 'Clothes in there – all damaged – plus wallet, keys and whatever else they retrieved from the pockets. My glasses are cracked but usable.'

'Don't worry, you're not going to be driving.'

Seeing them make tracks, a staff nurse in a crisp white uniform walked over. 'I'll go through the dos and don'ts so your daughter can hear them for herself.'

'He's not prone to taking advice,' said Sophie.

'This isn't advice, it's orders,' the nurse responded tartly. 'He has concussion, not bad enough to be kept here but enough to respect it. Paracetamol will help with headaches. I'll give you co-codamol too in case they're really bad. No drinking for a week.' Quine gave her a dirty look; she glared back, then allowed herself a quick grin. 'You'll throw up if you do. No audiovisual stimuli, it'll upset the brain till the concussion's fully gone. Otherwise, take it easy, rest, no sudden or violent movements or running up and down staircases. Or excitement.'

'Got it,' said Sophie. 'I'll put him on a lead.'

They found a Marks and Spencer where she bought a grey suit, white shirts, a couple of ties and enough other clothes for him to get by with, and then a Boots for a shaver and washbag contents.

'Right,' she announced. 'You'd better stay with Isla and me for a week at least so we can keep an eye on you.'

'I'll be fine,' he said, 'that fascist nurse was exaggerating.'

'Dad!' She slammed the door, silence fell briefly. 'That camper van was lethal,' she said a few minutes later. 'Not even a bonnet to protect you.'

'She'd never failed me.' He smiled, remembering journeys along other coasts and nights alone, glimpsing stars through the roof-window.

'Was it MOT'd?'

'Yes.'

'Insured?'

'Yes.'

'Then at least you'll get some money.'

'Yes, they're valued antiques.' He hadn't the heart to tell her that changing his insurance from third party only to comprehensive had been right at the top of his to-do list as soon as the first Sandford funds arrived.

As they headed inland, he had a constant urge to lean forward and peer through the left-hand wing mirror.

Sophie noticed. 'What is it?'

'Nothing. I'm just keeping a look-out.'

'A look-out for what?'

It had slipped out, he should never have let it. Too late –
even if he was digging himself a hole. 'Oh, I don't know, I was
just thinking it's odd the brakes failing like that.'

She glanced at him. 'What are you saying?'

'Just that.'

'If you're trying to suggest that rusty old heap was tampered
with, I want to know.'

'She wasn't rusty.'

'You're not answering my question.'

'OK, yes.'

'Who?'

'Deschevaux. Not him personally, one of his sidekicks.'

She frowned. 'Just to stop a book? Honestly, Dad, you know
any serious publisher's going to run a mile from it. We can't
afford to be sued these days.'

'I'm thinking of the web.'

'On the web he'll laugh it off as your invention. He doesn't
need to scare you for that.'

He reflected. 'You're right.' He needed to regain ground.
'Come to think of it, I remember those brakes not being too
clever once or twice before.'

'Unless it's anything to do with what you told Isla.'

'No,' he said quickly, 'definitely not that.'

'Good.'

Sun yielded to cloud hanging over Dartmoor. Sophie
replaced her dark glasses with tan-rimmed spectacles from
a case on the dashboard. Within seconds oversize drops of
rain bombarded the windscreen, the clouds darkening. She

turned on the wipers and headlights. The downfall eased as quickly as it had begun. He looked around – yesterday's *Mail on Sunday* was lying on the back seat.

'Thanks for getting the paper.'

'God knows why you read it.'

'I don't usually.'

'A vain politician, silly trophy-hunting girls and a headless torso. You'd think they could find just one thing in this world of greater significance.' She looked fiercely ahead.

A further silence fell. He had to tell her now, didn't he? It wasn't fair otherwise. It seemed every exchange with her was being based on a false premise. He stopped himself. Isla would never do that, would she? It was the best way, the sane way to ground their relationship. He must force himself to do the same. What possible good could it do her to know everything? And his daughter knew and understood the deal. Don't be weak, don't confess.

They were back at the flat by dusk, Isla arriving home shortly afterwards. 'You're a lucky boy, Joe,' she said, eyes popping.

After a few minutes, Sophie, as was now the rhythm of an evening, left them alone in the sitting room.

'Right,' began Isla, 'is the threat to you – let's hope it was intended only as that – a warning to lay off Deschevaux?' She clearly had no doubts the crash was not an accident. 'Or has someone discovered you're investigating the dead girl? Or are they connected?'

'Also,' said Quine, 'is Fowkes acting alone or with others?'

'Like the "friend",' continued Isla, 'assuming he exists, who removed the girl from the flat and has now resurfaced.'

'Is Jed being blackmailed by the "friend"?' asked Quine. 'And why?'

Isla walked over to the window. Darkness had set in. She drew the curtains. 'There seem to me two coherent explanations. One – Jed Fowkes is a frustrated fanatic who has a lust for power and a long-term ambition to impose his own stamp on the country. To this end, he's effectively blackmailing Sandford into becoming his creature. Two – he's acting for, or in concert with, a foreign power or movement or other outside force, either willingly or by blackmail, to create turbulence. Russia's the obvious one. Followed by Iran or other extreme Islamists. Murder hasn't worked, try something else.'

'There are other candidates,' said Quine. 'Take the EU. Wouldn't Brussels just love this country to fail? And Washington. The hard-core Trump rump have long been in cahoots with the right here. They probably view Sandford as a liberal commie. We're not short of options. You begin to wonder which is the worst.'

'That's easy,' said Isla. 'Fowkes's original story is true. The British Prime Minister killed an innocent girl.'

31

'You wanted to see me again, Jed. This time about M-C, I assume.'

'We can discuss that if you want but it's a side issue.' They sat on opposite armchairs in the sitting room at Number 10. Fowkes looked funereal; Sandford couldn't decide whether it was genuine, faked, or the natural darkness of a man who had never found much to enjoy in the world. 'I'd prefer to have met immediately after the weekend. Better not to allow these things to drag on.'

Sandford ignored the reproof. 'I see there've been three more since Sunday.'

'Yes, he'll have to resign. But that's not why I'm here. As I'm sure you realize.'

'Go on.'

'The discovery of the headless torso in Deptford is giving me nightmares.' Fowkes produced the *Mail on Sunday* front page from a jacket pocket and laid it on the table between them. On it was written in red, 'WHERE'S THE HEAD, JED?'

'Someone's after me,' continued Fowkes. 'For something I shouldn't be blamed for. I never touched that girl.'

'Don't rush to conclusions. It's obviously absurd that you or I could have any connection to the dismembering of a body.'

'Is it?'

'For God's sake...' Sandford told himself not to raise his voice. Remember Quine's advice. *Ride with it.* No confrontation or contradiction. 'You don't seriously believe that of yourself? Let alone me.'

Fowkes said nothing.

'Answer the question.'

Fowkes took a deep breath. 'As I said before, I asked someone for help.'

'OK. And as I said before, you need to pass on this person's identity to the police.'

'So he can tell them how you killed a girl and I became your accomplice in removing her body?'

'Jed, are you seriously claiming this "friend" of yours removed a young woman from our flat, cut her up and buried the remains?'

'The skeleton is evidence. That night will always be with me.'

'If threats are being made against you, report those too.'

'I can't. Because it happened.'

'No, it's your imagination.'

'Robbie, I don't need your denial, I need your support. We have to be as one.'

'Of course, you have my support. But, as far as I'm concerned nothing like this ever happened—'

'That's always been your good fortune,' said Fowkes, eyes rimmed with fatigue.

Sandford managed not to react. His fear now was Fowkes's state of mind. He was on an edge. But of what? Of violence himself? Or was his rage different? An internal cauldron that constantly simmered but had never yet quite boiled – until it came to the point when it destroyed them both.

Unless it was an act. But, perhaps, so rehearsed and honed that it had become some kind of reality.

'How can I help?' Sandford finally asked.

'Help?' Fowkes gave a short laugh. 'There's no help you can ever give me compared with what I once gave you. But yes, you can help me. Stop cutting me out. Bring me in on the Royal Speech. Let me write the key policy statements. Give me a veto. And when M-C resigns, give me a Chancellor who does what I say.'

He must show sympathy. 'Jed, I understand. Of course you must be involved. But you're not elected. Not accountable. You're asking a lot.'

'I *am* accountable,' he rasped. 'I understand what has to be done.' He took a deep breath and appeared to calm. 'Robbie, remember how we once thought of doing great things for our country. Now is the moment.'

Silence fell. Sandford stood, walked to a window above the Number 10 garden and stared out of it. Fowkes tapped fingers on knees. *Ride with Jed.* Finally, the Prime Minister turned.

'All right, Jed.'

Astonishment crossed Fowkes's face. 'All right?'

'Yes. We'll work together. And like the old days, you can take the lead.'

'And that arms, mercenary ban thing you've come up with?'

'I'll try to persuade you.'

'And if you don't?'

'It won't go in the speech.'

'Why the change, Robbie?'

'Because, Jed, when it comes to it, you're better on policy and strategy than me. Always were. I haven't gone soft. I know what this country needs. Thank God we can do it from the right, rather than those weasels on the left.'

'Who will replace M-C?'

'Who do you want?'

There was a glimmer in Fowkes's eyes. 'Margaret Lascelles?' he murmured.

Sandford just managed to stop himself laughing. Margaret Lascelles, Leader of the House of Commons – a job that, with a large majority, required little more than the sorting skills of a bin man – was an airhead. 'She's an idiot.'

'But a useful one.'

Sandford allowed himself a grin. 'OK, done.'

Fowkes frowned. 'One thing I don't understand is why you wouldn't let M-C follow the radical agenda.'

'What?' said Sandford. 'M-C was the one who got cold feet. We thought he was the iron man. He wanted to put the brakes on, not me.'

Fowkes couldn't hide his confusion. 'Why?'

'Maybe it's guilt after all the country's been through.

Stopping him facing up to what's necessary. Did he tell you otherwise?'

Fowkes hesitated, recalling the words of their curt argument. And how it was he who had jumped to a conclusion before allowing Morland-Cross to come to his own. 'I suppose not,' he admitted, 'now that I think about it.'

Sandford looked at his watch. 'Time waits for no man. And certainly won't be waiting for you now.'

Fowkes lingered. 'What about M-C?'

'I'm seeing him in a couple of hours. He'll fall on his sword.'

'What if he doesn't?'

Sandford smiled. 'Someone will have to wield it.'

Fowkes nodded. 'Good,' he said, turning on his heel.

The door clicked shut. Sandford checked his watch. His diary allowed him fifteen minutes thinking time about his next move – the conversation later in the morning with Henry Morland-Cross. Quine was right. Face to face, appease Jed. There remained this naïvety about him that seemed to defy all the lessons of experience and passing years. Perhaps this was the 'good' Jed, the idealist, too often blinded by apparent opportunity. And the 'bad' Jed was using a terrible story to get his way. A story that, as yet, showed no sign of being disproved. Instead, with every new turn, it seemed bleaker. Somewhere out there was a severed head.

32

'Welcome to the farm!'

Some farm, thought Quine, as the tall, broad-chested man in his early fifties strode towards him. Sandford had called Mikey Miller over the weekend with Quine's phone number and an explanation of his research for a biography. Miller rang his mobile while he was in hospital, leaving a curt message.

'Hello, Joe. Big man rung me. Come first thing Wednesday. Cheers, Mikey.'

The day was pure Indian summer, allowing Miller to wear an exotically flowery short-sleeved shirt, immaculate white shorts and flip-flops which Quine could swear had tiny silver studs in the rubber bands. His wavy blond hair reached his collar; a gold chain with a diamond pendant hung around his neck; a coral stud pierced one of his ears. Electronic security gates had opened to reveal a remarkably neat gravel drive – Sandford had passed on a rumour that it was laundered with an industrial cleaner and then blow-dried. The 'farmhouse' was an enormous, pillared Palladian-style villa with a central classical arch and frieze which reminded Quine of the Parthenon. As he walked towards Miller, it was impossible not to keep flicking his eyes between the arch and its creator framed beneath.

'Hello, Joe. Reckon I got my hundred millions' worth?' Miller stuck out his right hand, a chunky gold signet ring wrapped around the fourth finger.

'More than that, Mr Miller,' said Quine.

'My friends call me Mikey.' He pronounced it 'Moikey'.

Miller peered at the bandage on his forehead and remnants of cuts on his face. 'Blimey, Joe, you been in an argument with a pyrocanthus?'

Quine grinned. 'You could say that. No harm done.' He wore the new grey suit Sophie had bought him. He understood that, while Miller might himself adopt the Malibu cruiser look, he would take instant offence if a first-time visitor dared to dress down. In the company of very rich men, you began as their servant.

'So Robbie told me what you've come about – wanna see round the farm before we get down to business?'

'I'd love to,' said Quine.

'All right then. It's not uninterestin'.'

Miller set off, Quine at his side. 'I'll show you the agricultural side first.'

A flight of steps – apparently marble – rose to the centre of the villa. On each side was a long single-storey wing which Quine assumed must be staff quarters and utility rooms. All was built in the same gleaming white stone blocks. Narrow paths of the same immaculate gravel as the driveway wound through ornamental trees.

'We'll go this way,' said Miller, heading towards a glass door in one of the wings. They entered a corridor, crossed an informal lounge and went out into the back garden. The view was breathtaking: to the left a swathe of green stretching towards Oxford; to the right the foothills of the Chilterns.

'Not bad, eh,' said Miller.

'Gorgeous,' replied Quine.

Miller walked away from the house past what must have been at least a thirty-metre-long pool, with curved steps at one end and floodlights below the water level. Beyond were two tennis courts.

Miller stopped. 'You play?'

'Not for a while.'

'You should get going again.'

He walked on a couple of hundred yards, then stopped by a long rectangular field of plants. 'We're doing all sorts on the farm, but this is the future.'

'What is it?' Quine knew but still asked.

'Hemp.'

'Oh, right. I remember reading something about it.'

'Yeah, you might have. But hemp itself is all we're allowed at the moment. Lots of products from it but you know what'll be the clincher?'

'Cannabis oil?'

'Spot on. We're thinking we've gotta get ready for it. I shouldn't be telling you but hidden in the middle of all this we've got a bit of cannabis sativa underway. Just to see how it grows here.'

'It's not as if you need the… er—'

'Cash? No.' He clapped Quine on the shoulder. 'Trouble is I can't stop myself, can I? All right, let's go back and do our business. Then I'll show you the art gallery.'

He led Quine back into the house and, after asking him to take his shoes off – 'Don't wanna mix outside muck with inside muck, do we?' – he kicked off his flip-flops, attracting Quine's eyes to his immaculately polished toenails. He led Quine down a flight of stairs and turned right.

'We'll talk here in the intermezzo if that suits?'

'Of course.'

Miller seated himself on a sofa and directed Quine to a matching armchair. The walls inside were as pure white as the exterior. He hit an intercom. 'Can you come, Jimmy? Got a man here who's thirsty and starving.' He turned to Quine. 'So Robbie says I can tell you anything you wanna know.'

'That'd be great. Sounds like you and he have stayed close.'

'Dunno about that, more difficult these days. He's busy, I'm busy. But yeah. I give a bit to his party. Shouldn't say this, but I give to all of them. Butter every side of the bread.' Quine realized an appreciation of the joke was expected and chuckled. 'Hang on.' A slim, young Asian man had floated through the door. 'What d'you want, Joe?'

'Cappuccino?'

'Good, plenty of foam for him, and I'll have my usual. And some of them nice dark chocolate biscuits. Maybe a couple of chocolate croissants too. And Jimmy, warm them so the chocolate's nicely melted, all right?'

'Yes, Mikey,' he replied, floating away as silently as he had appeared.

'See, everyone's equal here. He's a good boy, that one. Might go far. Right, you ask, I'll answer.'

'How did you get to know Mr Sandford?'

'Just call him Robbie, eh?'

'Fine.'

'It was chance. We were in the same hall and began to pass the time of day. He was arts and I was maths but that didn't seem to matter. He got involved in the politics and all that. I used to go along and watch him once or twice. It wasn't my thing. But I thought he was good. Impressive. We just got on. Maybe because we were both state school boys, we stuck together.' He grinned. 'May have been up north but still plenty of posh boys.'

'Then after university?'

'We all did a bit of travelling and then we came home, started our jobs, me back in the bank, him in Parliament. He asked me if I wanted to share a flat with him and a bloke called Jed Fowkes. As it happened, it suited me, so there we go. Nothing to it really.'

'And your bank?'

'Yeah, well, that was strange. My first job was with Coulthard's – old-time City private bank, you couldn't get more traditional. But not stuffy, not really. I think they saw me as the grit in the oyster, if you know what I mean. And I thought, this is different, why not?'

Quine smiled. 'And you worked there all the time you shared the flat?'

'Yeah, I moved on soon after that. Later, of course, I had the hedge fund. Divested myself of that. And we've ended up here.' He waved his arms around. 'With all this.'

Quine turned a page of his notebook. 'You must remember Robbie went through a difficult period...'

For the first time, Miller's eyes narrowed. 'Yeah. We all do, don't we?'

'He wants the biography to include downs as well as ups.'

'Yeah, he told me that.'

'What was it really like over that time in the flat?'

Miller took a large bite of chocolate croissant which, almost unnoticed, had arrived on the table in front of him.

'I'll tell you,' he wiped chocolate from his lips, 'those times could get pretty hectic.'

'May I ask what sort of things?'

'Well, we were quite good boys in the week. It was the weekends. Always a party, often in our flat. Booze, girls, gear.' He paused. 'If I'm honest, I lost count of the number of girls I had. But this isn't about me.' He fell silent.

There usually came a moment when Quine would allow an interviewee to break a silence – to confess. The moment when the pearl was dropped. This was not yet it. 'What about Robbie and girls?'

'He was good-looking, still is. Charming. Good talker. Only problem was it sometimes fell apart when he'd drunk a bit too much and those pills he was taking for his nerves did their mischief. Didn't matter 'cos he just collapsed, then woke up next day, not a clue what had happened. Not that much ever did happen. Then there was Jed...'

As Miller moved on to Fowkes, Quine stayed silent and nodded encouragement. 'He was an odd one. He could do humour but it wasn't as if he enjoyed it. Always setting the country to rights. There was a rage inside him. He had trouble pulling the girls, maybe...' Miller hesitated.

'Maybe?'

Miller looked rueful. 'Sometimes I wondered if Jed was gay. But I never saw the evidence either way.'

'You mentioned gear,' said Quine.

'Yeah. That was coke. Me and some of the regulars. But not Robbie. Only ever booze with him.'

'What about Jed?'

'Yeah, he did a bit of weed. Nothing more.'

'Acid?'

'No. Don't remember Jed ever tripping. He wouldn't have liked that. Being that out of control.' His eyes narrowed. 'Thought we were talking about Robbie.'

Quine smiled apologetically. 'Sorry. My curiosity getting in the way. Just trying to get the vibe in the flat right.'

Mikey relaxed. 'That's all right. Just don't want you getting us all arrested.'

Quine chuckled and allowed him a moment for more coffee and croissant. 'Going back to Robbie,' he resumed. 'You mentioned not much ever happening when he "fell apart". Whether or not it ends up in the book, he told me to ask about anything that might have happened. I think he wants closure.'

did but none of them got anywhere. She was always up for a drink but nothing more. She was after bigger fish than us.'

'I don't suppose you know what happened to her?'

'Roisin? Yeah, if it's the same one, she's still there. A lifer. At Coulthard's. I think she became head of something.'

'What was her surname?'

'Can't remember. Anyway, I reckon she'd have got married. But there can't be that many Roisins at Coulthard's, can there?'

No, thought Quine, his heart now beating hard. 'Apparently there was one night when you, Jed and Robbie all met up in your usual pub. You had your own girlfriend in tow but you brought along Roisin and a Hungarian girl called Andrea. She was temping at the bank.'

Miller frowned. 'That's a bit precise.'

Quine knew he was treading the line that separated conversation from interrogation. Beneath the showmanship, Miller was a super-intelligent calculator.

'Yes, I suppose it is,' he admitted. 'It adds to the richness of any biography if you can sometimes pin down precise occasions and anecdotes rather than generalities.'

'Right, see what you mean.' He took another bite of croissant. 'Robbie took Roisin out once or twice and there was definitely times when we all had a drink together. But I usually went off with whatever girl I had. Sometimes to her place, sometimes back to ours...'

Quine grinned. 'To start the party?'

'To be honest, if it was party-time, I preferred to lock us away in my bedroom and get on with it.'

'And Andrea, the Hungarian girl, I just wondered if you remember her coming back to the flat with Robbie and Jed after the pub?'

'There you go again, trying to pin me down. Early nineties there was always temps coming over after the Wall fell. So could well have been.'

He remembers her, thought Quine. I'm sure he does.

'Apparently she was thin, pretty with reddish hair. Spent a month or so at the bank.'

'Sounds like you know more than me.' Miller abruptly stood and checked his smart phone. That was it, he'd get no more. 'Emails, don't you love 'em. We'll do the art gallery and cinema next time. Nice to meet you, Joe. Jimmy'll see you out.' Without shaking hands, Miller left the room staring at his phone, opening the door to a subterranean passage that seemed to stretch for ever.

Before Quine had time to react, Jimmy was at his side. There was no doubt – he had touched a nerve. Was Mikey Miller – self-invented Croesus of the people and creator of his own narrative – covering for the Prime Minister? Or for himself?

As Quine drove back down the drive, any delay before he googled the Coulthard's bank website seemed unbearable. He told himself to wait till he was out of sight and far away. The electronic gates opened to usher him through. He checked the brakes, then sped off, paying more attention to the rear-view mirror than the direction he was headed in. After a few miles, he pulled into a service station and switched on his phone.

Mikey Miller watched him go on CCTV. Was that *the* weekend? He had come back on the Sunday evening to find the shower curtain missing. When he remarked on it, Fowkes had cracked one of his occasional dark jokes. 'Sorry, mate, we had to use it to bury a body.'

'Ha, ha, very funny,' Mikey had replied. Was that when Robbie began to sort himself out?

33

For Henry Morland-Cross's return visit, Sandford not only provided freshly ground coffee in a cafetière and biscuits but a couple of chocolate muffins too.

'Thank you,' said Morland-Cross. 'Is this the condemned man's last indulgence?'

'No, that'd be champagne.' Sandford grinned as he poured. 'Milk and sugar?'

Morland-Cross, unable to recall seeing the Prime Minister so relaxed, could not interpret the friendly greeting. 'I thought you might want to meet immediately after the weekend,' he said. 'I hope you enjoyed yours.'

'Lovely, thank you. Chequers is delightful when no politicians are staying. And you?'

'Dorneywood.' He peered briefly down at the floor. 'Might be my last chance. Wish I'd made better use of the place now.'

'Hey,' said Sandford sympathetically. 'Did you have company?'

'I did. I think I might be transferring my affections again.'

'Happily, I trust.'

'This one might really last.'

Sandford slapped him on the shoulder. 'Good.' They sat down on facing armchairs. 'Let's drink our coffee to that.' There was an element of affection neither had felt before.

'But that's not why we're here,' said Morland-Cross.

Sandford had never seen him morose like this. 'No.'

'What's your feeling?'

'What's yours?' replied Sandford.

'Well, there've been no more coke allegations. That was a bloody lie.'

'I accept that.'

'Thank you. Which leaves a few women climbing on the wagon. It's only just into double figures. I don't think there'll be many more. It was all consensual. As I said, I've never once forced myself on a woman. I'll swear any oath you might choose. Even do a bloody lie detector.'

'Not necessary,' said Sandford.

'I suspect it depends on whether it's an orchestrated campaign.'

'One thing I can assure you. Nothing's come from Number 10. And nothing will.'

'Thank you. Which leaves Jed. Whatever he says he told that girl.'

'Which was?'

'That he tried to persuade her not to do it.' Sandford emitted a dry laugh. 'Quite,' continued Morland-Cross. 'I knew he was angry with me but I never thought he'd stoop to anything like this. He won't give up. So maybe I should go. I've prepared. I'll be OK. Take a break to seek forgiveness from the MeToo-ers, repent my wicked ways, and come back in a year. I'm not past it yet.'

Sandford straightened his back, put both hands on his haunches and leant forward. 'M-C, I want you to stay. I've thought about it. You shouldn't be driven out by this. You've committed no crime, you're just a victim of changing fashion. In the long term we'll be respected for taking a stand.'

Morland-Cross allowed a moment for it to sink in. 'Do you really mean that?'

'Yes. As long as we still have our deal.'

'Of course. We shook on it.'

'Jed won't be pleased. He had a different outcome in mind.'

'Yes, the little shit did.'

'Will you keep him as your Spad?'

'He'll have to grovel.'

Sandford stood and, in what had become this morning's habit, checked his watch. 'Good luck with that.'

As the Chancellor closed the Number 10 flat's front door, the Prime Minister took a deep breath. These recent dealings with Henry Morland-Cross were having an unimaginable result. He was feeling sympathy for him. It did not change the brutal reality. In a perfect world, he and Jed Fowkes would end up destroying each other.

*

There was a spring in Henry Morland-Cross's step as he strode along the first-floor Treasury corridor, bestowing broad smiles to left and right before entering the Chancellor's office and closing its door behind him.

Watching his return from Number 10, the Treasury permanent secretary rose from his desk, knocked on Morland-Cross's door and entered. After just a few minutes, he reappeared, looking puzzled. Instead of returning straight to his desk, he turned left, knocked on the Spads' door and leant in. 'The Chancellor can make time for you now, Jed.'

Fowkes marched down the passage with a few long steps, opened the Chancellor's door and shut it noisily behind him.

Morland-Cross looked up. 'Jed,' he said brightly.

'I understand the Chancellor can make time for me,' replied Fowkes coldly.

'Of course. As always.'

'And you, M-C, are still the Chancellor.'

'So it would appear.'

'How did you talk him round?'

'I didn't need to.'

Fowkes remembered Sandford's remark. *Someone will have to wield it.* Well, Sandford had certainly not wielded any sword. Too weak. Or too scheming. Unless it was a challenge to him to do the wielding. 'What do you mean, "didn't need to"?'

'I told him the coke story was a fabrication – which it was. I've never assaulted anyone, committed any crime. So here we jolly well are.' He was now beaming.

'Christ, M-C, you've got to resign,' Fowkes said quietly. 'You're a joke. You're seen as a serial predator. You're a weak compromiser too. You need to get the message. What do you want next, a stash of cocaine to turn up in your office drawer?'

'Is that a threat, Jed?'

'Read it any way you want. You must go now. No more delays. You're not fit for this office.'

Morland-Cross's brightness had vanished. 'What is it, Jed? What's driving you? Who's driving you? This is not the real you.'

'Unlike others, I drive myself.'

'I don't know what's eating away at you. I'll give you twenty-four hours to back off. And if you continue these threats, I'll report you as a plotter and a liar to the Cabinet Secretary. You'll be escorted from this building within seconds. Your computer, files, diaries and all other records will be impounded and inspected. If I were you, I'd think very carefully.'

34

Isla McDonald watched Fowkes leave the Chancellor's office and retreat towards his own. Even from twenty yards away, she saw a face icy with anger. At the Spads' door, he stopped and glanced around, swinging in her direction. Her eyes veered back to her screen and fingers to her keyboard. Had he noticed? Even if he had, surely a junior member of staff on attachment was entitled to take in what was happening around them. Still, it was a warning. She glanced through a window; storm clouds were gathering in the distance beyond Whitehall.

She imagined the female Spad looking up at her male colleague, feeling both fear and curiosity, perhaps adopting an expression of encouragement. She envisaged him refusing to engage with her. Whatever had taken place with Morland-Cross had enraged him. He wouldn't just sit in his office, twiddling his thumbs. Nor could he do anything that Thomasina would report back to the Chancellor. Surely he would soon leave the office and the Treasury building too.

Events, whatever they might be, were on the move. She was on her own – there was no time to weigh the odds. If he walked out of his office, getting up immediately to follow would not be smart. Better if, when he left, she was not at her desk. She had to assume he would leave through the main exit to Horse Guards Road rather than via some sinuous route twisting through the main HMRC wing overlooking Parliament Street or via the Foreign Office. That would be a change to normality and could draw attention.

She switched off her computer, picked up her coat and bag, murmured 'Hospital appointment' to the colleague beside her, went to the ladies – she might not have another chance for hours – headed downstairs into the lobby and then out into Horse Guards Parade. She crossed into St James's Park and took up a position by the railings at the south-east tip of the duck pond.

Thirty-five minutes later – longer than she had expected – he came. After he had left the building, she assumed he would turn right or left along Horse Guards Road. Instead, to her horror, he was ambling straight in her direction. She walked fast, west along the pond. Twenty yards later, she stopped, peered at the ducks and glanced right. A slim, male figure wearing a black leather jacket was rounding the corner she had just left, but in the opposite direction, back towards Horse Guards Road. She had to assume it was him and followed. If it was him, he had done a U-turn.

The man walked north past the parade ground. She kept him in distant sight. He gained speed. Changes of pace again. The detour via the duck pond must have been to check for a tail. She recalled her previous impression – Jed was not fully professional but not totally amateur either. Just like the man ahead. Ninety-eight per cent it was him. Perhaps the secret assignations over decades of political plotting had been sufficient in themselves to teach him how to take care of himself.

He reached the corner of St James's Park, crossed the Mall, and climbed the steps towards the Duke of York's statue. He didn't look round. She followed, hesitating halfway up the final flight, just before her face would come into the sight of anyone waiting beyond or using the statue as cover. If Fowkes had stopped to do this, he would expose her and she'd have no plausible excuse to offer.

She took a further step or two – an adult playing blind man's buff. Then she took off, increasing her pace as if she was rushing to a meeting. If he was waiting, she'd break into a run, ensuring she didn't catch his eye. As the full prospect leading towards Lower Regent Street came into view, there was no sign; her fear now was that she'd lost him. A hundred yards ahead, she just caught sight of the same figure in a black jacket turning left into Pall Mall. She ran as fast as her low heels allowed.

As she turned into the heart of London's clubland, she had come too close and allowed him to gain distance. She could hardly imagine Fowkes as a regular of the Athenaeum or Reform or, if he turned right into St James's, of Brooks's or White's.

The pavements of St James's Street were more populated than Pall Mall, giving better cover but a more interrupted line of sight. He reached Piccadilly, ignored a red pedestrian light and weaved skilfully through slow-moving traffic to cross. He headed left down Piccadilly. Stuck at the lights, the traffic having gained pace, she was in danger of losing him again. Once across, he must have been over fifty yards away. She ran, attracting disapproving looks from other pedestrians. At the north-side entrance to Green Park tube, he stopped. She ducked into a shop front. If the walk had all along been a ruse before he finally descended to the tube, there was no way of making up the distance – she'd have lost him. That's why you had teams.

He looked back, appeared less agitated, and walked on, turning right into White Horse Street. There the pavement offered no hiding place, the pedestrians no protection. He forged on, left into Shepherd Street, then right into a street she was unfamiliar with. She turned into it. Nothing. He had disappeared. Carefully, she walked the short street, risking a glance into its single restaurant. A few yards further up, she caught sight of a brass plate with the name and number of the street. A blue-suited man approaching from the opposite direction rang a doorbell; the door was opened for him. She saw enough to suggest that inside was a well-heeled private members' club. It had to be where he had vanished. She checked her watch – just after midday. How long would his meeting last? How could she secure evidence of who he was seeing?

The meeting surely could not take less than forty minutes. The restaurant almost opposite was yet to fill for lunch. She entered, reserved a window table for two for 12.45, left and calculated that if she walked fast, she could return to

Piccadilly, buy another scarf and cap to adapt her appearance, and be back within the half-hour. A lunchtime companion would help to complete the makeover. Even if it was almost certainly too late in the day, she texted the one person who might be able to help.

At 1.10 p.m. Fowkes reappeared. He had not stayed on for lunch – his rendezvous must have been strictly business, not social. Maybe his host had decided that sharing a bottle of overpriced burgundy with Jed Fowkes was no one's idea of fun. Now with a yellow scarf around her neck and a blue French beret on her head, Isla looked inwards while pointing her iPhone across the road. She clicked a flurry of pictures. One of them should be good enough to provide the visual proof of Jed Fowkes's destination; there was no need to tail him further. It might be a long drawn-out affair but somehow she had to stick to this seat until the last lunchtime visitor to the discreet establishment opposite had left.

She ordered, saying she feared her guest had stood her up. Hearing the 'he', the head waiter looked mournfully down on her. 'Perhaps a drink, madam.'

'Yes please,' she replied tragically, 'I'll have the whole bottle.'

'Yes, madam, of course.' One way or another, she would have to make her lunch last. She could safely assume that no one leaving the club would recognize her.

At 1.35 p.m. Quine entered the restaurant. 'Well done,' he said, seeing her face light up in surprise and the bottle of Gavi sparkle in its ice bucket, 'a glass of that would be very nice.'

The waiter brought over a menu and beamed delightedly at Isla. As he left, she said, 'I told him I'd been stood up. You got here quicker than you thought.'

'Sophie's car is surprisingly quick. We mustn't forget the congestion charge.'

They talked quietly about why she was here and he gave her the headlines of his conversation with Mikey Miller. Isla was facing towards the members' club entrance, able to see and snatch faces as they appeared; Quine, resisting any temptation to turn, could only watch the backs of figures heading south on the pavement opposite. There was something familiar about the gait of one of them, but he couldn't place it.

By 3.40 p.m., the waiting staff were becoming fidgety; it had been twenty minutes since the last guest left the club.

'Time to go?' asked Quine.

'I guess,' replied Isla reluctantly.

'At least it can go on the big man's expenses.'

'Let's hope it's value for money. I'm back to the office. You?'

'The flat. I need to confirm something. We may be on a roll.'

35

Isla re-entered the Treasury at 4.15 p.m. She responded to the inquiring eyes of her neighbour. 'All fine, thanks. Just the waiting. You know.' The colleague nodded in agreement.

The doors to both the Chancellor's and Spads' offices were closed.

Thomasina walked out coatless, presumably to the toilet. There was a second person in the office – Fowkes must have returned. Time dragged. The departmental head of the HMRC section had given her a research project that would familiarize her with tax avoidance and evasion schemes. They were nothing compared with the money-laundering iceberg they were drilling into at her MI5 desk. It was she who needed to educate them, not vice versa.

Fowkes was in the corridor, no jacket, heading quickly towards the stairs. Follow or wait? They were both a risk. She followed. It was 6.15 p.m., a time when the spacious lobby was crowded, mainly with leavers greeting evening companions. She was able to hang back within the inner precinct while

266

keeping the security barriers within sight. Fowkes swished his pass to allow two men through; all she could tell was that one had dark, almost quiffed hair, early forties or so and wearing a grey suit; she caught sight only of the back of the other's brown leather overcoat. He led them in the direction of the canteen. She itched to take a closer look, but there was no cover. There was only one way – take cover in plain sight.

She strode into the canteen, walked purposefully towards the tea and coffee counter, and ordered. As she waited for the cappuccino to be made, she did a 360-degree scan. No sight of them. There were three different exits from the canteen. If she waited, they might reappear from one of them. She took her coffee to a table and scrolled on her phone. Fowkes was returning to the canteen from the opposite direction to the one he had entered by. She did not dare look up immediately. After half a minute or so, she raised her eyes. No sign of him. Or the two men. She drained her cup, headed out and returned to her desk. Had he seen her sitting all alone with her coffee while most other staff were leaving for the day?

At 6.45 p.m., Fowkes emerged from his office, carrying his leather jacket and computer bag. He opened the Chancellor's door and looked in. 'Goodnight, M-C.'

'Goodnight, Jed,' came a distant voice. 'We'll put this damn thing to bed in the morning.' Isla guessed Morland-Cross was expecting comfort from Thomasina.

She waited for Fowkes to disappear down the corridor. He didn't. Instead she heard footsteps approaching. When they were too close not to ignore, she turned. 'Oh, hi.' She smiled, her stomach sinking.

'Hi,' he said, returning a pale imitation of a smile. 'I seem to keep seeing you round the place.'

'Hope that's not a problem,' she said.

'Of course not.' He lingered. 'You're new, aren't you?'

'New here,' she said. 'I'm on attachment.'

'Oh, right. Where from?'

'DTI.'

'Bad luck. What are you doing here?'

'Good question. Actually they feel underpowered whenever they're trying to argue for trade and industry concessions from HMRC. So they thought some expertise might help.'

'At least they're offering that to you.'

'Yes,' she said dubiously. 'A limited picture, I suspect.'

'What do you expect,' he said, smile just intact, 'this is Whitehall.' She laughed politely. 'I'm Jed Fowkes.' He stretched out a hand.

'I know,' she beamed. 'Spads are stars.' She stood and shook the hand. 'I'm Isla. Isla McDonald. Humble civil servant.'

'At least you'll be here when we're long gone.' He tried to match her beam. 'Do you fancy a quick drink?'

'Hey, that would have been lovely.' She checked her watch. 'Actually any other evening but my partner... she's expecting me home kind of now-ish. We've got friends coming for dinner.'

'Right. Cool,' he said, his smile vanishing like a punctured soap bubble. 'Your dinner's not stopping you working late.' His tone was sharper.

'I had to make up time. I spent three hours in hospital earlier.'

'Right. Maybe another time?'

'Yeah, that'd be great,' she said.

'Cool,' he repeated. Casting a short smile, he turned and stalked off. She felt her racing pulse and took a deep breath. Some kind of mangled come-on? An interrogation? Maybe the first had turned into the second.

The near empty open-plan offices seemed, for the first time, menacing. Who, and where, were Fowkes's guests?

She closed her computer and gathered her belongings. Walking down the corridor towards the lobby, she imagined the lean figure of Fowkes waiting around every corner. The sun was setting over Buckingham Palace west of the park. Recalling Fowkes's earlier manoeuvre, albeit subconsciously, she thought of feinting right into the park rather than turning left towards the tube. She told herself not to be paranoid. Was that hint of suppressed rage his factory setting? Or was it a forlornness, a deep-set disappointment in the course of a life which, however much he might deny it, had rendered him servant not master? Composing herself, she walked fast to St James's Park tube, refusing to cast any glances behind.

By the time she emerged at West Kensington, it was dark. The streets were lit by shop and street lights, lamps and chandeliers inside Victorian mansion blocks. Though the air had hardly cooled, she shivered. The walk to the flat was only some four hundred yards but it seemed a marathon. Taking a quick look around, she entered a Co-op on North End Road. No sign of anyone following her from the tube. She wished she could shake off that feeling. She also wished she had wiped the photos from her phone. Careless. She could easily have downloaded them. Basic rule – before walking alone down a London street in the dark, de-incriminate yourself.

She should buy something. She held up a pack of chewing gum from a pile beside the cash till. Why that? She despised the habit. She emerged again. No more nonsense. She increased her stride, gathering pace as she walked. Turning the corner onto the two hundred yards of pavement that led to her block, she broke into a jog, then a sprint, arriving breathlessly at the main door. Hands shaking and sweating, she flashed a quick look behind and inserted the key into the lock. She entered, closed the door behind her and, taking a deep breath, walked slowly up the three flights of stairs to the flat's front door. She slid in the key, turned it slowly and silently eased the door open.

The kitchen, bedroom and bathrooms showed no signs of life. The sitting-room door was closed, unusually, a weak shaft of light showing beneath it which could be coming from street lights or a corner lamp. She felt her heartbeat racing again, imagining Jed Fowkes or his two guests behind it, waiting.

The kitchen door, halfway down the corridor on the right, was open, its lights off. She crept down the passage, praying no floorboard would creak. Once on the kitchen's tiled floor, she felt on safer ground, but knew she must keep it dark. She went to a wooden block and quietly extracted the eight-inch stainless steel knife that was kept specially sharp for chopping onions. She paused to collect herself, then tiptoed back into the passage and towards the sitting-room door. She moved one hand to an inch from the handle, the knife in the other. There was no sound coming from inside. In one swift movement, she flung the door a hundred and eighty degrees open in case anyone was behind it waiting to pounce, leapt inside, knife held high and scanned the room. It was dim, the curtains undrawn, an arc light hovering over a single figure in an armchair. It rose.

'Christ, Isla, put that down,' said Quine. 'You look as if you've seen a ghost.'

36

Isla looked at the knife in her hand and placed it on a table. 'Hello, Joe. You saving on the electricity or something?'

He was staring at her. 'What's wrong? Are you OK?'

'It's fine. Is Sophie home?'

'Not back yet.'

'Never mind.'

'You're shaking.'

'It's OK. Over now.'

She went to the triple window and drew the curtains, then peeped from behind them onto the street and square below. A man wearing a brown hat was walking along the other side of the road towards the mansion block entrance. He stopped and looked up. She ducked her face behind the curtain. After a few seconds, she peered out again. He was twenty yards away, retracing his steps.

Quine joined her. 'I sensed someone following me,' she said.

He had never seen her jittery before. 'Or someone was lost and trying to find the flat where he's been asked for dinner.'

She sighed. 'Maybe.' She told him about Fowkes's unidentified guests and her later conversation with him.

'I get that,' said Quine. 'It's creepy. No wonder.'

'No, I overreacted. I'm a bit out of practice at this.'

'Enough's happened to take precautions.'

'Doesn't stop me feeling foolish. I could have assumed there'd be no one but you. And I've followed people a lot less nice than Jed Fowkes and friends in my time.'

'Don't bet on the friends.'

'Maybe not,' she said wryly, feeling better.

'How about I get us a drink, I'll update you, then we look through those lunchtime photos. I presume Sophie's working late.'

'Being bored by one of her authors, no doubt.' She thought of the lie she had told Fowkes. 'Yes, we'll have to make do for ourselves.'

'Good, I fancy a Chinese.'

'I'm still full from that lunch.'

'No, you're not. Just nerves. Food eases them. Give me your order, I'll phone, you go and have a soak.'

She lay in the bath, getting out only at the ring of the doorbell twenty minutes later. She tried not to jump at it.

They ate. Quine was right – she might not have felt hungry but food was the best ingredient to wind her down.

Quine went over his meeting with Mikey Miller in detail. 'I wondered at the end if he was hiding something, even if he was involved himself. I don't discount either. Before the interview turned tricky, he told me he remembered one of those two girls. She was a secretary at the private

273

bank where he had his first City job. Her name was Roisin. Has to be the same girl. He claimed not to remember the surname but thought she probably got married. He said she was smart. As far as he was aware, she'd stayed at the bank and done well.'

Quine put aside his plate, took his computer from a bag by his feet, placed it on the table and fired it up. 'This private bank was – and still is – called Coulthard's. Its headquarters is one of the last grand period mansions in Fleet Street.' He flicked through photographs on the bank's website home page and hit 'Our People.' Among the line of patrician-looking men, there were two women, one with curly greying hair and an unforced smile projecting a natural good humour. He double-clicked on her photograph.

'Roisin Osborne,' Isla read out loud. 'Head of HR. Roisin Osborne is a Coulthard's lifer. She joined out of college and was promoted to be the finance director's secretary in 1992. Her gifts of common sense and high intelligence quickly marked her out...'

'No other Roisins,' said Quine with quiet satisfaction. 'As Mikey Miller said, she was too good for young idiots who pissed about. I haven't found out yet who Mr Osborne is—'

'You don't need to. It's only the...'

'... Hungarian girl. Yes.'

'How do you know this Roisin will talk to you?'

'My "informant" will sort that.'

'Sure?'

'I'll email him, he'll see it late tonight. He should phone her first thing tomorrow morning. Your turn now. The photos.

Can we go into the sitting room? Congealing chow mein turns my stomach.'

Side by side on the sofa, she scrolled slowly, one by one, through the photographs on her phone. 'They're being analysed by the office. But let's see if you recognize anyone. They can be enlarged but that may not bring clarity, just increased pixellation.'

'You've got Fowkes anyway,' said Quine, looking at the first group.

'Have I caught him close enough to the club?'

'Yes.' He peered at each succeeding photograph for several seconds as the lunchers dribbled out in ones and twos.

'My God,' said Quine. He peered ever closer. 'Yes, I'm sure it is.' They moved closer to the screen. 'Yes. Quentin Deschevaux MP. Even from the back view I thought there was something familiar about one of them.'

Isla frowned. She looked at Quine for a long moment before continuing. 'He's probably just a member. No reason to think Fowkes was seeing him.'

'They're both on the right of the party so that could be a reason. But yes, you're right, no evidence.'

'That sort of club is where rich men go to show other rich men they're richer.'

Quine chuckled. 'That certainly fits Deschevaux.' She continued the display. 'What did Fowkes's mystery visitors look like?'

'I only saw one of them, early to mid-forties, wearing a grey suit and with a quiff in his hair.'

'What, sort of bouffant?'

275

'Yes, you could call it that.'

'Exactly the description of the man Mrs Trelight said came sniffing around, pretending to be from my publisher.'

'We've got to do better than hairstyle.'

Quine grinned. 'Why did I think you might say that?'

Isla grinned back. 'Are you setting me up, Joe?'

'Wouldn't dream of it.' He was pleased her sense of humour was returning.

'Ha! Right. We need tangible evidence of a suspicious Fowkes link. That's my job. Then we need Roisin Osborne to tell us about a red-haired Hungarian girl called Andrea. Your job.'

'I get the soft ones,' said Quine.

'If I try to tail Fowkes again, this could unravel. My luck won't hold for ever.'

'You could bring in someone to replace you.'

Isla's nostrils flared, the scares of the evening now oddly invigorating. 'Not a chance. With all this to play for?'

'Have you got these photos backed up somewhere?'

She rolled her eyes. 'Sophie told me you ask silly questions sometimes.'

A few minutes later, Quine emailed the Prime Minister.

*

JONATHAN MOORE
To: paulabcdreynolds@gmail.com
Re: latest

Hi Paul

Urgently need to speak to R person in attached link.
I understand she'll remember you fondly. If possible, please
phone her to give blessing first thing in the morning.

Need face-to-face catch-up with you after that.

Cheers
Jonathan

*

Sandford, reading it an hour later, was reminded of the impor-
tance of checking the email link at the end of each day. One
consequence was the need to spend every night at Salisbury
Square and face the daily catch-ups Carol always wanted.
He had never felt so alone. He had never had to hide such an
enormous secret from her. There were moments he felt he
should never have confided in Quine and, instead, just hoped
it would blow away and fade like a bad dream. That, for sure,
was not going to happen.

The email led him to think more about Roisin. He could not
recall the surname but, looking at the middle-aged woman
on Coulthard's website, it all came back. A lilting Irish accent,
curly dark hair, funny. It was not surprising she had done well.

He remembered his desire to see her again – which must have been after the weekend of Jed's story. Why had that wish been so strong? Just because he found her good company? Or did he have an inkling of something that had happened and a need to find out if she knew anything? Had Roisin discovered something about him?

Was there anything to fear from Quine seeing Roisin Osborne? Might she be able to put flesh on the bones of a Hungarian girl called Andrea? What a metaphor to be running through his head. But the prospect of Roisin being able to give her an identity presented a threat, however many years later. The thought of the torso with the chopped-off hand becoming recognizable as a once living, innocent young girl with red hair and her life before her was now constantly with him. Roisin had peeled off that night – but imagine if someone, as yet unknown, stepped out of the shadows of three decades and was able to give a lucid, accurate account of the company Andrea ended up in the night she disappeared.

He should stop speculating. Only the truth could make him safe. Or convict him. Yes, Quine had to see Roisin.

Carol peered over her glasses as he entered the bedroom. 'M-C all sorted?' As he looked at her, it was still Roisin he was thinking about. And her friend Andrea.

All sorted? If only.

*

Just after 11.30 p.m. Isla, laptop in hand, poked her head around the sitting-room door. 'I've had feedback.'

278

Quine, midway through converting the sofa to a bed, looked up, puzzled.

'Two IDs on the photos from outside the Mayfair club. Put that sofa back and I'll play it for you.'

Two men in dark suits advanced millimetre by millimetre on the screen. They had just left the club and were walking along the street. The bonnet of a large grey saloon crept into the left of shot; Quine could just make out the two-winged crest of a Bentley. The face of the man on the left was obscured. The man on the right's face was coming into focus. Isla hit pause, stopping the frame just before his face was covered.

'That is a guy called Lyle Grainger.'

'What!' Quine gasped.

'Wait.' She ran the sequence until the car's cabin just cleared the second face.

'And this is Herr Dieter Schmidt.'

'I never managed to find photos of either of them,' said Quine. 'It was as if they'd erased themselves from all records, physical and digital.'

'There's some further info,' said Isla. 'Once upon a time – late 1980s, early 90s – Grainger was based in London at the US embassy when it was in Grosvenor Square. Left the embassy end of '92, stayed in the UK. Schmidt is an East German who stayed in London after the fall of the Berlin Wall.'

'Deschevaux, Grainger, Schmidt. The three founding directors of International Personnel and Resource Management. Who all resigned as directors within a year of its operation in Freetown.'

'There's nothing to say they reduced their shareholdings,'

said Isla, 'no doubt all hidden in shell companies here or off-shore.'

'And all having lunch at the same Mayfair club on the day Jed Fowkes has an urgent need to go there.' Quine paused. 'I suppose you'll now say that Fowkes might have been seeing someone completely different.'

'No, but I'll say this. Those years after Communism collapsed were messy. And London was a honeypot.'

'Yes,' said Quine. 'A place where unholy alliances were the order of the day. We may just have fallen on one of the unholiest of all.'

37

Isla was at her desk by 8 a.m. The previous day's encounters showed that Fowkes was now on the move and not acting alone. The identities of his contacts were physically unproven, but the circumstantial evidence was powerful. Early starts were a norm for most Treasury and HMRC staff, but there seemed no sign of activity in the Chancellor's or Spads' offices. Thomasina and Jed operated by their own schedules and Morland-Cross often didn't appear before 9.15 a.m. She was in good time.

Thomasina arrived at 8.50, parked her coat and bag, reappeared nervously in the corridor and knocked on the Chancellor's office door. She waited for a moment, frowned, and retreated to the Spads' office. At 9.15, the time of the Chancellor's regular morning meeting with the private office, his principal private secretary emerged into the corridor. He approached the permanent secretary's desk in the open-plan and leant down to murmur something in his ear. The two men returned to the Chancellor's office door; a hesitant initial tap was followed by a loud, repeated knock. The PS turned the door handle and pushed. No movement. He whispered something to the PPS. Isla was just able to lip-read.

'Do you have a key?'

The PPS shook his head. He knocked on the door of the Spads' office and entered. He emerged with Thomasina holding a key. She looked nervously around the open-plan; Isla sensed her wanting everyone to go away and hide. She turned back and tried to put the key in the lock. It would not enter smoothly. She tried to force it.

The PPS touched her wrist. 'Shall I have a go?' he asked gently.

She handed him the key and he inserted it easily, opened the door a couple of inches and allowed her to enter ahead of him.

Isla, watching and feeling Thomasina's tension, felt a bead of sweat on her forehead as she disappeared behind the door.

A scream ripped through the corridor.

'Oh my God,' someone shouted.

Instinctively Isla jumped up and ran to the open door. 'I'm first-aid qualified,' she said calmly, 'is there a problem?'

'Yes,' began the PPS.

'Who are you?' interrupted the PS.

'I'm on a three-week HMRC attachment for the DTI,' she said.

The PS inspected her. 'All right, you'd better go in, we'll come with you.' In the corridor, Thomasina was making retching sounds.

Isla entered. A naked male body was seated in the

Chancellor's desk chair, its feet resting on the desk itself. The head was covered by a white plastic bag. Some kind of flex or ligature, tied to both feet, led back towards the plastic bag, disappearing beneath it. She approached the body. She understood the scene must not be contaminated but, in the unlikely event of there still being life, she bent down low and lifted the bag. She looked up to see the flopped head of Henry Morland-Cross. A lemon was stuffed in his mouth. The other end of the ligature was wound tightly around his neck. Purple spread from neck to cheeks. She stood and held his limp wrist, then put an ear to his chest. She had a quick look at the desk. A fifty-pound note lay on it beside a razor. There were remnants of white powder.

It was like a stage set. She already knew what had happened, and that it would never be proved.

She emerged. 'He's been dead for several hours,' she told the two civil servants. 'That young woman needs looking after.'

'We've called the emergency services,' said the PPS. 'A duty protection officer from Number 10 will be here soon.'

'It will help if he can be reassured there's been no disturbance to the scene,' she said.

'We're aware of that,' said the PS caustically, 'Miss, er...'

'Isla McDonald. I'll get out of your way. I'm very sorry.'

As she withdrew, the Number 10 protection officer, dressed in an ordinary civilian suit, arrived. She wondered how long she would be able to observe from the vantage point of her desk. Despite the chaos and confusion that would inevitably come, she needed him to follow correct protocol and ask all those present to stay in place while their details were taken.

Within a few minutes, police and medics were on the scene. A stretch of corridor outside the Chancellor's office was cordoned off. The only sounds were the shuffling of feet and the occasional murmur of voices. Thomasina, escorted by a policewoman holding her arm, was taken to her desk.

Jed Fowkes arrived, his face creasing as he neared the cordoned stretch of corridor. A policeman intercepted him. It was a brief exchange, then Jed retreated into the Spads' office.

'What happened?' he asked.

A pause and a sniffle before Thomasina replied. 'I don't know. He's dead.'

'What! How?'

She started sobbing. 'Sounds like he's been dead for hours.'

'Thomasina,' he said almost roughly, 'weren't you with him last night?'

'No. I popped in to see him. We had a few minutes together. He told me to go the flat – his own flat, I mean – and he'd try to get there later. He was buried in paperwork and if it was too late, he'd stay at Number 11.'

'Was that normal?'

'I don't know, I wasn't with him long enough. I usually stayed with him at Number 11.' A few seconds' silence. 'I wonder if he was meeting someone.'

'Why? Who?'

'It would explain it, that's all.' A further pause. 'I don't get it. He wasn't like that. Never.'

'Like what?'

'Christ, Jed.' Her voice was raised.

'Sorry, I didn't mean…'

284

'You'd better go and have a look,' she said.

'I won't be allowed. Too late.'

'At least you're spared that.'

He hesitated. 'Spared what?'

'You'll know soon enough. The whole world will know soon enough. Some kind of sex game. On his own.' She shook her head. 'It's just not him. It's not as if he ever needed anything like that. He wasn't in a weird mood or anything. He was pleased. He told me the PM wanted him to stay on.'

'Yes,' said Fowkes. 'He told me that too. When I saw him yesterday morning.'

'You didn't seem too happy after you saw him.'

'I was certainly happy for him. We were joined at the hip. Whatever the occasional argument. It just makes no sense. I mean, he lived life full-on but not like this.'

'I should have stayed with him.'

'It's OK. Don't blame yourself.' They fell silent.

Half an hour later, names and contacts established, staff were given permission to leave their desks and the building. Immediately the all-clear was given, Fowkes was in the corridor, carrying his bag, coat on, striding in the direction of the exit. Isla knew that she couldn't jump up after him, particularly in these circumstances. She went to the ladies, entered a cubicle, pulled out her phone and quickly dialled a number.

38

'Yes, Isla,' said Quine.

'I'll be brief. Major incident at the Treasury. Morland-Cross has been discovered dead in the office. Looks like a sex game gone wrong. Our man left in a rush. Clearly to see someone.'

'Without you behind?'

'Yes. Impossible.'

'Give me a second to think.' She flushed the toilet to create covering noise and hugged the phone to her ear. 'I'll use your car and drive to Mayfair.'

He gave her a street name, a different one from the private members' club, and a number. 'It's got to be worth a try. The building's in the middle of the west side. Get a cab. We'll assume he's walking. You might be there first. I'll stop just short of the north end coming from the west and you jump in. I'll be as quick as I can. Stay out of sight.'

'I'll know what to do.' She cut the call.

She walked calmly back to her desk and picked up her bag and coat. Staff not considered essential were drifting out; there was nothing unusual about joining them. She hailed a cab at the corner of Horse Guards Road and Birdcage Walk and told the driver to take her to the street running parallel to the one given by Quine. Though the chances of Fowkes spotting her inside the taxi were infinitesimal, she kept her head down. Fourteen minutes later – she tracked it on her watch – the cab dropped her off. Fowkes, walking fast, unhindered by traffic, might or might not have arrived. There was no way Quine, driving from West Kensington, could be there yet. Ignoring his advice she walked to the north end of the street. Unless Fowkes was taking a deliberately circuitous route, he would approach from the south side. She waited.

Twenty minutes later, Quine drew up alongside. She opened the passenger door and jumped in. 'I could see you,' said Quine. 'Doesn't that mean he could have too?'

'No. He either beat me here and he's inside. Or your hunch is wrong.'

'Any signs?'

'That black Mercedes with tinted windows drew up and someone, a male, got out. The driver's still inside. Waiting for his passenger to reappear, I'm assuming.'

'Has he seen you?'

'Who?'

'The driver.'

'No.' She hesitated. 'I don't think so.'

Her uncertainty alarmed him but he tried not to show it. 'And the man who got out?' he asked.

'I didn't see.'

'But his arrival could be related to Fowkes leaving the Treasury.'

'Clutching at straws. But the timing could work, assuming he's coming from within Central London. By the way, you gave me the number, you didn't actually tell me what the building is.'

'I assumed you'd know.'

'Sure, but I don't see a sign or plaque.'

'Quite. IPRM doesn't advertise itself.'

'I guessed that might be it.'

'Right. Where do you want to be to get the photo? If Fowkes appears, I mean.' Isla looked up and down the street. 'Do a circuit so we turn into the south end. Then find a space opposite the building. That will give me a good enough angle and direct line of vision from the passenger seat.'

'You'll have no cover.'

'It's the only way.'

'OK. How close?'

'Fifty yards or so. I'll judge it as we're lining up.'

'That camera can ID him at fifty yards?'

'I didn't buy it from Amazon.'

He reversed out of the north end and followed her instructions.

'There's a gap there,' she said.

'It's a double yellow.'

'I've got a police ID.'

Reversing into position, he realized that his manoeuvre might be visible to the black saloon car driver's wing mirror. Too bad – if he was the chauffeur, he was probably listening to music on earphones or reading the paper.

Thirty minutes passed. Quine kept an eye out for traffic wardens; it would be an interruption they could do without. Isla's eyes were trained unflinchingly on the exit. Butterflies buzzed inside him. It felt utterly different from the political journalist's standard stake-out.

Isla shifted, her phone camera whirring. He looked across. Yes. Clearly Jed Fowkes stepping out with another man. Not Deschevaux. Could be Lyle Grainger or Dieter Schmidt – they were of similar age – late fifties, dark hair, broad-chested. From this distance, neither was recognizable as one of the men in the old photos.

'Have you got the guy with him?' he asked.

'Trying.' She wound her window further down, shifting position again. Fowkes looked up in her direction.

'Shit,' she said. 'I think he's seen us.'

'Recognize you?'

'I don't know.'

Quine, now failing to hide his alarm, started the engine. 'Time to go.'

He accelerated. As they passed the black Mercedes, Fowkes and the other man were jumping in, gesturing to the driver, pointing. The saloon pulled out behind him.

'Jesus,' said Quine.

'Whatever else,' said Isla, 'they'll now have my number plate.'

'Where to?'

'Head into Park Lane. We're safest in traffic. Then circle Hyde Park Corner.'

She dialled a number, turning away from him. He could

make out some of what she said. 'AIT, cat 8. Hyde Park Corner.' She gave the number plate of the chasing car. 'Hostile black Mercedes. Heading for 125 SW.'

He reached the lights at the end of Park Lane. The Mercedes, at this point tailing rather than making any attempt to catch up, had fallen a few cars behind. Isla crouched beside the passenger seat. If he crashed, she had no protection. His hands felt sweaty on the steering wheel. He gripped tighter.

The lights at the junction with Constitution Hill were red. How long would this go on? How long could it go on? Were they just tailing, wanting to see where they were going? Or, if they saw an opportunity, would they try to intercept? With Jed Fowkes in that car, surely they wouldn't try anything stupid. Would they? He must stop asking himself questions, just concentrate on the road and the mirror. No more crashes. Don't screw this up.

'How far behind are they?' she asked.

He glanced in the mirror. 'About six cars.' He hesitated, looked again. Was it definitely the same car? Stop asking yourself questions, just get it right. His heart felt like a grandfather clock speeding up and out of control.

'OK,' she said. 'Do a full circle. There's no need to hurry. In fact, do the opposite. They can't try anything here. When we're back at these lights, update me on their position. I want to avoid looking round if I can.'

Negotiating the four sides of the square seemed to go on for ever. He was deliberately driving like an old lady, they were making no effort to catch up. What was their ultimate intention? Perhaps they did not know themselves and were just reacting. Quine started to see a funny side to it. The slowest chase in the long history of the motor car. Eventually, they arrived back at the Constitution Hill lights.

'I make it they're still six cars behind.' He calmed, feeling more in control.

'OK,' she said. 'We have a plan. Listen carefully. Approach the next lights slowly. Take a middle lane as if you're not certain whether you're turning left or right. Ultimately you're turning left but don't show it till the last moment. Don't leave room for a car to come up on your inside. Don't worry about people hooting. When you're near the lights, slow right down if they're green. If still green when you're there, stop. If they're red, also stop.'

They moved off. 'Fifty yards or so,' he said. 'They're green.' He looked in the mirror. They were closer, four cars behind. 'Twenty yards. Still green. The road's almost clear in front.'

'Good. Approach slowly.'

'They're going amber.'

'Go! Foot down. Turn left. Headlights on, hand on horn as much as you can.'

He did as she said. She raised her head and looked around. The car behind had stopped at the lights. The black Mercedes was blocked, two cars back.

'Brilliant. Now be bold. Take second right. Just cut across the traffic.' She felt the car swing right. 'Well done. Hand off horn. Lights off. Take first left.' He checked the rear-view mirror, no sign of the black Mercedes. He took the left. She sat up on the passenger seat. 'OK, left again at the bottom.

Twenty yards on the right into the mews, a garage door is open. Drive into it.'

He did. As soon as they were inside, the door came down and lights on. They were alone. 'Jesus,' he said, 'I almost hit a bus taking that right from Park Lane.'

'It's fine, you did it. Well done. Follow me upstairs and walk out through the front door. There's a car waiting to drop you at the tube. I'll see you later. You've never been here. This place doesn't exist.'

39

It would be perfect if they ended up killing each other.

Sandford could hardly believe he had used those words. What a firestorm. If he had imagined in a million years that it could lead to this, would he have played it this way? His predicament had been so critical that he could not, to his self-disgust, easily answer that question. Now he must see the game through. With Morland-Cross literally dead, Fowkes, at least figuratively, must follow.

The strange end of the Deputy Prime Minister and Chancellor of the Exchequer, the second most powerful man in the land, was bound to run and run. Even sixteen years on, the death of a rising but far more junior Conservative MP in similar circumstances was still attracting conspiracy theories. That, too, had included a lemon. No doubt it was a deliberate copycat. For the moment, because of Morland-Cross's reputation as a sexual predator, now supplemented by the allegations of violence, the media would have a field day. Every angle would be indulged: the perverted reaction to the shame of exposure; the fear of more women coming forward; the knowledge that his career was over, that he could never become Prime Minister; the resignation that was about to be forced on him; that he was deliberately flirting with death as his best way out.

It was a useful narrative for the authorities – police, intelligence agencies, civil service, the coroner, the state in all its manifestations. Sandford felt as sure of the sun rising at dawn tomorrow that no physical evidence would appear to suggest otherwise. Yet here he was, the Prime Minister, the apex of that state, one hundred per cent sure that it was murder. This time he was the conspiracy theorist.

He was trapped. To convince any investigator to dig deeper, he would have to tell a story that was impossible for him to reveal. Without implicating himself, he could offer nothing more than his hunch, his assessment of his colleague's state of mind. He would be courteously listened to and then dismissed, seen as wanting to protect a colleague and friend. Perhaps he would be asked what his alternative theory was. What difference would that make? If he began to hint at murder or conspiracy, eyes would roll, the pillars of the 'state' asking themselves whether there was a fantasist at 10 Downing Street.

I am not just alone, he reflected, I am powerless. A horrifying thought hit him. Was the death of Morland-Cross a coded warning? 'You fall into line, because what happened to him can happen to you too.'

The phone rang. 'It's Jed Fowkes, Prime Minister. Will you take the call?'

My God, what timing. 'Yes, Mark, put him through.'
A switch clicked.

'Thank you for talking to me, Prime Minister.' Both men
knew that the PPS would listen in to the call; this was government business on government phones.

'I could hardly not, Jed. A tragedy.'

'Yes, awful.' Fowkes hesitated. 'I'd never have suspected
M-C of that sort of thing.'

'Nor me,' agreed Sandford.

'Women of course, but never that.'

'Perhaps there's a part of everyone that we never truly know.'

'But a fine man. And a great thinker.'

'Yes, indeed.'

The line fell silent. The obligatory platitudes exchanged,
Fowkes broke the moment. 'But we can't stand still.'

'No,' agreed Sandford with uncharacteristic vehemence.

'Perhaps it was as well we had that discussion.'

Sandford wondered whether to give him what he wanted
straightaway or allow him to sweat. Just follow Quine's rule.
'Yes, it was.' He waited, curious to see if Fowkes showed impatience. For once, he did not. 'I'll speak to Margaret Lascelles
straightaway. Sort it out quickly, maintain confidence in the
markets and all that.'

'I couldn't agree more. In the meantime I'll keep an eye
on things for you.'

'Thanks, Jed, I really appreciate that.'

The call went dead. It was not yet noon; Fowkes had not
wasted a moment. Sandford rang Margaret Lascelles inviting
her to be Chancellor, with just one condition.

'Margaret, I'd like Jed Fowkes to continue as the senior Treasury special adviser. Chancellor is the hardest of all jobs to settle in to. I suggest that, effectively, you and I allow Jed to oversee things for two or three months. In the first instance this will be signing off Treasury input into the Royal Speech. I'll be closely involved myself too. In fact I intend that Jed and I will work together to achieve the final version of the full speech.'

She did not hesitate; perhaps she felt a sense of relief. 'Of course, Prime Minister, I know how far back you and Jed go. I look forward enormously to working with him.'

He put the phone down. Enter the puppet. Let Jed play it.

He reconsidered. No, that's not right. I'm the puppet Jed Fowkes is playing.

40

Back at the flat after a tube journey marred by nervous glances, Quine missed the first breaking of the story. Now he sat watching, flicking between Sky News Live and the BBC News Channel, as it snowballed into the full avalanche of speculation and motivation. Sandford had stepped out into a sunlit Downing Street, wearing a white shirt and tie so dark blue that it was almost black.

'I have just heard the sad, indeed tragic, news of the death of the Chancellor of the Exchequer, Henry Morland-Cross. He was a close colleague for many years. As well as his great good humour, he was a man of principle. In recent times he became a real friend as we steered our nation through turbulent times. No doubt much will be said and written about his death. But I hope the focus will be on his productive, energetic and beneficial life. I will remember, as I hope we all will, a gifted man who gave his best to his country when it needed him most.'

Yes, thought Quine, you haven't lost the knack, Robbie,

whatever your own troubles might be. Hearing his words and the tributes of others speaking with wildly varying degrees of honesty, he was shocked to realize the change within himself. A year or two ago, nothing would have excited him more than being at the centre of the story. Now it left him cold, repelled by the sheer volume of noise as every straw was clutched at to enhance sensation. Had he gone soft? Or was it the world, in thrall to instant and social media, that had gone hard? A lethally weaponized world.

He heard the click and creak of the front door and jumped up, his heart thudding again as it had on the journey home.

'It's just me,' came a familiar voice. He wished he did not feel so overwhelmed with relief.

Sophie walked into the room. 'You're back early,' he said, trying to look cheerful.

'It's my reading at home time.' She frowned. 'Are you OK?'

'Yes. Sort of.' He nodded at the television. 'It's just this. I thought I'd want to watch it all. But I can't stand it.'

'Switch it off.' She grabbed the zapper from the sofa and did it for him.

He stretched out an arm. 'I'd better have it back.' She handed it over. 'Trouble is I can't stand it but, once it's on, I can't stop myself.'

*

'We've hit a wall,' said Isla that evening.

'A wall?'

'Yes. I might be exposed from Fowkes first spotting us.

So I guess that's the end of my attachment to HMRC.' She smiled ruefully. 'You might be too. Hard to be invisible in the driver's seat.'

'Are we safe?'

'I can look after myself. Let's work it through for you. Assuming IPRM stroke Deschevaux was behind your camper van crash, we don't know if that was because of your book or because they'd found out you were involved with this. Maybe someone told them you were nosing around Deptford. They may have ID'd you watching them today. But they've also exposed themselves by coming after us with Fowkes in the car. So they won't be stupid enough to come for you again. Not in this country anyway. They'll assume you have protection. Though I wouldn't be having a holiday anytime soon in a lawless country where IPRM has a presence.'

'Thanks, Isla.'

'My pleasure. Advice comes free.'

'You said we've hit a wall.'

'Yes, unless...' Deliberately, she did not finish the sentence.

'Unless what?'

'Before I answer, let's sum up. One, Morland-Cross had an explosive argument with Fowkes. Two, Fowkes had a covert meeting with Christine Patterson two nights before her TV confessional. Three, the combined surveillance and photos outside the Mayfair club means Fowkes has a relationship with that company's two founding directors and with Deschevaux. It also means that they're still part of that company. Four, Fowkes was seen allowing two unidentified men into the Treasury on the evening of the night Morland-Cross died.

We have no evidence but it's possible, maybe probable, they killed Morland-Cross and made it look like an accident. Five, when Fowkes spotted the car you and I were in outside the IPRM head office, the car ferrying him followed us in a way that indicated hostile intent.'

Quine sighed. 'But it's hardly going to hold up in court. Is that the point?'

'No. Not yet anyway. Unlike the law, we're trying to find the truth.' They shared a wry smile. 'But we have a missing element.'

'Which is?'

'You have to persuade a certain person to agree a particular course of action.'

'No more riddles. What do you mean?'

'Come on, Joe. Robin Sandford must fully bring in the intelligence services. Right now. You and me can't get to the truth alone.'

'He won't,' Quine said flatly, his face a picture of gloom.

'He has to.'

'He'll never tell them the real nature of Fowkes's threat.'

'He doesn't need to. All the factors I've just listed would be seen by any intelligence chief as potential indicators of a criminal conspiracy at the heart of government.'

'We don't have clear evidence of the network. It's still our theory.'

'It may not add up to enough for police investigation. But it does for MI5 to intervene. That's our job. To anticipate and prevent.'

Quine's phone rang. He started. Seeing the reflex action,

300

Isla observed him closely as he answered. 'Yes, of course… this morning – before today's tragic news emerged… well, why not?… Your head office in Fleet Street… Ten thirty. Excellent, I look forward to it… Yes, goodbye.'

Quine looked up at Isla, excitement in his eyes. 'Roisin Osborne. Sandford's delivered. She may hold the clue to what he truly has to fear.'

'Now it's my turn to ask, Joe. Are *you* OK to carry on?'

'Sure. What have I got to lose?'

*

Sandford, home half an hour after midnight after a day unlike any other in his entire life, read the latest email.

*

JONATHAN MOORE

To: paulabcdreynolds@gmail.com

Re: Urgent

Hi Paul
Am seeing R tomorrow. After that, need to meet without delay and review.

Cheers
Jonathan

*

The bedroom door was ajar, Carol's bedside lamp on. In her hands she held a few sheets of A4 paper.

'Weirdest day ever,' he said, approaching to give her a kiss.

She pushed him away. 'Yes, everything's changed, hasn't it? I want to know what's going on, Robbie. The lot.'

'You mean M-C.'

'We can start there if you want.'

He felt queasy. There was a sternness, a tone of the interrogator in her voice. He had never heard her speak so sharply. He realized how tired he was. He must not rise to her.

'I guess we take it at face value,' he said. 'M-C had a fetish none of us knew about.'

'Not the M-C you've ever described to me. He liked fucking women, not himself.'

Something was coming; she never used language like that. 'Many people have secret lives.'

She shuffled the sheets of paper. 'Exactly, Robbie. It's not M-C I'm interested in now.'

'Sorry, I'm not with you.'

'You're not levelling with me in any way. I've looked at your email exchanges with Joe Quine.'

'Carol, you've no right to go there. Please give them back.'

He put out a hand to receive them. She didn't move. 'We're married. We share our lives.'

'I'm asking you again. Don't do this.'

She started reading. 'Artefact. No sign of other supporting material. Our friend exploiting emergence for own purposes. What's the artefact, who's the friend?'

'Stop it,' he murmured.

'Our friend left his boss's office looking upset. Sounds as if there'd been an angry discussion.'

'Don't.'

'Now this last one. Urgently need to speak to R person in attached link. I understand she'll remember you fondly. I hit the link and googled her. What's going on, Robbie?'

His chest was tight, his stomach cramped. Glaring, he squeezed the hand he'd stretched out towards her into a fist. He was suddenly short of breath. He turned and went into the bathroom. Splashed water into his face, then rested his hands on the basin, trying to take deep, slow breaths.

Watching him go, she realized that, for a split second, she actually thought he was going to hit her.

41

'I couldn't resist,' she said. 'I was just amazed he'd remembered me.'

Roisin Osborne had come down to meet Quine as, overseen by a top-hatted commissionaire, he signed Coulthard's leather-bound visitors' book in reception.

'Goodness,' she continued, 'the Prime Minister on the phone. To me! It must be thirty years.'

'It sounds like you remember him well too,' said Quine.

'I wouldn't quite say that.'

A twinkle in her eyes made her easy to warm to. But there had to be toughness underneath in order to rise from secretary to director at an institution that had survived the centuries like Coulthard's private bank. She led him up two flights of stairs, talking as they walked. 'But how did he track me down to here? Or maybe that was you?'

Quine had decided not to mention Mikey Miller – an instinct told him he was not someone Mrs Osborne would recall with approval or fondness. 'No, all him. He'd forgotten your surname but, once he looked back, a girl called Roisin was as fresh in the memory as yesterday. And he recalled Coulthard's. I took pot luck and checked if there were any Roisins working there. And here we are.'

'Well, would you believe it?'

They reached a square landing, corridors running off to the left and right and two doors ajar. She entered one of them. 'The dining room. Where men once traded fortunes over port.'

It was a grand, wood-panelled rectangular room, its floor-to-ceiling windows overlooking a courtyard garden. At its centre stretched a mahogany table, carver chairs at each end, broad uprights along each side – he counted seating for twenty.

'Do they still have such things as directors' lunches?' he asked.

'Only occasionally. And women directors are allowed.' She swivelled. 'Right, tour over. We'll go to my office.'

This turned out to be along one of the corridors, through a small ante-chamber, and into a generously sized room, all with the same wood panelling as the dining room. She directed him to a sofa and placed herself on its other end. 'So how can I help you, Mr Quine?'

'Joe, please.'

'Roisin, likewise.'

'How much did the PM explain?'

'Well, he said you were researching a biography and he trusted you and wanted to help. He wanted all the ups and downs, good times and bad. I said I wasn't sure how much

I could help. He said he'd always remembered me most fondly
– which was rather sweet of him – so maybe I might remember
something of him.'

'Good.'

'Though I couldn't quite help wondering why he thought
my memories would be any use.' The smile remained but the
observation was sharp.

'I think I can give you an answer,' Quine replied. 'Robbie,
if you and I may call him that, is trying to fill a gap in his
memory. There was one year of his life – as he was starting
work at the Commons after a very bad car accident – that
he remembers very little about. Except for certain people
like you who stand out. He believes there was perhaps an
element of post-stress trauma as we now understand it. He
wants to understand the person he then was and how he
came across to others.'

'Well, he was fun.'

'Not a bad start.' As they exchanged comfortable smiles,
a young man arrived carrying a silver tray, laid with china cups,
coffee and a plate of biscuits.

'Thank you, Duncan,' said Roisin in a tone of grateful
surprise, even though she must have known it was on its
way. She watched him leave before pouring the coffee and
resuming. 'I only met him a few times.'

'What do you remember?'

'Well, on the first occasion,' her Irishness coming through
with the lengthened 'o', 'it was a Friday night. End of the week
and all that. I always felt part of the fun of this place was being

in Fleet Street, not the City. Journalists' pubs were – how can I put it? – a little salty. Pity they've gone.'

'A tragedy,' Quine concurred.

'I was young and… perhaps the word is cautious. By the end of an evening, things could get a little hectic. So I tended to make my way home.'

'Sensible.' As he said it, he realized how much the word fitted her. A woman of no-nonsense.

'Too sensible perhaps. Sometimes I feel I missed out. Anyway, I think it was the Monday or Tuesday after one of those pub evenings Robbie asked me out to dinner. He was a nice boy, well-mannered, good-looking. We went out to dinner twice, maybe three times.' She paused. 'Drink seemed to affect him. So I wrapped the evening up after we'd eaten.'

'Did he ever tell you he was suffering from anxiety issues after the car crash? It seems the pills he was given and alcohol didn't mix too well. It appears to have caused the issue with drink that you noticed.'

'No,' she said, taken aback. 'Never.' She shifted uncomfortably. 'I wish he had. Is he happy for us to discuss this?'

'Totally. As he told you, he truly wants to know all the ups and downs. We'll see later what should go in the biography.'

'Well, if you're sure.'

'There's no question of it.' She relaxed. 'Perhaps this is my curiosity,' continued Quine with a smile, 'but if there hadn't been this issue, do you think something more might have come of your relationship?'

She laughed. 'Well, if I'd known he was going to be Prime Minister…'

'But you found someone else.'

'Yes, I did.' Did her body slacken just a millimetre? And the smile fade? Perhaps she was aware of it. 'And that's been good,' she continued. She waved her arms around the room. 'And this is where I've ended up.' A brief silence fell as they sipped coffee and admired their surroundings.

'So, going back to those first Friday nights,' resumed Quine, calculating that any submerged ice had been sufficiently broken, 'Robbie remembers one evening when there was a group of you – it might have included Michael Miller, Mikey they called him…'

She frowned. 'He didn't used to hang around. He was too desperate to get away with whatever poor girl he was about to let down.' His calculation had been right – no further mentioning of Mikey.

'And Robbie sort of remembers a Hungarian girl, she might have been called Andrea—'

'Good heavens, I was thinking about her just the other day.' She paused. 'In the way you do sometimes. Do you ever have that?'

'Yes,' Quine lied.

'She was only here a few weeks if that, waitressing and cleaning. Sweet little thing.' She grinned. 'Sylph-like. That made me envious.'

'What happened to her?'

'I've no idea. One Monday morning, she just didn't turn up. Disappeared.' She clicked her fingers. 'Just like that.'

'When did you last see her?' asked Quine lightly.

'I think it may have been one of the Friday evenings.' She straightened, screwing up her eyes. 'As I said, I would have gone home, probably left her with Robbie and a couple of others. Maybe his friend, Jed, he used to come sometimes.'

'Jed Fowkes?'

'That's right. I never really knew him. He was Robbie's other flatmate, wasn't he?'

'Yes. You *do* have a good memory.'

'Amazing how it comes back, isn't it?'

'But then you heard nothing more from Andrea.'

'No, I was a little upset. I'd tried to be a friend to her. But that was not unusual, not with the temps, particularly the foreign ones. They'd come and go all the time. Change jobs. Fly home, never to return.'

'You don't happen to remember her full name, do you?'

'Why?' She looked puzzled. 'Do you want to track her down?'

'I don't know,' said Quine, trying not to arouse too much curiosity. 'This is the job Robbie's asked me to do. Any meeting can bring a connection, and then an anecdote, and then an enjoyable paragraph about misspent youth. The sort of thing that might even make it readable.'

'Yes, I can see that.' She drained her coffee, jumped up. 'Follow me,' she said, setting off along the corridor and down four flights of back stairs, arriving at a semi-basement office with a single window.

'Welcome to Coulthard's private bank archive,' she said. 'No other bank has anything like it. We used to have a full-time archivist, now she only does a day a week. It comes under me so I can come and go as I please.'

She took a key from the drawer of a bare desk, opened an internal door and hit a couple of switches to reveal a long room, illuminated by rows of strip lights.

'Three hundred years of history,' she said with pride. 'It's held a record of every individual who's ever worked at Coulthard's in whatever capacity. I say "held" because under data legislation, we have to try to find them and obtain their written permission. Most don't mind.'

She paused, then gave Quine a withering look. 'Because of those laws, I'm not allowed to tell you that Mikey Miller was one who did mind and insisted on his file being destroyed.'

Quine wondered if Mikey had once tried it on and not taken no for an answer.

'Where we've been unable to contact people,' she continued, 'I made the decision to keep their file. I checked with our lawyer and he reckoned no one's ever going to contest that.'

She wandered in and out of sliding shelves holding rows of metal boxes. 'Some used to be in wooden boxes, even cardboard. I had them all transferred.'

'What about digital storage?'

'Oh no,' she said, 'that's not for the Coulthard's archive. Not yet anyway. It's bad enough the business has gone digital. Now the exact year we're talking is what? 1991?'

'Most likely,' he replied, 'though it could also be part of 1992.'

'Right, let's begin at the beginning. Won't take long. A year's box or boxes refers only to those entering that year. However big their file builds, it stays in that one year.' Near the end of a row, she stopped and started rifling through a box. 'Andrea's folder will be thin, just a single sheet or two.'

Triumphantly she withdrew a card file. 'Eureka!'

The file identifier was simply the name 'Takacs, Andrea'. Pinned on the inside was a black and white, passport-sized photograph. Quine swallowed, allowing Roisin the space to enjoy her discovery. The image was faded but it showed a pretty thin-faced young woman.

'Yes, that's Andrea.' She lingered, staring at the picture. 'I wonder what happened to her.'

Inside were two cards. One gave start and end of employment dates, the second a line showing three weekly wage payments.

Moving alongside Roisin, Quine tried to scrutinize the two cards, searching for an address. All he could immediately make out, handwritten in capitals on the first card, was 'BUDAPEST, HUNGARY'.

'There's a word written before Budapest,' he said.

She brought it closer. 'It's hard to read, almost illegible.' She handed it to Quine.

'Do you have a magnifying glass?' he asked.

Her forehead creased. 'Does it matter?'

'I'm incurably inquisitive,' he said with a grin.

'In that case…' her voice tailed off. She turned and walked back towards the office, he followed with the file. She searched a couple of drawers and pulled out a small case, opening it to reveal a round glass. She handed it to him.

He stared through it for at least half a minute before giving up.

'Give it to me, that word could be my writing,' she said. 'My first job was junior secretary in Personnel – as we used to call it. We added extra information as and when we obtained it.' She concentrated for a moment. 'Hmm, I could have done better. Looks to me it begins with something like P, u, s, z...'

Quine had a final look for himself. She could certainly be right about the capital P and lower-case z. He handed the file back to her. Was this the end of the trail?

'So are you going to fly off to Hungary to find the Prime Minister's girl who disappeared?' she asked, eyes sparkling.

Quine almost shuddered at the way she had put it. He forced a smile. 'I'm afraid the budget won't extend to that. Not even for the long-lost redhead. What a shame! A Prime Minister's love that fate cut short. I can hear myself writing it.'

'Hold on, Joe, he only met her once. As far as I know.'

'Sorry, getting carried away.'

'And I thought it was me he fancied,' she said with mock offence.

'I was a journalist, Roisin. Never let the facts get in the way of a good story.'

She replaced the file and they returned to the office. He did not want to appear to make too much of the discovery by leaving curtly and they chatted for a while.

Then, suddenly, she stopped in her tracks. 'You know,' she said, 'going back to Andrea, maybe it *was* her Robbie had a soft spot for. I remember him asking more than once when he took me out those couple of times if I knew what had happened to her.' She paused. 'It was almost as if he was anxious about it.'

'Or sad that she'd gone?' added Quine.

'Who knows?' Leaving the question hanging, she looked at her watch.

Quine took the hint and rose. They walked companionably down the stairs to the reception hall.

'No,' said Quine, taking his coat from the commissionaire, 'I reckon it was you he had the crush on.' He grinned. 'I think you'd have been a very good first lady of Number 10.'

She returned the grin. 'I dare say I might have.'

*

Sandford flicked a surreptitious glance at his watch: 11.44 a.m. Forty-four minutes into Cabinet Economic Committee, sixteen minutes to go. At times like this, it was not just the aloneness, but the sheer tedium; the sitting, apparently watching intently, his mind utterly elsewhere. He glanced at his new Chancellor, wisely nodding at every utterance. He wondered how many of them she understood.

His mind kept returning to the ugly scene of the night before. He told himself it was Carol's fault, she had no right to root around his private correspondence. He wasn't levelling with her because he couldn't. She should accept that and trust him, not suspect him. But he shouldn't have reacted the way he did. Jed's story was turning him into a person he did not recognize or like. The argument even made him begin to wonder if he was someone with the capacity for violence.

Truth remained the only solution. Quine's email insisted they meet face to face after his meeting with Roisin Osborne. Like it or not, he must go through with it and allow Quine to get as far down the trail as he could – whether it ended up destroying him or not. That night he sent an email from Salisbury Square.

*

PAUL REYNOLDS

To: jonathan1234moore@gmail.com

Re: meet

Hi Jonathan

Sorry about the short notice. 7.30am, Archbishop's Park, main gate. Jogging gear. We'll do a couple of circuits. Forecast good.

Cheers
Paul

*

Quine read it twice, murmured, 'Thanks, Robbie,' and set the alarm for 6.15 a.m.

42

Quine rolled out of bed at the alarm's first repeat. He crept
unsteadily to the bathroom, filled the basin with cold water,
buried his face in it for a few seconds, then harshly brushed
his teeth. The cab was booked for 7 a.m.; plenty of time to get
to Lambeth. As for jogging clothes and trainers – those had all
gone up in flames along with Beatrice. It was another reminder
that he was losing condition all too quickly. He dressed in what
he had: jacket, trousers and brown moccasins.

The cab dropped him at 7.25 a.m. as the main gate to the
park was opening. He saw Sandford approaching with a jogger
on each side – protection officers, he assumed – and an escort
car creeping along the road behind. As the party reached the
gate, Sandford slowed down and inspected him.

'Did I catch you unprepared?' he said.

'You might have to slow down. No Saturday lie-ins for the
Prime Minister then.'

'Got to keep fit.' Sandford slapped him on the shoulder.
'We'll walk to the nature garden.'

They found a bench surrounded by rhododendron bushes. The jogging escort took up positions nearby. 'You said it was urgent,' said Sandford quietly. 'Ten minutes, OK?'

Quine first summarized the tracking of Jed and his movements on the eve of Morland-Cross's suicide.

'You think the two men he allowed in killed him?' asked Sandford.

'We've no evidence. But yes. They disappear inside the Treasury, then no further sign of them.'

'They'd need to have been passed out.'

Quine calculated. 'Then Fowkes's movements that evening need to be looked at. There might be something on CCTV.'

'I can't go there. Not yet,' said Sandford. He saw Quine's frustration. 'I've an update too.' Sandford gave a full account of how he had played Fowkes and Morland-Cross off against each other.

Quine would never have suspected him of such low cunning. 'So that explains Jed's fury.'

'Yes,' agreed Sandford. 'If I'd known this was going to be the consequence—'

'Been and gone now,' said Quine more roughly than he meant.

'I've done what you said, Joe. Jed should now be thinking he's controlling me. Not a position I like much.'

'I understand. Now we have to see where it leads. We've been keeping an eye on him.' Quine described Fowkes's visit to IPRM in Mayfair and the ensuing car chase. 'That means the

MI5 operative may be compromised. It also means MI5 is now more officially involved, like it or not. They take against their people being tailed. Robbie, you've got to bring the security services fully onboard. It's impossible otherwise. Tracking Jed has to be a professional operation.'

Sandford sighed, then caught the eye of an escort. This was going to take longer than he had bargained for. He held up the outspread palms of both hands to indicate ten.

'I can't tell them everything.'

'No. But there's enough on Fowkes after yesterday to justify full-scale surveillance. Whether Fowkes's contacts include Deschevaux, or are just Grainger and Schmidt, we don't know.'

'Where are we on Jed's fantasy?' Sandford did not hide his anxiety.

Quine knew he was bound to ask and, even up until this moment, had been unsure how to answer. He chose his words carefully. 'I've not yet been able to find anything that disproves it. Which in no way means it's not an invention.'

'Just do the facts, Joe.'

'OK. Since we last talked, I've met Mikey Miller and Roisin Osborne. Mikey says there might well have been a Friday evening group at the pub as Fowkes described. He later went elsewhere with a girl. Roisin Osborne also recalls an evening beginning as Fowkes says and that she left when it became a bit "hectic" as she put it. Finally, Coulthard's private bank archive records that a Hungarian girl called Andrea Takacs worked there in 1991. After just a few weeks – three in fact

– she didn't return to work on the Monday morning and left no contact address. She's never been seen again.'

Quine tried not to look too piercingly at Sandford. But even a glance told him the man sitting beside him was near breaking point.

He closed his eyes for several seconds. 'I see.'

'I did ask Mikey Miller about whether there had been any instance of group sex in the way you described. He said it happened once when he wasn't there. It was organized by a friend of his who claimed the girl was a willing part of it. He was extremely angry with him. The friend said you had no part in it and ended up comforting the girl.'

'That's something, isn't it,' said Sandford. 'Prime Minister not part of gang-bang. God, what have we come to.'

'Remember there's no proof whatsoever of Jed's Andrea Takacs accusation,' continued Quine. 'Or that the skeleton has anything to do with her. The next step has to be Budapest. I've a freelance on standby there—'

'Is that wise?' interrupted Sandford.

'His need to know will be extremely restricted. It's the obvious avenue to explore.' Quine saw his reluctance – or was it plain fear? 'Robbie, you and I are the only people with this information. It remains speculative. Without Fowkes's story – a man whose recent actions vastly reduce his credibility – there's no need for anyone else to know. If the remains do turn out to be Andrea Takacs, there is still no evidence of you playing any part in what happened to her.'

'Except Jed's story.'

'Precisely.'

Sandford allowed himself a few seconds to consider. 'OK. Go to Hungary if your freelance finds anything. After that, let's see. My God, I wish I could remember that night.' He buried his head in his hands. 'Or is it better that I don't?'

43

Gazing up from the tarmac three mornings later at the massive curved roof of Budapest airport's Skycourt, Quine thought how much must have changed since Andrea Takacs, hardly out of her teens, had embarked on her adventure to London nearly three decades before. Her own country had barely emerged from the iron grip of the Soviet bloc; a two-and-a-half-hour flight would have transported her to a throbbing hub of western capitalism with all its excesses. He felt a wave of sympathy for her.

He had asked a former colleague, the foreign editor at *The Post*, if he could point to a reliable freelance in Budapest with good research skills. The colleague knew Quine well enough not to ask for details and recommended a stringer, Pete Kovacs, who filed for *The Post* when a story either in Hungary itself or the neighbouring countries needed a body on the ground. At Quine's instruction, Kovacs held up a board at arrivals saying simply 'I'm Pete'. Even though IPRM did not appear to operate in Hungary, he had not forgotten Isla's warning.

He approached the fair-haired, smiling young man holding up the sign and stretched out his hand.

'Pete?'

'Sure, that's me.' He sounded Californian.

'Great. Call me Joe.'

Kovacs looked at his watch. 'One thirty, only ten minutes behind. You can relax.' Kovacs had assured him that afternoon was the right time to make the move and he could do it as a day trip, as long as the target showed. Two and a half hours in the air, allow for an hour's delay, a one-hour time change, twenty minutes through the airport and a one-hour drive. 'Welcome to Hungary,' said Kovacs, 'even if you'll only see how flat most of it is.'

Leaving the short-term car park, Quine cast the occasional surreptitious glance over his shoulder. They headed east, carving through the northern stretches of the great Hungarian plain. 'Cowboy country,' said Kovacs.

'You enjoy westerns?'

'Sure, I learnt my English from Clint Eastwood.'

Quine chuckled, relaxing as flat fields floated by, dotted by the odd tree and low farmhouse, sheep and horses, but disappointingly few cattle.

Kovacs finally broke the silence. 'Thirty minutes to Pusztaszabanya.' Kovacs had located four villages in Hungary beginning with the first four letters identifiable from Coulthard's archive entry. All were within two hours' driving distance from Budapest and he had visited each one. Only in Pusztaszabanya was there evidence of the family Takacs.

'Good.' Quine checked his jacket pockets for his iPhone and a separate mini-recorder.

'School finishes at four p.m.'

'And you've made no approach.'

'No, I only asked at the post office if there was anyone called Takacs in the neighbourhood as a friend wanted to contact them. That's where they told me.'

'Will they be suspicious?'

'Maybe curious. Nothing ever happens in places like this.'

At 3.55 p.m. Kovacs parked his dented Škoda on the main road running through the village. The school was easily identifiable, its main building, resembling a three-storey Dutch barn, the largest in the street. At 4 p.m. excited children burst through the gates, some into the arms of waiting mothers, others old enough to walk home alone. Within a few minutes, they had all vanished, followed at intervals by teachers leaving in ones and twos. Quine assumed that the deputy head would be among the last. They waited.

A dumpy figure came into sight, whitened hair gathered in a straggly ponytail hanging well below the shoulder. She seemed a far cry from the slim young redhead in the photograph. Her walking speed suggested she might be no more than fifty-ish. The right age. Yes, this must be Andrea Takacs. Quine could hardly believe it. The entire story was about to be turned on its head. A triumph of good over evil.

As she exited the school gate, they intercepted her. Kovacs addressed her with the agreed introduction. *'Takacs Kisasszony?'*

She stopped, her face creased in puzzlement. *'Igen?'*

'Van egy látogatóm Angliából, aki szeretne találkozni veled. Beszélsz angol?'

'Yes, I speak some English.' Kovacs nodded to Quine.

'Miss Takacs, my name is Joseph Quine. I have been asked to try to make contact with you by someone who was a friend of yours in London when you were briefly there in 1991. You may remember her. Roisin Osborne. She is still at Coulthard's bank – she now keeps the archives. She is trying to track down everyone still living who ever worked there, even for a very short time, for a company history.'

With each succeeding word he spoke, Quine noticed a cloud of incomprehension gathering in the plump round cheeks and grey eyes of the short woman rooted to the spot opposite him.

'Excuse me, I was never in London,' she said quietly.

Quine's elation gave way to a sinking in the stomach. 'You are not Miss A Takacs? Miss Andrea Takacs?'

The cloud on her face suddenly cleared. 'No, that is – sorry, was – my sister. My younger sister. I am Abigél Takacs.'

'And you were never in London?'

'That is correct.'

'Then I am very sorry about this mistake and to have troubled you. You may remember your sister Andrea was briefly in London. The friend I mentioned would be very grateful to know what happened to her.'

'I do not think so,' said Abigél Takacs, her words and face devoid of any expression.

'I'm sorry,' said Quine. 'I don't understand.'

323

'I do not think any friend of my sister will want to know.'

The buzz of the village seemed to turn to silence. All three heads bowed. Kovacs turned to Quine. 'I think perhaps we should leave Miss Takacs alone and go.'

She suddenly raised her head. 'No!' The word came out burning with anger. 'You follow me.'

She walked briskly along the pavement until they reached the town's modest church, its walls rendered grey and featureless, a short bell tower overlooking low-slung electricity cables. She led them through a wooden gate and around the church. In the foreground were neat rows of headstones; beyond lay the flat, unyielding expanse of the plain. Nowhere could have been more quiet or more distant from London.

She stopped by a headstone rising from the tip of a grave covered with white gravel and marble edging. A small oval frame showed the photograph of a pretty, smiling teenage girl with waves of deep red hair. Below was written:

*

ANDREA LILIANA TAKACS
SZÜLETETT 1971. MÁJUS 20-ÁN
MEGHALT 1992. JANUÁR 1

*

Beneath was a short inscription. 'I am so sorry, Miss Takacs,' said Quine. 'Are you able to tell me what this says?'

She stood with tears in her eyes, staring into the fields. 'It says, "In loving memory, a life cruelly cut short."' She took a handkerchief from a pocket, wiped her eyes and turned to face him. 'She was twenty years and seven months old.'

'I'm so sorry. Could you tell me what happened to her?' There was no reply. 'I think her friend *would* wish to know. They were very fond of each other.'

'There is a bench.' She walked towards it; Quine gestured to Kovacs to hang back. They sat while she prepared herself. Quine needed the fullest account possible and kept silent. For several seconds, while she stayed rigid, he pleaded with whatever spirit inhabited this place that she would go through with it.

'When Andrea arrived home,' she finally began, 'it took her some weeks to tell me. I wanted her to go to the police here. She said there was no point. Nothing would ever be done. London was far away. She would not tell our mother. And then it was too late.'

'Too late?'

'Of course.' She nodded her head in the direction of the gravestone. 'And why should I trouble my mother with it then?'

'Have you told others what happened?'

'Later I went to the police myself. They said there was nothing they could do. No evidence, no witnesses, just – what do they call it in English...'

'Hearsay?'

'Yes, that's right. *Hallomás*. If your friend knows anything about Andrea's time in London, maybe she can tell the police there.'

'I will ask her,' said Quine. He tried to imagine a circumstance in which he could ever reveal what was to come to Roisin Osborne.

'Good. Then I shall speak.' She looked away from him, as if finding some distant presence to address. 'Andrea was my only sister. We had no brothers. She was pretty – much more than me. She was curious about the world. When the chance came for people like us to travel, she wanted it. The year before she went to an island in Greece with a friend. She loved it. Above all, she wanted to go to London. The most glamorous city. She had a schoolfriend who had been there. She told her it was easy – there were many places with noticeboards with jobs and flats. Two weeks after she arrived we had a postcard. It was all "great", she wrote. She had a job in a bank and was living in a youth hostel. That was all we heard until the phone call.'

She fell silent, looking towards the sky, holding back tears. 'Phone call?' he prompted gently.

'Yes. She said, "I am at Budapest airport. Can you come?" She sounded scared. My father died the year before but we kept his car. My mother had gone by bus to visit a friend. I was still learning to drive but I took the car on my own. I drove as fast as I could. She was sitting on her suitcase. She did not smile. I knew there was something bad from the phone call. She managed to stand and walked to the

326

car. She wouldn't tell me what happened. We arrived home, my mother was angry. She did not know where I was. We fed Andrea and put her to bed. I said to my mother that she seemed to have caught some illness. Over the next few days, she was eating better, getting up, but she was quiet, staring out of windows, not wanting to do anything. Then one day, she came into my room and sat on my bed. "My life is over," she said.'

Abigél Takacs stopped, turning her head away from Quine.

After a few seconds he spoke. 'There's no hurry.' This time he was not lying. In one sense, he already had enough. Andrea Takacs had left London alive, not dead. The headless skeleton with the severed hand was not her, but another unfortunate young woman.

'I wish to say everything.' She swivelled, now looking him straight in the eye. 'She told me the bank she worked in was good. She made friends with a girl from Ireland called Roisin. They went out for drinks. She and Roisin were talking to a boy called Robbie. She said he was nice. He was with his flatmate – he was called something like "Jet". He was quieter, not handsome. It was getting quite late and Roisin said she would go home. This Robbie invited everyone to his flat for a last drink. She thought, why not? They got a taxi and went across the river. They reached the flat, she didn't know where, but not too far. She was not used to drinking too much and asked for something like lemonade. The other boy went to the kitchen to bring drinks. She and Robbie kissed. She drank some lemonade and was a little sleepy. The other boy said he was going to bed and left. Then Robbie took her into his bedroom. She said she was so sleepy, a little faint, the room was going in and out of focus.'

She breathed deeply; Quine prepared himself for the worst.

'The next thing she remembered,' continued Abigél, 'she was lying on the back seat of a car. A driver and a second man were in the front. There was pain between her legs and around her parts. She felt down. It was wet. She did not dare say anything. One of the men looked round. "OK, Andrea," he said, "we're going to look after you. Do everything I say and it will be fine."'

Quine hesitated to interrupt but two questions shrieked. He might not have another chance. 'Can I ask you something?'

She nodded.

'Did your sister know why she felt so faint and passed out?'

'Pass out?'

'Yes, it sounds as if she was unconscious.'

'No, she said she had not drunk too much. I asked about drugs. She said no. Later I thought it myself. Maybe something was in her drink.'

'Did she say whether the man in the car spoke with an accent?'

Abigél Takacs hesitated, Quine's heart missed a beat.

'She said he was not English. She thought he was American.'

'I'm sorry, I interrupted.'

'It is OK. I will continue. Andrea said these two men took her to a place – she did not know where. She was allowed to rest, have a shower, eat. The American told her it was better she did not stay in London and went home. They had bought her a ticket to fly to Budapest the next day. One of them took her to get her things from the youth hostel. He said she must leave her purse behind with the other man. Andrea said she was frightened of them. If she did not do what they said, she was even thinking they might kill her. She collected her things, put them in her rucksack, and went back with the American to the flat.

'The next day they took her to London airport. The American went with her all the way to check-in and baggage search. When she reached the front of the queue, he told her not to tell anyone about what happened. She said they watched her until she got on the plane. As she went through passport control, she turned and could still see him watching.'

Abigél rose and headed back towards the grave. Quine drew alongside her, both silent, looking at the pretty girl in the photograph.

'That was not the end of it,' he said.

'No.' She closed her eyes. 'I do not know whether to tell you this part of it.' She walked back towards the gate leading to the next-door field and leant on it. Quine found himself dropping to his knees beside the headstone. He examined every feature of the girl in the photograph, clasped his hands together and prayed. Hearing footsteps, he stood.

'She told me she was sure she was pregnant. She was crying. She said, "My life is over." We lived in a small Catholic village in a traditional, God-fearing part of our country. I tried to encourage her. There would be no shame in having the baby after what had happened. If she did not want to, I said I was sure we could go to Budapest and find the right doctor. I needed to help her. I tried to keep discussing the possibilities with her but she would just go silent.

'On New Year's Eve, my mother, Andrea and I joined our village in the church hall to celebrate our Lord and the coming year. She was trying to look happy for us. In the early morning I heard footsteps in the house and a door open and close. I thought nothing of it, my mother was often up. It was a cold, sunny morning. I looked out of my bedroom window at our small garden and the cherry tree in the middle. I saw something terrible. I rushed down. A rope was wound around her neck and tied to a branch. She was hanging from that tree. I thought again and again of those words. "My life is over."'

Quine, himself now trying to hold back a tear, wondered if he should place a comforting arm round her. He sensed not. There was a residual toughness of spirit in Abigél Takacs that might not welcome it.

'It broke my mother. Andrea spoke just to me. I sometimes thought I should tell her.'

'You did the right thing,' said Quine, 'there is nothing more anyone can do. I am sorry. I am so very sorry for what my country did to your sister and your family.'

'I will go to my home now. You may go too.' She looked up into his face and cupped one of his hands between her own. 'It is good we have spoken. Please tell her friend.'

Watching her disappear behind the church, Quine remembered something important. He removed his phone from his

330

chest pocket, leant down and took a sequence of photographs of Andrea Takacs's grave and headstone. He had journeyed here to solve a mystery. Instead, it had become darker and more impenetrable than ever.

44

Quine arrived back at the flat around 10 p.m. Sophie and Isla were both home. After quick hugs he said, 'Before anything else, I've got to send an email.'

*

JONATHAN MOORE
To: paulabcdreynolds@gmail.com
Re: trip

Hi Paul

Need to talk without delay. Not unhelpful developments. Now have jogging shoes and shorts if easier!

Cheers
Jonathan

*

He looked up. Sophie was standing over him. 'Drink, Dad?'

He brightened. 'Yes, please.' She turned to Isla.

'Me too, please.'

'Do you two need to talk?'

'Yes, but let's have some downtime first.'

'I'm amazed…' began Quine as his daughter reappeared, carrying a tray laden with glasses and snacks. 'I'll start that again. I really admire how you manage not to ask us what's going on.'

Sophie smiled. 'I'm used to it. That's the deal. It would drive us both mad any other way. Not to mention the worry.'

'Wouldn't you like to know? I didn't even tell you where I was flying to this morning.'

'It's up to you, not me. You can tell me what you want.'

'Sometimes I do just that,' said Isla. 'It's usually when I feel a moral choice. And I put it as a hypothetical question, changing the details.'

'And you find that helpful?' said Quine.

'Yes, it can be very helpful.'

'What about you, darling?' he said, turning to Sophie. 'Isn't that frustrating?'

'No. Why? It would be like me discussing every new book that comes my way. But like Isla, sometimes there's a dilemma that makes the conversation interesting for both of us.'

'It would never work for me,' said Quine.

'Of course not,' said Sophie. 'You're a journalist. Your curiosity's insatiable. Gossip and rumour's the food of life. You'd be a hopeless spy and an even more hopeless partner of one.'

'I'll drink to that,' he said. 'By the way, since you didn't ask, I've been to Budapest and back in search of a missing person.'

Sophie lowered her eyes. 'Dad, there is no God-given kudos in being the contrarian. In fact, one might even argue its main effect has been to make you broke.' She smiled sweetly. 'Now, I have work left to do.'

*

'This is a world of half-truths,' Quine began as Sophie left the room.

'Tell me something new.'

'I will.' He described in every detail the encounter with Abigél Takacs. 'So Robin Sandford is off one hook,' he concluded.

'He didn't actually kill Andrea Takacs,' said Isla.

'Not directly. Nobody killed Andrea Takacs.'

'Except herself. It still leaves open the question of what he *did* do to her. Which, from his sister's account, sounds like rape.'

'Maybe. Unless it was someone else—'

'Come on, Joe, Andrea told her sister she went with Sandford into his bedroom.'

'Am I supposed to tell Sandford that?' asked Quine despairingly.

'That's your call. My job is different. Andrea Takacs is long buried in Hungary. As the Hungarian police told her, her sister's only a hearsay witness. Her evidence, particularly on something as long ago as this, is pretty much worthless.

Legally, I mean. Jed Fowkes is the only eyewitness. And he is now caught lying about the identity of the skeleton—'

'He may not think he's lying, he could have been misled, either deliberately or not.'

'Perhaps. The point is it's hard to imagine a scenario where this ever becomes a cold case of rape that turns hot and ends up in court.'

'So, back to my question. What do I tell Sandford?'

Isla shrugged, offering no further answer. A ping sounded as an email dropped into the Jonathan Moore inbox. It was brief.

*

PAUL REYNOLDS
To: jonathan1234reynolds@gmail.com
Re: update

Repeat in the morning.

P

*

'Out on the streets early again,' said Quine, closing the laptop. He looked longingly at his glass. 'Better take it easy.'

'All of this leaves a load of questions,' said Isla, as if there'd been no interruption. 'The most obvious being who the skeleton with the severed hand and missing head is.'

'Any ideas?'

She huffed. 'I might need a minute on that. Possibly a year. Is Fowkes confusing this with another similar incident? Or using the chance discovery of a skeleton to scare Sandford? Or is there a totally different explanation?'

'You tell me.'

'At least we know Fowkes is not flying solo. That creates three possibilities. One, he is in control and the one with the plan, the others are back-up. Two, they are equal collaborators. Three, those others are using him.'

'Keep going, I'm tired.'

'What is Fowkes trying to achieve? Power? Some kind of vengeance? Money?'

'Unlikely with him. He's never shown any interest.'

'Ideology?'

'Which goes with power. He assumed Morland-Cross would be his front man. But he turned out to be malleable in a way he never expected.' Quine sighed. 'If only we knew what was said in those conversations between Fowkes and Morland-Cross.'

'We would if Sandford had allowed my organization in from the outset and bugged them,' said Isla.

'Whatever it was made Jed think M-C needed to be killed.'

'Not necessarily. It may just have been an attempt to frighten him and bring him back on board. But it went wrong. Or he resisted. So they set up the self-asphyxiation.'

'Skilled work,' said Quine.

'Yes, but doable by two strong professionals who know how not to leave bruises. You don't need much gear. Ligature, plastic bag and something to stuff in his mouth.'

'God, what a world.'

'Finally,' said Isla, 'there are the two most dangerous scenarios of all.'

'It gets worse?'

'The first we mentioned before. Fowkes is collaborating with foreign governments or agencies to damage this country.'

'Or?'

'We're facing some kind of attempted coup. Whether internal or external. But it feels different. You don't need to depose a leader, you just need to control his mind and actions.'

'You're scaring me, Isla.'

'But we're in the game,' she said, ignoring him. 'At all costs, Fowkes mustn't know the skeleton's not Andrea. We have to see how far he wants to go.'

*

Sandford was only mildly cheered by Quine's appearance at Archbishop's Park in brand-new jogging gear. He suspected the email had been worded to reassure him; if so, it had not worked. He dreaded the report back from Hungary. The chances of disproving Fowkes's story seemed as remote as ever – it would dog him for the rest of his life.

He stopped at the gate, the security detail hanging behind as usual. 'Good morning, Joe, ready to go?'

'Not sure I can run and talk at the same time.'

'We'll do half a circuit.'

They stopped at a different bench, less discreet. Quine had a sense of Sandford tiring of the security, desperate to recapture his freedom. With a shadow like this hanging over him, the oppression must be stifling.

'Tell me about Budapest.'

Quine told the full story without interruption. 'Thanks,' Sandford said. 'So I didn't kill this poor girl.' He spoke bitterly. 'But I raped her and made her pregnant. Is that what you're saying?'

'Did you?' asked Quine sharply.

He turned on him fiercely. 'For Christ's sake, what do you think I am?' Quine stayed silent. 'Sorry, you're right, it's a question I have to address. For my own sake if no one else's. I have to find another explanation.' He paused. 'There has to be one.'

'Have you spoken to the Cabinet Secretary about Fowkes's covert visit to the IPRM office and his presence during the car chase that followed?'

'Yes.'

'Did you ask him to bring in MI5 officially?'

Sandford shifted uncomfortably. 'No, I still thought it best to wait till you were back.'

'There's enough to go on. There'll be no issue about the Home Secretary issuing a warrant for electronic surveillance.'

'He'll enjoy that,' said Sandford sourly. 'He might jump in his chair but he was always an enemy of M-C and he loathes Fowkes.'

There was one more button Quine had wondered whether or not to push. It was as much out of curiosity as anything else that he did.

'Robbie, shouldn't you now tell the security service, perhaps even the police, about Jed's allegation? He's been shown to have lied. Anything else he claims will also be assumed to be a lie. Whatever happened to Andrea in the flat will never be more than Jed's story. Andrea's sister's story will stay in Hungary and never constitute legal evidence. You're off the Andrea hook.'

Sandford seemed suddenly agitated. 'No, I can't. Ever.' He leant forward and stared blankly at a clump of trees. 'Anyway you're wrong. How can I ever be off that hook?'

45

'I've been sent back in,' said Isla.

'What!' Quine exclaimed. 'Or, rather, where?'

'My desk at the Treasury.'

'That's crazy.'

'Actually, the way my boss worked it out, it made sense.'

Isla described how she and her head of desk, whom she named as 'James', had spent the morning analysing every angle. The overriding problem he identified was that Fowkes would now be on his guard. They needed him to make a big enough error to nail him. By this he meant sufficient to have him expelled from the Treasury as a security risk and discredited. The latter was the priority. Criminal charges could come later if they were warranted.

James interrogated her about the exchange of glances with Fowkes in the Mayfair street of IPRM's head office.

'Did he definitely ID you?'

'He appeared to catch my eye.'

'But you were parked some way down the street.'

'Yes, seventy-five metres or so. Maybe more.'

From this James concluded that there was only one way to relax Fowkes. 'You see, it's no good replacing you with someone else. Fowkes will smell a very large rat. So we have to assume,' he told Isla, 'that while Fowkes might have believed he saw you in the car, he has no concrete evidence. You yourself are the best person to reassure him. You need to be in regular contact with him. Smile at him. Say hello when you have the chance. Never follow him. Always be in your seat when he returns. He'll begin to doubt himself. Because if you really were tracking him, you'd have to stay out of his sight for ever more. Wouldn't you? So what we need, before it's too late, is to return you to the lion's den. Get you back in your Treasury seat. Right now. And then, however long it takes, when the moment comes – you'll sense it – then you move. Then you follow. Then he must *not* see you.'

'So how was it?' asked Quine.

'Squeaky,' Isla replied. 'And unreal. As if I was on a film set.' She saw him notice the bandage on her right wrist. 'I thought it might help. Make it seem I'd had some kind of injury. Had to take a few hours off. The woman who sits beside me spotted it. "Fell off my bike," I whispered.'

'Smart.' Quine was coming to enjoy each new Isla ruse.

'You always need a story. You know that. Even if it's as weak and cobbled together as this one.'

'And Fowkes?'

'Showed at five. God knows what he'd been doing. But at least I was there. He flicked a glance in my direction just

341

as he was opening his office door. His expression was utter mystification.'

'And you?'

'I saw him come in – I'm sure he didn't spot me at that point – and glued my face to my screen. At the opportune moment, I looked up, made it seem I'd just happened to catch his eye and gave him a sweet smile. He returned it with a twitch of the mouth.'

'The other Spad?'

'You mean Thomasina?' He nodded. 'I assume she's out.'

'Mourning the man she'd thought would make her a star,' said Quine.

'She was using him,' said Isla. 'Five thirty,' she continued, 'he went next door to see the new Chancellor. The bugs went in last night. It must have been their first meeting since Morland-Cross's death. Want to listen?'

'Am I allowed?' he asked.

She laughed. 'Don't ask.'

She inserted a stick into her computer, allowed a few seconds, clicked on an icon and upped the volume.

*

JED FOWKES: Welcome, Chancellor.
MARGARET LASCELLES: Thank you, Jed.

*

The opening words were followed by rustling and footsteps, indicating her rising to shake his hand and both sitting down at a meeting table.

*

ML: Hardly the circumstances anyone might have wanted. I was enjoying my role as Leader of the House but I felt I couldn't refuse the Prime Minister.

JF: I'm glad you didn't. However terrible it all is.

ML: Jed, I'm greatly hoping that you'll stay on as my special adviser.

(A short silence.)

JF: I don't know, Margaret. It feels raw right now.

ML: I understand. It doesn't have to be permanent. Perhaps if you could tide me over for the next three months at least. Then see how you feel.

JF: Who else are you thinking of bringing in?

ML: No one. No one else knows this place as well as you. And how to work the civil servants.

JF: In broad terms, how do you see it panning out?

ML: I need a minimum three months' lead-in time. I'll follow your advice and the policies you wish to implement.

JF: That's very generous.

ML: It's not generosity. It's practicality. And it assumes that you would want to bring about the radical changes that you and M-C – and others, including me, of course – always spoke of.

(A longer silence.)

JF: Does the Prime Minister understand this?

ML: My reading is that he wants it.

JF: He didn't always.

ML: Indeed. M-C's death has had a huge impact. He feels he owes this to him. And, I suspect, it has reminded him of what he entered politics to achieve. That we weren't doing this just to compromise once we had power.

JF: Yes. I'm often sad about the trimming and tacking.

ML: Not now. The future is ours to take. Only a week to go to the Royal Speech. The Prime Minister told me he wants to work hand-in-glove with you personally to finalize it. He intends it to be our blueprint for the next four years.

JF: He said that?

ML: He was most emphatic about it.

JF *(after a long pause)*:

Margaret, Chancellor, I am delighted to accept your offer.

*

'Sandford's laying a trap,' Quine said. 'I don't know what it is. He's keeping it close. Not a word to me.' He is also playing one hell of a risky game, he thought to himself. He had better be able to control its ending. 'What happened then?'

'I heard a movement of chairs, guessed the conversation was over and I started packing up my stuff. I wanted him to see me leave as he was walking back to his office. To know I wasn't waiting for him. I couldn't risk searching for any expression on his face. I left without a single glance behind.'

'Are you OK?'

'None of us are machines. I was twitchy. Waiting for the tap on the shoulder. Not a big deal.'

'You don't need to do this.'

'I do. It's what we're paid to do.' She looked at the stick. 'They've got all this back at Thames House now. That's not what I'm there for any more. I'm just the honeypot.' She breathed deeply. 'Oh, one more thing. There's someone you should try to see. He's more clued up than anyone on those unholy alliances you mentioned.' She passed him a card with a name and phone number.

'He never talks to journalists,' said Quine. 'I've tried a few times. Always turned me down.'

'Wrong,' she replied. 'He never talks to *political* journalists. He occasionally talks to a certain type of security correspondent. You know, the ones who sniff MI5's bum and print what they're told. But you're neither now. You're a historian exploring a changing world three decades back. He might just bite.'

Quine's phone rang. An unrecognized number. 'Hello.'

'Is that Mr Q?'

'Mrs T, how nice to hear from you. I'm so sorry, my phone didn't recognize the number.'

'Yes. Well, I'm phoning from a neighbour.'

'Oh?'

'I thought it might be safer.'

Quine felt a sudden fear. 'Has something happened?'

'Nothing to worry about. No one's hurt or anything.'

'Do go on.'

She hesitated. Unlike her, he thought. 'There's something

345

I think you should know. There was a break-in at the house when I was out shopping this afternoon.'

Oh no, thought Quine, surely not. 'I'm so sorry,' he said as calmly as he could, 'that's horrible. Very frightening for you to come back and discover it.' He held his tongue. He must allow her to speak and not show alarm.

'Well, it was a bit of shock at first, but I'm all right now. I just wanted you to know. And also to say,' he sensed her putting her lips next to the mouthpiece, 'everything's all right. If you see what I mean,' she whispered. 'I thought better to use another phone. Just in case.'

'That's extremely clever of you, Mrs T.' Relief surged through him. 'Yes, do be careful on your own phone. I'll make sure the right people check it's not been tampered with.'

'I'd be most grateful.'

'No, it's me who should be grateful. Did they take anything else?'

She chuckled. 'There's nothing of any value. Mind you, the place is all topsy-turvy and I'm afraid your room got quite a going-over. We'll be needing some new floorboards there—'

'Then I must refund you for those,' interrupted Quine. 'And any other damage.'

'Mr Q, don't even think of it!'

'We'll see about that. You're a wonder, Mrs T. I'm so grateful to you and very much hope to see you again very soon.'

*

Two hundred and seventy miles away, Mrs Trelight, bursting with pride, returned to her house and paid another visit to the freezer chest. She lifted the lid, pushed several items to one side and pulled out a package from the bottom. On the freezer bag, written in heavy blue ink, were the words 'PORK BELLY'. Within were several layers of wrapping – waterproof plastic, bubble wrap, white masking tape and more waterproof plastic. At the heart lay six brown files. She put the pack back at the bottom and above them a large frozen package marked 'PIG, SHOULDER, LEG, CHOPS, KIDNEYS'. Above that she placed further small packs of frozen produce. The burglar had not even opened the freezer lid.

She must keep those chops for when Mr Q was next passing by.

*

Sandford arrived home at 11 p.m., having hosted a Number 10 dinner for the American ambassador, most of which he spent listening to the ambassador's wife. It had been tedious but not arduous, allowing his thoughts to wander. These days they only seemed to land in unpleasant destinations.

In his box was his bedtime reading, including a transcript of the day's Treasury intercepts. He had argued with the Cabinet Secretary over access to the raw intelligence, finally resorting to history.

'It has always been the prerogative of a Prime Minister to call for this, Kevin. You may remember the precedent established by Winston Churchill. Particularly with regard to Ultra.'

'Yes, Prime Minister.'

'I am capable of understanding and interpreting this material in the case of Jed Fowkes. I've known him a lot longer than anyone around here.'

'Yes, Prime Minister,' conceded the normally genial Sir Kevin Long.

As it turned out, rather than anything said by Fowkes, he was most drawn to Margaret Lascelles's remark about him.

*

ML: It has reminded him of what he entered politics to achieve. That we weren't doing this just to compromise once we had power.

*

Well, she was never going to survive his next reshuffle anyway. As for Jed, his ambition was frightening. His plot seemed to be unfolding smoothly, scene by scene, whereas he still had no clear resolution in sight.

Five days, excluding the weekend, to the Royal Speech. He had ordered all previous drafts to be excised, citing the death of Morland-Cross as his reason. He recalled Quine's words about 'endplay'. Was the speech part of it? Or just a step in the plan? He calculated the timing. Back him against a tight deadline or allow him leeway? It had to be now. Let's see what you've got, Jed.

It was just after midnight. He went into the bedroom and collapsed on his side of the bed, looking briefly at Carol. There was no acknowledgement or response. Silence filled the room. She turned a page of her book; he always asked her what she was reading. Not tonight.

'We have to move on, Carol,' he finally said. Her eyes stayed glued to the page. 'I'm sorry for my part in the argument we had. That wasn't the real us.'

'Your *part*?'

'Yes.'

'You're saying *I* had a part in it?'

'It's a private email.'

'Which I set up for you.'

'I said before. I'm grateful to you.'

'I felt you were threatening me.'

'I didn't mean to.'

'So that's all right then. You didn't mean to.'

He breathed deeply, went into the bathroom and closed the door behind him.

46

Quine rang the bell of a handsome block of mansion flats just by Westminster's Roman Catholic cathedral. The door buzzed. He entered and gave his name and that of Sir David Vaughn. The porter phoned an internal number, received approval and directed him to the lift.

Vaughn, a career MI5 officer who had retired as Director-General in 2007, was notoriously discreet. Quine knew of several journalists who had asked for off-the-record meetings, both during and after his tenure, and been rebuffed, some more courteously than others. One, the *Guardian* security correspondent, presumably not of the right sort, had managed to distract the porter and ride the elevator to the sixth floor to ring the bell of the flat itself. He had returned to his office a nervous wreck with a clearer understanding of the menace a former spymaster could convey.

Vaughn was waiting, front door of the flat open. 'Mr Quine.'

'Yes, Sir David.'

'Come in,' said Vaughn, his accent mildly Lancastrian.

'We'll have coffee in the kitchen. My wife is away rehearsing this morning.' He paused. 'A Prokofiev quartet. If you like that sort of thing.'

Quine inspected him, trying to measure the reality against the photographs and occasional televised appearances in front of parliamentary committees. He was thick-set if slightly stooped, dark hair only beginning to grey at the edges, a sturdy man, at heart still the Manchester Grammar schoolboy who had got into Balliol and been talent-spotted by an MI5-connected don. A man a million miles away from the public schoolboys who had once disgraced British intelligence.

'I don't,' said Quine.

'Me neither.' The Lancastrian accent strengthened. Quine felt he had passed a test. With careful deliberation Vaughn put on the kettle, measured two tablespoons of coffee and dropped them into a cafetière. Quine suspected he was never a man to appear in a rush.

'I tend to stop at the end of the nineteenth century.'

'Yes, when the tunes ran out,' said Vaughn.

Vaughn seemed uninterested in further small talk. He finished making coffee with the same even deliberation; all in marked contrast to Quine's impatience.

'We'll go into the sitting room. If you spill a drop on her carpet, you're a dead man.' A bushy eyebrow twitched.

The drawing room displayed a softness in contrast to the man facing Quine. Pale pink fabrics, the perfume of fresh flowers, a Persian cat on the window sill.

'Right, Mr Quine, why are you here?'

'Firstly, I appreciate you seeing me.'

'We'll see about that. But I'll say this for you. Your newspaper never posted scouts to watch me come and go. And you personally understood the word "No". Unlike others.' A quick glare caused Quine to ponder if any other journalists had been thrown down the stairs. 'You say you're now a historian.'

'I'm researching a book on the decade from the mid-1980s to mid-1990s. I'm thinking of calling it "Unholy Alliances".'

'Not a bad title.'

'Thank you.'

'There's something I'd like to say to you on my own behalf, Mr Quine.' He paused. Quine waited. He had not expected anything but answers to his questions. 'I was sorry for what happened in your case against Deschevaux. In retrospect, I wish I'd been able to agree to your request for a meeting while you were researching him.'

'I didn't expect it.'

'No, you're not on the list.'

'List?'

'Yes. The approved list. Don't ask me to tell you who's on it.'

'Of course. Yes, I'd like to have discussed it with you.'

'I couldn't have proved your case for you or given you documented evidence, but I might have warned you never to trust Greeks bearing gifts from that man.'

'Yes,' said Quine ruefully. 'But I know my source was genuine. Until they got at him.'

'That was your failure of the imagination, Mr Quine. So many things are. 9/11. What followed the Iraq War. History is full of them.' Vaughn stopped, turned his head and stared out of the window, apparently captivated by the brick walls of Westminster Cathedral. A picture, Quine reflected, that he must see every day.

'In my history,' said Quine, 'I'd like one chapter to revisit the origins of International Personnel and Resource Management.'

'Would you?' Vaughn chuckled. 'Unholy alliances indeed.'

'Can you tell me more?'

'Tell me what you know first,' he said firmly.

'It began with three men. Dieter Schmidt, an East German who came to the German embassy in London in late 1987 and stayed on in the UK. Lyle Grainger, an American who worked in the US embassy in Grosvenor Square in the late eighties and early nineties and also stayed in the UK. And Quentin Deschevaux who joined very soon after the company was set up. What I don't know is who those three men were. Their origins, their histories. It didn't seem to matter for my newspaper pieces because I had enough for the specific allegation of the massacre. Until my source reneged.'

Vaughn sighed. 'I'm afraid once that happened, Mr Quine, you could never win. However "unholy" these three men might have been.'

Quine hid his excitement. He had hit a nerve. 'Can you expand on that? Who they really were.'

'You mean "Who they are?" They're still there. As I understand it. In the shadows of course.'

'Yes.'

Vaughn sipped his coffee. Quine held back. 'Why don't you first try to expand on it yourself?' Vaughn said. 'You have clues.'

Quine frowned. 'Right,' he said, 'let me try with Schmidt. Unholy. German intelligence?'

'Good,' said Vaughn. 'Which side of the Wall?'

'Unholiest is east. Stasi.'

'Correct. You've done enough for me to fill in some gaps. Dieter Schmidt rose to be a Stasi colonel, initially in East Berlin, then posted to Leipzig. He was stationed at the London embassy – East and West Germany were both represented there. He arrived in late 1987. From London he watched the Berlin Wall fall in 1989. He negotiated his way through the new Germany and left the embassy in 1990. Schmidt was a character of interest to us.

'I'll give you something else. A younger woman, Anneliese Bluthner, joined him in London in early 1989. We were unsure of her rank, her post was described as secretarial. Given her apparent closeness to Schmidt, we were sure she was Stasi too.'

'Do you know what happened to her?'

'No. After Germany was reunified, Stasi boys and girls went off here, there and everywhere. Their day was over. We had no need to waste resources monitoring them.'

'What about Schmidt?'

'With the help of his new colleagues from the BND—'

'West German intelligence—'

'Yes. They supported his application for British residency. Apparently he was helpful to them. Maybe they just liked him. Didn't want to send him home to face the music. We had no problem.'

'Fascinating,' said Quine. 'Thank you.'

'Back to you now.'

'Lyle Grainger,' said Quine. 'An unholy bedfellow of Schmidt. Once based in the American embassy in London. So CIA.'

'Correct again. It's surprising sometimes what you can work out when you put your brain and memory to work. Lyle Grainger was CIA with London station. To some extent like Schmidt, he was part of a changing world. From '88 to '92 his nation's President was a former head of the CIA.'

'George Bush,' said Quine.

'Yes.'

'Then Clinton takes over.'

'Precisely,' said Vaughn. 'Old hands like Grainger, perhaps with old methods, were no longer flavour of the month. He left the Agency after Clinton's election and stayed in the UK. I suspect he was already making plans with Schmidt. It was a small world in turbulent times. Ripe for those "unholy alliances" you're writing about.'

'And then Deschevaux,' said Quine. 'I've nothing to go on.'

'I'll give you a clue. I'm not playing games, Mr Quine. It's cleaner if you get to base one without me holding your hand. The Berlin Wall fell in November 1989. Give me another world-changing series of events around then and the months after.'

It did not take Quine long. 'South Africa. De Klerk nego-tiating with the ANC. Mandela released early 1990. End of apartheid.'

'Getting there. Put it together again.'

'Unholy.' He thought. 'God I'm slow sometimes,' he said suddenly, 'Deschevaux was BOSS.'

'Third time correct. Not bad. The man we know as Quentin

Deschevaux was born 1956 in South Africa. Birth name Quintin – spelt with two "i"s – de Chavonnes. In 1978, he joined BOSS, Bureau of State Security. When BOSS was renamed NIS – National Intelligence Service – after an internal scandal in 1980 de Chavonnes stayed on. Stationed South African embassy in London 1989. February 1990, Nelson Mandela is released. The ban is lifted on the ANC, the new South Africa is born. Chavonnes doesn't like it. He leaves the embassy. Goes to ground and resurfaces with the amended name Quentin Deschevaux in 1992.'

'And together they start International Personnel and Resource Management,' said Quine.

'Yes. The unholiest of all your alliances.' Vaughn drained his coffee. 'But, as you say, now a matter of historical interest.'

'Not entirely.'

'You mean you have more?' said Vaughn raising his eyebrows and displaying surprise. Quine assumed it was feigned.

'Evidence has come my way that a senior Treasury adviser called Jed Fowkes may have a present relationship with Schmidt and Grainger – perhaps Deschevaux too.'

Vaughn, with the faintest of smiles, slowly shook his head. 'You're trespassing onto contemporary ground. I can be of no assistance.'

'Perhaps I could ask you a purely historical question?'

'You may try.'

'Does this relationship have its origins during the period of global change that we've been discussing?'

Vaughn rose from his chair. 'Mr Quine, if you are to be a historian, you must study history. What a subject writes himself is a source. Often an entirely open one. And some-times, after the decades pass, you can find new meanings in the subject's words. The young Fowkes once wrote – for publication – the story of a visit he made to East Germany in the summer vacation of 1987. I suggest you visit the Student Union library in Oxford and comb through back copies of *Cherwell* magazine for that year. If you have any specific further questions arising from this research, I may consider answering them.'

'I'm very grateful to you, Sir David.'

'As I said, I was sorry you failed. It was a good try.'

'I don't consider it over yet,' said Quine.

Vaughn led him out of the sitting room, collected his coat from a hook and handed it to him. 'We've never talked.'

'Of course.'

Quine stretched out his hand. Slowly, Vaughn shook it. 'Good luck.'

'Thank you, Sir David.' As he spoke the words, Vaughn was already shuffling back to the sitting room. 'Thank you very much,' repeated Quine, now to thin air, as he closed the front door of the flat behind him.

Its click triggered a flashback to the fears Isla had felt. *Honeypot. Tap on the shoulder.* And the burglary at The Waves. Suddenly distrusting the lift, Quine raced down the stairs with Vaughn's words ringing in his ears, needing to note them all down immediately. For the benefit of others, if not himself. The unholy alliance of Schmidt, Grainger and Deschevaux had emerged from a previous world and its lethal spy games played out between nations and ideologies. Thirty years on, it had adapted itself to a new world of private armies, oligarchs and kleptocrats, where hiring a killer was as easy as renting a car. Stepping out into Ashley Gardens, there was the perfect refuge in sight. Quine headed towards Westminster Cathedral, trusting in the Virgin Mary to keep watch over him.

47

'Jed Fowkes has gone quiet,' said Isla. 'No reappearance by Thomasina so he's on his own in the office. And after that first conversation with his new boss, there's been no contact.'

'From what you can hear, what's he actually doing?'

'God knows. Writing Treasury input into the Royal Speech presumably.'

'That shouldn't take long. A thousand words max.' Quine grimaced. 'Jed's small page of history.'

He and Isla had fallen into a regular evening debrief. He knew he couldn't stay in her and Sophie's flat for ever and felt a mounting regret that he had never spent enough time with his daughter. At least events had created a fondness for the person she had vowed to spend her life with. He now saw that he had become too consumed by work and his pursuit of Deschevaux to appreciate the life that lay beyond his obsessions.

'However...' Isla continued.

'Yes...'

'It was around eleven-ish. I saw his door edging open and thought, why not. I jumped up and headed towards the stairs in the direction of the canteen. It was a sixth sense.'

'And he followed…'

'He joined me in the queue. "Oh, hi," I smiled. "Hi," he said. It was like finding himself beside me was a total surprise.'

'Which was good?' mused Quine.

'Of course. If he was sure it had been me in the car with you, what would be the point? He offered to buy me a coffee, said we should have it in the canteen. I made it sound like I was worried about taking time out, and he said, "It's not Amazon here, you know." I quite liked him for that.'

'What did you talk about?'

'He asked me about the DTI. I gave him some flim-flam about what I did and how it all seemed a bit humdrum compared with the Treasury. "The last few days here haven't exactly been typical," he said. "Oh, I didn't mean it like that," I said. I tried to sound embarrassed. "It's OK," he said. For the first time, I felt a twinge of sympathy from him.' She paused. 'I began to hope he was seeing me as just another second-rater from an inferior department.'

'And then?'

'That was pretty much it. He obviously wanted to get away. I'd succeeded in boring him. And he knew I wasn't available. It's possible I'm off his radar.'

'But not certain?'

'No.' She rose to look out of the window, following the lengthening shadows thrown by the evening sun. 'Certainty. The privilege of the deluded.' She swung round. 'And you?'

'I met an interesting man today.' Quine briefed her on his conversation with Vaughn. 'I wrote it up straightaway in Westminster Cathedral. Reckoned the only surveillance there would be the angels.' He stooped to fetch a pad of A4 from his case, stripped off a few pages and handed them to Isla. 'Put them somewhere safe.'

He outlined the different career paths that ended with Grainger, Schmidt and the reinvented Deschevaux converging at International Personnel and Resource Management.

'And now they've added two front men for today's new markets,' said Isla. 'A Russian who once worked at the Federal Treasury in Moscow. And a Chinese man who has links to the Beijing government. Exact nature yet to be confirmed.'

'What we still don't know,' said Quine, 'is the origin of Fowkes's relationship with them all.'

'Which must be a pretty tight one,' said Isla, 'given he was in one of their cars chasing you and me through Central London.'

*

'It's good, Jed,' said Sandford. 'Really good.'

Fowkes's twitch of the mouth almost looked like a smile. Sandford had asked him to finish his redrafts by the end of the weekend. Now, at 8.30 a.m. on Monday morning in the Prime Minister's study in 10 Downing Street, with the principal private secretary, Mark Burden, in attendance, they were putting the Royal Speech to bed.

'Thanks, Robbie, I appreciate it.'

'You said it. This is the moment.'

'I thought you might reject the ambitions for health.'

'No. We have to look at the long term. The past year may show how wonderful our doctors and nurses are, it says the exact opposite about the organisation above them. You're right, Jed. Free health care at the point of delivery in a centralised bureaucracy is not sustainable. We have to move towards a private insurance system.'

'And the tax measures?' asked Fowkes.

'Income and corporation tax cuts are spot-on. Abolishing inheritance tax will be controversial—'

'But essential to the message we have to convey,' interrupted Fowkes.

'Yes, I can see that,' acknowledged Sandford.

'I know it will be tough on some. But we simply can't keep social security and pensions rising in line with inflation. There's no alternative to pegging them at the present rate for the next four years. Arguably we should be cutting them.'

'Is that what you really think we should do, Jed?'

Fowkes hesitated. 'Let's be honest with ourselves. If we're going to finance the big infrastructure projects and keep the tax cuts, someone's got to pay for it. And economic common sense says that should fall on the unproductive sector.'

Sandford allowed himself time to reflect. 'I guess they're not our voters.'

Fowkes's eyes flickered. 'No. They're not.'

'In that case, we'll do it. You draft the final adjustments. An hour enough time?'

'Plenty.'

'That leaves just one matter,' said Sandford. 'If we do this, wouldn't my arms and mercenary idea send a message that, despite these necessary measures, we remain a government with a soul?'

The eyes opposite opened wide in alarm. 'It sends a message that we're idiots. We truly can't.'

'There's nothing I can do or say to persuade you,' said Sandford unhappily.

'I just can't go there.'

Sandford sighed. 'It will embarrass me.'

'It needn't. Just brief that industry-wide consultations are to take place. Hint at a voluntary code.'

'All right. We'll take it out,' said Sandford, with a defeated smile. 'All done then. It'll be printed on Monday. Thursday, the brave new world begins.'

'Exciting new world,' said Fowkes.

They stood. Fowkes hurried out of the room, as if ensuring his prize could not be taken from him. As the door closed behind him, the Prime Minister and his principal private secretary exchanged a look.

*

Quine arrived at the Oxford Union library just after noon. He had imagined himself browsing through dusty back copies in an ill-lit basement. A phone call to the helpful librarian had revealed a more convenient, if more mundane, search. The tall green bound volumes of *Cherwell*, the university's student newspaper, were the most prominent display on entering the library's reception area.

He asked for the years 1987, which Vaughn had mentioned, and 1988 in case whatever he was looking for had been delayed in the writing. He took them to a table, sat down and leafed through. The link from past to present was uncanny. These were the years of David Cameron wearing tails and bow tie, embracing a pretty girl in a marquee; Boris Johnson also in tails, blond hair neater, stomach smaller; Michael Gove defending elitism in the Oxford Union. Somewhere among them was an obscure figure called Jed Fowkes who was on a summer student trip behind the still intact Iron Curtain.

He reached November. On the banner above the magazine title, there it was. 'Conversion in Leipzig, by Jed Fowkes, page 6'.

*

I am a student of my generation. My teenage school and student years have run in parallel with the Thatcher years. To me, like the vast majority of others, the word Thatcherism became an abomination. We believed we saw the cruelty of capitalism all around us. In response I began to understand that socialism, real socialism, was the only answer for a better society. To that end, this summer I was accepted by the East German govern-ment on a short student summer course at the University of Leipzig. I went with high hopes. Here I would find fairness, equality, a generosity of spirit and a contentment. It did not turn out that way.

*

The article continued with a description not just of material poverty but of psychological and spiritual poverty. A depressed people labouring under a repressive government, fear in their eyes, shortages in the shops. Then came a passage which Quine found himself reading with mounting fascination.

*

During my stay in Leipzig, I met an attractive young woman whom it is better for me not to name. She was a postgraduate student, a few years older than me. We became friends – I won't dwell on how far our friendship went. Two weeks into it she said that she would like to introduce me to her uncle, who she described as a fascinating man with a deep understanding of the future evolution of the socialist world. We had a drink, a meal a few days later, and then I was invited to stay the weekend at his cottage in a farming village outside Leipzig.

It was during those two days that I realized an attempt was being made to recruit me. It became clear that this 'uncle' was a member of the Stasi, East Germany's intelligence service. He asked me, when I returned to Oxford, to assist the spread of the socialist ideal by helping his nation. It was to be a lifelong arrangement with a financial retainer. He flattered me by telling me that I had been spotted (by whom, I wondered) as a future high-flyer in British politics, in whatever capacity that might turn out to be.

For my own safety, I played for time. I now realized that the young woman was not the person I thought her to be. I was not invited to see the 'uncle' again. I told the young woman that I was seriously interested in the suggestion but needed time to think it over. She appeared satisfied with this and said I would be contacted after I returned to England. This attempt was made after my return and I rebuffed it.

I now understand that I made a mistake and I write this as a warning to others.

On my return, having undergone a political conversion as a result of this visit to a sad and corrupted society, I joined the University's Conservative Association. I have made good friends, one in particular who has encouraged me to write this article as a warning to others.

Do not fall for false gods as I so nearly did.

*

Quine finished his third read of the article, raised his eyes and looked blankly into space which resolved itself into the captivating pre-Raphaelite murals of the Oxford Union library. Yes, there were questions arising to ask Sir David Vaughn.

He read on. Over the rest of the university year, Fowkes's final one, he became a frequent contributor to *Cherwell*. The article had clearly laid the ground for a career inside the Conservative Party. He might not have been attractive or smooth enough to seduce the constituency backwoods men and women who selected parliamentary candidates. But he had remained a mover behind the scenes. If power not fame was his ambition, he was tantalizingly close to achieving it.

48

Isla watched and listened. Within his Treasury office, Fowkes continued to be careful. The hidden microphones were revealing no indiscretions, no whispered phone calls, just the silence of a serious man working at his desk. Running into her in the canteen the previous afternoon, he had suggested another quick coffee. It certainly was quick – perhaps it was a further check, perhaps he just needed to converse with another human being. His lack of interest in her now seemed real.

At 10.15 a.m. on the Tuesday morning he was summoned by the new Chancellor to her office. In the exceptional circumstances, a warrant had been granted to permit bugs there as well. Isla, earphones on, watched him walk along the corridor and enter.

*

Margaret Lascelles: Welcome, Jed, have a seat.

Jed Fowkes: Good morning, Margaret.

ML: It's arrived. *(Sounds of something being rustled.)* The Royal

Speech. One copy for you, one for me. I understand it's gone to the Palace this morning. Circulation is extremely restricted until time of delivery on Thursday to prevent leaks.

JF: Of course.

ML: I congratulate you. It's a remarkable document.

JF: Thank you.

ML: More than radical. In its way, revolutionary. How did you manage to get the Prime Minister's approval?

JF: I think he remembered the hopes and ambitions we once had. To truly change the country.

ML: Amazing. Wonderful really. And no sign of 'moral' government, arms sales bans and all that.

JF: I think he realized he hadn't thought it through.

ML: Well... Thursday will be a game-changer.

JF: We've finally done it.

*

Isla heard footsteps and made a show of intense typing, raising half an eye to see Fowkes emerge. He seemed excited as he re-entered the Spads' office. Silence fell. She imagined him sitting, calming himself. Within a couple of minutes, there were sounds of movement. They had to be preparations to leave. The Spads' door opened. He reappeared, leather jacket on, left arm clamping something to his chest, no case. He headed towards the stairs.

Flexibility, the ability to take your own decisions on the ground – key qualities drummed in from day one. *You'll sense it*, James had said. The moment Jed takes his risk. The moment the days of allowing him to relax means he drops his guard. She jumped up from her desk, grabbed her coat, beret, phone and mini-recorder. With no time for explanations to her colleagues, she followed. As she reached reception he was leaving the building.

He turned right and right again past Clive's statue, left when he hit Whitehall. The autumnal sun was low but the day not cold. He walked fast. She broke into a jog to keep him in sight, sweat gathering beneath the beret and around her neck and chest. He did not stop, did not look around. Surely he must at some point. He crossed Whitehall, continued north past the Banqueting House, right into Horse Guards Avenue, left into Whitehall Court, right into Whitehall Place, approaching Embankment tube. He was not heading anywhere near Mayfair or IPRM. She took out her phone, hit two digits and spoke briefly.

A few yards from the tube station, he halted abruptly. She was close but able to swivel and stare at Big Ben in a tourist trance. He did not turn, just stood, as if he might be considering his options. He took off again, scampered up the steps of the Hungerford and Golden Jubilee bridge. At the top, he had only two ways to go. It must be a rendezvous. She reckoned a pick-up somewhere on the South Bank, perhaps by a black Mercedes.

He stopped again. She turned her back to him, then sneaked round for a glance. He was looking downriver towards St Paul's and the City, hitting a number on a mobile. She switched on the recorder, edging ever nearer, trying to keep her side or back to him. Maybe he was just organizing the rendezvous. There could not have been an advance plan for this – he would not have known when it was coming.

She was within yards – enough people scurrying on the bridge to give some cover. She tried to get close enough to pick up even odd words from his phone call. Nothing.

He lowered the hand holding the phone from ear to midriff, the conversation over. Was this the moment? Just one short, secretive phone call. A message he did not dare give anywhere near the office or Treasury. A burner phone. A venue with a deep river flowing beneath it.

His other arm felt the leather jacket. A reflex action – he must be checking that something was still lodged beneath. She made her decision. More to come, leave him alone. He had a quick look around and, with a slight movement, moved his hand over the railing. He released a small black object – it could only be the phone. She imagined it plopping into the river below. Was that the vital piece of evidence?

He turned, heading back towards her. She turned at the same time and walked fast, getting well ahead of him. She, and he, had nowhere to go but back down the steps onto the Embankment. She could cross the road, find cover just inside the tube station hall and keep an eye out for him coming down.

She saw him scurrying down and onto the pavement, now heading towards Parliament. She crossed back over the road and followed, texting as she walked.

He reached the lights at the junction of Embankment and Westminster Bridge. The pedestrian light was red. She hung back, wondering if he would ignore it and skip between traffic to get to the other side. He waited, not drawing attention to himself. The light changed, he walked and turned right. She assumed his destination was the House of Commons. He rounded Big Ben, then turned left. He passed the members' entrance; perhaps it was not the Commons after all. Unless he was bluffing.

He stopped, looked west and, this time jumping between traffic, crossed St Margaret's Street. He walked straight on, Westminster Abbey to his left. She crossed, keeping him in sight. He was nearing the north door. Avoiding a couple walking towards her, she was momentarily distracted. She looked up and he had disappeared. Must have turned right, back towards St Stephen's Green.

She ran, stopped at the corner beyond the entrance to St Margaret's Church and peeped round. No sign. Inside St Margaret's, had to be. She turned back. A single security guard and a guide manned the entrance. She asked a tourist's question about the statues on the Abbey's north door and then if she could walk around St Margaret's. Of course, she was told, it was open to all, and free. But no photography please. She pushed open the central door of the triple arch and entered, immediately turning left and inspecting a memorial plaque. Cautiously she glanced around. A handful of tourists, a verger wandering around. She moved to the back of the nave for a broader view.

A figure was kneeling in the front pew of the left side aisle. She took up position in a right side aisle pew near the back. She had a good diagonal view. Discreetly she took a photo.

After a couple of minutes, the figure rose. It was wearing a black leather jacket. It had to be him. Rather than walking down the side aisle, he walked to the nave, stood in front of the altar for a few seconds, crossed himself, bowed, swivelled and headed down the nave towards the exit. Jed Fowkes was surely not a believer.

For a split second, she was caught by indecision. She needed a clearer photo. Each step was bringing him closer. She raised her iPhone above the top of the pew and clicked. He stopped, swinging in her direction. Something, perhaps just that tiny movement of the iPhone, had alerted him. There was a flash of recognition in his eyes.

Think. Think fast. Like her, he must make a decision. Go back to where he had placed his package or follow her. His priority surely was to get to her first. She was nearer the exit than him. Better that she lured him outside. A confrontation inside the church could jeopardize everything. She got up and walked fast enough to ensure she reached the exit before him. Outside the church, she turned right towards St Stephen's Green, not running, still not wanting to attract attention, not wanting the security guard and guide to notice anything amiss. As she rounded the church, out of sight of the entrance, she slowed down. In a couple of seconds he caught up with her. She allowed him to grab her.

'What the fuck are you doing here, you little bitch?'

'Oh hi, Jed, fancy seeing you here.'

'I said, what the fuck—'

Two pairs of arms, one from each side, seized him.

'This woman tried to rob me!'

'I'm sorry, sir,' said a well-built figure in jeans and T-shirt. 'Could you release her please?'

'We're here to protect you, Mr Fowkes,' said a second similarly dressed figure. 'It would be safer for you to come with us. If you understand what I mean.' They each took one side, arm-locking him. He submitted. An unmarked car was waiting on a double-yellow line just a few yards away.

Isla watched him disappear inside, then returned to the entrance of St Margaret's. 'I think I may have left my gloves inside,' she said to the security guard. 'What an idiot, eh?'

She re-entered and headed to the front left side aisle. It was marked number 60. Nothing was immediately in sight. He had been kneeling on the left edge. There was a half- to one-inch gap between the wooden end of the aisle and the stone of the cathedral wall. She put on her phone torch, shone it down the crack. A thin package. The oldest tradecraft in the game – a dead letter box. A good one too.

She prised it out. A brown manila envelope. She needed photographic evidence. It was sealed with a metal fastener and added staples. She cursed. She wondered how long she had. Surely, at the very least, the timing would be sufficient for them to get Fowkes away. She undid the fastener and slowly, one by one, unpicked the staples. She slid out the single object inside. A bound advance copy of the Royal Speech. She photographed it, placed it halfway into the envelope and photographed the two together. With great care, she reset the staples and attached the fastener. She replaced the envelope in the crack and photographed it there too.

She walked out of the church, now turning left and left

again, back to St Margaret's Street and right past the House of Lords to Thames House beyond. Two watchers took up position inside St Margaret's Church. On this day, its 'No Photography' rule would have to be broken more than once.

49

Thursday, 8.30 a.m. The day of the State Opening of Parliament, culminating in the Royal Speech.

Sandford had decided the less said to Margaret Lascelles, the better. He lifted the phone. 'Mark, could you get the Chancellor on the line?'

A few clicks and she was there. 'Good morning, Prime Minister. An exciting one too.'

'Ah,' said Sandford. 'Margaret, I'm afraid there's been a mistake.'

'Oh?' He detected the flutter in her voice.

'Yes. The wrong version of the Royal Speech was sent to you.'

'But it was properly bound. Just as the final document always is.'

'Yes. I had samples of two versions printed – the one Jed Fowkes contributed to and also my original. I wanted to read them against each other.'

'I see.'

'I'll investigate with the Cabinet Secretary what went wrong. And how only one version ever got to you.'

She hesitated, he waited. 'May I ask which, erm, version you decided on?'

'I appreciate Jed's work,' replied Sandford. 'But I've decided steady as we go is the right option.'

'And the legislation about arms sales and private security and military operations?'

'Oh, that's a commitment,' said Sandford as if it could never have been in doubt. 'Did I not make myself clear at Conference?'

'Yes, Prime Minister. Of course.'

'Good. Have you seen Jed in the past couple of days?'

'I haven't. He seems to have gone missing.'

'I expect he thought his work was done. He must need a break after everything that's happened.'

*

Quine, head buried in the *Financial Times*, was having a leisurely breakfast with Sophie and Isla, who had been given a couple of days off to recharge batteries.

'Look at this,' he said, handing them a folded-over inside page. 'Bottom right. My old foes back in action.'

*

IPRM, the international private security and military conglomerate, has announced a major contract with the Chinese government to provide support services in Africa. It is understood that this will take two forms. Firstly, the protection of Chinese personnel and infrastructure projects throughout the continent. Secondly, the provision of support services to African governments with whom China is collaborating.

Michael Ho, chief executive officer of IPRM, said the deal was a game-changer for the company. 'We will now be looking at a potential flotation to help finance our further global ambitions.' Asked about the Prime Minister's recent speech on a potential ban on companies like IPRM trading with non-democratic regimes, Mr Ho was confident. 'Our information is that there is no prospect whatsoever of this leading to what would be unenforceable legislation. We believe that a voluntary code is the way forward and will take part in industry-wide consultation to achieve the right outcomes.'

*

'So our nice Prime Minister's morality crusade is over before it began,' said Sophie.

Quine and Isla exchanged awkward looks. 'Don't take it as given,' said Quine. 'You can't believe a word you read in the press, can you? And you certainly can't trust anything that comes out of the mouths of IPRM.'

His phone pinged. 'Well, here's a thing.' He turned to Isla. 'You and I have been invited to an early supper with the Prime Minister at his home in Notting Hill. I suggest you bring that recorder of yours.'

50

At 9 p.m. the bell rang at the Sandford family home in Salisbury Square. A protection officer opened the front door to reveal a visitor. The Prime Minister stood a few feet behind.

'Hello, Jed,' said Sandford, 'thank you for coming.'

There was no handshake. Fowkes wore a suit which appeared to have been recently pressed – probably the same one he was taken in – a white shirt and red and pink striped tie. His hair was neat, his face clean-shaven. His narrow chin jutted out more than ever. Only in his sunken eyes was there any sign of distress. He was presenting himself as a successful, professional political expert, dressed for work – a man who did not yet accept that he had been beaten.

'Did I have any choice?' he asked.

'I told them not to force you to come.'

'They didn't. Except for illegally kidnapping me, I can't fault their conduct. Their "safe house" is comfortable and well-equipped. They even offer a cleaning service. Though I didn't appreciate being blindfolded.'

'No doubt they have their rules.'

'No doubt.'

'Come on in.'

Sandford led him through a door leading off the hall into a double sitting room, the protection officer taking up his seat outside. He gestured Fowkes to an armchair and sat himself on a sofa beside it.

'Drink?'

'I trusted you,' said Fowkes, not responding. 'Like I always have. And now you do this. Deceive me. Not just some tiny deception. I watched the speech today. That's it. That's me done. Career... life over.'

'You were blackmailing me.'

'Blackmailing you! I was telling you the truth.'

'You weren't, Jed. There's another truth. God knows how long it goes back, but you're in the pay of IPRM. Mercenaries killing for profit. You knew that if their big China deal came off, you'd be in for millions. But then I announce I'm going to clip their wings. And you come up with your lie to try to stop me. Was it really worth M-C dying for that?'

Silence fell. A buzzing fly hit a window pane. The buzz ceased. The rumble of traffic reduced to a distant echo from a different world. Jed Fowkes glowered. 'Do you seriously, honestly think, knowing me all these years, remembering where we go back to, that's what this is all about? That I have even the slightest interest in money. As for M-C, you killed him. Your squalid little deal led to that.' He paused. 'I thought it would only be a warning. Get him back in line. But stuff happens. Those sort of people can get carried away.'

'A warning?'

'You made it necessary. You were the cause.'

'Jed, are you saying you knew about it in advance?'

'We're past all that. What does it matter now?'

Behind the closed double doors of the sitting room, Quine swiped the edge of his hand along his neck to signal to Isla to switch off the recorder. She returned the gesture with a frown. He grabbed a piece of notepaper. **He's confessed. We've got him. No more on record.** She shrugged her shoulders and touched a button.

''Fess up, Robbie,' continued Fowkes. 'I grant you, M-C was at one remove. But that poor girl, that was hands-on.'

Sandford sighed. 'You're not going to revisit that fantasy, are you?'

'We've been over it. It's not fantasy. I don't know exactly what happened in your bedroom. Maybe you were into weird stuff. Maybe you just happened to go further than intended. You killed her, Robbie. And I saved you.'

Sandford allowed a silence. On all accounts, he must keep calm. 'There's someone I want you to meet,' he said. He left the room, to be instantly replaced by the protection officer.

Fowkes eyed him with contempt. 'I'm not going to set fire to the house.'

A couple of minutes later Sandford returned with Quine, the protection officer retreating. Fowkes's face dropped. 'I imagine you two had dealings over the years,' said Sandford.

'Occasionally,' said Quine, offering a hand to shake. 'Hello, Jed.'

Fowkes didn't move. 'It *was* you, wasn't it? In the car. The girl too. I felt sure of it. Then she came back to the office. So it couldn't have been her.'

'As you said, Jed, we're past all that,' said Sandford quietly. 'Take a seat, Joe.' He gestured to a chair. 'Jed, your lie began at the party conference. I needed the truth. I asked Joe to help me. A few days ago he made a visit to Hungary. To a village called Pusztaszabanya. Joe, please tell what happened.'

Quine described his meeting with Abigél Takacs. As he finished, Sandford rose from his chair, walked over to a bureau, opened a drawer, returned with a photograph and handed it to Fowkes. 'Take your time.' Fowkes inspected the photograph for several seconds and put it down. 'It's a gravestone,' continued Sandford.

Fowkes swallowed. 'I can see that,' he said quietly.

'It's the physical proof of what Joe has just said.' Fowkes took back the photograph and stared silently at it. 'The proof that Andrea Takacs did not die in our flat or my bed. The proof that the remains in Deptford Dockyard are not hers.'

'Yes,' said Fowkes, putting the photograph down again. 'I know.'

'Excuse me?' said Sandford.

'I know what happened to Andrea Takacs. Nothing that's just been said is news to me. It just wasn't factored in that you'd ever track her down.'

'Jed, could you stop playing these games?' Sandford looked at Quine, who shrugged his shoulders.

'Not games, Robbie,' said Fowkes. 'My friend who came to the rescue was well-connected. Andrea's return to Budapest was observed by one of his company's associates in

Hungary. At that time, in the early days after the collapse of Communism, there were opportunities there. Not any longer, its present leader can look after himself. This associate followed Andrea and her sister to her home. He kept an eye on further developments. We were informed of her sad end.'

'Then what the…' Sandford stopped himself. 'Then the skeleton, the severed hand, has nothing to do with anything.'

'In one sense, you're right. The identity of the body's irrelevant. You killed Andrea just as surely as if you'd plunged the knife into her heart. Her suicide is one hundred per cent your responsibility.'

'There's a simple fact,' said Sandford. 'It's not her remains that were found in Deptford.'

'I agree. So tell me whose they are,' said Fowkes.

'I don't know whose they are.'

'I believe you, Robbie. That's why we're talking about Andrea instead.'

'My God,' said Sandford almost despairingly, 'you're some trickster. I've kept asking myself why you've made these false accusations against me. Because I couldn't have done these things. I know I couldn't – and didn't. I've thought long and hard about it. Tried to overcome the loss of memory and work out what must have happened. Over the last few days, it's finally come to me.' Fowkes briefly caught his eye, then looked away. Sandford stayed focused on him. 'You were always interested in the power of drugs. Weren't you? You used to talk about them. Benzodiazepines for example. Remember them?'

'What is this, Robbie?'

'Flunitrazepam.'

'So?'

'It was branded and commonly known as Rohypnol. It began to become infamous in the early 1990s as the so-called "date rape" drug—'

'You are heading so way off—'

'Girls went for me, they didn't go for you. It must have been difficult for you. Painful. But, maybe just once or twice, maybe more, you found a way round that.'

Sandford stood and began to walk up and down the room, now the barrister delivering his closing address, glancing between Quine and Fowkes.

'It was you who always brought the drinks from the kitchen. And it was always just after that I totally lost my memory. Went into the black hole. It wasn't only my pills and alcohol, was it? It was Rohypnol – or whatever benzodiazepine you were using – to knock me out. And a smaller dose for the girl so that for the next couple of hours she wouldn't resist and later wouldn't remember. Then you did whatever it was you liked. But what you liked doing caused one of them to fall unconscious, panicking you into thinking she was dead. It all makes sense. Remember those porn mags you had—'

'What the fuck—'

'I saw one once, you'd left it out by mistake. You're the one who's mentioned weird stuff, not me.' Sandford returned to his seat, his voice softening. 'I finally get it. Yes, I had a problem, but in reality this was your problem. You did that to me, Jed. You harmed that girl and organized the cover-up. And thirty years later you tried to turn it against me.'

Silence fell.

'You're a persuasive man,' said Fowkes. 'Always were. Something of the escapologist about you. Maybe you've even persuaded yourself. But your idea is delusion. Pure fantasy.'

'Jed, stop the lying.'

'Why would I lie? I've lost.'

'I think it's because you always wanted power over me.'

Fowkes shut his eyes and, clenching his fists, lowered his head. An oppressive silence fell. It was interrupted by a bang from the square. A car backfiring.

Fowkes stretched out his palms. 'Don't try to provoke me.'

A further silence. 'Truth.' Quine had been quiet long enough for that single word to cut through the ice. It was only a theory and he had wondered whether to raise it. *What* happened was just part of the story. This could prise open *why*.

51

'Sometimes we look at things the wrong way round,' continued Quine. 'Upside down. Often because we're blinded by a wrong assumption.'

'What are you talking about, Joe?' asked Sandford. This was not in the script. Not that there had been time to prepare one.

'There's still a body. Or parts of one. Who is she? The burial is dated to between twenty-five and thirty-five years ago. A full ten-year spread. Why not cast the net wider?'

Quine removed his wallet from an inside jacket pocket and extracted a small black and white photograph. He walked over to Fowkes and handed it to him. 'Do you recognize her?'

Fowkes screwed up his eyes. 'It's poor quality.'

'It's taken from a photograph of postgraduate students sitting around a table at the University of Leipzig in 1987. Does that help?'

'You tell me.'

'When you were on summer vacation in Leipzig, doing a short course at the university called "The Humanity of Socialism".'

'I remember it well. I wrote about it.'

'You did. Earlier this week I read the article. I found it fascinating.'

'I'm glad you liked it. That visit changed my entire outlook on life.'

'I've since made some checks. I understand that British intelligence read your account and asked to see you. You agreed and told them, with complete openness, that the Stasi recruiter was a certain Dieter Schmidt and the young woman was called Anneliese Bluthner. In early 1989 Anneliese, now a committed Stasi officer, was seconded to London. She would have renewed contact with you. Times were changing. Some more flexible Stasi like Dieter Schmidt saw what was coming and made plans to suit themselves. Others, like Anneliese Bluthner, remained committed to the socialist paradise. I suspect she felt betrayed that you'd sold your soul to capitalism.'

'Intriguing,' said Fowkes.

'Perhaps you were even lovers. And, one night, there was a reckoning. She accused you of betrayal and double-dealing. Or threatened to chuck you. Either way you attacked her. Even raped her. Did you kill her? What's known for sure is that Anneliese Bluthner disappeared in late 1989 during her secondment to London – never to reappear. This has been confirmed by the German embassy.'

'She wouldn't be the only Stasi officer to make themselves scarce,' said Fowkes.

'Have another look at the photograph.' Quine handed it back to Fowkes, along with a magnifying glass. 'I have copies. There's no point in destroying it.'

Fowkes peered through the glass. 'I see nothing. Her hands are cupping her cheeks so you can't even see the face properly.'

'That's the point. Look at the fourth finger of the right hand.'

Fowkes had a quick look, then handed the photograph and magnifier back to Quine. 'And?'

'That looks to me remarkably like the ring found on the fourth finger of the hand unearthed in Deptford Old Dockyard. There's a further connection. Why is it that in recent days, thirty years on from these events, you've been seen with Dieter Schmidt? You're close to him now, you were close to him then. If Anneliese's body needed getting rid of, he was the one person you'd think of in London who had the know-how to do the job.'

Fowkes was wearing a most unusual expression. It was a smile. A real smile. 'I have to congratulate you. That's good. Completely and utterly wrong. But really good.' He chuckled, seeming genuinely to enjoy the moment. 'You began with the word "truth". I actually like truth. As I said earlier, what's there to lose anyway? I didn't think I was going to do this, but why not? The full truth.'

Quine exchanged glances with Sandford. He seemed nervous again, beads of sweat glistening on his forehead.

52

'Let's go back to 1987,' continued Fowkes. 'I went to Leipzig in the German Democratic Republic. As I wrote in my *Cherwell* article, the visit changed my life. But not as I wrote. Here's the truth. I loved it there. It had its faults but essentially it was a country of equals. I met Anneliese Bluthner. I liked her very much. She introduced me to Dieter Schmidt. I swore a lifelong loyalty to the socialist ideal and agreed to work for the Stasi. We made a plan which would allow me to infiltrate the British Conservative Party.'

He turned to Quine. 'You've read its first move – the article. After it, MI5 did indeed ask to see me. As agreed with Dieter and Anneliese I complied with that request and answered all their questions. The MI5 interviewer took me at face value. I suspect they were interested in recruiting me.'

'But they decided you were unreliable,' said Quine.

'Shut up,' said Fowkes. 'It's for you to listen now. Anneliese came to London, we resumed our friendship. After the Wall fell, she told me she was reinventing herself and returning to Germany to become part of the new nation. Schmidt stayed in London. Our professional relationship was over, my retainer lapsed. But he and I kept in close touch. I remained the socialist, he became the capitalist. It didn't matter. We understood each other. He introduced me to his CIA friend, Lyle Grainger.'

He turned to Sandford. 'After you raped and almost killed Andrea, Schmidt and Grainger personally came to our flat to take care of her.'

'You mean you raped her,' said Sandford.

'I'll ignore that,' said Fowkes. 'From that moment on Schmidt, Grainger and I were allies, whether we liked it or not. As it happens, we did like it. We knew each other's secrets. If they needed my help or I needed theirs, there was never any hesitation.

'There was one difference. They exploited capitalism to make money. I had no interest in that. My political ideals never wavered. As we're having this conversation, there's a further secret I'll let you in on. Back in 1987, the Stasi recruited a second English student. I was tasked to the Conservatives. His – or her – job was to be their agent within the Labour Party. That person is still there, like me, committed to real socialism. Nobody knows the name. Except Schmidt and me. Look how that party was turned into a vehicle for revolution. Look how close it came to power. Sadly it failed. But there are other means of creating upheaval and revolution. Attack not from the left but from the right. The extremes meet around the back, don't they?

'Wind the clock forward thirty years. My one-time friend, Robin Sandford, becomes Prime Minister. Nine or so months in, I begin to realize he has no ideology at all. He's a man of straw. But I know this is my one opportunity to do something incredible. His party, if not him, is now hard-core far right. So is his Chancellor who I control. This Prime Minister, this government, this party can impose a radical agenda that will bring such division and strife to this wounded nation that the revolution truly might come. Initially from the right. Then triggering a counter-revolution from the left.

'I have a hold over this Prime Minister because I – Schmidt and Grainger being the only others – know of an incident in his past. They also know of the remains of a young woman buried in Deptford Dockyard around the same time. They are in possession of one part of the body, a hand with a ring on its fourth finger, for possible future use. Maybe they got that idea from the Mafia and horses' heads. Maybe it was standard Stasi practice. I don't know.

'I propose a plan which will allow me to put a gun to the Prime Minister's temple and persuade him to follow my agenda. It suits my friends as their business benefits from political volatility.

'My friends retrieve the severed hand, repack the bones to display its shape clearly and bury it beneath a mains water pipe laid just a couple of feet below a service road in Deptford Dockyard. They leave evidence of a dangerous sinking in the road and alert the local council to it shortly before the party conference. It's one of the very few occasions when I know I can get an audience, however brief, with the Prime Minister.

'I create a narrative from this hand and, as will appear later, the body it was severed from. I choose to centre it around the incident with a young Hungarian woman called Andrea. I make that choice because I myself was there from beginning to end and remember the details. I also think the Prime Minister will be able to remember this girl and at least some of that evening. Enough to know that what I'm telling him may be real. And, as it happens, *is* real to all intents and purposes. After all, there is no point in choosing an alternative incident which he may not remember at all and I have not fully witnessed. There's no threat in that.

'My plan brings an unexpected bonus. In his speech the Prime Minister, out of the blue, makes a proposal about arms sales and the private security business that could have a damaging impact on IPRM which my friends partly own. Another owner is Quentin Deschevaux with whom I have occasional dealings. They all, Deschevaux included, ask me to ensure this proposal is dropped. I'm happy to oblige. But for me it's a side issue. I will gain nothing from any advantage to their company. I have no financial interest in it whatsoever.

'As it has turned out, my plan was thwarted. I lost. I have no regrets that I tried. As for you, Robbie, whatever side you're on, you've ended up in love with mediocrity. You arc a false leader without point or purpose. You will achieve nothing. You were once my friend. I was fond of you. I saved your skin. All for nothing.' Fowkes stood. 'That's it. May I go please?'

'Thank you for that, Jed,' said Sandford. 'The door's open. The car that brought you here is still outside with instructions to drop you off wherever you wish. If you've made other arrangements, no one will get in your way.'

Fowkes turned to Quine. 'I heard about your accident, Joe. I told them you and your book would never be a threat and to leave you alone. Looks like I got that one wrong.' He walked to the door and stopped. 'By the way, who was that young woman who acted as your spy?'

Quine shrugged his shoulders and displayed the empty palms of his hands.

Fowkes nodded and looked at Sandford. 'Goodbye, Robbie,' he said softly. He allowed a moment and then spoke softly. 'It will come.' He paused. 'One day, it will come.' He turned on his heel and exited through the front door held open by the protection officer.

The square was darkening, street lights brightening. Quine and Sandford watched Fowkes stride purposefully past the car that had delivered him. As he reached the corner, a different black car drew up beside him. Its passenger door opened from inside. Fowkes got in.

'My God,' said Sandford, 'he's mad.' He walked back into the house.

Quine said nothing. Lingering behind on the doorstep, he looked again at the photograph. The ring could have been a silver coin of the same era. Had there been a flicker of recognition in Jed's eyes when he looked at it? No. Wanting it, he had imagined it. He had craved finality but it was not to be.

He returned to the sitting room. Isla had not appeared which was good; Sandford might want to unwind with him alone.

He was standing, staring at the street through the front window. 'What do you think?' he asked, not turning. 'Is he mad?' Now he swung round sharply. 'Or am I?'

Quine knew what his role had to be. 'You're not mad. Whether or not he's mad, he's certainly deluded.'

'Is that certain? I suppose if your theory about the German girl's true, then it would show what he was capable of. And it would mean he also raped Andrea. I know I'm right. He was drugging me.'

'There's no reason,' said Quine, 'why the German girl theory shouldn't be any more or less true than any other theory.' And, he thought, she could at least be an alibi body if one were ever needed.

Sandford shrugged. 'My God, he must be bitter. I've always said he was odd. But this is another level.' He paused. 'All this stuff about revolution and counter-revolution. Does he honestly believe that? Does he still think it could ever happen like that?'

'Oh yes,' said Quine with feeling. 'And he's not alone. Not by a long chalk.'

Sandford slumped on the sofa. 'I'm tired. Unusual for me.'

'It's not surprising. But it's done. Nothing Jed ever says again will be believed. He's right. His career and life are over.'

Sandford looked up at him. 'Am I a mediocrity?'

Quine felt a curious relief that this was the question at the forefront of his mind. 'No, Robbie. You're not a mediocrity.'

53

The day after the State Opening of Parliament and the reading of the Royal Speech, simultaneous dawn raids were mounted on Quentin Deschevaux MP's Westminster office and his Chelsea home in The Boltons. Joe Quine later realized it was one of the grand houses he had passed on his first day back in London.

Deschevaux had been successfully photographed retrieving the package containing the Royal Speech from the gap by the side aisle of St Margaret's Church where Fowkes had dropped it. It was decided to delay his arrest until after the speech was delivered in case it spurred him into further illegal action. The statement released by IPRM on its China deal was strong evidence but only circumstantial. The raids revealed a series of confidential government documents dating from the time Fowkes had joined the Treasury. Deschevaux was charged under Section 22 of the Theft Act with handling stolen goods, which carried a maximum sentence of fourteen years' imprisonment, and released from custody on substantial bail.

The already sensational media coverage of his arrest was enhanced by a further knock-on effect from the Royal Speech. Quine had felt an inevitability about it.

*

'SENIOR TREASURY MAN FOUND HANGED AT BLACKFRIARS BRIDGE' and variations on the theme were the headlines on the front pages of the Sunday newspapers.

Quine could not help admiring the elegance of the reference. Jed was found at the very spot where on Friday the 18 June 1982, Roberto Calvi, the man who became known as 'God's Banker', was also found hanging by the neck. Calvi had been chairman of Banco Ambrosiano; the Vatican was its major shareholder. The year before, he had been convicted of illegally spiriting tens of millions of dollars of bank money out of Italy. At the time of his death, the bank was collapsing with a billion dollars of debt it could not repay. Calvi's death was initially recorded as suicide but, in the years to come, it became a fertile source of conspiracy theories. He had fallen foul of the P2 Masonic lodge; or the Mafia; or the Vatican itself. The facts that, the previous day, his secretary had thrown herself from her office window in shame at the bank's collapse and Calvi had already attempted suicide in prison became lost.

That evening Quine dissected the fallout with Isla.

'If Jed killed himself,' said Quine, 'it was a deliberate choice of location. He wasn't just disappearing, he was becoming a story. A legend. Fueller of conspiracy theories for years, even decades to come.'

'It also suited plenty of people to have him dead,' Isla said. 'IPRM for one. He was carrying a lot of secrets.'

'And he'd failed. No use to them any more.'

'There were other interested parties.'

'What do you mean?'

'Our Prime Minister for one. If the skeleton ever gets traced to that flat, it must be Fowkes, mustn't it? The weird one. The one who committed suicide. Who felt such shame he couldn't go on living.'

Quine allowed the unspoken implication to drift by in silence. 'Oh, I never asked,' he finally said, 'I guess you must have listened in to the rest of the Fowkes/Sandford discussion.'

'You bet.'

'But it's our secret, yes? You didn't switch that recorder back on.'

'No, I didn't,' she replied firmly. It was not a lie. It might have looked like it to him when her finger hovered over that button, but she had never switched it off in the first place.

*

Carol was upstairs lying on the bed, waiting. Ever since the girls were old enough to know not to barge in, it had always seemed the place for their most private chats and few rows.

'I got your message,' she said as he entered. 'So, you've cancelled all your evening engagements to spend time with your wife.'

Sandford sat down beside her and allowed a second of silence. 'I can tell you everything now.'

'Everything?'

'Yes, everything.' He pursed his lips. 'I won't even ask you to sign the Official Secrets Act.' A glimmer of a smile – a small softening.

The version he contrived for her told of many things that were true and some that were not. Others were omitted altogether. There was no mention of skeletons or severed hands or incidents in a South London flat three decades earlier.

'You're saying that right from the beginning it was all about Jed and his one-man revolution with Deschevaux his partner-in-crime,' she said, as he came to the end. 'And the story Jed first told you about M-C and his Spad having it off in his office was because M-C was getting in his way.'

'You've got it,' he said. 'Though no one, not even Jed, I suspect, could have foreseen the chain reaction.'

'Poor M-C.'

'Yes, poor M-C.'

'Robbie,' she said, 'why didn't you share it with me? The strain you must have been under. I could have helped.'

'Carol,' he said, smiling with a certain sadness, 'I couldn't have done that. Say a single hint had slipped out, however accidentally. The monitoring of Jed had to be watertight.'

'I realize that,' she said, 'but I'd have been there for you.'

'Yes. I know you would.'

'I'm sorry. Truly sorry.'

'There's a lesson in it for both of us.'

She frowned. 'Forgive me for asking this, it will finally clear the air. Couple of things on those emails. The R woman. I checked the link but didn't see where she fitted in.'

'Yes, Roisin Osborne. She's a director at Coulthard's private bank. Jed and I met her way back through Mikey Miller. She'd kept in touch with Jed more than me over the years so I asked her to see Joe. We were trawling to see if Jed might have let slip anything with his friends and contacts. Without making them aware of it, of course. Turned out Roisin had rather a crush on me. I'm afraid I didn't reciprocate.'

'I'm very glad you didn't. Just one more. "Artefact".What was that?'

'You and your memory!' He kissed her on the forehead. 'It might be funny if it wasn't so tragic. There was an element of code. Joe and I were both aware emails could never be fully secure. If you really want to know, the artefact was a sex aid found in M-C's office by a cleaner. It was handed in to the head of property. I think in that email "boss" and "subject" were being used to describe the same person—'

'You mean M-C.'

'Yes.'

'And the sex aid?'

'Come on!'

'Don't be shy.'

'All right. It was a deflated and folded rubber doll. How on earth it was left there remains a mystery. Just imagine what the tabloids would have made of it.'

*

Peace has been finally restored, reflected Sandford, lying in bed an hour later. Carol's even breathing and rising and falling chest the only sound and movement in range. The apology and reconciliation. He had been careless, not anticipating that she would drill down into the emails. He should have known her better. Roisin was easy enough to explain away but he had felt himself stumbling on 'Artefact'. He had no idea how the sex aid suddenly came to the rescue. Perhaps it was just thinking about Morland-Cross.

Please forgive me, M-C, if you're looking down from above or up from below. Your final service as a cover story is gratefully appreciated.

54

One month later

Quine could not decide. Was he enjoying being back in the limelight? Or did he miss the peace of life in exile?

Certainly he was in demand. Deschevaux's arrest had rekindled interest in the circumstances of the libel case. With the fallen MP now so disgraced that he had no reputation left to damage, journalists could throw caution to the winds. One serious investigative journalist, guided by Quine, was about to be funded by Channel Four to go to Sierra Leone to re-investigate the massacre. Once he had hoovered up all the available evidence and any witnesses on the ground, the ultimate prize would be to persuade Jack Edgerley to go on the record.

Quine also had a head start on the Jed Fowkes story. Even without any reference to young women disappearing from a South London flat where a future Prime Minister had lived, it was a remarkable one, not least the Stasi connection. Sir David Vaughn had been as good as his word in helping with Quine's questions arising from the *Cherwell* article. Vaughn had, in his twilight years, become a man of great moral rectitude, he concluded. Perhaps he always had been.

That morning, sitting in the editor's office of *The Post* newspaper, there had been a further surprise as he opened an envelope handed to him by the editor himself. It was headed 'Private and Confidential' and addressed to 'Joseph Quine, c/o The Post'. The stamp was foreign. Inside was a postcard showing a beach in Brazil. On the back was a handwritten message.

Sorry I let you down. They gave me no choice.
Don't give up.

The world seemed suddenly full of possibility.

'What are you thinking about, Dad?' asked Sophie, interrupting his thoughts.

He looked at his empty wine glass. 'A top-up would be nice. What about you?'

'Your book. I've persuaded my boss to join the auction.'

'Brilliant. Though I think I remember once saying you weren't the target publisher.'

'Maybe you did. But now Deschevaux's neutralized, we're suddenly feeling brave.'

'Riley says it could go for a lot of money.'

'We'll have to beat the competition, won't we?'

He chuckled. 'Be fun, wouldn't it, Sophie?'

'Yes, Dad, it'd be fantastic.'

Isla walked into the room. 'What are you two plotting?'

'Dad and me working together,' said Sophie.

'Aye well, he's not a bad ally,' said Isla.

They lapsed into a companionable silence. What next, Quine asked himself. Sandford was ever more serious about pursuing the biography. Another option was the events of recent weeks that had given him a hell of a story if he was ever allowed to tell it.

He thought of Cornwall and Mrs Trelight. And then he thought of Robin Sandford, the 'good' Prime Minister. Was he? Had he ever truly known him? The only certainty was that, somehow, he always managed to come out on top. As for what had happened in that flat, it was better not to think about it.

*

One a.m. The Prime Minister sat alone in the 10 Downing Street flat. A night of rest from his family, his staff, his colleagues.

He had survived. Henry Morland-Cross and Jed Fowkes had not. He missed neither of them, but they would not let him go. Spectres in the night. Women in the night. Carol. Roisin. Andrea.

It will come.

Who was she? Surely he could remember the name. Because, as it grew on him in the days and weeks after Jed died, the image of the ring became ever more vivid. She had flaunted it at him. 'It's valuable, posh boy. Silver coin, hundred years old. Hungarian boy give it me, then I give 'im what he wanted.'

One day, it will come. Jed's parting words. The girl from that sweaty, crowded, alcohol, drug-fuelled club, appropriately called Hell's Bunker. The memory was growing. They bumped into each other just before closing, both far gone. On the walk back to the flat she talked. How she'd had years in care – father raped her, beat her mother up – but now she was nineteen she was out and had her freedom. 'Owe nothing ('nuffink') to no one', 'no old hag of a foster mum any more', 'fuck off to care homes too', 'I can have the life I want, I can fuck who I want', 'I can even have a good-looking lad like you if I want.' 'What you do anyway, posh boy?' The words, the accent, the high-spiritedness all came back, the fun. And he had replied, 'I'm just chilling too. Between things.' There would not have been much more chat than that. And then they arrived at the flat.

With Jed waiting.

What would happen if – when – the skull was discovered? The police would investigate, revisit all missing persons around that time. She would be on the list – even if no one cared about her. No family keeping a watch, written off by the state, transient friends. But yes, they would investigate. Chopped-up bodies could not be ignored. There would be records – including dental records. Care homes and foster parents would have made her go to the dentist. So they would have a name. Maybe one of those transient friends would say the last they knew of her she was off to Hell's Bunker. They would ask for witnesses. That long back, the dates vague, the chances would be one in a thousand. But just say someone did remember. Say they could track the date. Everyone was made to sign in at Hell's

Bunker. But that would be all right. There used to be hundreds there on a Friday night.

Say, even, someone saw her leaving with a boy who looked just like him at that age.

That would be all right too.

There would be no witnesses to what then happened.

Because Jed is dead.

Sandford closed his eyes and allowed his head to relax into a cushion. Waves of fatigue began to wash over him, that exquisite moment when, at last, he could bury his memories and his conscience and tip into the black hole of sleep.

Acknowledgements

My thanks to those whose expertise, insight, support, inspiration and introductions made such a difference; Julian Alexander, Tom Burton-Page, Sue Carney of Ethos Forensics, Hugh Dent, Joanna Frank, Paul Greengrass, Val Hudson, Sophie Nelson, David Penn, Tom Smith, Laura Westbury, Robert Young. All at HQ have been as terrific as always, Clio Cornish, Finn Cotton, Melissa Kelly, Lucy Richardson, Fliss Porter and Darren Shoffren. I owe special thanks to the brilliant Bill Massey who, by a set of chances, became my editor on this book and to Lisa Milton for all her continuing support. And, as always, Penelope, Helena and Olivia, thank you so much for everything – patience, love, editorial insight, support, the list goes on.

ONE PLACE. MANY STORIES

Bold, innovative and
empowering publishing.

FOLLOW US ON:

@HQStories